Peter Watt has spent time as a soldier,
deckhand, builder's labourer, pipe laye
investigator, police sergeant and advis
Guinea Constabulary. He speaks, re
and Pidgin. He now lives at Maclean, on the Clarence River in
northern New South Wales. Fishing and the vast open spaces of
outback Queensland are his main interests in life.

Peter Watt can be contacted at www.peterwatt.com

Also by Peter Watt

Cry of the Curlew
Shadow of the Osprey
Flight of the Eagle
To Chase the Storm
Papua
Eden
The Silent Frontier
The Stone Dragon

Excerpts from emails sent to Peter Watt since his first novel was published:

'Stand proud, Peter Watt. Your stories have touched one . . . may they touch a nation.'

'There was not one boring chapter in [*The Stone Dragon*] . . . Just fantastic reading.'

'Thanks for many hours of enjoyment . . .'

'I read one of your novels, *Shadow of the Osprey*. I was hooked from the very first page and I had to go out and buy what other books of yours I could find . . . I would say "move over Wilbur Smith" . . . yours are something special and I hope that you continue to write for a long time yet.'

'I started reading the first of your books . . . and before you knew it I had read them all . . . Thank you for writing novels that have history attached; it is wonderful.'

'. . . you tell a very good story, so good in fact I cannot put them down.'

'I heartily agree with the comments from readers that are printed in your books. I also have read Wilbur Smith and Bryce Courtenay and am very pleased to add you to the list of my favourite authors. Keep up the good work.'

'. . . brilliant reading . . . you have a great gift.'

'I have just read *The Stone Dragon* and I have to say that the first page made me smile so much because you resurrected a favourite character in John Wong. Then reading the story of Peking made me think about your recommendation of other books on this sad saga and I am now going to broaden my horizons on different countries. But I know you have many more stories to tell and I cannot wait.'

'I re-read *Eden* and it has not lost its suspense and reality . . .'

'I picked up *The Stone Dragon* at my local library in Western Australia, and after a couple of chapters am delighted to have found a new good author to add to my favourites. I'll be reading your other books and confidently pay for them at the bookshop.'

'Inside the cover you have emails sent to you and I would like to add my compliments. Thanks for many enjoyable hours of reading.'

'Peter Watt is one of the best authors I have ever read and his ability to take you with him on the journey is wonderful.'

'I am an avid reader of your books . . . I love your work.'

'I could not put [*Cry of the Curlew*] down – great stuff, terrific story and a great feel of Australia permeating through the story . . . Thank you for writing these stories of the early settlers in this land of ours.'

'I have thoroughly enjoyed your entertaining and informative books . . .'

'Thank you so much for *Shadow of the Osprey*! I could not put it down.'

PETER WATT

THE FROZEN CIRCLE

MACMILLAN
Pan Macmillan Australia

First published 2008 in Macmillan by Pan Macmillan Australia Pty Ltd
1 Market Street, Sydney

National Library of Australia
Cataloguing-in-Publication data:

Watt, Peter, 1949–.
The frozen circle / Peter Watt.

ISBN 978 1 4050 3854 6 (pbk.).

A823.3

Set in 13/16 pt Bembo by Post Pre-press Group
Printed in Australia by McPherson's Printing Group

Papers used by Pan Macmillan Australia Pty Ltd are natural, recyclable
products made from wood grown in sustainable forests. The manufacturing
processes conform to the environmental regulations of the country of origin.

To Naomi,
for her love and support

PROLOGUE

Ipatiev House
The Siberian city of Ekaterinburg
Ural Mountains, Russia
Evening of 16 July 1918

Comrade Yakov Yurovsky paced the small room. A tall, sturdy man with a neatly trimmed goatee beard, dark short hair and intelligent eyes, his face was now twisted with anxiety. He stopped pacing to remove his pince-nez spectacles and lay down on the couch in his office, applying a wet cloth to his brow. In his forty years on earth he had experienced war, prison and exile under the Czar's tyrannical rule and now the Czech White Army was rapidly approaching the city of Ekaterinburg which he knew would inevitably fall into their hands. If so, his wife, children and widowed mother who shared his small flat would be at risk if the White Army learned they were related to the leader of the local Soviet.

But that was not his only concern. Comrades Lenin and Trotsky in far away Moscow wanted to keep their prisoners alive against the wishes of the local Soviet. Trotsky wanted

1

to place the Czar on trial and humiliate him; Lenin, to use the royal family as pawns in his vicious civil war. But Comrade Lenin had given in and signed the death warrant. Only Trotsky protested and he was not a man to be ignored in the Revolution. Moscow was a long way from Siberia and the pressing matter of possibly allowing the Czechs to overrun the region and rescue the royal family was here and now.

A knock at the door stirred the commander of the grand old house now being used as a private prison for the Czar, his family and their personal servants.

'Comrade Yurovsky, the party has been assembled and pistols issued to each man.' The voice from the doorway was that of the foreman of the twelve-man execution squad.

'Just wait one moment, comrade,' Yurovsky waved from the couch. 'I will join you soon.'

Had he made the right choice, Yakov asked himself. What was at stake in the next few hours was the very fate of his family and the history of the Revolution. He knew that he would forever twitch at every footfall outside his office or apartment for the lie he would have to live. But Yakov had proved his loyalty to Comrade Lenin and Trotsky's revolution. This was a personal matter and the audacity of it must forever be hidden not only from those he supported, but also from history itself. Not only Comrade Lenin was capable of using pawns, Yakov thought as he rose from the couch to join the execution squad. He knew there was no going back but the faces of his own family flashed before him as he followed the foreman down the stairs to the cellar where nine unsuspecting, innocent people waited to have their photograph taken for posterity. But instead of looking down the lens of a camera the Romanovs would be facing a row of revolvers and smelling the stench of cordite mixed with the acrid scent of blood as they died in a hail of gunfire

2

in the tiny cellar. When it was all over, Yakov would make his report to Moscow and Comrade Lenin informing that he had carried out his revolutionary duty. After all, who would question the man responsible for ridding Russia of the evil tyranny of the Czar and his family?

But Yakov was also human. He knew that he needed what the American imperialists called 'an ace up the sleeve' should the Czechs overrun his home and threaten his family. Good luck had sent him his ace.

20 kilometres west of Ekaterinburg
23 July 1918
One week later

Although it was the middle of summer, with the disappearing light of the day the temperature was falling. The young woman, bedraggled by her flight from the city, struggled in the dense forests of the taiga. Her strong body had been sapped of strength as she had escaped the besieged city where she had been held prisoner after the execution of her parents by the Bolsheviks under the command of Comrade Yakov. The White Army was fighting fiercely for possession of the city but Maria had taken advantage of the confusion brought about by the fighting, slipping from the house where she had been held captive.

She collapsed on the spongy mosses of the forest floor to rest and thought about her future. She knew that she had a long journey ahead of her through war-torn territory and the fortune in jewellery she carried in a cloth belt around her waist was as much as a liability as an asset. Should she fall into the hands of bandits or Bolsheviks she knew that she would not fare well. Her only hope of survival was the identity papers she also carried, declaring her as the Princess Maria Romanov – if she could reach the Allied or White Army lines around Archangel. Surely the English royal family would do everything to rescue her from the Bolsheviks, she thought hopefully, if only she could reach Archangel. For now the city in the Arctic Circle could have been as far as the moon itself and her chances of survival very slim in a land as vast as the Russias.

She was sure Yakov had only kept her alive because she might prove valuable as a bargaining chip should the Czechs overrun the city and threaten his family for his role in the execution of the Russian royal family. If the Czechs failed then her life too would be forfeited. She could not take the chance of remaining and had seized the first opportunity to slip from under the guard placed on her with a bribe of one of the many precious stones concealed in her corset.

'I'm cold,' Maria whimpered, shivering as the short darkness of summer descended in the tree tops and a wind sighed through the pine needles to sing away her hopes of survival.

Maria was not only a very pretty young woman, with deep blue eyes and rosy cheeks, she also had a toughness of spirit that would see her continue the journey west towards Europe. She had her indomitable spirit and a small fortune in gems. All she needed now was a lot of luck in seeking out the right people who could help her reach the safety of France. She still remembered the stories of her French mother painting images in her mind of a fabled city called Paris. She would reach Paris and declare to the world that the bestial Bolsheviks had not been able to kill all the Romanov family, she thought with a fierce determination, ignoring the fact that that Paris lay thousands of kilometres to the west.

The sun was gone and Maria huddled into the gnarled roots of a large tree, where she shivered through the night despite the many layers of clothing she had been wise enough to take with her on her escape. She was at least grateful for the fact that it was not winter for she would have surely died of exposure. The young woman curled up and quietly sobbed herself to sleep.

When the warming sun finally returned to kiss her cheeks Maria awoke. As her eyes focused she sat up with a start. Standing over her was a tall, bearded man with shaggy hair and wild eyes. Worse still, he held an ancient rifle in his hand. Maria wondered if death had come to take her.

London, England
Armistice Day
11 November 1918
Three and a half months later

The din outside the walls of the Regimental Officers Mess was deafening. It had been so all day and continued into the night as the masses on the streets of London celebrated the end of the Great War, singing, dancing, beating anything that could make a sound in lieu of drums, blowing whistles, horns and drinking.

The normally busy mess was empty, save for two uniformed officers sitting in their respective leather chairs at opposite ends of the room. The place was heavily adorned with the trophies of past wars: lances, shields and tattered flags festooned the dark wood veneer walls while sepia photos of English officers wearing pith helmets took up any spare space. The mess had an ambience of tradition and serenity: a place where time had stood still since the Battle of Waterloo. Even this just finished war with its rude intrusion of science and technology to aid the killing had not yet intruded with its trophies.

The noise outside tapered off as the night drew on. Now the turning of the pages of the London newspaper could almost be heard as the tough-looking captain wearing the uniform of an Australian officer continued to peruse each and every article, oblivious to the explosive excitement that had been the announcement the war was over.

The young, second lieutenant at the other end of the room also wore the uniform of an Australian officer. In his early twenties, he was tall and had what many would call an aristocratic appearance. Sandy hair and pale blue eyes set off his fine features. He was not reading a paper. Instead, he gripped a gin and tonic in his hands and stared morosely at the emptiness of the room. His melancholy thoughts were interrupted when the Australian captain walked over to him.

'Another G & T, Mr Littleton?' the officer asked.

George Littleton appeared startled. 'Thank you, sir,' he replied. 'That would be bully.'

The captain walked over to the bar and went behind to pour two gin and tonics, ticking off the drinks on a chit. The stewards had all deserted the mess hours ago to join the deliriously happy crowds in the streets. Captain Joshua Larkin, MC, DCM, MM did not think they would be reprimanded for leaving their posts as most of the citizens of London were with them, also away from their places of employment. He returned to the junior officer with the drinks and sat in a comfortable, well-padded leather chair next to the younger officer.

'Thank you, sir,' George said, accepting the drink. 'I would have thought from what I can see of your decorations that you would be out on the streets celebrating the end of the hostilities.'

'And I would have thought that it would be you, Mr Littleton,' the captain countered. 'A handsome, dashing young officer such as yourself could do very well tonight with the ladies.'

George swigged heavily on his replenished drink as if attempting to swallow the decorated captain's comment. 'I never had the chance to see any action,' he replied. 'I had just arrived in England and was waiting to go over when the Armistice was called. Hardly call that the attribute of being the dashing officer,' he added bitterly.

'Count your blessings that you missed the show,' Joshua said, leaning forward and fixing the young man with his grey eyes. 'I know that most of my cobbers who are still over there, under the mud or hanging on the wire, would have preferred to bemoan the fact that they missed out than experience their fate. You have the chance to return home – sound in body and sane in mind – to start a life.'

'I'm sorry, sir,' George faltered. 'I did not mean to sound petulant. It's just that I so much wanted to serve my country and to be denied the opportunity to do so has been a great disappointment.'

Joshua eased back in his chair and smiled. 'You look and sound like you come from a bit of money,' he said.

George glanced at the obviously battle experienced soldier whose perceptiveness was surprising. He himself had summed up the captain as a man from a working class background who had risen to a commissioned rank. Captain Joshua Larkin had the open, ruggedly honest face of a man one could trust although it was etched with the lines that bespoke of too many days exposed to moments of sheer terror. This was particularly apparent when one looked into the grey eyes; there was unspoken horror there.

'I suppose you could consider me as having had a fortunate life, thanks to my heritage,' George answered the captain in a bemused tone. 'My family owns a substantial amount of property in Australia and I know my father will be pleased to see me return to eventually assume the reins of power. He was against me enlisting in the first place. And when I insisted he ensured that I was given a commission. Only right that the son of Harold Littleton be an officer and a gentleman.'

'Wise bloke, your old man,' Joshua said, raising his tumbler in a mock salute. 'The only thing he did wrong was letting you have a commission as an infantry officer. Your life expectancy would have been very short over there. But that is all a moot point now that the war is over.'

'I suppose that you are looking forward to returning home, sir,' George said. 'Do you have a family waiting for you?'

Joshua Larkin bowed his head and seemed to stare into his glass. George sensed that he had touched a raw nerve with the officer and regretted his question.

'Nothing to go home to,' Joshua finally replied. 'I have been in it since Fromelles and that seems a lifetime ago. I worked as a clerk in Sydney before the war.' Joshua did not elaborate and the young, well-educated officer guessed that in his last statement the man beside him had said it all. The war had provided this man with something he could not have found as a clerk working in a dreary civilian job.

'No, I won't be going home,' the captain continued, swigging his drink. 'Tomorrow I swap my uniform for a Pommy uniform in the Royal Fusiliers. It seems the English have another war going and have been recruiting men around London who'd been discharged to go home.'

'Another war?' George queried, his interest suddenly apparent at the Australian captain's statement.

'Surprised that you haven't been approached already,' Joshua answered. 'The English, along with the Yanks, French, Czechs, Japanese and Canadians have an expeditionary force campaigning in Russia against the Bolsheviks. Mr Churchill and his mob feel that the Bolshies have to be taught a lesson and they are putting together another force to reinforce those already there.'

In his excitement, leaning forward toward the captain, Second Lieutenant George Littleton almost spilled his drink. 'I presume the regimental orderly room would have the information I require to volunteer,' he said.

'You're a fool, Mr Littleton,' Joshua said. 'You should call it quits and go home to your life back in Sydney. Believe me, I was once like you and just as stupid to volunteer. If I knew then what I now know I would have stayed at home.'

'But you have proved yourself,' George countered. 'You would be welcomed home as a hero.' He was suddenly aware of a dark, angry expression in the captain's grey eyes.

'I know enough to tell you that now the war is over hardly any civilian is going to give a damn about returning soldiers, let alone a government,' Joshua retorted bitterly. 'Every man over there was a hero to just survive so we are as common a commodity as the bloody rabbits in the country. No, there will be a parade or two then we have to try and get jobs back that are now occupied by the blokes who chose to stay at home, rather than volunteer to join us. Oh, sure, they will slap us on the back and say what a courageous thing we did and even buy us a beer but when it comes to giving us any compensation that will be a different story. But at the end of any war the treatment of soldiers is to praise them – and then forget them. It has always been the same. At least I know soldiering and if another war is there to be fought it may as well be blokes like me who have no reason to go home straightaway.'

George was taken aback. The captain's reply had shattered his notion that people would always respect men returning from war. He could see an opportunity to prove himself in battle and was counting the hours until the orderly room was open to hand out applications for this expeditionary force destined for Russia. He was no longer feeling despondent and his drink suddenly had a taste rather than being simply a liquid to drown his regrets.

ONE

Valley View
The Central Highlands, west of Sydney
Present day

A gentle fall of snow during the night had settled to become a blinding sheet of white under the clear skies of the following morning. From where Senior Constable Morgan McLean stood on the verandah of the 19th-century police station, steaming mug of tea in hand, he could see the sweeping panorama of the slopes marching up to the timbered hills to the north of his rural domain.

Valley View township was the home of around 700 people but gradually growing with the influx of the tree-changers from Sydney seeking affordable housing in a rural setting. The town had been cut off from the steady flow of traffic between Sydney and Melbourne for at least a hundred years and had retained a feeling of belonging to the past. With its old, sandstone buildings and well-established willow trees proliferating along the gently flowing creek behind the town it was clear that time had well and truly left Valley View in its wake.

Nestled in the hills above the snowline, it enjoyed a claim to little crime other than the usual disputes over fences, a few dog complaints and the occasional domestic violence offence. Occasionally, Senior Constable McLean was called to one of the two local hotels to settle an argument over the use of the pool tables or evict a drunken patron. Most of the calls for law enforcement were settled on the spot, ruling out the need for the half-hour trip to the small city on the Hume Highway where any offenders could be processed and bailed to appear before the magistrates' court.

Morgan McLean had experienced enough excitement in his days to warrant the peaceful life of his current posting. Recently divorced, he was now forty-two years of age. Eighteen years earlier he had served with the Special Air Services Regiment in the Gulf War. At twenty-five the SAS trooper realised he was reaching a point where he would have to either remain with the army in a non special forces posting – or seek another career. As each birthday came and went his body told him that the rigorous standards required by the regiment made it harder for him. He had always had an interest in policing and chose to enter the NSW Police Force.

Standing on the old wooden verandah looking out at the serenity of the snow-covered pastures he had no regrets about not remaining in the army. Here, he had a small sense of belonging; the normally suspicious and conservative rural community had come to accept him after a couple of years' policing the district. Morgan was a man who had the knack of commanding respect. Just above average height he could not be called handsome, but he had a strong face and the build of a heavyweight boxer in his prime – a legacy of his days with the regiment and its emphasis on physical and mental toughness.

The tea consumed, Morgan turned to walk back inside to the warmth of the cramped office that also served as the main reception area for visitors to the police station. Today he would have a chance to fill in the backlog of returns. He was considering another mug of tea when the telephone rang.

'Senior Constable McLean, Valley View police,' Morgan answered, slumping into a chair behind his desk.

'Constable McLean,' a worried female voice said at the other end. 'You have to come out to our place. My partner has found a body . . . Well, at least a skeleton.'

'Ms Dawson, is that you?' Morgan asked, recognising the voice of Monique Dawson. He had met the attractive young woman when she had visited the police station a month earlier to update her car licence and in idle conversation Morgan had learned that she and her partner, David Greer had moved from Sydney to renovate an old sandstone house outside of town. Monique had also informed Morgan that she was a professional artist while her partner was involved in some kind of financial service. Most of his work could be done via the internet, she had explained, and they had always desired a plot of land with a lot of trees. They had hired a team of workers to rebuild the house and its outbuildings.

'Yes,' she answered. 'I think you know where we live, out on the old valley road.'

'Yes, I know,' Morgan said, quickly glancing at his wristwatch, a habit developed by experienced police for noting the time in future reports on any incident. 'I will be straight out. Just don't touch anything, okay? We need to preserve the scene as much as possible.'

'I have seen those shows on cable TV,' Monique replied with just a hint of amusement. 'But I don't have any of that police tape to seal off the scene.'

Morgan smiled. The young lady had a sense of humour. He remembered that she had also mentioned that she had once been a registered nurse before finding that she could use her artistic talent to make good money.

'I will be straight out,' Morgan repeated, placing the phone in its cradle and grabbing his leather jacket from the hatstand. Probably not much in it, he thought as he lifted the keys to the police four-wheel drive from inside the drawer of his desk. Old settled areas could produce the occasional skeleton of some pioneer who'd been simply buried in a paddock. The discovery would probably be of more interest to archaeologists than law enforcement after a coroner's report.

A cold wind whipped the air around the three people standing beside the partially excavated hole where the skull and chest bones could be clearly seen.

'I thought that I might take advantage of the break in the weather to clear the ground here for a future footpath,' David Greer explained.

Morgan had already summed up the man as a product of an exclusive private school. He just had that look and sound about him. Tall, with sandy, curly hair and the fine features of an aristocrat, he exuded the lazy arrogance of one used to getting whatever he went after and Morgan had no doubt that the man looked down upon those he considered tradesmen.

'You can imagine the shock I got when I scraped away the ground to reveal the skull,' David concluded in his cultured voice.

To lessen any chance of further contamination Morgan had ensured that he did not handle the partially exposed skeleton wrapped in what remained of a pile of rotted clothes. The wonder science of DNA analysis required this. Instead, he stared at what was obviously a bullet hole in the centre of the forehead. 'Has anyone else beside your self handled the remains?' he asked, glancing up at David.

'You didn't go near the body, did you, Monique?' David asked.

'Good God! No,' she replied.

Morgan could see a slight shudder ripple through her body at the suggestion. She had a pretty, oval face framed by lustrous red hair that was being blown about by the wind. Her green eyes were a feature noticeable to any man, as was the shapely outline under the pleated skirt and jumper she wore. 'I don't want whoever this is to haunt us.'

Morgan stood. 'I am going to lay out an inner and outer perimeter around the body,' he explained. 'That means that we keep away from the remains until the experts arrive to do their job. I hope it will not inconvenience you too much.'

'I have seen enough of those cable shows to know that the hole in the head was probably caused by a bullet,' Monique said quietly. 'Does that mean the man – or woman – was murdered?' she asked.

Morgan frowned. 'A good guess,' he said. 'But the coroner will make a decision on that matter.'

Morgan turned and walked away a short distance to make a call on his mobile phone. His first call was to the detectives whose office was located in the rural city a half hour away, and his next to the chief inspector's office to inform him of the find. Now, it was only a matter of waiting until the detectives and the forensic people arrived to take over. He laid out his tape around the yard, connecting it to small trees and garden posts. His work was done simply reporting the matter and protecting the scene.

'Could I make you a cup of coffee or tea?' Monique asked when Morgan returned to join the couple standing a distance from the partially excavated grave.

'That would be nice,' Morgan beamed. 'I can't see why we have to stand out here when I have a good view of the scene from your kitchen. I can get your statements about the discovery a little more comfortably out of the cold.'

It did not take long for the local detectives led by the detective senior sergeant to arrive. Morgan briefed them as to the circumstances of the discovery, adding that he had taken statements from the house's occupants.

Detective Senior Sergeant Ken Barber was a big, burly man who was from the old school of policing. He was facing retirement but this had not diminished his love for the job. 'You don't think they have any involvement?' he growled in Morgan's ear, eyeing the young couple standing in the doorway of their kitchen that opened into the backyard.

'No way, Ken,' Morgan answered. 'They have only been here a few months and it is obvious to even a garden variety copper like myself that the body has been buried for a fairly long time.'

Barber nodded. From experience he trusted the knowledge of the local police. 'Not a bad looking sort,' he said, eyeing Monique.

'A bit old for you, Ken,' Morgan snorted. 'She is at least thirty years old.'

'Yeah, you're right,' the detective senior sergeant sighed. 'I prefer them around twenty.'

Morgan smiled at the retort. Ken was currently being investigated for a complaint of yelling at a young police-woman who had been seriously derelict in her duties. The

16

issue had not been that she had almost cost the life of a colleague but that he had caused her trauma in his dressing down. He was, after all, a policeman from the old school.

'I've got onto the forensics people from Sydney to get down here,' he said. 'They can figure this out.'

'I don't have any reports of missing people,' Morgan added. 'From what I can see the body seems to have been in the ground a fair while.'

'My thoughts also,' Ken mused. 'Maybe we have to go back in the records a bit to see if we have any missing persons in the district. I don't know why but I figure this one is worth a bit more of a look at. I might get one of those ground-penetrating radars here to poke around the house. In the meantime I will send the boys back to your station and set up a command post. Hope you have a good supply of coffee and bikkies on hand. How are the counter meals at your local?'

'The bottom pub does a good meal,' Morgan said. 'Body discoveries are certainly good for the town's economy.'

'Need to get a PR officer to look at a press release,' Ken continued as he ticked off a mental checklist in his head. 'But not much in this until we get something back from forensics. It could be an old suicide.'

'Yeah, but who buried the body?' Morgan asked.

The burly detective senior sergeant glanced at Morgan from the corner of his eye. 'That, my son, is the sixty-four thousand dollar question.'

His role finished at the scene, Morgan gazed up at the foothills behind the sandstone double-storey house. His eyes settled on the ground floor and then on Monique who was still standing in the doorway of the kitchen. For a moment their eyes locked and Morgan felt that she was appraising him in some way. He smiled, and his smile was returned.

He turned and walked back to his vehicle. The lady was certainly as interesting as she was beautiful, he thought idly.

For a couple of days the team of local detectives used Morgan's tiny station as a command post until the crime scene police carefully removed the skeletal remains and the earth around the body for transport to their laboratories in Sydney for forensic analysis. Morgan had little to do with the investigation as it was prepared for the coroner – other than his initial witness statements and his own search through the records for missing persons. Once all those he uncovered for the past twenty years had proved to be accounted for, he would join the local detectives down at the pub for a good meal, a cold beer and a catch-up on police gossip from Hume City.

The discovery stirred intense interest among the local community and when Morgan attended a meeting of his Returned Services League sub-branch at the community hall he was beset by curious veterans – from World War Two to the latest members from conflicts in the Middle East.

'Can't say much,' Morgan would reply. 'It's a coroner's matter now.' He was not trying to avoid any sensitive matters; his answer was truthful. Nothing would be known until the forensics had been done. Not even the local media had shown much interest in the discovery. It had featured only as a headline in the local papers, and only rated a paragraph in the national media. All that was about to change as Morgan was returning to the police station and a call came in on his mobile phone.

'Young Morgan?' Ken Barber asked.

'Speaking.'

'Our case has kind of hotted up,' the detective said. 'The radar turned up another body late this afternoon, not far from the first one. This one also has apparent trauma injuries. You might have a case of the Valley View serial killer on your hands. And if it was a serial killer, the case looks like being almost ninety years old. I've got a feeling that the second one is going to cause a bit of a stir in the papers.'

Morgan's face registered little surprise. Even he had deduced the bones had lain under the earth for a long time. What secrets did this little town virtually isolated from the rest of the world hold? He prepared for another onslaught of coffee-swigging detectives at his police station and knew that the media would not be far behind them.

TWO

Archangel
Northern Russia
May 1919

The great blocks of ice reared up against the hull of the transport ship steaming its way into the Russian port of Archangel. Sergeant Joshua Larkin stood at the bow and drew the collar of his greatcoat more tightly around his face to ward off the chill blowing off the ice-logged sea. For a moment he was reminded of the bitter cold winters on the Western Front when the shell fire was made worse by the icy ground allowing the artillery shells to explode on instant impact, scattering shards of red hot steel across a greater expanse of the battlefield. At least when the mud came with the thaw the artillery rounds had a habit of burying themselves before exploding, thereby muffling the deadly effects of shrapnel.

But this was supposedly summer in the Arctic Circle – a place where the sun was over the horizon for up to twenty-two hours a day – and Joshua was pleased that Elope Force had steamed from England now and not earlier when he resigned from the Australian Army to re-enlist in the British force destined for the Front in Russia.

'I've never experienced anything like this,' Corporal George Littleton said, stamping his feet to keep warm on the frozen deck of the transport steamer. 'Nothing like this back home.'

Joshua fumbled in his greatcoat for his battered old pipe. It had been a comfort for the last two years of the war and he had come to see it as something of a lucky talisman. Finding it at last, he thumbed in a plug of tobacco and hunched against the wind to light the pipe. Satisfied that it was drawing well he blew the blue-grey smoke into the frigid air. 'France could be a bit like this,' he replied, staring at the approaching busy port. 'Bloody cold and wet.'

George Littleton stood beside the man who he had befriended after he too had resigned from the Australian Army to enlist in the British expeditionary force. A condition of their enlistment was that they were forced to relinquish their previously held commissions and enlist as non-commissioned officers. Joshua's outstanding record in France and Belgium had quickly earned him a sergeant's stripes, while George's family connections in England had gained him corporal's chevrons. Joshua still remained his senior in the army but George was pleased that this was so. Although an odd pair, during their training for the Russian expedition the two men had gravitated together; Joshua, of a working background, combat-experienced and older, George having come from money with connections in the mother country. In a strange sense the friendship was more like a brotherhood for George who looked up to Joshua as one would a respected brother. George's utter admiration for his friend had been cemented in a London pub one

21

night when he found himself cornered by a couple of cockney toughs whose claim to fame was that they had avoided military service in the war. A comment by George and the blood and beer flowed on the dirty floor of the public house as Joshua, swearing, waded in swinging fists to flatten both men in defence of George.

Standing over the two badly beaten cockneys, Joshua swung around to challenge any other man in the public bar to join the two on the floor. None accepted and both soldiers left to seek a quieter pub to drink in. Joshua said nothing of the fight but George realised that his friend had unhesitatingly come to his aid. He was grateful; he knew he was no match for the two toughs who had confronted him. All Joshua had said on their walk along the London street was, 'Careful what you say about a bloke's service in the war. As far as the people here are concerned it's all over and who we are is of no consequence to them.' It echoed the former infantry captain's statement on the night of the Armistice.

George's family ties to England had ensured that when leave came for them both he was able to open some doors. They joined the better landed aristocratic families for weekends of parties, dinners and fox hunts, although Joshua would decline joining the actual hunt, excusing himself as a poor horse rider. He would be simply satisfied to avail himself of the patron's library and liquor store while the rest rode the countryside, trailing the hunting beagles in pursuit of the fox. George had been intrigued to see his friend scribbling in a journal whenever he had the chance.

'I started this one to record a new campaign,' Joshua explained when he noticed George watching him. 'Against orders I also kept a journal recording the war.'

The war had decimated the ranks of the English

aristocracy. Many heirs to the family name and manor now lay as rotting cadavers in foreign soil on the other side of the English Channel. Those left behind recognised that English society had changed forever and a new mood prevailed now that the working class had proved its mettle. So it was accepted that a couple of colonial non-commissioned officers could be allowed to join in the activities of those who once considered that men of their lowly rank should use the tradesmen's door to the manor. It made it easier for them both that they had, at least, once held the King's commission before displaying their patriotic zeal in volunteering to fight the growth of Bolshevism now perceived as an insidious threat to all that was still sacred to the remaining traces of the aristocracy. The Bolsheviks had already proved their brutal disregard for the established rules of Western civilisation by executing the Russian royal family. After all, the Russian Czar had been related by blood to their King and that almost made him an Englishman. Comrade Lenin had attempted to deny the outright slaughter but word had gradually spread that he had ordered the dreadful murder of innocents. If the Bolsheviks were not stopped now the creeping disease of socialism might infect the working classes of Western Europe.

Joshua spoke very little about himself or his past. As close as George had come to his friend he still did not know whether the man was married or single, or why he would even consider remaining in the army to risk his life in another campaign. While he had to prove to himself that he was capable of facing death and acting like a man, Joshua didn't – he had already done that. George had some while back ascertained that Joshua Larkin was a highly intelligent man, one who had succeeded in teaching himself the French language to the point that he could almost be considered fluent. George's own school-taught French was no match for his friend's grasp of the language.

One of Joshua's most outstanding characteristics was his ability to lead men who instinctively sensed his courage and compassion. George had also become aware of his friend's attractiveness to women of all classes, and thought it strange that Joshua seemed to step aside whenever a lady made it known she was interested in him. At those times George was sure he would see an unfathomable pain in his friend's eyes. Was Joshua Larkin one of those *kind* of men? He shook his head. No, Joshua's manner around women did not speak of fawning courtesy.

As the shoreline of Archangel drew closer Joshua tapped the ash from his pipe on the frozen rail. 'Time we got ready for the big parade, George,' he said with one of his cheeky grins. 'Got to show the Poms and Ruskies we are as good as them.'

With a tight knot in his stomach Corporal George Littleton followed his friend below to prepare for disembarkation. Several months had passed since the end of the Great War and the letters from home had begged him to return. But here he was, ready to land on the shores of a country still steeped in mystery and revolution. He knew that he was about to go to war when the rest of the Western World knew only the respite of the Armistice. If he had any regrets about his decision to risk it all they were strongest now as he knew there was no turning back. Corporal George Littleton of the Sydney Littletons was about to learn what Joshua Larkin already knew. There was no glory in war – only the chance of surviving to see the fruits of peace ripen on the vine of life.

★

1 Melbury Road
West Kensington, London
July 1919

Major James Locksley, DSO flipped open his umbrella
against the grey sleet of the London spring. A tall, well-
built man in his early thirties, he cut a distinguished figure
in his army uniform emblazoned with a row of colourful
riband on his chest. Horse-drawn wagons carrying groceries and kegs of beer plodded alongside the fume-spuming
cars that now jostled for space on the narrow city roads as
he hurried towards the large, red-bricked mansion with the
innocuous address of 1 Melbury Road.

The carefully sealed letter hand-delivered to his exclusive gentleman's club had intrigued him. It had said little
other than offering an invitation to meet with a naval captain. Mansfield Cumming was the chief of a department
that Locksley only knew as the Secret Intelligence Service,
and having recently returned from the Russian campaign
the British major surmised that he was required for some
kind of debriefing. Upon reaching the headquarters of the
SIS, Locksley closed his umbrella and entered the building
to be met by a young man wearing civilian clothes.

'Major Locksley?'

'I am he,' Locksley replied.

'Captain Cumming is expecting you, sir,' the young
man replied, gesturing for the major to follow him along a
dark corridor.

Locksley shrugged, shaking off some of the sleet, and followed the man to a door. He knocked, and poking his head
inside announced Major Locksley's arrival before turning
and nodding to the soldier to enter.

Locksley stepped inside, noticing that the thickly set

man behind the heavy wooden desk was not alone. Locksley immediately recognised an old friend, Captain George Hill sitting in a comfortable leather chair to one side of the room. Neither of the two men in the room bothered to rise when Locksley entered.

'George, old chap,' Locksley said. 'My congratulations on your Military Cross. I saw it gazetted only yesterday.'

George Hill rose to accept the extended hand.

'Thank you, James,' he said. 'I should introduce you to Captain Cumming who has asked for you to attend this meeting.'

Cumming rose with some awkwardness and Locksley was quick to observe that the chief of intelligence had a wooden leg. Formalities aside, Cumming gestured for Locksley to take a chair, placing the three men in a triangular formation.

'Major Locksley,' Cumming said, 'Captain Hill is actually the man who has recommended you for this meeting. It appears that he thinks very highly of you and your own experiences in Russia in recent times.'

So it was a debriefing, Locksley thought.

For a moment Cumming seemed to be deep in thought. 'What is about to transpire in this room is not to leave this room on pain of court martial or death,' Cumming finally said.

Locksley felt a twinge of apprehension – this was not a debriefing.

'Captain Hill's MC was recently awarded for his outstanding service in Russia with another one of our people, Sidney Reilly. That is about all I can say on the matter as Captain Hill is for the moment also sworn to secrecy on their mission there. As you can probably surmise you have been summoned by His Majesty's government for a mission that has political and military ramifications far beyond anything you could imagine. I know that you have been assigned a posting on the Persian frontier but if you are prepared to swear your loyalty to what I may propose I can safely promise a colonelcy for your commitment to the mission. You will command your own regiment.'

Locksley felt his head swim . . . mission, colonel rank and regimental command, court martial and death all came together. He shifted in his seat.

'Sir, I am a commissioned officer of the King and am prepared to undertake any mission that the King's representative should offer,' he replied dutifully as was expected of him.

'Good,' Cummings huffed. 'I expected no less of you, given your sterling record of service in France and Russia. George has been passed certain vital information while in Russia. Only we are privy to what he and Reilly learned from our agents there about the barbaric execution of the Czar and his family last year.'

'Terrible matter,' Locksley said, agreeing that the execution of royalty was the sign of civilisation – as he knew it – in decline. Major James Locksley DSO was an ardent royalist, devoted to the principles of traditional monarchy no matter where it may be in Europe.

'The world has been told that all the family were executed at the same time but reliable sources have informed us that in fact one of the children was spared – to be used as a bargaining chip should the White Army forces overrun Ekaterinburg. It seems that the man in charge of the execution has filed a false report to his comrades Lenin and Trotsky. Our sources say that the child is on the run, seeking asylum in France.'

Locksley listened with intense interest. Already the

ramifications of what was being said to him were sinking in. If one of the Russian royal family were still alive then that person could be a real rallying point for opposition to the Bolsheviks. From his own experience serving in Russia with the White Forces he knew just how much the news would raise morale in their struggle to defeat Bolshevism. 'Which of the children is still alive?' he asked, leaning forward in his eagerness.

'It seems that the Grand Duchess Maria Nikolaevna was spared.'

'The Grand Duchess is also the Grand Princess,' Locksley said.

Cumming smiled for the first time in their meeting. 'No doubt you would know this because of your parents, Major Locksley, or should I say, Sakharov.'

Locksley smiled sheepishly at the identification of his real family name. His parents had immigrated to England for financial reasons and changed their name and religion to fit in with the establishment. Alexander Sakharov had been able to take some of the family wealth with him and soon made a small fortune in his adopted land. It had been substantial enough to put his son through Britain's most prestigious schools and finally Sandhurst, where the young officer cadet was accepted as a true Englishman. Locksley very rarely announced to his friends that he was fluent in the Russian language. But the dispatch of British forces to Russia to assist the Royalist White Army in fighting the rebel Bolsheviks had allowed the Russian-speaking English officer an opportunity to see the land of his birth and use his lingual skills.

'Yes,' Locksley replied. 'The princess enjoys a high status among those who know something of Russian royal traditions. If we were able to rescue her we would have a rallying point against the damned Bolshies.'

28

'Captain Hill was right in recommending you,' Cumming said, picking up a pen of green ink. 'I am going to authorise you to be attached to us for a short time, Major Locksley. I am sure that we will be able to get permission for you to carry out a mission on behalf of His Majesty's government, one that will be of vital importance to the very future of democracy in Europe.' With his words Mansfield Cumming placed one letter on the already prepared paper requesting Locksley's secondment to the SIS for an unspecified mission. Cumming's single 'C' in green would become renowned in British intelligence.

Before returning to his digs in London Major Locksley was invited to have afternoon tea with his old friend Captain George Hill. Cumming excused both officers and watched them leave the room. Neither man saw the frown on his face when the door closed to his office.

The portly, one-legged English naval officer took a deep breath and sighed. He had not briefed the major on every aspect of the mission. Those matters would come in due time. 'Bloody damned politicians,' Cumming swore, glancing down at the photograph of a beautiful young woman in her late teens with long flowing hair and huge wide eyes. Even now Grand Princess Maria was somewhere in the deep, dark forests of northern Russia. Alive, she was worth much to the fight against the growing threat of this new thing called communism. Dead, she was worth even more to those in the British government.

THREE

Valley View
Present day

The thin layer of snow had melted and the earth beneath had turned into a slush in the backyard of the residence, now a declared crime scene, albeit it apparently a very old one. Morgan McLean stood beside Detective Senior Sergeant Ken Barber who puffed on a cigarette, eyeing the two open graves only a few metres apart. A chill still hung in the air but the sun was shining in a clear, blue sky.

'We got back a pretty comprehensive report from our forensics people,' Ken said. 'Our first body has been tentatively identified from the World War One identity discs they found in the grave beside him as a bloke by the name of Joshua Larkin. It seems from the military records that he was last reported serving as an Aussie in Russia in 1919 with the British army. I have a copy of his military service records from the War Memorial people for you to have a look at. So far it appears that he had no descendants in

30

Australia. Our crime scene people reckon from the way they found the body that it was buried with some respect for the deceased. They also recovered the bullet that appears to have killed him and think it was fired from an old Scott & Webley revolver.'

'Service issue in World War One,' Morgan observed.

'Figure with your own military service you would be of great help on this case,' Ken said, drawing on his cigarette and watching the smoke dissipate in the chilly air. 'So I have asked the boss to put you on our team. It will be worth a bit of overtime to you.'

'And a few long lunches,' Morgan added with a grin, knowing the social ways of detectives.

'Could be,' Ken smiled back. 'But it is not a case we are ever going to solve, considering the apparent age of the crime. Doubt that there is anyone alive today we could put in the dock.'

'What about the second body?' Morgan asked.

'Identity not known and buried with little respect for the deceased,' Ken replied. 'From what forensics could ascertain it was that of a male aged somewhere between twenty and forty. Also shot through the head. They were lucky enough to find a bullet in the earth taken with the body and ascertain that it was also a .38 – but not from the same gun.'

'Possibly a souvenir smuggled back by a returning soldier,' Morgan commented. 'I doubt that I will be much more help on this one,' he continued.

'Thought you might give the PR officer from Sydney a hand in putting together a press release,' Ken said. 'The media are about to descend on the scene. Some bloody idiot in the press is calling it an old serial killer case just discovered. If you ask me it was probably nothing more than a garden variety double killing. But the phrase serial killer gets papers

31

sold so they are going to try and milk this one all they can. If we were to turn up another body I might agree with them, but two bodies does not constitute a serial killer.'

Morgan had to agree. What they had was simply two bodies, possibly killed at the same time for what could have been a variety of reasons: robbery, anger, jealousy, or even an accident for that matter. What was of more interest considering the time that had elapsed was the identity of the person who had buried the bodies. Whoever that had been must be long dead by now, Morgan mused.

'Go through everything we have on the running sheet and come up with some info for our PR lady from HQ,' Ken said, finishing his cigarette. 'With any luck we will wrap this up to the satisfaction of the coroner in a week or two and continue chasing cases a bit fresher than this one. In my experience this case isn't just cold, it's a bloody frozen circle we aren't likely to break.'

Morgan silently concurred and walked back to his vehicle. He would return to his station and assist the public relations officer to put together a press release. Not that they had a lot to go on; the discovery of the discs with one of the bodies was not considered conclusive proof as to the identity of the deceased.

In front of the local television team, a newspaper journalist, a current affairs program reporter and three crews from national TV networks, the no-nonsense police PR officer delivered a statement on the steps to Morgan's police station.

A policewoman who had previously been a journalist before joining the NSW force, she had carefully collated the facts and just as carefully deleted any possibility of speculation on the discovery of the two long-buried skeletons. She did, at least, release the name on the military ID discs. It was something she knew her former colleagues could get their teeth into – an angle like this for a story would mean they would not indulge themselves in creating stories that could cause irritating interference to investigations down the line. No doubt the reporters would rush off to learn more about this Captain Joshua Larkin but learn no more than the police already knew anyway.

When the press conference was over Morgan nodded to the PR officer. She had done well and he guessed that the story would fizzle out with a short story on page ten and not even get to TV. As for his role, Morgan felt the least he could do was locate Mrs Harrison from the local historical society and ask some questions about former residents of Valley View. He knew that the small group met on Wednesday nights at the CWA hall. He suspected that the ladies simply got together for the tea, scones and gossip rather than compiling a history of the area but it was worth a try. At least he could then do his bit for the investigation by writing up his findings for the coroner.

Morgan was somewhat surprised to see that not all the members of the local historical society were little old ladies, knitting baby booties between bouts of gossip. Also sitting around a trestle table were the local school principal, a man in his thirties, a couple of senior high school students and, most surprising of all, Monique Dawson. When he entered the hall there was a momentary pause in the conversation but that fell away when Morgan greeted all who stared at him with a broad smile and a warm greeting. 'Good evening ladies and gentlemen,' he said.

Gladys Harrison, a warm matronly lady in her late six-ties, hurried forward to guide him to a table covered in old black-and-white photos where the small group sat around fingering the records of the past. 'Constable McLean, what a surprise to see a member of our local police interested in our group. I assure you that we are not serving intoxicating liquors,' she said with a wicked grin.

'Wish you were,' Morgan retorted. 'I could do with a beer. Hello, John, I didn't think teachers had any interest in history anymore,' Morgan added facetiously.

'That's our students you are thinking of,' John Peters replied with a broad smile. 'I have a feeling that your inter-est in our little group has been prompted by the recent grisly discoveries at Monique's place.'

Morgan glanced at Monique sitting beside the two young girls from the local high school. She returned the look with a faint, challenging smile.

'Spot on,' Morgan answered, taking a seat opposite Monique.

'Well, we have beaten you to the punch,' Mrs Harri-son said proudly. 'We have addressed the recent find at this meeting and are examining all we know about the old Lar-kin residence – that's the place Monique and her partner are currently renovating. Monique has joined our meeting to assist with our research.'

'I will appreciate anything you come up with for the coroner's report,' Morgan said. 'I doubt that we will ever solve the case but maybe at least we will be able to give some kind of closure to any living relatives we may be able to find as a result of the investigation. There may be a possi-bility that someone in Valley View is related to one or both of the people whose bodies were uncovered.'

'We don't think that the body identified in tonight's six

o'clock news is that of Joshua Larkin,' John Peters said quietly. 'It doesn't fit the description we have found in our records. The man you said was Joshua Larkin was far too tall to be him.'

Morgan was taken aback by the school teacher's statement.

'You see,' John chuckled. 'We amateur historians need to be as thorough in our investigations as you coppers. According to his military records, Joshua Larkin was only around five foot ten, yet your skeleton was measured at around six foot one. I doubt that Captain Larkin could have grown so quickly in a year.'

'Interesting,' Morgan said. 'We do not say categorically that the body we found the identity discs on is that of Larkin but there must be some link with him.'

'Joshua Larkin was certainly a resident of the district,' Mrs Harrison said. 'But, only briefly.'

'What do you know about him?' Morgan asked, turning to her.

Gladys Harrison shuffled the papers before her, adjusted her reading glasses and cleared her throat. 'Joshua Larkin had once served as a soldier of some distinction in France and won a Military Cross as an officer as well as a Distinguished Conduct Medal and Military Medal as an enlisted soldier. He was eventually promoted to captain. In 1918 – instead of returning to Australia – he took his discharge from the Australian army to enlist in a British regiment, the Royal Fusiliers where he was given the rank of sergeant. He then served in Russia with an expeditionary force sent to oppose Lenin's Bolshevik forces. There is an intriguing gap in his record of service in Russia but we know that he returned from Europe in 1920 with a French wife, Marie, and purchased the property where his alleged body was found.

35

From our records it appears that both he, and his French wife, mysteriously disappeared in 1921. At the time there were rumours that they had been murdered and buried on the property.'

'The second body we found was that of a male,' Morgan said. 'Not female, but your information will be very worthwhile for the coroner.'

'We can go one step further, Constable McLean,' Gladys said. She flourished a photograph before Morgan's eyes of a man and woman dressed in early 1920s clothing: she with her hair piled on her head under a hat, and he with his stern features supported by the starched collar of a good shirt. It appeared that the couple were posing at a picnic beside the creek that ran behind the town and Morgan could see others in the background with wicker picnic baskets beside blankets on the grass.

'The photo was taken for the local paper in 1920 for the centenary celebrations of the founding of Valley View by the famous Macarthur family,' Mrs Harrison continued.

Morgan continued to stare at the two faces in the photo. Whoever the photographer was, they certainly knew their craft. He dwelt on the face of a very pretty woman, possibly in her early twenties, and that of a man in his early thirties and thought he detected just the hint of haunted expressions on the faces of the couple in the photo.

'Shortly after the photo was taken the couple disappeared,' Mrs Harrison said, taking back the print and replacing it in the folder marked, *Larkin Mystery*.

'You should have been a copper,' Morgan grinned.

Mrs Harrison puffed up with pride. 'Well, we do our best,' she answered. 'And we are still digging into the history of the Larkin mystery. It truly caused some interest to the town way back in 1921.'

Morgan looked across the table at Monique who had remained silent. 'As current resident of the Larkin house you do not have any further information, do you?' he casually asked.

Monique seemed taken off foot by the question. Maybe she did know something worthwhile.

'The property has always been in my family,' she uttered, as if reluctant to reveal the fact. But under Morgan's unrelenting stare she found herself divulging more. 'I was born in England and came out to Australia when I was only a baby,' she explained. 'The property is now in my name.'

'How far back has your family owned the property?' Morgan asked, his interest piqued by the revelation.

'I think that is a personal matter, Constable McLean,' Monique answered, her face flushing red. 'I would not rather speak of it in public.'

The exchange had caught the attention of all at the meeting and it was clear Monique wished she could stand up and leave.

'Sorry, Ms Dawson,' Morgan hurried. 'I was talking like a copper and did not mean to intrude.'

'Apology accepted,' Monique said, relaxing a little. 'You can probably understand that it is not every day bodies are dug up in your backyard with implications of murder that might be related to my family.'

The meeting continued with Mrs Harrison delegating tasks to the members in further research on the Larkin mystery – as she liked to call the file. Before Morgan could intercept Monique at the end of the meeting she disappeared quickly to her car. Gladys Harrison took Morgan's arm and pulled him into the kitchen for tea and scones with the other members of the society. But Morgan was preoccupied. His instincts told him that there was a link between the bodies in the ground and Monique Dawson's family history. He would arrange to meet with Ms Dawson as soon as possible and attempt to get her to reveal more of her family's past.

Tea-and-sconed out, Morgan returned to his residence attached to the station and resumed his duties, unaware that the name of Joshua Larkin had set off a red flag in the distant offices of a department of British Military Intelligence. A casual news item transmitted on the website of a national Australian television network had filtered through a computer system in the UK. Although both Joshua Larkin and the campaign in the dark woods of Russia were now beyond living memory they were not beyond the interest of a modern intelligence department. The Larkin file still carried the stamp *Top Secret* and was classified as *Not to be closed until 2020.*

Whatever the classified file contained required a century to close. In the opinion of those who had come and gone in the highest echelons of the British government since the end of the Great War the matter had to be so sensitive that it had the potential to alter history. But now a lowly employee of Military Intelligence 6 was just about to open the file with the simple act of pushing a key on his computer.

FOUR

West of Onega
Northern Russia
July/August 1919

Corporal George Littleton felt his hands sweating. Although the air was bitterly cold in the dank, dark stands of the almost silent pine forest he felt a hot flush on his cheeks. Fear – he knew he was feeling fear – as the platoon edged forward, rifles ready. Beside him extended in a sweep were the men of his section and just behind his section Sergeant Joshua Larkin moved with the platoon headquarters.

For weeks since their arrival the Fusiliers had been deployed to patrol the massive clearings in the forests for enemy activity. They had been assigned to strengthen the positions along the road and rail stretch towards Onega in the west. Some local White Army units had proved to be on the side of the Bolshevik revolution and had either deserted or been disarmed and replaced by the arriving British expeditionary force. Until recently Joshua and he had carried out mundane garrison duties in the cold and mud of northern Russia, but now George was about to face his first real action. A Bolshevik machine gun post had been spotted and the platoon he was a member of would attack and destroy the crew of the deadly weapon.

The order to halt came and George signalled to his section of eight men to go to ground and wait. Joshua moved cautiously forward towards him.

'You and I are going to have a closer look,' Joshua whispered in his ear. Together, the two men slithered forward on their stomachs until they were able to insert themselves in a tangle of fir tree limbs that lay on the ground. It was then that George felt real fear knot his stomach; he could smell the acrid scent of tobacco and hear the muffled voices of the Russian enemy just yards away.

Joshua carefully peeled aside the dying foliage to see the object of their stealthy advance. The fur caps of five Russian soldiers appeared just above a small rise in the muddy ground. Among them he saw the thick barrel of a water-cooled machine gun. Joshua guessed that the enemy crew must be poorly trained as they displayed little discipline with their noise and smoking. He tapped George on the shoulder and indicated that they should make their way back to the platoon, where he would brief the young British officer on the situation.

Although the young lieutenant with no combat experience had said that he would reconnoitre the weapon's pit, Joshua had convinced him that he, as the platoon sergeant with combat experience, should carry out the task. The young officer happily agreed, accepting his sergeant's rationale; the majority of the platoon had not seen action and this would be their first taste of it. Best that those with expertise be given the task of making sure nothing went wrong. Joshua had sized up the young man. He was not one of the toffy-nosed twits from the upper class but rather a boy from a middle class family who had proved his intelligence and leadership abilities to tough, war-seasoned instructors before he was granted his commission. Lieutenant Randolph Jones's family were originally Welsh and his father had worked his way through a coal mining company to a position of authority and minor comfort. He had encouraged his son to take a commission in the army as a way of furthering his son's future in an English establishment. Short and stocky, the young officer had no airs and was prepared to listen to those experienced in combat.

Three section commanders, the platoon sergeant and the platoon commander huddled together over a hastily sketched map on the floor of the dark forest. Joshua provided a brief on the layout and location of the machine gun pit and closed by commenting that he did not think the enemy was expecting them. They had numbers and surprise on their side.

Joshua was pleased to see that his platoon commander lay out a sensible plan of attack and mused that the British army had come a long way in recognising martial talent over class representation. They would attack the post from the front with two sections while holding the third section in reserve. It would also be in a position to provide a withering cover fire from its own heavy machine gun set up on its tripod. George's section would be in the assault group to attack, armed with the hand grenades they had been issued.

George returned to his small party of white-faced soldiers to inform them of their role in the attack. They listened silently and on the order, quietly attached the long bayonets to their rifles. A couple of his men were veterans of the French and Belgian battlefields and they helped settle the others of the unit with their easy banter about how this show was a pushover. There was nothing really to fear, the veterans reassured the younger, untested soldiers. George was secretly happy to hear his veterans accept the situation with such ease; it helped his nerves just as much as those of the section who had not seen real combat.

Hand grenades primed and trailing rifles with bayonets fixed, the Australian soldiers inched their way forward at a crouch, moving carefully in the direction of the tiny clearing where the Russians were located. On their left flank the other men of the platoon also moved forward. They were only twenty-five yards out when the whistle blew to indicate that they make their first move. With practised fingers, pins were pulled from the grenades and each man hurled his lethal casing of explosive towards the enemy which they could clearly see once they stood.

A rain of bombs fell on and about the nest, catching the defenders offguard. Barely had the Russian cursing began when the fuses on the grenades spluttered into lethal blasts, hurling metal fragments in all directions. The last grenade had hardly exploded when George found himself flinging towards the wisp of smoke, his bayonet-tipped rifle extended forward. His men and the accompanying section followed with strangled war cries. In seconds George was at the lip of the rise and looking down into a pit. The gun crew had not had the chance to get the deadly machine gun firing and George could see blood running down the face of the huge man before him. Without thinking, he thrust the tip of the bayonet into the wounded man's chest as he attempted to wipe away the blood from his face. The man let out a scream of pain and terror, then gripped the blade of the bayonet embedded in his ribs. He fell, taking George into the mud at the bottom of the trench with him. Desperately, George attempted to pull the bayonet from the man's chest, aware that a Russian soldier on his left was raising his own rifle to club him. The man's bearded face was a mask of fury and George let go of his rifle to shield himself from the crushing blow.

But suddenly, the soldier with the raised rifle toppled forward and bloody gore splashed over George's face. A bullet had taken off the top of the enemy soldier's head. Around him, George could hear the grunts, curses and sobbing of men caught up in vicious hand-to-hand fighting. Reeling backwards, George tripped over a dead soldier and caught sight of a patch of blue sky through the tiny gap in the fir trees. For a second he could smell the antiseptic scent of the forest. Everything seemed surreal. A hand reached down to grip his elbow and George saw Joshua's grim face staring at him.

'It's all over,' he said, hauling George to his feet. 'No casualties to report on our side. Bloody well done, cobber.'

In a daze, George blinked, glancing around to see his section, some drenched in blood, watching him. At their feet were the bodies of not five but eight Bolshevik soldiers. The extra Russians had been concealed in a small trench just behind the machine gun post.

'You did well for your first real action,' Joshua continued, wrenching the bayoneted rifle from the chest of the huge Russian now looking at the sky with lifeless eyes. It came out with a soft plopping sound. 'I think your section will have a bit of faith in their commander from now on.'

George accepted the praise without comment. One minute he had been waiting for the whistle, his stomach

43

on the verge of strangling itself; and next he was stabbing a total stranger to death. He noticed that his ears were still ringing from the very close explosions of the Mills bombs. The young lieutenant was now by his side.

'Well done, Corporal Littleton,' he said, slapping George on the back. 'But one could expect such an achievement from a fellow who once held the King's commission. I think it would be wise if you had your men do a thorough search of these chappies and their position to see if there is anything of worth to be retrieved for our intelligence chaps. Corporal Jackson will be in charge of recovering the Bolshies' arms. We don't have time to bury the Ruskies.'

'Sir,' George acknowledged, waving his section to him as the reserve section swept past them to probe further into the forest in case the machine gun post had been a forward element of a deeper defence. He had finally tasted combat and was surprised to see that his hands did not shake as badly as those of his friend, Joshua Larkin. But then, he had not been at this for as long as the former Australian captain.

Crouching in the cold rain, George wondered at the sanity of volunteering for the British force serving in Russia. Night was falling and around him the men of the battalion attempted to keep warm if not dry. Weeks had passed since his first action and since then he had engaged in other situations that brought him face to face with death. They had been heavily attacked in their defensive positions along the road and rail track and fallen back. But in a counterattack they had seized the lost ground, and in one attack the mostly Australian company that he belonged to had stumbled on a large force of Russian Red Army preparing to counterattack them. With fixed bayonets and hands full of Mills bombs they had pre-empted the enemy move by counterattacking themselves and routing the Bolsheviks, inflicting heavy losses. Within a week, George was involved in an attack on an artillery gun emplacement located at a railway siding. Again, they had swept aside the enemy, captured the gun and two hundred Russian prisoners. Now, his hands shook as much as those of his friend, Joshua Larkin.

'Want some cha, corp?' a soldier of George's section asked. He was a boy from a small country town who had arrived in Britain – as George had – to also miss the war. Like George, the young soldier volunteered to fight with the British in northern Russia. A British commander had generously allowed his Aussie volunteers to wear their Australian army uniforms and they had quickly established their national identity within the ranks of the British soldiers around them.

'Thanks, Fred,' George replied, huddling inside his greatcoat against the sleeting rain. 'Wouldn't mind if I did.'

The soldier slipped away to fetch the welcome mug of tea as Joshua appeared beside him. He and George were never far from each other although Joshua's duties as the platoon sergeant kept him busy with the platoon commander.

'G'day, young George,' Joshua said, squatting beside the corporal. 'All section commanders are wanted at platoon HQ at eighteen hundred hours for a briefing.'

'What's up?' George asked, shivering as he spoke.

'Looks like we are in for a big show,' Joshua replied. 'Seems that all up to now has been no more than a bit of skirmishing. General Ironside has decided that we have everything under control in this part of the world and he will be going after the Bolshies along the Dvina River. I think he wants us to come with him,' Joshua added with a wry smile.

Inwardly, George felt stricken. If what he had endured until now was little more than skirmishing he had no desire to confront a real battle. Why had he not taken Joshua's advice to go home when he had the opportunity? Right now he could be sitting at the family table tucking into a beautiful meal of roast lamb and baked potatoes. That would be followed by a round of port in the library of the family mansion and a good cigar. Instead, here he was, a mere enlisted man in someone else's army fighting a war very few outside Russia even knew about – let alone cared about. The prevailing atmosphere was of peace that was expected to last forever – after the devastation of the war just gone. And why was it that Joshua who had experienced so many years of war on the Western Front would opt to volunteer to continue soldiering? Maybe one day he might tell the truth.

'Are you okay?' Joshua asked, noting his friend's melancholy.

'Nothing much,' George shrugged.

'I always said you were a fool for volunteering for this stunt,' Joshua said with just a note of anger in his voice. 'You have so much to go back to in Aussie.'

'What about you?' George flashed. 'You have so much to leave behind on the fields of France.'

Joshua sat back on his haunches and stared up at the blackening sky. Rain poured down his face and George could see pain there. 'My wife died just before the Armistice,' he said quietly. 'Bloody Spanish flu got her. She was the only real thing worth anything to me in my life. I prayed that if there were a God He might take me instead of her – considering what I had come through. Jessie was waiting for me and in all the years I was away it was only her letters that stopped me going mad. You see, what was behind me in France was the knowledge that I would survive to return to Jessie.'

George was stunned by Joshua's admission. He could never imagined that this tough, taciturn man had a gentle side. He had witnessed the sergeant in battle roaring orders and exposing himself to the hottest of fire without any consideration for his own safety. It was no wonder the man had been recognised in the past for his courage. But was his courage simply the act of a man who no longer cared if he lived or died?

'I'm sorry, old friend,' George replied. 'I was not even aware that you had been married.'

Joshua rose to his feet, his rifle in his hand. 'Although I may be in danger of sounding like one of those romantic poets I have read,' he said, 'I was fortunate in this life to have met a woman who I could give my very soul to.' George could see that Joshua was considering saying more but true to his more usual style, he dropped into a silence.

'I will see you at the briefing,' George said awkwardly. He realised that Joshua's admission as to why he was in Russia was an act of faith towards him as a friend. War had a way of cementing bonds between men that could never be duplicated in times of peace. They were men apart socially but George had to admit that, given different circumstances of birth, Joshua Larkin could have been anything in life other than the clerk he had been as a civilian. Still, as a soldier, he was second to none in the battalion.

FIVE

South London
Present day

The architecture of the imposing building on the banks of the Thames River was typical of the 1960s, when it was constructed. Tall and angular with telecommunications towers atop the levels of concrete and glass, it housed Britain's elite MI6 offices. The Military Intelligence Section Six organisation had been charged for almost a century with protecting the UK against those who would do Her Majesty's people serious harm. Over the years the organisation had undergone many changes but its basic structure of counterintelligence work of foreign powers remained at the heart of its operations.

The young man who had been assigned a watch on foreign media broadcasts could hardly believe his eyes when one of the department's special icons flashed on the screen indicating some Aussie item about the discovery of a skeleton – possibly being that of one Captain Joshua Larkin. It had to be a mistake, he told himself as he leaned forward in his ergonomic swivel chair. As an employee of the secretive organisation even his family and closest friends did not know that Samuel Briars was in fact on his way to being installed as a fully fledged agent. He had answered an intriguing ad in the paper while finishing his IT studies at university. It led him to an interview and he was snapped up when his course results were revealed. Sam Briars was considered a leading expert on encryption programs and breaking firewalls. His skills were badly needed by his potential employers and the young man of twenty-five years jumped at the chance of joining the secretive organisation and possibly becoming a real James Bond. At least that was his expectation – but the more he worked at his desk the more he realised intelligence work was less than glamorous and more bureaucratic. For now in his career at MI6 as in any other civil service job, it was a matter of doing the tedious grunt work of news watches before further training for work in the field.

When the icon had lit up the name Joshua Larkin Sam presumed the computer system had thrown a wobbly; it was apparent from the news item that the man had been dead almost a century. Either that or someone should have updated the files to delete all outdated information. Sam dutifully noted the code that the icon flashed in his log-book and clicked to another website broadcasting Aussie news items. He hoped that one of them might display a picture of an Aussie beach and a few scantily clad girls in bikinis when he remembered that the former colony south of the equator was emerging from a very cold winter. The next broadcaster also had a small feature on the discovery of two skeletons and once again the special icon flashed on the screen highlighting Captain Joshua Larkin's name. This time Sam could not ignore the warning and, stretching his long legs, stood to alert his supervisor that something rather unusual was happening on his watch.

His supervisor was equally perplexed.

'Could be a bloody mistake,' he muttered, taking down the flashing code. 'But I will push it upstairs and see what they have to say about this Larkin chap.'

Sam shrugged. He had done his bit and now someone on another level could make a decision. He did cover his backside by downloading every item he could find on the Aussie police investigation, for in the press releases were names, places and times and his was the business of taking raw information and possibly turning it into intelligence. He glanced at his watch and was pleased to see that he only had another hour to go before he could stand down from his shift. But before he did, he would transmit what he had found to the woman he most dreamed of getting into bed with. The mention of a Russian connection would be of interest to her when she clicked on his encrypted attach- ment. She was, after all, in St Petersburg on assignment working undercover. Being an awkward young man, Sam believed that demonstrating his prowess with a computer had to impress beautiful and intelligent women. This inter- esting find would at least entertain Sarah Locksley when she clicked on to receive information from her supervisor in the UK.

The four men who sat around the shiny mahogany table represented the powerful forces of British intelligence. Before them were carefully prepared folders of copies of original, yellowing papers held in the archives. The meet- ing had been called to discuss the almost forgotten matter raised almost ninety years earlier by their predecessors.

The president of the committee, Harry Stanton, was in his late fifties. His energies were now diverted to collecting information on the disturbing rise of neo-fascist organisations in Europe, but in his early days with the service, he had been assigned to the Cold War department. He spoke Russian fluently and vaguely remembered the old file from when he had commenced his duties on the Russia desk. At the time it appeared so improbable of ever being activated on account of the time that had passed Harry had relegated its memory to passing interest. But the opening of an old grave in far-off Australia had also opened a door to the modern world of international intrigue in Europe.

'Gentlemen,' he said, clearing his throat. 'I never thought I would see this again.'

The other three glanced at the open folders before them.

'Do you think it has any relevance today considering the time that has passed?' one of the men asked, frowning.

Harry screwed up his face as if agonising over the question. 'One would consider the matter dead and buried,' he replied, 'considering the changes since the end of the Cold War. But it is those very same changes that have made this file as relevant today as it was when it was first raised back in 1919. In fact, I believe the issue could cause more instability in Russia today than it could have back in 1919. It is bad enough that we have a premier antagonistic towards the West, let alone that we give him an excuse to ride on the back of a new militaristic surge of Russian nationalism.'

'Do you think that if the information was somehow released to the world it could affect us?' one of the men asked, leaning back in his chair and rubbing his forehead.

'Considering the basis of the information,' Harry replied, 'I fear that the danger is posed closer to home than we can afford. There is a chance that the matter will die a simple death – that the Aussies know nothing of Captain Joshua Larkin – and by the end of the week it will not be reported any further in their press. If so, then this file will be relegated to the archives and forgotten to history. What is intriguing, but may answer some of the old questions raised by the file, is if what eventually happened to Captain Larkin according to the police findings is true. It appears he met a sticky end,' he added as a postscript.

'*If* is a word we should consider,' the man leaning back in his chair said. 'I think that we should take pre-emptive measures to ensure that the matter has not the slightest chance of being uncovered – either by accident or investigation.'

Harry could see that the other two members of the meeting were nodding their heads and a look of doubt crossed his face. 'I think that the matter should be pushed upstairs to the PM's department for a decision,' he said, using the civil servant's out to any sticky situation. 'His people can take responsibility.'

The three men nodded with some vigour and closed their folders.

Valley View
Present day

The discovery of the two skeletons was now two weeks old and the initial stir it had caused in the town was tapering off. Gladys Harrison was still vigorously pursuing any information on Captain Larkin however, and DNA samples from the bones had been sent by the NSW Police Department to an American laboratory for a possible profile. There had been no clue on the second body discovered and Morgan had been convinced that the first, tentatively identified as Larkin, was not in fact the man. As far as he was concerned both bodies were a mystery and would probably remain so forever.

As it was Saturday night Morgan was out on patrol, cruising the main street of the village as a warning to would-be drink-drivers. Spring was around the corner and the cold nights had less of a bite. The police frequency mostly relayed information for the cars in Hume City and Morgan's experienced ear blocked out anything that had little interest to him.

'Valley View One,' the female dispatcher called. Morgan grabbed the mike on the dashboard, acknowledging the call.

'You have a call to a possible prowler at a residence . . .'

Morgan recognised the address immediately. It was the old sandstone house. He immediately put his foot down, choosing not to hit the lights and siren in the hope that he might catch the reported prowler by surprise.

The house was not far out of town. Within a couple of minutes he slewed the four-wheel drive to a sideways halt while reporting off on his police radio. The house was well lit. Gun and torch in hand, Morgan quickly scanned the backyard that still bore the scars of the excavation. The dense shrubbery would give a prowler many places to hide, he realised.

A light went on, flooding the yard with a weak glow. Morgan could see Monique standing in the doorway, a silk dressing gown wrapped around her and a worried expression on her face. Joshua slipped the Glock pistol back into his holster.

'Are you okay?' he called, walking carefully across the yard to greet her.

She nodded. 'I may have called you on a wild goose chase,' she said when Morgan stood before her – her breath a mist in the air. 'I thought I heard strange sounds outside but I think I may have been imagining things. I'm sorry.'

Morgan shook his head. 'You don't have to apologise,' he said. 'Better to be wrong than be right and not call us.'

'It's cold outside and I think that I owe you another apology for appearing so rude towards you at the meeting some nights back. Can I offer you a hot drink?'

'Is David here?' Morgan asked, prompted by a sense of concern for the young woman who had faced the threat of a prowler on her own.

'He is away in Sydney on business,' Monique replied, turning her back on him.

Morgan followed her into the warm kitchen heated by an old-fashioned, wood combustion stove of cast iron. The kitchen had an air of not having progressed into the 21st century, and even the furniture was dated to sometime in the late 19th century.

'Tea, coffee or hot chocolate?' Monique asked.

Morgan felt just a little uncomfortable for accepting the invitation. 'Coffee will be fine,' he replied. 'White with one.'

Monique reached for a jar from an open wooden shelf above the sink. 'I am afraid it is only instant,' she explained. 'I feel that I was a bit short with you the other night at the meeting.'

'That's fine,' Morgan said.

'You should sit down,' Monique invited. 'You look a little awkward standing there.'

Morgan grinned and sat down at the small wooden table. It looked like it had seen many years of service, nicked and scratched as it was.

The coffee was served in a heavy mug that was obviously

handcrafted, no doubt by Monique. 'You have nothing to apologise for,' he said, sipping the steaming brew. 'I just need to know as much as I can to write off the investigation so that the coroner can conduct a hearing.'

Monique sat down opposite Morgan, her coffee mug before her. 'It is hard to explain a lot of things,' she said. 'I guess the discovery of the bodies in our backyard has had an unnerving effect. It may sound silly but I think the spirits of the two men who were buried out there are haunting this place. I truly heard some strange sounds tonight . . . at least I think I did.'

Morgan did not scoff at her fears. 'You might have had a prowler – someone curious to see the place where the bodies were found,' he reassured. 'I doubt that they will hang around after my arrival.'

'You certainly have a reputation among the locals for being a man not to be crossed,' Monique said with a smile. 'Mrs Harrison has the utmost respect for you. She said that you were a veteran of the Gulf War.'

'Yeah,' Morgan replied, glancing away self-consciously. 'I like it here. The people are a bit reserved but when you get to know them, they are all right.'

'This place has been in my family for many years,' Monique said. 'I was born in the UK and my parents brought me here when I was a baby. I grew up in Sydney and it was only shortly before my dad passed away that he revealed the existence of the house and land. He said it would be a gift for me when I met the right man to settle down with. It happened that David was able to leave Sydney with me to settle here. At least I thought this would be our dream house but now I am not so sure.'

'How is it that if your family are from England they could have title to this place?' Morgan asked, his interest aroused.

'I am not sure,' Monique said. 'Only Dad knew the full story about our title to the house and I didn't bother asking. And now I wish I did, but at the time I was so excited about being able to move here away from the rat race that the offer of title over the place was enough. Now I have also inherited a couple of murdered ghosts.'

'You can't murder ghosts,' Morgan said with a broad grin. 'You can only exorcise them.'

Monique broke into a smile at Morgan's gentle correction. 'I did not know that policemen had a sense of humour,' she said.

'Believe it or not, when the uniform comes off we are just people in our underwear and socks,' Morgan said. 'But that is not a pretty sight.'

Monique laughed softly. 'I doubt that would apply to you, Constable McLean.'

'You may as well call me Morgan or Mac,' Morgan said.

'I believe the locals refer to you as the sheriff,' Monique replied. 'But I will call you Morgan. So, Morgan, what is happening with the investigation?'

Morgan took a long sip from his coffee before answering. 'So far, not a lot. Like Gladys Harrison, I don't think the first body unearthed is that of Joshua Larkin, and the second still remains unidentified. Forensics has at least identified the bodies as those of males between twenty and forty years of age. It also appears that the bodies have been buried for some time – maybe just under ninety years ago, which would make sense considering that the previous owners of the property, Captain Larkin and his wife Marie, disappeared around 1921. About all we know is that the men were killed by separate weapons, and that the first body appears to have been buried with some reverence. Other than that we don't have much else. I have a feeling that Mrs Harrison and her historical society will provide more information for the coroner than any of our efforts. I have been assigned the task of liaising with her during the ongoing inquiry. I can see that you have a vested interest in the matter as well.'

'As the house has been in our name since 1920 I suspect that this has something to do with my family,' Monique said quietly. 'I don't have a clue what that is but I almost feel a closeness to Joshua Larkin and his wife that I cannot explain.' She stared into Morgan's eyes as if seeking some doubt as to her sincerity but found none. 'Is it possible that his is the second, unidentified body?'

'We won't know that until we get a DNA profile back from the States, and find someone living to match the sample,' Morgan shrugged. 'The second skeleton certainly fitted Larkin's height and build as described in the old military records when he was alive.'

'I intend to carry out my own research,' Monique said. 'It is as if this Joshua Larkin is asking me to seek an answer as to what occurred here so long ago. I would like your help, if that is possible.'

Morgan wondered how he could help other than keeping her abreast of the official police investigation without divulging anything that may arise of a sensitive nature. But what could be considered sensitive in a murder so long past? 'I will do all I can to help you,' he answered. 'Can't see how it would interfere with the report for the coroner.'

Monique seemed to relax and smiled sweetly just as Morgan's mobile phone rang. It was a call from Hume City police HQ informing him that a job had come in for his attention: a noise complaint of a rowdy party in town. Morgan finished his coffee and rose from the table.

'You will have to excuse me,' he apologised. 'I have a job – the coffee was great.'

Monique escorted him to the back door. 'Thanks for answering my call for help,' she said. 'If I have to I will call a priest or pastor to perform an exorcism if the ghosts get too noisy.'

Morgan smiled broadly. Monique had remembered his small joke. He hated to admit it but she was the most attractive woman he could remember meeting in a long time. Certainly, she had an unsettling effect on him. But she was with another and Morgan had no intention of showing his interest in Monique Dawson. After all, she had not displayed any in him other than calling for his assistance as a policeman.

He walked through the chilly but clear night to his vehicle, pausing only once to look back at the young woman framed by the kitchen door with her arms wrapped around her breasts. He waved and continued to the vehicle.

Monique watched as Morgan drove away. She turned and locked the door behind her, wishing that David were home. This night she would sleep with all the lights on. The house had certainly taken on an eerie feeling since the two bodies had been disturbed and she wondered at her imagination conjuring up ghosts. But before she retired for the night she would go on the internet and find out as much as she could about Captain Joshua Larkin. Little did she know that her search would not go unnoticed.

In a room of MI6 in London a young man watched Monique's keystrokes in cyberspace. Sam Briars was

58

becoming intrigued by his task of monitoring everything and everyone identified by the Aussie press in the matter of the two bodies found in some obscure little village. In the course of his considerable searches he had ascertained that the property where the bodies were found belonged to Monique Dawson – and belonged to her family dating back to Captain Joshua Larkin's purchase.

As much as they tried to bluff it out, the kids were scared. Morgan knew fear when he was in its presence. Both young men stood by their respective hotted-up cars in the main street outside the town's only café. The lamplight reflected off the two vehicles that had been reported for doing noisy burnouts just outside the town limits.

'Young Steven and Mark,' Morgan drawled. 'How about you produce your licences?'

The two youths rifled through the pockets of their baggy trousers and handed their licences to him. Morgan knew both boys, each barely eighteen years of age. 'You realise that if I start writing out tickets you will be both walking to work next week.'

Neither boy replied, more shame-faced at being caught rather than at having been a dangerous nuisance to the public.

'But I am in a good mood tonight and you know the alternative,' Morgan added.

'Mr McLean, do we have to,' Steven protested.

Morgan flipped open his book, pen poised to commence writing out the traffic infringement notices. 'Your choice,' he shrugged.

'I will do it,' Steven blurted.

'Me too,' Mark joined in.

Morgan closed the book and grinned. 'See me at the station Monday after you knock off work, and I will give you the papers to fill in.' The boys' expressions of fear were replaced by looks of despair as they took back their licences.

'Don't forget,' Morgan said as he turned to walk back to his police vehicle. 'I will see you both at the station on Monday and don't let me find either of your cars on the street tonight – go home, now.'

Morgan slid into the driver's side of the four-wheel drive, placing the dreaded TIN book beside him on the passenger seat. His last view of the two boys was in his rear-vision mirror. Two faces reflecting sorrow for what lay ahead of them.

The good citizens of Valley View were not going to be kept awake by the screech of tyres, and justice had been meted out in an appropriate way to this couple of testosterone-driven young men. Morgan had just coerced them into enlisting in his old army reserve unit, where they would undergo a military training that would knock the edge off their excess energy and expose these small-town boys to the bigger world. Respect for themselves and others would become part of their culture. Morgan knew both boys were undergoing apprenticeships and had a future should they survive their wild ways. Their army service would also provide them with extra cash, which he hoped they would spend wisely. So far he had recruited a full section of the town's lads to his old reserve unit which he had joined after his discharge from the regular army. The boys had returned to town after training as different men, with a more positive attitude to life. The people of the town loved their sheriff for his commonsense approach to policing their tightly knit community – albeit not always according to the strict rules and regulations of the law.

★

60

It was after midnight when Morgan drove into the yard of the police station. He tidied up his paperwork for the shift, rubbed his tired eyes and reflected on the events of the night. For some reason Monique kept appearing in his thoughts. It had been a long time since Annette had left him. His former wife had grudgingly given up her well paid and glamorous life as a high profile public relations officer to a well known federal politician to travel with Morgan to Valley View. But life in a small country town had not suited her and, without warning, one day she was gone. Occasionally Morgan saw her on TV, standing behind the politician at one of his interviews, and the pain would stab him all over again. He had tried to contact her when she left but Annette made it very clear that she no longer loved him. The divorce came through in a pile of official papers.

Morgan McLean had been trained to be tough both physically and mentally. It had been the only way to survive the many missions he had gone on, to places in the world he would never be able to speak of, undertaking tasks so dangerous that he did not want to remember them anyway. And he had fallen back on his inner toughness to survive the agonising separation.

He knew that Annette leaving him had been the talk of the town but no-one dared approach him to offer their condolences. After all, according to popular perception, cops were a special breed of person and not subject to the same feelings as their fellow humans.

Returning to the police house after the decree nisi had at first been an almost impossible thing to do. He was reminded constantly of Annette's past presence. Little things he would find in the house that belonged to her would cause him terrible grief. It was true that time was a healer of both physical and mental wounds. The very fact that he had been having thoughts about Monique helped reinforce this for him.

With the last entry done for the car log Morgan rubbed his eyes and headed for his quarters – a house standing behind the station, provided for the local officer. He would make a cup of tea, watch some late night movie and then go to bed. Hopefully, the phone would not ring for a call out. He had a feeling that with young Steven and Mark being caught out the word would spread among the rest of the town's youth and they would either disperse or take their burnouts well out of town where no one would hear them.

SIX

Archangel
Early August 1919

The faces on the streets were pinched with cold and hunger. Major James Locksley had seen similar expressions on the faces of refugees in Belgium and France. Confused and frightened men, women and children displaced by a war they had not asked for. But the city of Archangel was nothing like anything he had seen in those former places. He instinctively recognised the influence of the Vikings on the place of his birth, and not only the Vikings but also an Asian influence seen in the towering church cupolas unlike anything in the West. Orthodox priests with their long beards and long black robes still could be seen in the muddy streets as evidence that the city remained loyal to the memory of the Czar. Colourful Cossacks on horseback and armed with lances rode in columns past him as he hunched against the almost forgotten cold of the city that lay in the Arctic regions. The

Russian troops were not alone; the British major recognised the uniforms of American, French, Czech, Canadian and British soldiers.

He arrived at his destination and showed his pass to a British soldier standing to attention in the cold. The soldier allowed him to pass and Major Locksley found himself in a spacious, marble-floored room where another British soldier sat behind a carved wooden desk with his head down, shuffling papers.

'Major Locksley. I am here for a meeting with Colonel Kingston, sergeant.' Locksley said, causing the soldier to look up, sit to attention and salute.

'Yes, sir,' the sergeant said, glancing down at the roster of the colonel's appointments. 'I will tell him you are here.'

Locksley waited, gripping the briefcase in his left hand that contained the papers and maps he would need for his mission. Glancing around the huge room he could see the ornate gilding, the work of past artisans, on the roof and walls. This had once been the house of a wealthy resident of the city, he mused.

'You can go through, sir,' the sergeant said, marching back from a door at the far end of the room. 'Colonel Kingston is expecting you.'

Locksley knocked once on the door and a voice within boomed, 'Enter.'

Locksley stepped into another large room to be met by a tall, aristocratic man wearing the uniform of a staff officer. The colonial wars campaign ribands on his chest gave away his maturity, despite the colonel's smooth skin that made him look much younger. The colonel offered his hand.

'Good to have you aboard, Major Locksley,' he said with a warm smile. 'I believe you have had service with our earlier efforts to help the Whites.'

'Yes, sir,' Locksley replied, letting go the firm grip. 'Last year in Siberia.'

'I have been told that Siberia is a tad colder than here,' the colonel said. 'But the ways things are going for us I doubt that we will be here for much longer. The damned ranks of the White Army can't be trusted. You know, we have had mutinies in the ranks of so-called loyalist troops and some of our own chaps have been murdered who were attached to those units. Bloody treacherous lot, the Russians, can't trust any of them.'

Locksley felt his cheeks flush. He wondered how well briefed the colonel was on him, and his unspoken question was answered when the colonel suddenly checked himself. 'I should apologise,' he said. 'I was informed from Whitehall that you are actually Russian by birth.'

'A man has no choice in where he is born,' Locksley tactfully replied. 'Only where he dies. I can assure you, sir, that I am British to the King's commission.'

'That I do not doubt, Major Locksley, considering your sterling service to the King and Empire. But so much for chitchat, time to get down to business. I believe that you were briefed on your mission in England and that I am to provide you with any assistance that I can, so that you can get about doing your job, whatever that may be.'

'Thank you, sir,' Locksley said. 'I realise that you have not been told anything about my role in this matter but I can assure you that its importance has major ramifications to the overall mission of us assisting the Royalists in their war against the Bolsheviks. I am sure that you understand the need for all this cloak and dagger stuff.'

Locksley could see that the British staff officer was not really convinced that he should be kept in the dark but he was a good soldier and obeyed orders.

'Well, where do we start?' the colonel asked, his hands behind his back.

Locksley opened his briefcase, producing a large scale map of the northern Russian region which he placed on the colonel's desk. Both men perused it.

'From my latest briefing in London I am to travel to this part of the front,' Locksley said, placing his finger on a place marked Emtsa.

The colonel peered at the name. 'It's a village that lies behind our current deployment,' he said. 'As far as I know it is in Bolshie hands.'

Locksley let out a breath of disappointment. It would take time to travel in this country to meet with the contacts originally established by the spy master, Sidney Reilly. That the village where the contact was supposed to be made was in enemy hands made this mission even more dangerous.

Colonel Kingston walked over to a map pinned to the wall of his office. It displayed the deployment of the British and Allied forces in the northern Russian campaign. He ran his finger along the Dvina River and stopped. 'General Ironside has forces deployed along the river around here,' he said to Locksley who had joined him. It was originally a Russian-produced map and Locksley could read the Cyrillic writing beside the English translation of locations. 'From the latest intelligence report, the general intends to push the Bolshies off the banks of the river. It will be a devil of a job as Lenin's men are well dug in and fortified.'

'It makes sense that I travel to join up with General Ironside's headquarters on the Dvina,' Locksley said, seeing no other option. 'I will need the appropriate clearances from your HQ to do so.'

'That is not a problem, old chap,' the colonel replied. 'You will be able to leave tomorrow morning with a column going up the rail to supply Ironside. I will have your papers ready and all you have to do is be at the rail station at zero six hundred. An NCO from my HQ will meet you there with the papers and pass. I am afraid that for the moment I cannot suggest any place of interest for you to fill in the time before you depart.'

'Thank you for your thoughts, sir,' Locksley said with a wry smile. 'I am sure that I can entertain myself in the city.'

With the business completed, Locksley saluted smartly and left the presence of the staff officer. He had rough and ready accommodation with a logistics unit near the harbour but was in no hurry to go back there. Instead, he dropped into an Orthodox church with its rounded cupola like an onion half. There amidst the echoing gloom and incense, the British major crossed himself and kneeled to pray. Old habits died hard despite his conversion to the Church of England. He was not alone and the many scarfed women – young and old – hardly gave him a glance, so preoccupied were they praying for those they had lost in this terrible civil war.

Major James Locksley, DSO had much to consider and needed to seek advice although he knew there would be no easy answer. He would offer a prayer for his wife and two children in England. When James Locksley had married a good, English girl from a wealthy family he had told her very little about his Russian roots. His children were growing up as English as any and only the war had brought him back into contact with his previous life. He also prayed for success. If his mission was successful he could change the course of the war and possibly history. As a Russian-born national, now working for the Secret Intelligence Service, it was within his power to do this. But, as a British officer sworn to uphold the oath of his commission to the King of England, Scotland and Ireland, he would have to forget the ties to the country of his birth. It was not an easy thing to put aside the Russian blood that flowed in his veins. Although growing up in England, he had been forced to deny his Russian identity, the smell of the giant fir trees and the vastness of this cold and troubled country was a part of his soul. His body belonged to the British army but his soul belonged to Mother Russia. His memories from his childhood were of endless seas of flowers growing across the steppes in the spring bloom. It was not a memory he could forget but nor could he neglect his duty to his adopted country of England.

Sludka village
Northern Russia
Early August 1919

There was a rumour floating around the battalion that they were to be evacuated back to Archangel, and then home to England. George Littleton prayed that there was substance to the whispers of hope as he had recently witnessed the terrible effect mustard gas had on its victims. The artillery barrage that preceded their assaults on the villages of Chudinovka, Kochimaka, Borok and Gorodok had poured in the deadly gas-filled shells – along with a mix of smoke and high explosive – before the Fusiliers launched their attack with rifle, bayonet and grenades. The two villages had fallen and George had again felt the almost paralysing fear before each battle.

The village of Sludka had also been taken by force of arms and the Russian dead still lay where they had fallen in the muddy, rutted streets. Smoke and flames billowed from the burning logs of the wooden houses and spent cartridge cases lay everywhere. Physically and mentally exhausted, George half kneeled in a former Russian trench, using his rifle as a prop, and took stock of the situation. His section had two men wounded – but not seriously – and he himself had not sustained a scratch so far. The rumour that they would be going home seemed to make his thoughts of survival even more moribund. Maybe God was going to play a cruel joke on him and snatch his life away just when it looked like he would live to see Australia again.

'George, get your section up and moving,' Joshua said, hurrying towards him. Sergeant Joshua Larkin was temporarily platoon commander as Lieutenant Jones had been laid up with a bout of dysentery and evacuated to a rear medical unit. 'The Bolshies are mounting a counterattack and we don't have the men to hold them. We are posted in the rearguard.'

George's morbid thoughts intensified when he heard the phrase 'rearguard'; it implied that they would be the last out and in constant contact with the Bolshevik troops pursuing them. It was a dangerous position to be in. Almost on cue George could hear the rattle of a machine gun and staccato of rifles from the edge of the village. The Bolshie attack was on and already the battalion was falling back, leaving Joshua standing beside George with his rifle tucked into his shoulder. George's men were well trained and now experienced soldiers. Each man knew his job and faced the yet unseen enemy. Suddenly, a group of Bolshevik infantrymen rounded a corner of the street that Joshua had organised the platoon to hold until the last moment.

'Fire,' Joshua yelled and the platoon's rifles opened up on the advancing infantry who did not have time to take cover. They were cut down but quickly replaced by their comrades surging forward. 'Sections one and three, up and move,' Joshua screamed. 'Section two, covering fire.'

Two of the platoon sections rose and raced for the end of the street, leaving their comrades to lay down fire on any foolish enemy who might try to follow them. When Joshua was satisfied that the first two small parties of men had gone far enough to take up secure firing positions to cover their retreat he bawled the order for the remaining section to move.

Gasping for breath, George flung himself behind a burning building and peeked around to see if the remaining section was joining them. He could see that they were, with Joshua ensuring that he was the very last man to take cover, flinging himself beside George. Sweat poured down Joshua's face despite the cold. The crash of gunfire was almost continuous.

'We have to get across the swamp,' Joshua panted, indicating with a nod of his head the direction of the Sheika River. 'Your turn to move out,' Joshua continued, turning his attention back to the last streets of the village before they were in the woods and heading for what was more like a swamp than a river.

George nodded and called out to his section to make a break for the edge of the forest beside the river wetlands. He could vaguely make out Joshua's booming voice shouting orders to provide covering fire. George and his section penetrated the dense and gloomy forest where many other soldiers were milling around seeking their NCOs and officers, before making a dash across a narrow plank that bridged the deep and murky waters below. The sound of rapidly approaching enemy soldiers firing behind them spurred him and his men on. Fear had pumped adrenalin through their systems and they managed to make the other side of the watercourse.

70

Safely across the plank, George took count of his men and was relieved to see that even the two wounded had been able to make it. They might be fighting a rearguard action for the retreat but they were winning in their task, he consoled himself just as Joshua and the remaining men of the platoon also struggled into the cover of the dense forest beyond.

Half crawling, half staggering, George made it to the trees and collapsed behind a fallen log to catch his breath and recover a little. It was then that he noticed that they were not the last to cross the river. The calls of distress were in English and when George propped himself up for a look he could see that around four British soldiers were floundering in the water, one an officer George recognised. Their heavy equipment was dragging the Englishmen under as bullets squirted waterspouts around them. Then George noticed a young, fellow corporal leap into the water and swim towards the drowning men. The Russians had reached the edge of the swampy river and were firing at the rescuer with everything they had, but one by one, Corporal Arthur Sullivan, dragged the men from the water, saving all four. A cheer went up from the throats of the Australian and English soldiers who had witnessed the courage of the young Aussie. Four men owed Sullivan their lives.

'Bloody fool should get a VC for that,' Joshua muttered. 'If I had been his officer I would be recommending him for one. Up and out of here,' Joshua ordered the men of his platoon. 'We still have a job to do.'

Exhausted but less fearful, George and the others rose from the soft, pine-needle forest floor and followed Sergeant Joshua Larkin in retreat to some place safer. They marched through the night to put distance between themselves and the pursuing enemy who Joshua suspected had called off the chase to seek whatever they could scrounge in the village that had fallen to them. Eventually they were able to collapse, thankfully into a location being prepared by another British unit as a defensive position further down the line. Only sleep mattered now and it came quickly to the soldiers wrapped around their rifles and huddling under their warm greatcoats.

George did not know how long he had been asleep when a distant voice seemed to be calling him from the end of a long white tunnel. At first he tried to ignore the call but a boot kicked his own and George slowly opened his eyes to stare up at the strained face of his friend, Joshua Larkin.

'Sorry, George. But you and I have been summoned to HQ.'

George accepted the hand that was offered to help him on his feet. 'They want to give us medals or what?' George cracked a tired smile.

'Don't think so,' Joshua replied, reaching down to pick up George's rifle. 'It seems we are to meet with some Pommy major by the name of Locksley. Don't ask me why but from past experience when majors summon you to a meeting it usually means trouble. I got briefed on him a little while ago when the brigade runner caught up with me. It seems that he is fresh out of London by way of Archangel.'

Passing George his rifle, Joshua turned and trudged wearily towards the centre of the sprawling impromptu camp, where he knew he would find brigade headquarters and the mysterious Major Locksley.

SEVEN

MI6 offices
London
Present day

Sam pressed the button to the printer and spat out all the hits on the name of Joshua Larkin. With a set of coloured highlighters he commenced identifying the individual enquires, attempting to place them into categories. His considerable skills in the world of cyberspace had equipped him to the mission very well although he was not briefed on why he had the task. He was aware that he worked in a world of 'need to know' and that all he needed to do was identify who was asking about this long-dead Aussie soldier. He was vaguely aware that his task was of some importance as he had been called into a meeting being chaired by the head of a section two levels above his and briefed on what he was to report.

Most of the hits could be tracked back through the ISPs to media outlets and this he considered normal. Many others were from private persons, no doubt curious at the past items in the media about the apparent murder mystery. Even the extensive searches originating from the address of the residence where the bodies were found appeared normal to him. After all, if a couple of skeletons turned up in your backyard you would have to show some interest in who they had once been. But, as a matter of course, he flagged the computer's signature and when he turned back to view his screen noticed that the resident of the house was on another search. This time it was about the 1919 campaign in Russia. Still, nothing unusual, he mused, reaching for the cup of coffee on his desk.

Sam keyed in his advanced program to continue monitoring any hits on websites pertaining to Joshua Larkin and sat back. 'Christ!' he blasphemed softly and leaned forward to activate the icon to trace the ISP from Russia. Though the program he used for tracking users was sophisticated, the source of the hits was disguised by cipher. Sam smiled to himself. This was not the first time in his career that he had seen similar firewall blocks. He had a good idea who was hitting on Joshua Larkin and his tedious task on the watch had just provided him with a challenge. Sam did not ask himself why one of Russia's foremost intelligence services would be making the search. The fact that they were was of note in itself and he duly logged the occurrence. Before the end of his shift his interest would again be piqued when a second hit came in from the Russian Federation. This one stirred a vague memory of a briefing he had once attended as part of his training for MI6. The firewalls were a lot easier to bypass and now Sam's log was slowly showing a strange but sinister pattern emerging. A known, neo-Nazi organisation was tracking Monique Dawson.

★

Harry Stanton read the internet results the trainee agent had left on his desk. The younger man sitting opposite Harry in the conference room had also read a copy of the same report and awaited his supervisor's comment.

'The Aussies have certainly stirred up more than they would ever realise in a million years,' Harry said, looking up from the folder in front of him. 'It seems that our old friends in Russia are aware of the implications of the Aussie find.'

'How would they know?' Daniel Kildare asked. He was only thirty-eight years old and a graduate of a prominent British university. He had the studious appearance of a young Oxford don and had only been with the agency for the past five years. Prior to that he had commenced a career in foreign affairs and from there was recruited for work in MI6. Daniel Kildare also held a commission in a territorial army unit and was fluent in three other languages besides English – Russian being one of them. He was an unmarried man without any real girlfriend, which he blamed on the long hours he spent developing his skills in intelligence work. His dedication had been noted by those above him and he was marked as a man who would go far in the service of his country. Some of his colleagues said behind his back that he was a fanatic, but grudgingly admitted Daniel Kildare could get the job done.

'According to the old records we suspect that Kim Philby passed on the file to Stalin just before the war,' Harry said, reminding his colleagues of the irreparable damage the former British intelligence traitor had done to England's security, before being exposed.

Kildare nodded. The home-grown spy web was now part of intelligence folklore.

'Apparently, when Stalin learned of the contents of the

file he was said to have placed it at the top of the list for attention by Beria,' Harry said. 'Such was the threat he saw in the matter and in due course, as the result of Beria's investigation, thousands of people were arrested, tortured and executed. Nothing was uncovered but we have since learned that in Stalin's paranoia he would often drag Beria before him and berate the sadistic head of the secret police for his failure to produce results.'

'The PM's department has sent the file back to us for actioning,' Kildare said. 'Where do we go from here, since it appears from the wording in their reply that they don't really want to know what is going on?'

The senior intelligence man pursed his lips. 'I still think that nothing will come of the Aussie's finding of the bodies, but it may be wise to send someone to monitor the situation on the ground, considering that the Ruskies are showing interest. I will discreetly feel out if the Aussie domestic intelligence services have wind of the Larkin file.'

'Do you think that is a wise move?' Kildare asked. 'How much would they know of the contents of the file?'

'Nothing that I know about,' Harry answered, glancing down at the growing pile of papers in his folder marked *Top Secret*. 'This file is restricted to only those I personally nominate for inclusion on the team.'

Kildare nodded. He hoped that his boss might nominate him to travel to Australia. After all, spring was already in the air in that part of the world and spring was followed by summer, whereas winter was coming to England. 'What about our friends in the USA?' Kildare asked.

'They need not have any involvement in the matter,' Harry replied. The last thing he wanted was for the Yanks to become involved in a purely British affair – well, an Anglo-Russian affair. The Cold War was long over but that did not mean old animosities were dead. The file had been sealed and was not to be opened until the middle of the 21st century. It was not unlike the American papers on the JFK assassination in that respect, except the file on the table in front of him had the potential to raise a lot of questions about the department's past dirty secrets and even reach as far as the behaviour of the revered former king of England, George V.

'If there is nothing else,' Harry said, 'you may as well do some homework on that Russian nationalist movement the Russian premier is so keen to stamp out.'

'I will get on it,' Kildare said, recognising that the meeting was over and rising from his chair to leave Harry Stanton rubbing his forehead.

It was hard to believe that matters almost a century old could be accidentally exposed by the unearthing of a couple of bodies on the other side of the world, Harry mused, watching Kildare depart from his office. But then who remembered the name of the Serb nationalist who fired the fatal shots at the Austrian heir and his wife in Sarajevo so long ago? Shots that would spark the terrible conflict of the Great War. And somehow not all the ghosts of the Great War were exorcised. They still had the power to wreak havoc on the early part of the 21st century. Harry Stanton had to monitor the disturbing rise of neo-fascist movements in Russia. The seemingly criminal gangs of skinheads were emerging with the trappings of Hitlerism in a country where the Great Patriotic War had lost so many of its people to the same scourge in World War Two. How strange it must be to the grandparents of the tough gang members now sporting tattoos of the swastikas their grandparents had despised and feared as the emblem of their annihilation.

Harry appreciated that the threat these same gangs

could perpetuate in Russian politics. The gangs had been virtually overlooked, but if organised and led by a strong person bearing a powerful icon, they could destabilise European geopolitics. Harry was learning from his sources within the new Russia that the influence of the gangs reached into the psyche of many Russians yearning for the symbols of the old imperialist Russia of the Czars and the gangs had the tacit support of many wealthy business-men who also desired a nation modelled on that of Nazi Germany in the 1930s under fascism.

Nothing would come of the discovery of the bodies in far-off Australia, Harry convinced himself. But he would feel better if he had someone on the ground to monitor the situation.

Valley View
Present day

Morgan could not believe his luck. There, in a fading brown carton were the police records for the station dating back to 1905. The string that tied them in bundles had left a faint stain like rust on the outside edges of the paper and it was clear that they had remained untouched since some police officer stationed at Valley View had filed them some time in the 1950s, according to the protruding slip of paper. Many officers had come and gone in their postings to the town but the box of old records had been undisturbed. Morgan was surprised that they had survived. He knew from experience that such papers were often consigned to the fire by police little interested in the history of policing in the area.

Carefully, he flipped through the bundles, each marked

with fading red ink on the outside page of yellowing paper, until he found the year he wanted – *1920–1921.* Removing the thin file he walked back to his office and sat down at his desk. As it was early evening and he was off duty he hoped that he would not be disturbed. He glanced around to ensure that he was alone and then placed his booted feet on his desk.

The papers contained records of lost and found property receipts, wanted posters and, most importantly, occurrence page entries. The occurrence pad was the log of incidents in the town that brought police attention or action. Morgan smiled when he read the names of culprits picked up for drunken and disorderly behaviour, many of them leading families in the district whose ancestors had not been so upright. He soon found himself absorbed in reading the day-to-day life of a country policeman who had once ridden a horse to attend call-outs, and whose duties went beyond simply enforcing the law. The local policeman was also the ex officio officer for about every government department that existed at the time, issuing licences and collecting monies on their behalf. But he sat up suddenly, removing his feet from the desk when he came across the name of Joshua Larkin. The entry was mystifying. The constable reporting the matter in his fine copperplate writing wrote in his stiff, formal reporting style:

20 December 1920
I proceeded to the recently vacated residence of Capt. Joshua Larkin at one o'clock this day as a result of a complaint from a Mr William Crawford of 2 Main Street, Valley View who expressed his concern for the security of the residence of Capt. Joshua Larkin and Mrs Larkin. I proceeded to the said residence and made a thorough search of the grounds but

did not find anything untoward. I informed Mr Crawford of my inquiries and he was satisfied with my report to him. No further action required in this matter.

It was time to try to find the missing persons reports – almost a century out of date. Morgan returned to the property room and rifled through the remaining stored papers but this time he was out of luck. But at least he had confirmed that Joshua Larkin and his wife had either left Valley View around November 1920 – or that one of them remained as one of the bodies discovered in Monique Dawson's backyard.

EIGHT

**Northern Russia
August 1919**

Sergeant Joshua Larkin and Corporal George Littleton
stood outside the tent sign-boarded as the headquarters
of the regiment. A tall, well-built major with a polished
brass-tipped wooden swagger stick tucked under his arm,
stepped out and eyed the two Australians. Joshua, as the
senior of the NCOs saluted.

'Are you the two chaps who are to report to me?' asked
the major, returning the salute.

'Sergeant Larkin and Corporal Littleton, sir,' Joshua
answered.

'Good,' the major grunted. 'I am Major Locksley and I
have a task that may suit you both as, I believe, before volunteering for the British army you were both commissioned
officers in your own army. I will need to speak to you both
privately and separately. You first, Sergeant Larkin,' he said,
turning his back and returning inside the tent.

Joshua followed and the British major sat down on a camp chair, leaving Joshua standing. The major planted the swagger stick between his legs, toying with the symbol of his field rank.

'Your commanding officer nominated you and Corporal Littleton as soldiers who have proved your mettle here. I believe that you have already done so for the King in France and Belgium and have been decorated for your bravery,' Locksley said, as if reviewing an invisible file.

'Yes, sir,' Joshua answered.

'I have requested two men to accompany me on what could be a dangerous mission behind the Bolshie lines,' Locksley continued. 'You were chosen because both of you are men who understand the meaning of loyalty to the Crown. You have sworn your allegiance to the King and his heirs in the past – and I would presume that the oath of office you once took still stands.'

Joshua was intrigued by the conversation. Where was it going? 'Yes, sir,' he replied. 'I may now be a non-commissioned officer but I still adhere to my oath to the King.'

'Good,' Locksley commented. 'Once an officer, always an officer, eh?'

'Yes, sir.'

'I am going to request that you volunteer to accompany me on this mission of utmost importance to the outcome of this war – and to the British Empire itself. At this stage I am unable to tell you anymore and will rely on you being discreet in all matters pertaining to your secondment. I can promise you that if we are successful there will probably be another gong in it for you and possibly restoration of your commission in the British army, Sergeant Larkin.'

'I am not going to volunteer for another gong, sir,' Joshua said stiffly. 'But I will volunteer if you say that the mission

82

is of great importance to the outcome of this war, because from what I can see, we are losing it very badly.'

Locksley shifted uncomfortably in his seat and stopped tapping the end of his swagger stick. 'I am sure that you have heard the rumours that we will be evacuated very soon.'

'Yes, sir. The rumours have been circulating since we heard that General Ironside has been replaced by General Rawlinson.'

'Well, it's true,' Locksley said. 'It appears that at this stage we will be out before Christmas. We cannot see any victory in this campaign against Lenin and his Bolsheviks. But if my mission is successful we might just turn things around.'

Joshua had no idea how this could be done but from his manner and demeanour had summed up the British major as no fool. There was just something a little un-British about the major he could not put his finger on. Something about his face and build.

'When do I commence my secondment to you, sir?' he asked.

Locksley stared at Joshua for a moment, examining his expression. Finally he spoke. 'You start immediately after you answer one question, Sergeant Larkin. Would you be prepared to kill your friend and colleague Corporal Littleton if I so ordered it?'

At first Joshua was stunned by the question. It was a test and he did not believe the British major was really serious – just one of those things the army did to test a man's blind obedience to the service. 'Yes, sir – if the conditions at the time warranted it,' Joshua answered. 'And I would expect Corporal Littleton to do likewise.'

'Good chap,' Locksley said, rising from his chair and tucking the swagger stick under his arm. 'Get your kit together and report back to HQ within the hour. The paperwork will be pushed through to your unit HQ. You can send in Corporal Littleton.'

Joshua saluted and stepped outside the tent to see George's questioning expression.

'The major just wanted to know if I was prepared to shoot you,' Joshua whispered. 'I said I would.' He was rewarded with a stricken look from his friend which melted when he saw the broad grin spread across Joshua's face.

'Your turn to see the major,' Joshua continued in a louder voice and dropped his voice to add as George stepped past him, 'Don't forget to promise the major that you will also shoot me.'

Confused, George entered the tent, leaving Joshua to wait for him. Joshua suspected that George would receive the same speech and like him, volunteer for the mysterious but intriguing mission, although the promise of a medal might be the main inducement for George. After all, the only reason the former Australian officer had elected to lose rank and go to war was for a taste of glory. Like so many other young men he had quickly learned that there would always be war – but no real glory. Just mud, exhaustion, bad dreams and the fatalistic knowledge that death might ruin any plans of returning home. One's name etched into a marble memorial in the middle of town was no consolation to being alive and living a full life.

Joshua waited for around fifteen minutes and George finally stepped out of the tent with a bemused expression on his face.

'I promised to shoot you,' he said with a grin.

'That means you were as stupid as me to volunteer for services with the mad major,' Joshua said, slapping his friend on the shoulder. 'Whatever the bloody mission might be. How come you volunteered?'

'Because you did,' George replied, puzzled that his friend should ask such a stupid question. 'You can't let your cobbers down.'

The answer echoed in Joshua's mind. How many times had he heard the same words in France and Belgium? How many times from the lips of dead men?

'Maybe we made a mistake,' Joshua grumbled.

'No,' George answered, checking his pace to step in with Joshua as they marched back to their portion of the Allied lines. 'I feel that whatever the major has planned is of vital importance to this war. And if that is the case then it is only proper that you and I be of assistance in any way that we can. It's just the right thing to do.'

'What in hell do you think the mad major is up to?' Joshua asked, shaking his head.

George screwed up his face. 'I bloody well don't know,' he replied, shrugging his shoulders. 'But whatever it is I have a feeling that you and I are going to see a bit of the countryside before returning to Australia.'

Joshua remained silent as they reached their lines. He suspected that his friend was right.

Even as the three scruffy-looking men, wearing the clothes of Russian peasants trudged through the shadows of the tall, silent trees, around them the Australian members of the British army were fighting a pitched battle near Emtsa village.

Joshua, George and Major Locksley each carried little other than a Scott & Webley revolver, along with two hand grenades and a razor-sharp knife, all carefully concealed beneath the many layers of clothing they wore. Each man also carried papers in case they were stopped by the

Bolsheviks, compasses, and tins of bully beef with packets of hard biscuits for rations. Locksley had revealed to George and Joshua that he spoke Russian and that they were to remain silent, feigning to be deaf and mute if questioned by any Russians they should meet on their trek. He would have a story that he was a relative in charge of them if any questions were asked.

Even at this stage – when they were two days from their last position inside the British defensive lines – neither of the Australians had been informed what their mission was. All they knew was that they were acting as a kind of body-guard to the British major and that if he should be killed they were to attempt to get the message back to London of his failure to complete the mission. They were to inform only one man in that eventuality and that was the chief of the British Secret Service. This did not surprise either George or Joshua. Everything about the way the mission was conducted smacked of intrigue at the highest levels of government: the threat that either could be killed by the other on orders from the mad major; the fact that they were no longer wearing their Australian army uniforms and were setting out to travel deep into territory occupied by Lenin's forces.

They walked in silence with the major leading, occasionally stopping to shoot a compass bearing. Satisfied, he would signal to continue.

'We should reach a village before nightfall,' Locksley said on one brief stop. 'There, we are to make contact with the village priest.'

'I don't suppose you are going to tell us why, sir,' Joshua said, rubbing his mittened hands together against the bitter cold.

'No, sergeant,' Locksley answered. 'The least you know

the better it is for us should you happen to be captured and tortured.'

Joshua had to agree with Locksley's logic. There was no doubt the enemy could torture him to death and he could tell them nothing of why he was out in the forest trudging around with a mad Pom and an Aussie mate. So far that possibility had been remote, as the vastness of the forests of northern Russia had concealed them from any sighting by the enemy. If loneliness lived anywhere in the world it had to be in these forests, Joshua mused.

Eventually they stumbled onto a rutted and winding track. Locksley said that they would follow the track, paralleling it in the cover of the forest rather than walking along it in the open. They did so, moving cautiously until they came to the edge of a clearing and saw the log houses of a tiny village. Smoke rose from the chimneys, hanging in the air above the houses, and in the muddy, rough streets thin, cloth-wrapped figures moved slowly, pulling wooden sleighs stacked with firewood.

Locksley removed a small pair of opera binoculars from his pocket and scanned the village. Beside him, Joshua and George waited for a decision.

'A warm bed tonight, boys,' the major said. 'This looks like our destination. But I will wander in first and have a little look-see, to confirm we are at the right place. If anything happens – you know the way back to our last location. From there, just make your way to Archangel and report to a Colonel Kingston at Logistics HQ. He will look after things from there.'

'Sir,' Joshua acknowledged. 'Good luck.'

Locksley lowered his binoculars and looked at the two Australians. 'Thank you, Sergeant Larkin.' The brief moment of warmth between the three men was a break from the rigid formality of the past days in each other's company.

'You can hang onto these,' he added, passing the glasses to Joshua. 'I will get them when I return for you both after dark.'

With his parting words, Major Locksley stood up and walked into the muddy clearing. Hardly anyone looked at him as he approached the cluster of buildings. This was a time when displaced persons on the run from either side often stumbled into the village, which had attempted to remain neutral in this bloody civil war. Through the binoculars Joshua watched the major disappear behind a building.

There was little they could do for the moment except open a tin of bully beef and eat the fatty meat cold. No fires or lights to show their location – just a hope that the mad major would return for them after dark.

Chewing on the salty meat, George wondered how the hell he had let himself volunteer for this insane mission when he was so close to going home. He had proved himself in the brief time they had spent on the Russian front and had no need to stay. Maybe he was catching Joshua Larkin's disease of being just plain suicidal. George had meant it when he had told his friend the only reason he was also volunteering was because Joshua had. It had not been the possibility of a decoration that had induced George to remain behind in the lonely, cold and desolate forests of Russia. It had been friendship.

The night came as an eerie twilight followed by darkness. Joshua dozed as George lay in position on sentry detail awaiting the return of the British major out of the night.

'Joshua! Wake up!'

Joshua woke quickly, gripping the butt of the pistol. He blinked away the remnants of sleep to see a file of flickering lights. Tapers of flaming sticks marked a column of Russian infantry snaking its way into the village. From their dress he could see that they were most probably Bolshevik forces and they preceded a team of horses towing a large artillery gun. The situation had just turned very bad. Locksley had not returned.

NINE

Valley View
Present day

The first that Morgan heard about the papers and journal was from Cheryl, behind the counter of the local service station, when he had refuelled the police car.

'G'day, Morgan, did you hear that Gladys was given a heap of papers and stuff concerning those skeletons you found up at the Larkin house?' the forty-ish, peroxide blonde with the sun-tanned face said, pushing the police petrol account towards him to sign. Monique and David's residence had quickly earned the title of the Larkin residence since the media attention. 'Seems that the Crawfords found the stuff at their place.'

Morgan looked up sharply. He had only just seen the Crawford name the night before in the old police report. 'No, I didn't know,' he replied, scribbling his signature in the account book. 'Has Gladys still got the items?' he asked.

'As far as I know,' Cheryl answered, filing the account book in a drawer behind the counter.

'Thanks Cheryl,' Morgan said, leaving the office with its displays of trucking magazines, cassette tapes of Country and Western music and racks of lollies. Morgan always wondered why Cheryl stocked goods more at home on the busy highway north of Valley View. At least the C & W tapes sold to the locals.

Morgan slipped behind the steering wheel and set his thoughts on visiting Gladys Harrison. It was possible that the items she had in her possession might help the coroner ascertain the identity of the two bodies. It was only a three-minute drive to Gladys Harrison's residence. Hers was a sandstone cottage, a relic from the 19th century but well maintained and one of the tourist attractions in the tiny town snuggled in the hills. English climber plants covered one half of the front wall and the wooden verandah belied the age of the house.

Morgan checked himself off the air over the radio and walked up the paved path. His knock on the door was answered by a balding man in his late seventies who Morgan recognised as Gladys' husband, Stanley. 'Hello, Stan. Is Gladys in?' Morgan asked with a reassuring smile.

Stan stared through rheumy eyes for a moment and called back into the house, 'The wallopers are here to take you away, Gladys.'

Morgan winced at the old man's attempt at humour.

'Constable McLean, come in,' Gladys said cheerily, appearing behind her husband, wiping her hands on a worn tea towel. 'I have just baked a batch of scones and can put the billy on for us.'

Morgan winced again but what could he expect from the president of the local Country Women's Association in

Valley View. She was not famous as a scone maker, despite her years of trying. 'Thank you, Mrs Harrison,' he answered with as much conviction as he could muster. 'I would really love a scone.'

Morgan followed Gladys to the kitchen with Stan shuffling along behind. 'You're a bloody good liar,' he grumbled so that only Morgan could hear him. 'You can have my share too. I'm going out the back to read the paper.'

Morgan ignored his comment and sat down at the 1950s Formica table. Gladys bustled around, producing tea pot, scones and her locally conserved apricot jam which Morgan smothered on his rock hard scone.

'I suppose you are here about the papers and journal Betty Crawford has given me,' Gladys said, pouring the tea for them.

'That, and your wonderful scones.'

Gladys stood up and disappeared from the room to reappear with a shoe box from which she lifted a pile of very old-looking papers. She passed them to Morgan. 'This is what she found when she was cleaning out their back shed yesterday. I'm afraid the cockroaches have done some damage.'

Morgan glanced at the papers. They were eaten away around the edges and the black spots denoted cockroach excreta. Still, he was pleased to see that they were still relatively intact despite the years they had been stored.

'You know,' Morgan said, turning over the battered, leather-covered journal in his hands. 'I was only last night reading about a Mr William Crawford who back in 1920 had the local constable have a look at Captain Larkin's house.'

'That would be Betty's husband's grandfather,' Gladys responded. 'He was a great friend to Captain Larkin. Old

Bill Crawford was also a veteran of the Great War and it seems that they had been in some of the same battles on the Western Front. His name is inscribed on our local war memorial to all those who volunteered from the town and served overseas.'

Despite being a member of the local sub-branch of the RSL, Morgan had not really taken much notice of the list of names of volunteers from the town and district on the memorial, or of a Great War soldier resting on arms reversed planted at the end of the street. He felt just a little guilty at his oversight and took a small bite from his scone.

'Do you mind if I take temporary possession of all these papers?' he asked politely. 'They might prove invaluable to the investigation.'

'I was going to take them down to you,' Gladys said, sipping her tea. 'I have already photocopied everything and have sent off the copies to a university where they have someone who can translate the Russian writing for us. Hopefully when the coroner has concluded his investigation we will get the journal and papers back for our museum.'

'I am sure you will in no time at all,' Morgan replied, peering at the thick documents stained by time and wear. They carried ornate symbols of a double-headed eagle with a crown on both heads and in the back of his mind he remembered having seen such an emblem somewhere before. Possibly in a book on Russian history, he thought, as he stared at the Russian writing on the documents. 'Maybe you could keep me informed of what your Russian translator has to say,' Morgan added.

'I certainly will,' Gladys said. 'Monique tells me that we should have something back fairly soon.'

Morgan was jolted by the mention of Monique Dawson's name. 'Ms Dawson knows about the documents?' he asked.

'Of course,' Gladys said, placing her delicate tea cup on its saucer. 'She and I have formed what in your business you would call a task force – to enquire into the happenings at Larkin House in 1920. She is a lovely young lady and a credit to the community.'

Morgan was slightly annoyed that he did not know of the happenings going on around him without his knowledge. Gladys Harrison and Monique Dawson were getting themselves involved in a police matter, albeit with good intentions.

'Well, I just want to thank you for all your help in the inquiry, Mrs Harrison,' Morgan said, rising from the table with the papers and journal. 'Have you had a chance to read the journal?'

'My goodness, no,' Gladys answered. 'The handwriting is very hard to decipher and the words written in such small size I would need a new pair of eyes to read what Captain Larkin wrote. Monique has promised to provide me with a full transcript as soon as she has gone through the copies I gave her.'

Morgan nodded. Gladys stood up and went to a sideboard. 'Being a single man I am sure you would always appreciate something home-cooked for your larder,' she said, producing a plastic container of her scones for him.

'Mrs Harrison,' Morgan answered diplomatically. 'I cannot thank you enough for your wonderful gesture. I am sure that they will go to a good cause.'

Morgan accepted the gift noticing that Gladys' husband had shuffled into the kitchen with a wide grin on his face. The two men exchanged meaningful looks as Morgan left the house with scones in one hand and the collection of papers and journal in the other.

★

The telephone call came as a surprise. Morgan shook his head, placing the phone back on the receiver. He was officially off duty and the invitation to have coffee in the town's one and only coffee shop that also doubled as the general store was not something he was called to do every day.

When he walked in Morgan greeted the proprietor, a rather overweight young man whose real love was in the world of cyberspace rather than groceries and coffee. Monique sat in a corner, sipping a mug of instant cappuccino. She was staring absent-mindedly through the large glass window at the town's memorial to the fallen.

'Monique,' Morgan said, standing over the table. 'Your invitation is a pleasant diversion from my duties.'

'I like coming here,' Monique smiled as Morgan pulled out a chair to sit opposite her. 'It may not have the sophistication of the cafés in Sydney but there is something very homely and honest about Rick's coffee shop.'

Morgan laughed at her description of a corner of a general store with its three tables and rickety chairs allocated for snacks. A panel of the latest video releases provided a partition from the rest of the store. 'I am sure Rick would be flattered by your description of the space near the window,' he said as Rick ambled over to take an order.

'A mug of coffee like the one Miss Dawson has thanks, mate,' he said to Rick.

'No worries, Morgan,' Rick answered. 'Right away.'

'So, to what do I owe the invitation?' Morgan asked.

'I don't know if you have had a chance to read Captain Larkin's journal yet,' Monique said, turning her attention to Morgan. 'But I think you may be able to help me with some of the material he has written. A lot of it seems to be in a military language I have no experience with. He seems to have used a lot of abbreviations.'

'Normal stuff,' Morgan replied, glancing down at the typewritten sheets she slid across the table towards him. It was obviously a transcript that she had made on a computer and printed out. Morgan could see dates to each entry commencing in 1919 and it looked as if Monique had done a good job of transcribing what Morgan remembered of the soldier's seemingly scribbled notes. 'This is for platoon and this one for brigade major,' he said, pointing to a couple of abbreviations. 'I see that you have been busy,' he added.

'I was so engrossed in the captain's journal that I sat up all night translating as best as I could,' she said clearly weary from the effort. 'I am up to where he returned to Australia in 1920. His story is fascinating and so sad. So much suffering he must have seen in war and yet he had time to reflect on the occasional moments of beauty he saw around him.'

'In the Great War we lost more soldiers than in World War Two and all wars since,' Morgan said. 'It was a terrible time.'

'You have been a soldier in a war,' Monique said. 'It is sad that we civilians give little thought to what you must see and have to do.'

Morgan shifted in his chair. He had once been a soldier but that was another life, one he knew he could never explain to one who had not been there. 'Kind of good that you don't,' he shrugged. 'Soldiering is something outside all the good we know in our society.'

'I guess so,' Monique sighed.

Rick placed a mug of steaming coffee in front of Morgan.

'Well, if I can be of help with your work I will be,' he said, raising the mug. 'You are at liberty to drop into the station at any time.'

'You know this town,' Monique smiled. 'The fact that

96

I am sharing a coffee with you here will be gossip around town tomorrow that we are having an affair.'

'Probably,' Morgan said, returning the smile. 'The town could say worse about me.'

Monique looked away at his light-hearted comment. 'I may take you up on your offer,' she said. 'I feel that the captain's story is going somewhere very important.'

'Why do you say that?' Morgan asked.

'Because I have read his epilogue and if what he has said is true then his story is one of the most explosive of our times.'

'In what way?' Morgan asked, leaning forward.

'Gladys has informed me that you have the captain's journal. When you get a chance, read the last pages and you will understand,' she said softly, glancing at her watch. 'I have to go, David will be home from Sydney by now.'

'Sure,' Morgan said, rising to his feet. 'It has been nice sharing your company and conversation.'

Monique extended her hand. 'Thank you for your help,' she said. 'But I must get home now.'

Morgan watched her leave then walked over to the counter and paid for his drink, knowing that Rick would be telling the next local to walk in that Morgan McLean and Monique Dawson had been having coffee together. Such was life in a small town.

As soon as he returned to the station, Morgan pulled out the journal from the drawer of his desk. He flipped to the last pages and what he read made him gasp. Monique had grossly understated what she had discovered.

Across the world in the offices of MI6, Sam Briars was also sitting up in his swivel chair as he read Monique Dawson's file of the transcription she had made. The trojan virus he had planted on her computer was working well and he was able to access her files without her even knowing. 'Bloody hell!' he swore, scrolling down the pages. It was no wonder that any mention of the Aussie Captain Joshua Larkin caused such a flurry in the levels above him.

This time, however, what he had on his screen would cause more than a flurry – it would cause the perfect storm.

TEN

Northern Russia
August 1919

Joshua watched the flickering lights and could hear voices raised in fear as the Bolshevik soldiers went from house to house in search of food and possible young men to swell their ranks for the revolution, whether they wished to or not. He lay on his stomach and used the binoculars to ascertain how many of the enemy had accompanied the field gun. He swept the binoculars across the village and could see the Bolsheviks smashing in doors. Had Locksley had time to escape? He hoped the English officer had some warning of the arrival of the enemy soldiers in the village.

Major James Locksley did not have time to slip out of the priest's residence. The enemy had arrived unexpectedly in what he had wrongly assumed was an isolated village too far removed from tactical advantage to the Bolshevik army.

The door had burst open and five ragged men carrying rifles tumbled in to shout orders for all within the priest's house to stand where they were. James Locksley stood at the centre of the room and immediately raised his hands to show that he was not a threat to the men menacing him with their rifles. Beside him, the bearded and black-cassocked priest also raised his hands while the priest's dumpy wife sat frozen with fear by the fireplace. She was forced with a rifle butt blow to the back to stand with her husband where she trembled uncontrollably.

'I am a commander from the 6th Lenin Brigade,' Locksley said with a voice of authority, at the same time praying that the papers he carried from the real – but dead – Bolshevik commander would work. He reached with one hand to his pocket to produce the papers just as a sixth man entered the room. He was a huge, bearded man bearing a fresh scar above his eyes. Unlike the other men in the room he carried only a pistol in a shiny leather holster strapped to his hip. Locksley immediately guessed he was the commander of the forces outside. The big bear of a man glared at Locksley, accepting the papers and perusing them quickly. He did not hand them back but stuffed them in the pocket of his fur-lined jacket.

'What business do you have with this enemy of the people, comrade Sihkorsky?' the commander asked in a cold tone.

'I am here recruiting the people of this village for the glorious revolution, comrade commander,' Locksley answered, returning the cold stare. 'Your arrival is unexpected. What is your unit, comrade?'

For a moment the bear did not answer and with a speed belying his size he smashed Locksley in the face with his fist. The British major knew then that his bluff had probably not worked. He fought to remain standing. The blow had broken his nose, splashing blood on his assailant. Locksley was vaguely aware that the priest's wife had screamed. As he reached up to wipe the blood from his face with the back of his sleeve he saw the Bolshevik commander draw his pistol from the holster, raise his arm, and level his weapon at the head of the screaming woman. A single shot caused her last sounds on earth to cease. She crumpled to the floor at the feet of her petrified husband. Snapping from his frozen fear, the priest let out a wail and bent to cradle his wife's bloody head in his arms. Another shot followed and he fell lifeless across his dead wife.

'Two less class traitors to the revolution to feed,' the bear grunted, swinging his pistol on Locksley. 'But you are a different matter. I don't know who you are but it has been your bad luck to assume the identity of a comrade I know was killed fighting the British near the village of Onega. I will spare you for questioning. Then I will kill you.'

With a gesture, the Bolshevik commander had Locksley searched, his weapons taken, and his hands tied behind his back.

Locksley knew that he was a dead man. He only prayed that he would not reveal what the priest had told him minutes earlier but also knew torture was inevitable at the hands of a man who could so casually take life. He hoped that the two Australians would be able to avoid the Bolshevik patrols and make their way back to Archangel and brief Colonel Kingston that the mission had failed.

Throughout the bitterly cold short night both men swapped sentry duty in the hide that they had made from fir needles and logs. Although they were around a hundred yards from the village they were well concealed from view. However, Joshua knew that the Bolsheviks might be well trained enough to mount a clearing patrol of the area in which case their hide would probably be discovered. Already he had formulated a fall-back position for himself and George some half a mile from their present location in more heavily timbered country to their rear.

The short night gave way to an equally bitter morning with low, grey clouds. Joshua nudged George as he lay curled on the floor of the forest until he came awake and handed him the binoculars to take over surveillance duties.

George wriggled forward, lifting the binoculars. 'God almighty!' he swore, pressing the eyepieces of the binoculars closer. 'I can see the mad major!'

Joshua took the glasses from George and focused on the hand-tied man being led between two armed soldiers. Even at a distance he could see the signs of brutal treatment; the British officer could hardly walk and blood stained his shirt. At one stage Locksley stumbled and was immediately struck around the head with a rifle butt by a guard. They led him to one of the houses and thrust him inside.

'Looks as if the major is finished,' George commented. 'His orders were for us to make our way back to Archangel.'

'Don't be in a rush,' Joshua grunted. 'From what I have observed of the Bolshies so far it seems that they are not a very professional mob. Probably just peasants snatched up by their revolutionary masters. So far all I have counted is around a dozen armed soldiers guarding the gun. And from what I can observe the biggest bloke out there is the commander, and the only ones with any professional appearance are three of the gun crew. They look like they know what they are doing around their piece. You notice that they didn't send out a clearing patrol this morning. They must be pretty confident that they have nothing to fear in this part of the country.'

George listened warily. He sensed from the way Joshua was speaking that he might be formulating some hair-brained scheme to rescue the major.

'You know that we are under his orders to get out if anything happens to him,' George said lamely. 'After all, we don't even know what the hell we are doing out here. Whatever the mission was is as dead as the major will be soon enough.'

Joshua put down the glasses and rubbed his eyes. 'I'm not going to pull rank and order you to help me,' he said wearily. 'But I wouldn't want to face the fate in store for the major. It's always been our way to help our mates.'

'He's a bloody Pommy officer,' George attempted to rationalise.

'And we swore to help him,' Joshua countered. 'Do you want in?'

George rolled his eyes to the grey sky above. 'What in hades do you think,' he sighed.

'Thought so,' Joshua grinned. 'It's going to be easy with these blokes. All we have to do is hope that they don't do away with the major before nightfall. Then we will make our move and rescue him.'

'That easy?' George said sarcastically. 'The Bolshies mightn't be real soldiers but they outnumber us with real guns and a semblance of being alert. What do we have?'

'Surprise, four bombs and two pistols,' Joshua replied. 'And a chance for you to take home a Victoria Cross to impress your family.'

George knew his friend was attempting humour in a moment when he had put their lives on the line. No deco-ration for bravery could replace just being alive.

103

For the rest of the day the two Australians lay in their concealed position, taking turns to rest, eat and watch the enemy move about the village. Joshua thanked the gods of war that the village had been occupied by relative amateurs. Had they been trained troops, he knew his plan would have little chance of succeeding.

The beatings had gone on all day it seemed to Major James Locksley as he lay on his side of the earthen floor. He had trouble seeing out of one eye, now closed by a blow, and knew that he had lost teeth. It hurt when he breathed and he suspected that his captors had broken some ribs as well.

The Bolshevik commander was not as stupid as he appeared, Locksley concluded. Finding the British-made hand grenades and pistol on him, the bear, as Locksley named his captor, concluded that Locksley was probably a spy for the White Army. Fortunately, he had not discovered Locksley's British identity. In the end, Locksley had given away some information to his inquisitors, if only for an interlude from the beatings and burning of his skin with a glowing, fire-heated poker.

They were careful not to take the torture to the point of death, the bear realising that his captive was probably a man of importance to the White Army, maybe a high-ranking officer with much to tell on their enemy's military dispositions. He had some regrets for killing the priest who might have given helpful information on the man they were brutally interrogating. But his hatred for the Russian Orthodox Church, dating back to his early life in his own village in southern Russia, and for those who preached subservience to the Czar was enough to make him act impulsively.

The prisoner had finally confessed that he was attached

104

and the two men with the commander stood back near the door observing the interrogation. They were armed with rifles slung carelessly on their shoulders.

A grim smile of satisfaction creased Joshua's face and he hefted one of the two grenades into his hand. Everything now depended on the British major's ability to comprehend the events of the next few seconds.

'Major Locksley, sir,' Joshua yelled from outside knowing that his voice should carry through the window but not be understood by the Russians inside. 'I am about to toss a grenade inside. You have to get the table over and stay behind it.'

Joshua's shouted command startled the Russians who reacted by unslinging their rifles. Swearing, the commander stood up from the table, unholstering his pistol. But Major Locksley seemed hardly to react to the command. He lifted his head and blinked at the movement in the small room. Joshua pulled the pin on the grenade and stepped to the window. It sizzled and smoked as the internal fuse burned its way down. Experience had taught him just how long he could hold the grenade before it went off. Locksley heard the sound and instinctively dropped to the earthen floor, painfully knocking the heavy wooden table on its side to act as a shield.

It was the commander who saw Joshua's face framed by the window. He snapped off a shot that threw splinters, causing him to flinch away.

Joshua tossed the grenade inside where it thumped onto the earthen floor and rolled to stop at the Russian commander's feet. For a second, Joshua could see utter terror in the big man's face but he reacted quickly by bending down to pick up the grenade.

Joshua ducked his head back just as the blast ripped

through the room, the shrapnel from the exploding grenade tearing flesh in the confined space. He kicked in the
door, praying quickly that the major was still alive and that
the grenade had done its job. When the door flew open
he was rewarded by the sight of all three Russians lying
on the floor. One of the men stirred, groaning in his pain
from the terrible shrapnel injuries. Joshua shot him in the
head with his revolver and stepped over him to look behind
the upturned table. It had absorbed much of the grenade's
shrapnel, shielding the major, who was lying on the ground
curled into a foetal position. Joshua reached down and was
rewarded by the major staring up at him with bleary eyes.
Joshua helped him to his feet.

'Are you okay, sir?' he asked but the major only blinked
at him without comprehension. Then he shook his head.

'Sorry, old chap,' the major said loudly. 'Can't hear a
damned thing you are saying.'

The major's deafness was confirmed when a second loud
explosion shook the cabin to its foundations. He did not
appear to have noticed although the explosion had caused
Joshua to jump. George's grenades had set off the ammunition wagon, causing confusion among the ranks of the
Bolshevik soldiers. Joshua doubted that many would spill
out of the safety of the villagers' stout homes to investigate
the cause.

Quickly, Joshua stripped a Russian for his clothes. The
British officer dressed with irritating slowness but Joshua
understood that his injuries were causing him great pain.

'Time to get out of here,' Joshua yelled into the major's
ear. 'They aren't going to stay quiet for very long.'

Although Locksley could not understand a word the
Australian sergeant was saying he had enough of his wits to
realise that they had to flee the village.

Joshua placed his arm under the major's shoulders and helped him through the door into the night, now alive with frightened shouts from one cabin to another. Joshua guessed that the survivors were discussing what to do next.

In the cover of darkness the two men made their way back to the rendezvous point Joshua had established outside the village and were greeted by George.

'Let's go,' George said, assisting Joshua with the British officer.

Behind them they could hear the sounds of men organising a search. They were far from safe.

ELEVEN

MI6 HQ
London
Present day

Harry Stanton's mug of coffee had gone cold. He hardly paid it any attention as he thumbed through the report that had been compiled for him by young Sam Briars and added to by Daniel Kildare. From what he could ascertain a journal had been kept by the late Captain Joshua Larkin detailing the events in Russia. Jason's considerable skills in hacking other people's computers had provided the MI6 department head with all the information he needed for a first rate ulcer. Secrets that should have lain buried for eternity were now staring him in the face and the transcription of the journal lifted from Monique Dawson's computer on the other side of the world were as clear as the headlines in any leading British tabloid. Stanton knew that if what was before him leaked out to the media it would make front-page news in every Western paper, easily displacing even the latest scandals of the young royals.

But worse still, was the impact the information could have on the stability of an already rocky Russian Federation. With his hands behind his back, Harry leaned back in his comfortable leather chair and looked through the double-glazed window of his office onto the city of London below. It was a bleak day outside with sleeting showers of rain but not as grim as the way he felt. He knew that the Prime Minister's department would scurry for shelter and leave his department out to dry if he did not nip the situation in the bud. Careers could fall on whatever decision he made next.

Leaning forward, Harry flipped over the pages of the report. So far the secret appeared to be confined to a tiny and internationally insignificant part of the world that, he had been briefed, was relatively cut off from the mainstream of events in Australia. That he had the information before him was good but what the young intelligence analyst downstairs had warned him about was the inordinate interest being shown by a Russian website well known for its extremist right-wing politics. Harry strongly suspected that they had the same information sitting in a report somewhere in Russia and would most likely act swiftly. That meant he could not delay. The contents of Captain Joshua Larkin's journal must be destroyed before they leaked out to the media. The total elimination of the journal was now of highest national priority.

Harry Stanton took a deep breath and sighed. He cursed the regulations forbidding smoking in the building. He had given up ten years earlier but right now he would have killed for the nicotine rush to sooth his nerves.

Breathing out, Stanton picked up the phone and dialled an internal number. As he did he scribbled a name across the front of the folder containing the explosive report.

'Kildare?' he queried. 'I want you in my office in fifteen minutes. We have to talk about Operation Cleaner . . . I know you have not heard of it . . . That's right, its existence will be severely restricted.'

Stanton replaced the phone. Maybe ghosts are real, he thought. Because the ghosts of a lot of long-dead people were haunting him now.

Valley View
Present day

The first signs of winter giving way to spring were appearing in the rolling hills of Valley View. Flowers were thrusting through the earth and the sweet sound of native birds were more apparent in the blue skies.

Morgan McLean had read the transcripts of the journal and wondered cynically if it could have been some elaborate hoax by the late Australian army officer. After all, the incident of the *Hitler Diaries* had fooled a lot of experts. Three weeks had passed since he had been given the transcripts and in that time Monique had disappeared from town. She had left a message that she would be in Sydney visiting her parents and that her partner, David would be travelling to Los Angeles on a business trip. But life had gone on as usual for Morgan who policed the district with a firm but friendly hand.

He finished the paperwork on the three young learner drivers who had nervously chewed their nails while sitting on the front verandah of the police station awaiting their turn to be tested. The two girls passed their driving tests easily but the young man had failed; reversing onto the footpath and running over the sign in front of the town's only general store and café had not helped his cause.

The relevant paperwork completed, Morgan glanced at his in-basket and lifted the first file from the pile. It was a folder from district headquarters with attached coroner's papers on the two as yet to be identified bodies. Morgan reflected with a touch of guilt on the fact that he had Larkin's journal in his possession and had not as yet informed anyone in the police service of its existence. Was it really relevant? He opened a drawer to his desk and removed the well-worn journal with its dog-eared pages and stared at the book in his hand. The phone rang and Morgan placed the journal on his desk.

'Valley View police. Senior Constable McLean speaking,' he answered.

'Senior bloody Constable McLean,' the irritated voice of Detective Sergeant Ken Barber drawled from the other end. 'Do you hicks in Valley View ever get newspapers?' he asked in a not-too-friendly tone.

Morgan sat up straight, leaning into the phone. 'What the hell are you going on about?' he asked.

'Well, if you had read the *Sydney Morning Herald* today you would have noticed the headlines.'

Morgan instinctively glanced at the journal on his desk with a gut feeling that whatever had the detective sergeant upset had something to do with the contents of Joshua Larkin's writings. He did not know why he thought that – except he had a good copper's nose for such matters. 'Sorry, Ken,' he replied. 'I have been taking driving tests all morning. What's this about the paper?'

'Do you know anything about a diary kept by one Joshua Larkin?' Barber asked.

Morgan hesitated. His instinct had proved correct; he placed his hand on the battered journal. 'Er, sort of,' he hedged. 'I saw some transcripts of its contents.'

113

'Do you know where the original document is?' Barber questioned.

'It could be with our historical society. I will chase it up,' Morgan lied, not knowing why he would cover up the existence of the journal. He was not comfortable lying to the senior detective he counted as a friend but something deep inside told him that the book on his desk had suddenly taken on an importance beyond anything he could imagine. Was it possible that everything the former army captain wrote was true? The hair on the back of his neck stood up. For whatever reason, Morgan knew that he had to delay the book being passed to another party until he had time to sort out its implications. Was it a former special forces soldier's instinct for danger that made him not tell the truth? 'Besides, what is in the headlines?' he asked.

Barber paused. 'It seems that someone in your town gave a university lecturer in Russian language copies of documents for translation. The translator contacted the media to say that the papers related to a Russian princess by the name of Maria. He told the newspapers that he had information from his source in Valley View that there was a journal written by this Captain Larkin bloke to corroborate the documents.'

Morgan immediately knew what the matter was about. He found that his hand was trembling – just as it used to after a contact in the deserts of Iraq. 'So what?' Morgan countered, hoping that his voice did not give away his rising apprehension.

'So, according to some half-baked investigative journalist the documents and journal prove that not all of the Russian royal family were killed back in 1918. That this princess Maria survived and not only survived but came out to Australia – and to Valley View of all the godforsaken

114

places. According to my hunch, the diary has to have something to do with those two bodies so you need to find that bloody book as quick as you can.'

'Leave it with me, Ken,' Morgan said, placating the irate detective. 'I will dig up the journal but it might be a couple of weeks before I track it down.'

'A couple of bloody weeks! It would be better if you said a couple of days!' Ken Barber exclaimed. 'How busy do you get out there?'

'I have a fair bit of paperwork to catch up on,' Morgan offered lamely. 'I have a station inspection coming up next month.'

'I will keep you to your deadline,' Barber growled. 'Have the journal and documents on my desk this time in a fortnight and be prepared for a barrage of phone calls. I suspect that you will probably have all those bloody current affairs programs hammering on the door of the station wanting to prove that we had a real live princess living the rural life in Valley View.'

Morgan suspected that the detective sergeant was right in his expectation of publicity. 'I will get down to the pubs and general store to warn them to stock up for the invasion,' he said lightly. 'It will be wonderful for tourism around here.'

His view of the looming situation caused the detective to chuckle. 'Don't expect me to sign off on any overtime for all the interviews you do,' he said. 'I will be out in two weeks to pick up the journal. It's part of the coroner's file now.'

Morgan placed the phone on its cradle. No sooner had he put it down than it rang again. It was a prominent TV reporter wanting his comment on the article in the morning paper. Morgan was polite when he said he had no comment to make and put the phone down. He quickly switched it to the answering machine and hoped that the media did not have his mobile phone number. He needed time to think. First, he must get in contact with Monique which might not be easy. But his instincts told him that whatever was going down had something to do with her.

St Petersburg, Russia
Present day

The concrete was crumbling, revealing the rusting re-inforcing steel rods behind the walls. The promise of the great Soviet dream to build factories had been achieved by taking short cuts and the three-storey building that had been intended for use as a factory producing consumer goods was never occupied. But now it provided the ideal training ground for Petrov Batkin's youth group of starry-eyed idealists dreaming of a new order in Russia.

Batkin watched the party of nine predominantly young men pretending to be warriors as they ran and shouted through the decaying corridors of the deserted building. He knew that they were attempting to impress him with their bravado, balancing precariously on exposed steel girders as they crossed the gaps a storey above the jumble of broken glass and rough concrete blocks below. A fall could incur serious injury – or death.

Batkin had the muscled body of a man half his forty-eight years on earth. The scars on his back and chest were a legacy of a Taliban RPG-7 blast many years earlier in Afghanistan when he had been part of a Spetnaz team infiltrating the valleys and mountains of his country's enemy. That had been a time of despair, when he saw his country care little for the sacrifice of its young men. Batkin grudgingly admitted that he had comrades in the West who had served a decade earlier in a war in a place called Vietnam and they too had died for an ungrateful nation. Batkin did not like the West. He could see its decadent influence in the streets of his beloved Moscow corrupting the youth born after the end of his military career. At least these young men and women balancing on the exposed beams had displayed some sense of what Russia could be given the right circumstances; to rise once again as a super power, not in the failed tradition of the Communists, but that of the ancient Czarist times, before the disastrous revolution of 1917. Most of his old special forces comrades called him a foolish dreamer, swigging the rotgut vodka at reunions rarely held now. After all, either the vodka killed them or they chose to take their own lives, forgotten and unmourned by their country as they lay in morgues around the new Russian Federation.

Oh, but he would have dearly loved to tell his students of new developments in the future of Russia. He watched a young woman, older than her comrades, wiping the sweat from her brow as she descended from the balancing exercise on the girders. Under the grime she was very beautiful, Batkin mused. More importantly, he calculated she was potentially one of the most important students that he was grooming for future operations. No longer would simply the bashing of the inferior races from the former impoverished republics flocking to Moscow in search of employment be their trademark. Those nationalist expressions of extreme violence against helpless immigrants were seen by some bleeding-heart liberal Muscavites as being on a level with the rising racist, skinhead groups of Europe. No, all his group needed was genuine legitimacy in the political system and then the average Russian would flock to their cause. After all, had not Adolf Hitler risen to power in Germany by promising the defeated nation its rightful dignity in the world? Symbols were all powerful in man's search for meaning in life and he had learned of the most powerful symbol for his cause.

Batkin removed a mobile phone from his coat pocket and made a call. He had found his ideal candidate for the mission to a far-off country. All he needed now was the backing of his secret admirers and financial supporters.

Sarah Locksley felt the muscles in her thighs cramp. She was not known as Locksley to her Russian instructor but rather as Sakharov. Her mission to infiltrate the neo-Nazi gang in St Petersburg for MI6 had been achieved on account of her fluency in Russian and her profile as a young English woman of Russian heritage being disillusioned with the ways of the West. Like many misguided children of radical immigrants she feigned an idealism for the past glories of the Russian Empire of her ancestors. The leader of the St Petersburg chapter had accepted her loyalty to their cause and Sarah knew that her model-like beauty had helped her win him over. As tough as Petrov Batkin was however, he was still a man, and over the weeks of demanding physical and mental training he had come to accept her as a trusted member of the gang of young men and women preparing for urban warfare in the coming revolution.

Batkin knew that his English student resided in one of St Petersburg's better hotels but that was expected of a woman used to the luxuries of the West. She openly spoke of her family's wealth in England and so he was not suspicious of her. He had been able to learn from discreet inquiries made by his organisation that she was a twenty-nine year old former model and now freelance journalist for a radical right-wing magazine in Germany – and that she was single and had never married. For his upcoming mission, the girl had a perfect profile.

Sarah bid her companions a good day and left for her hotel. Here she would flip open her well-hidden laptop and report all that she had learned of the organisation's aims, leadership and methods. In return she could scan her email.

Sitting on the edge of her bed Sarah opened the encrypted email from Sam Briars. She frowned as she had no romantic interest in the gawky computer expert whose sending of bits and pieces of information were intended to impress her. She was impressed, however, by his blurted confession to her at a wine bar that he was able to monitor even his superior's so-called secure cyberspace mail. She knew that he had made the indiscreet confession to show off his considerable intellect in the field of Information Technology. Had she done her job she should have reported him, but she had filed away what she had learned for her own use in the future. After all, the old adage that knowledge is power was very valid in the universe of intelligence gathering. Sam Briars was nothing more to her than an awkward boy infatuated by her. She could use his expertise when it suited her although she had been, at least, impressed by his ongoing emails outlining the Larkin affair in Australia. It had echoes in her own family history. Sarah Sakharov aka Locksley read the latest information and her eyes widened. A journal had been discovered and there was a hint that a member of the Czar's family had survived the massacre to travel to Australia. Sarah took a deep breath. Could this be the answer to the little spoken

119

of scandal concerning her great-grandfather? If so, then a matter of family honour cried out for vengeance. Sarah Locksley did not know it but even as she clicked off her laptop circumstances were conspiring to resolve the matter of her family honour.

TWELVE

The taiga
South-east of Archangel
August 1919

The stabbing pain came even when Major Locksley breathed.

'Broken ribs,' he winced, gripping his chest.

'They really did you over,' Joshua said, examining the British major's head for any sign of injury. 'Other than that, you seem fine.'

'Thank you, sergeant,' Locksley said with a touch of sarcasm. 'I am sure that your medical credentials are impeccable.'

'About the best you will get out in the taiga,' Joshua said, standing and scanning the gaps in the thick stands of forest behind them. The temperature was dropping and the three men felt the cold bite through the layers of clothing they wore.

'What is our situation, Sergeant Larkin?' Locksley asked.

'Down to our last four tins of bully beef, one packet of biscuits and a tin of jam,' Joshua answered. 'No bombs left and thirty-six rounds of ammo for the two pistols.'

'Not good,' the British officer grunted. 'But we have to go on.'

George cast Joshua a questioning look. 'Would it not be better that we call off the mission, sir,' Joshua offered quietly. 'Considering the extent of your injuries.'

Locksley gritted his teeth against the shooting pain in his chest. 'You were once an officer, sergeant, would you call off the mission if you were in my position?'

'No, sir,' Joshua sighed. 'Well, we still have a compass and all we need to do is keep a bearing of due east. That course will eventually bring us to our rendezvous point about twenty miles away.'

'What do we expect to find there?' George asked.

Locksley turned on the Australian corporal. 'It is not up to you to ask that question, corporal.' He replied. 'All you have to do is complete the mission.'

What bloody mission? Joshua thought. From the beginning all they had been briefed was that they were to escort Major Locksley on a mission behind the Bolshevik lines. What they were going to do there was left out of the briefing – other than that the British major might make it clear why they were risking their lives if his position became untenable.

'Sir,' Joshua said. 'In my opinion your injuries have seriously impaired your ability to complete whatever mission that we are on. Either we take you back or you brief us now as to why we are out here.'

Locksley grimaced. 'I was careful to pick you and Corporal Littleton for this task,' he said. 'The mission is so important that if I cannot go on you must carry out any

122

orders that I give you without question. The mission is so important that it is worth more than our lives. That you were once commissioned officers gives me faith that you have an understanding of your sworn oath of loyalty to the King. But at this stage I am not considering going back so will rely on you and Corporal Littleton to help me complete what we have set out to do. Is that clearly understood?'

'Yes, sir,' Joshua answered, frustrated by the air of mystery surrounding why exactly they were in the middle of a dark and almost silent forest deep in enemy territory. 'But what if you are killed?'

'Should that situation suddenly arise, I have taken steps to cover the event,' he answered. 'I am going to write out an outline of what you are to do upon identifying the reason for us being out here,' he said. 'Should you be in possession of the briefing paper, because of my inability to go on, you are to immediately destroy the paper after accepting its contents. My outline will be clear and concise. The paper will be in my top pocket.'

Joshua shrugged and turned away. It was time to march east to whatever awaited them.

Although Joshua and George had left the village occupiers in a state of turmoil after their short but brutal attack, the Bolshevik militia were able to reassemble. The survivors knew that they would incur the wrath of the supreme council of the district for the loss of the precious artillery gun and needed to hunt down those responsible.

The killing of their commander had caused enough confusion to give the three invaders time to put a reasonable distance between themselves and the village. But they were travelling with a man slowed by his injuries. A party was organised immediately to go in search of whoever had done the damage to their section. They had the advantage of knowing the region. It was only a matter of time before they would catch up with the three enemy soldiers.

The three soldiers did not make more than five miles before the sun began to set. They had moved cautiously but the distant sound of their pursuers drifted on a brisk breeze towards them. Major Locksley hobbled at the rear, supporting himself at times with a stick that they had fashioned into a crutch.

'Stop,' Locksley commanded. 'We need to reassess the situation.'

George and Joshua slumped down beside the major who rested with his back against a tree.

'It appears that the Bolshies are on our trail,' Locksley said. 'With the way I am they will catch us before the sun rises.'

'We will have the darkness to conceal our position,' Joshua offered.

'You well know that even if they overshoot any hide we make for the night that will only put them in front of us and the chances of stumbling on them tomorrow is too well stacked in their favour.'

'I can lead them off,' George said with an expression of reluctance, secretly cursing the British major for persisting with his mission when they should have turned around and headed back to Archangel.

Joshua glanced at his fellow Australian. 'Or I can.'

'You're the senior non-com,' George said with a weak grin. 'You should have volunteered me to lead off the Bolshies.'

Joshua shook his head. 'You only do it if you promise me that you stay out of trouble.'

'Corporal Littleton's volunteering to lead the enemy away from us makes sense,' Locksley said. 'You have my permission to do so.'

George stood up and stretched his long limbs. 'Time I got going then,' he said. 'I will double back and take a course north for about five miles and then the same east before going south. According to my calculations, that should put me in the area of the rendezvous point.'

'Do you think that you can do it?' Locksley asked.

'The compass and paces will keep me on track,' George said, raising a compass to his waist to shoot a bearing north. 'Needless to say I will leave enough clues as to my panicked flight north.'

'We will cover all traces of our tracks here and pray that your ruse works,' Locksley said. 'What you will be looking for at the contact point will be a couple of log huts in the woods. Good luck, old chap,' he added.

'A bit like Hansel and Gretel finding the gingerbread cottage,' George quipped. 'But hopefully without the wicked witch.'

He flashed them a grim smile and began his trek north. He would continue marching through the short night until he was certain that the hunters had peeled off to follow him, allowing Joshua and the mad major to continue east. But as confident as he had appeared briefing the other two on his intention to set a new course, George realised that finding the meeting point would be like searching for the proverbial needle in a haystack. He would be alone in enemy territory, potentially sacrificing his life for a mission the purpose of which he was completely in the dark about.

★

125

Joshua and Locksley were careful to retreat into the forest, concealing any traces of their movement. They had gone a mile when darkness fell and they set about constructing a hide under fallen timber and moss clods.

The two men took turns staying awake to guard against a surprise attack but it seemed that either the pursuers had camped for the night or that they had continued to follow George's trail into the forest. Joshua guessed that the Bolsheviks would have halted. Tracking a man at night in the dark forest was near to impossible. But if George continued marching he would be exhausted by the time the sun rose over the taiga. Joshua hoped that his friend had enough sense to consider his options. He felt responsible for the affable young man.

When the sun returned to warm the vast forests of Russia Joshua helped the major from the concealment of their hide. In silence they threw down the last can of bully beef and drank from a clear pool of water. As neither had detected the sound of their enemy it seemed that George's courageous ploy of luring off the enemy had worked, although the weather was setting in with a sky black and ominous. And the temperature continued to drop.

Locksley appeared to be recovering from his injuries and Joshua was amazed by his resilience.

'Time to go, Sergeant Larkin,' the major said, taking a bearing east with his compass. 'I think that we should be seeking shelter before the storm is upon us.'

As they set off Joshua found his thoughts drifting to George. He had grown to respect the young man's toughness as he had proved himself to be a fighter since they had disembarked at Archangel and fought their way through the Russian campaign.

'How far, sir?' Joshua asked.

'I am not sure, sergeant,' Locksley replied. 'But I pray we will reach our destination before dark. It will require a cracking pace.'

Joshua shrugged. He would see if the English major had the strength to do it. If not, he would take possession of the paper Locksley had placed in his pocket and go on alone.

Corporal George Littleton was at the end of his tether. He had forced himself to stay on his feet during the night but exhaustion was setting in. Just before dawn, as he stumbled through the forest his legs gave way. Groaning, he collapsed into the soft bed of pine needles where he lay, breathing in the antiseptic smell that mingled with the richness of the damp soil.

Despite attempting to stay awake, George drifted into a dreamless, deep sleep. Time lost all meaning until his world of slumber was rudely shattered by a painful kick in his ribs. He awoke, confused, and for a moment did not know who he was or why he was lying on the ground in some place that could have been anywhere in the world. He sat up and blinked at the hazy figure. A uniformed soldier was pointing a pistol directly at his head. As George's vision cleared he could see a row of about forty armed and mounted horsemen staring down at him.

The soldier pointing the pistol at him shouted something in a foreign language. George presumed it was Russian. At least he had led off the hunters from the village and given Joshua and the major time to continue their journey. At least he hoped so – otherwise his death would be meaningless.

'Okay, you've got me,' George groaned and noticed a look of surprise on the soldier's face.

'You speak English?' the soldier said.

George turned his attention to the man who from the way he was dressed was obviously an officer. 'I should,' George replied. 'I am Australian.'

'Australian?' the man with the gun queried.

'British,' George answered, realising that nationality was probably more understood in this campaign.

'I speak English,' the officer said with a heavy accent.

A few Russians might, George guessed – not that it helped his chances of surviving a firing squad or a long and tortuous journey to Siberia.

'You have . . .' the officer hesitated, searching for the words. 'Identify,' he finally said, pleased with his recovery of the word.

George reached inside his shirt to produce his identity discs, which the officer leaned forward to examine. George could smell a trace of vodka on his breath.

'What is name?' the officer asked.

'Corporal George Littleton of the British army.'

'I am Lieutenant Andrej Novotny of Czech cavalry.'

George could hardly believe his luck. A weary smile broke across his face. 'Good to meet you, Mr Novotny,' he said with a sigh of relief. 'You came at the right time.'

'I need to take you as prisoner,' Novotny said without any sign of malice. 'We need to make sure of your identify.'

George nodded, understanding the protocols. He was sure that he would be released when they contacted the British authorities. The Czechs, who were allies in the fight against the Bolsheviks, would have liaison officers attached to British HQ. 'I am sure that you will have my identity and status confirmed when you contact the British army,' George said confidently.

A frown crossed the Czech officer's face. 'That could be problem,' he said. 'We are cut off and trying to reach

Archangel. We have mission but mission hopeless. Now, all armies go home. War lost.'

No sooner had the officer made his statement than one of the mounted soldiers shouted something, causing the Czech to look beyond George into the depths of the forest. A rifle bullet cracked past George's ear, followed by a volley and the distinctive burst of a machine gun. A horse neighed in pain and collapsed with its rider.

George instinctively fell to the earth, reaching for the pistol concealed in his clothing. The officer dropped beside him, searching desperately for the source of the sudden attack on his patrol. He shouted in his language and the horsemen galloped away leaving two horses and two dead soldiers behind. It was obvious that the Bolshevik militia had caught up and carefully laid out a line to fire on the Czech patrol.

'We have to get out of here,' George shouted in the Czech's ear, gripping his sleeve to drag him away.

Novotny did not resist and the two men wriggled along the ground towards a fallen tree, which George hoped would provide them with temporary cover. From behind the rotting log George peered cautiously to see figures flitting between the tall trunks. 'Must be a company of the bastards,' he said aloud. 'Doesn't look good. We need to get further away.'

Novotny wiped away dirt from his eyes. 'We stay,' he said. 'My men have orders. We stay. It safer.'

George frowned. As far as he could ascertain they were pinned down and the Russians were manoeuvring in the forest to outflank their position. To confirm his pessimistic opinion that they were trapped a Russian suddenly appeared only a few feet away, running at them with a rifle. George popped up from the log, exposing himself to snap off two shots from his pistol. The Russian collapsed and tumbled to stop at the edge of the fallen trunk. A hail of machine gun fire raked the log, chopping away the rotting timber as if it were paper. George knew a bullet would eventually find them. It was all over but at least he would go out fighting, albeit in some forgotten part of the world, against an enemy hardly anyone back home knew about since the cessation of the War. It all seemed so futile.

Then he heard the shouts and increase in gunfire. It was coming from their flank.

Novotny grinned victoriously at him. 'They good men, my men,' he said. 'They do what I say.'

George had a sudden respect for the fighting abilities of the Czech army. It was obvious that the officer had commanded his men to retreat and redeploy for a dismounted assault on the Russian flank. The Czechs had fitted bayonets to their carbines and charged along the line of Russians with the fury of devils possessed. The Bolsheviks had seen the mounted patrol retreat and presumed that they had frightened them off but they had underestimated the discipline and courage of their enemy and were now paying the deadly price.

George now knew he was safe even if he was in the company of the Czech soldiers who'd become cut off from the main forces retreating to Archangel. Unwittingly the Czechs had aided his own mission – whatever it was – to assist the British major and Joshua in having a clear run to their objective – wherever it was.

THIRTEEN

Valley View
Present day
Two weeks later

Morgan realised that the battered journal in his hands was probably worth its weight in diamonds to a collector. But it was also as deadly as if he held a small atomic bomb in his hands. As far as he could ascertain the book belonged to the Crawford family as they had possession of it for so many years.

Morgan knew the family as hardworking and deserving of a break; they were, in the Australian vernacular, 'battlers'. So he would return the journal to them with strict instructions to keep it somewhere secure until a time when they could possibly sell it. As far as he knew, the original documents that had caused the interest by the media were still with Gladys Harrison. She also would have to ensure those documents were kept in a safe place.

The Crawfords and Gladys Harrison listened to Morgan's story and agreed to follow his instructions, as well as safeguarding their secret for the moment.

When he returned to the police station Morgan was met by Detective Senior Sergeant Ken Barber who stomped out a cigarette before following Morgan inside.

'You've got the diary?' he asked with a pained expression. 'Or those other documents you mentioned?'

'Sorry, Ken,' Morgan replied. 'I can't seem to locate anyone who knows about them.'

The burly policeman stared at Morgan as if sizing up a suspect. 'What about this Mrs Harrison sheila?' he asked.

'I went and saw her,' Morgan answered. 'She seems to have misplaced the documents and the only record she has of the papers she sent the university are her own copies. She thinks that someone may have stolen her originals. You know what it is like around here – everyone trusts everyone and no one locks their doors. But I would not put it past someone in the town to have knocked them off hoping to make a quid at a later date.'

Barber stared at Morgan. The experienced copper had not been fooled by his lie.

'You know we need everything we can get for the coroner,' Barber said. 'That means all documents that may be pertinent to our investigation.'

'Don't get me wrong,' Morgan protested. 'I am part of the investigation and the bodies are on my patch. I have just as a strong reason as you or anyone else to close the case.'

Barber sighed. 'I get the feeling you are not playing it completely straight with me, young Morgan,' he said. 'But you aren't a bad copper and for whatever reason you have to be fudging this one I will go along with you to a point. All I need is for you to come up with some evidence that will give us the identities of the bodies and we can put it all to bed. How have you been handling the media?'

Morgan felt a little less anxious. The switch in topic indicated that the matter rested for now.

'Most have given up,' Morgan replied. 'I have given them the stock answer that we have nothing to confirm their stories about any Russian princesses living in Valley View – that the whole thing appeared to have a basis in a prank perpetuated by locals to encourage tourism. You know the media, no crumbs and it seems that their interest has been diverted to some Hollywood gossip about some actress having a baby.'

The slightest smile crossed Barber's face. He well knew the attention span of the average TV or newspaper journalist. When the chance of a Russian princess being an inhabitant of some out-of-the-way Australian town in the 1920s was balanced against a well-known Hollywood starlet being pregnant, the average punter would go with the story about the Hollywood actress. History had no interest to the average punter, Barber thought, reaching for his packet of cigarettes.

'Well, that's about it,' he concluded. 'Just keep me up to date on anything that you might come across that's relevant to the investigation.'

'No problems,' Morgan answered. 'You will be the first to know of anything of importance.'

Barber pulled a cigarette from the packet and wandered out of the police station trailing a stream of smoke. He stopped beside his car to gaze around at the surrounding hills and sky as Morgan watched him from the doorway of the station.

'I have a feeling that it's gonna be a hot summer this year,' Barber smiled. 'Hope your hippies behave themselves for the festival.'

The festival! Morgan suddenly remembered that the

week-long folk festival was in two weeks' time and it was his duty to organise the policing for the event that attracted thousands to the small town and district.

'They're not hippies,' he called down to Ken Barber.

'In my book, anyone with long hair is a bloody hippie,' Barber said, hoisting his massive frame into the driver's seat.

As Morgan well knew, the big policeman had been a national serviceman fighting in the rice paddies and hills of Vietnam when many of his former friends had avoided military service and run off to communes. From that time on, all people Ken Barber despised were labelled 'hippies'.

Morgan watched him drive away before going back to his office. He slumped into his chair and stared bleakly at the wall. A poster proclaimed some young person as missing in Sydney and another advertised Neighbourhood Watch. He had hated lying about the journal and papers but there seemed to be more to this case than just the two unidentified bodies found at the old Larkin residence.

A knock at the door brought Morgan back into the present. A young boy of around eleven years who Morgan recognised as one of the primary school seniors entered nervously. Morgan vaguely remembered his name as Christopher.

'Senior Constable McLean,' he said in a quiet voice. 'Tommy has my bike and won't give it back.'

Morgan rose from behind his desk and walked over to the boy, placing his hand reassuringly on his shoulder. 'Where is Tommy now?'

'He is down at the café, with the other boys from his school,' Christopher answered.

Morgan grabbed his police cap from the front desk and ushered the boy outside, closing the door behind him. He

134

was back in the real world of police work. He had a dispute to resolve.

Sydney, Australia
Present day

The organisation's financiers had been relatively generous in allocating funds to the mission, Petrov Batkin mused, checking into the plush hotel overlooking the harbour.

'You are in Room 364, Mr Olev,' the prim, young Japanese receptionist said, passing Batkin a plastic keycard.

Batkin accepted the card without answering. His English was good but the less he said the less he gave away. His passport was false but well enough forged to fool the best in any customs service.

He had only one suitcase. He picked it up to carry it to his room, waving off the hotel's porter service. At the third floor Batkin exited the lift. He smiled at a Filipino lady, obviously a cleaner with her trolley of equipment. It paid to blend in with the others around him and a smile was expected.

Entering his room, Batkin stepped out on the balcony to admire the view he had of the harbour below. He had never visited Australia before and his knowledge of this continent so far from Europe and Russia was limited. Observing the tranquillity of the harbour now and the openness of the busy city on his bus trip from the airport he could not help but envy the city's citizens for what seemed an easy life compared to his experiences in Russia. They were soft, he thought, staring down at a green ferry-boat plying the calm blue waters. The people of Australia were very much like the Americans: obsessed with materialism and their TV shows.

This would be an easy mission compared to the many he had once undertaken for his country. He could not foresee any problems in some little Australian village west of the city on the harbour. There would no be roadblocks and demands from machine gun toting border guards demanding identity papers. Nor shadowing by a ruthless internal security service bent on imprisoning him. The very open nature of the society he was operating in made his task easy.

Batkin returned to his room, stripped off his clothes down to his underwear and sat on the floor to complete his daily rigorous exercise regime of push-ups and sit-ups. Only then would he allow himself sleep.

When he awoke refreshed from the jet lag of the long flight, he would take out his laptop and find a website that would give him an overview of Australian culture and customs. He had work ahead of him. He needed to hire a car and then wait for Sarah Sakharov who was due to fly in the next day. But most importantly, he was scheduled to meet the leaders of Russian organised crime in Sydney and brief them on the help that they were to provide as his backup. It would be they who would outfit him with a weapon.

Valley View
Present day

As usual it was Cheryl at the local service station who informed Morgan that Ms Monique Dawson had returned to the town from a trip to England. Cheryl was a fountain of intelligence for anything happening in the district.

'You looking forward to the festival?' she asked Morgan as he signed the petrol book.

136

'Like another hole in the head,' he growled without looking up. For him, the folk festival meant little sleep and a lot of work policing the many visitors to the town. But his seemingly ungrateful comment was in part spurred by the knowledge that the coroner's investigation was still his priority in policing. When he glanced at Cheryl he could see his comment had hurt her feelings. After all, the festival brought a lot of money to her service station. 'I suppose it will go well,' he added with a weak smile. 'I just have a bit of work on my plate.'

To further please her, Morgan paid for a Weiss bar. The ice confectionary would go down well on this unseasonally warm day. The news about Monique having been in the UK had taken him unawares. The last thing she had told him was that she was travelling to Sydney – and the UK was a long way from Sydney.

Morgan closed the car door and shifted the four-wheel drive into gear. He knew his next stop and drove north out of town until he came to the old Larkin residence. Wildflowers sprouted in the surrounding sloping fields and the sky was studded with fluffy white clouds. Spring was well and truly settling on the Valley and even the house seemed to have taken on an air of waking from a winter slumber.

Morgan pulled into the gravel driveway and radioed off the air. He was hardly out of the vehicle when the front door opened. Monique greeted him with a warm smile.

'Heard that you made a trip to the UK,' he said by way of his greeting.

'It was not originally on my agenda,' Monique answered. 'And hello to you, too.'

Morgan flinched. 'Sorry,' he said with an embarrassed smile. 'Kind of good to see you back safe and well.'

'Would you like to come in for a coffee?' she offered. 'David will be home tonight.'

Morgan took a breath as if considering the invitation, although he knew he would accept. 'That would be nice,' he said. 'We have a bit to talk about.'

Morgan followed Monique in to the living room, which was crowded with cardboard cartons. It was hard to tell if she was unpacking or packing. Items were strewn about all over the place.

Monique quickly boiled a jug and prepared two coffees. When she had placed a steaming mug in front of Morgan on the polished coffee table she settled onto a vintage settee opposite him. 'My trip to London was prompted by some things I learned in Sydney,' she said as if answering his silent question. 'It was not planned when I last saw you here.'

Morgan felt uncomfortable. 'I did not mean to appear to be interested in your personal life,' he apologised. 'It's just that I too have read the journal and it did not escape my notice that if this house has been in your family since the 1920s then that would have to mean you are somehow connected to the late Captain Joshua Larkin.'

Monique took a sip from her coffee and looked past Morgan's shoulder to a newly framed photo of a handsome couple on the wall. 'I went to England to look into some old records,' she replied, looking back at him. 'And from what I could find in my research I believe that you might be correct.'

Morgan leaned forward, expecting her to continue. 'Is there some kind of link?' he asked.

'I cannot say for certain,' Monique answered. 'I am waiting for some information to be sent to me from a DNA test I did in the UK, but it will take some weeks to get back the results. What I learn may help identify who was buried outside our house – if your American DNA specialists are able to get a sample from the bones recovered from here.'

'I am about one hundred per cent sure that Joshua Larkin is not one of the bodies that we found,' Morgan countered.

'How can you be sure?' Monique asked, slightly frowning.

'Because I have access to old police records. You see, I have a piece of the jigsaw puzzle just as you too have a piece.'

Monique placed her mug on the coffee table and stared at him. 'I wish I knew you better,' she said. 'But if my information is correct it has the potential to cause more trouble in my life than it is worth. Please trust me to keep my silence on what I may learn from the results of the DNA test.'

Exasperated, Morgan stood up. 'Would you tell me if you were a blood relative of Joshua Larkin?' he asked bluntly.

Monique paled. 'I have a feeling that if the world were to learn that it would cause a lot of distress in my life,' she countered.

'I'm sorry for appearing a bit less than tactful in my questions but I have to know as much as possible to close this case. I suspect that if we can cross Joshua Larkin off the list that is a start, and the fact that I strongly suspect that you are a descendant of his helps me further.'

'If what you say is true, then you must go that one step further,' Monique said, her eyes wide with what Morgan thought was fear.

He frowned. 'You mean Larkin's wife, Marie,' he said.
She nodded.

'Bloody hell, I think I now understand what you mean. You know it's my job to protect members of the public,' he said lamely. 'So, if you need any kind of help you only have to ask. I am only a phone call away.'

The young woman looked at him with just the hint of tears in the corners of her eyes. 'I can handle it,' she said. 'But thank you for your offer.'

Morgan knew instinctively that it was time to lay off. In a sense he would still leave with the information he had come for. 'I have to go back to the station now,' he said. 'Just remember my offer.'

As he drove away Morgan pondered what he strongly suspected: that Monique Dawson might be the great-granddaughter of the last princess of Russia. And that had dangerous ramifications from what Joshua had read in Joshua Larkin's journal.

Morgan logged onto the net as soon as he got back to the station. He needed to conduct his own research on the Princess Marie. He was surprised to find some evidence by modern-day scientists in Russia that two bodies had apparently been missing from the mass grave outside Eka-terinburg where the Bolshevik executioners had disposed of the remains of the Royal family and their servants. He was intrigued by a report he read that in the early 1990s a Rus-sian forensic team came to the conclusion that the bones and DNA of the young Prince Alexis and his sister Maria were absent from the communal grave. All others had apparently been identified. A disclaimer in the article also warned that there was a dispute among the scientific community sur-rounding the DNA results. What was most intriguing was that Joshua Larkin had mentioned an incident related to him of how Maria had been held hostage but escaped in the confusion during the fight for the city. How could Larkin have made up such a story? It was only now that modern science was revealing the possibility of the missing pair.

Morgan was soon aware of the fraudulent impersonation by a woman known as Anastasia in the pre–World War Two period in Europe. DNA had proved the impostor to be a Polish peasant girl but it had not stopped people at the time swearing she was the Princess Anastasia. There had been numerous best-selling books claiming her as the lost Russian princess and inevitably a Hollywood movie.

When Morgan had completed his research on Princess Maria he was amused to think how the world had been led down the garden path by this Polish impostor when the truth was most likely in the pages of Joshua Larkin's journal all along. If what Morgan had read was true, then he had a sneaking suspicion that Monique Dawson just might be the sole claimant to the Russian throne should the monarchy be re-established in the new Russia. But he also knew the possibility of that happening was about as probable as winning the lottery.

FOURTEEN

Joshua could see that the major was suffering from his injuries. He had trouble keeping up and stopped often to ease the pain in his chest. Sweat beaded his brow in the cold air.

'You want to go back, sir?' Joshua asked.

'No, sergeant,' Locksley answered, doubled over with the pain. 'According to my calculations we should not be far from our destination. Just keep going. I will keep up.'

Joshua shrugged, eyeing the pocket in which he knew the major kept the scribbled details of the mission. But he turned and continued walking among the tall trees of the silent forest. Cold, sleeting rain bit at his face as they slowly trudged east.

Joshua heard it first. A rhythmic sound to their front. He halted, listening to identify the sound. It seemed like an axe chopping timber.

'Must be close,' Locksley wheezed, stumbling up to join Joshua. 'At least close to some form of habitation. Go on, sergeant.'

Obeying, Joshua continued, moving cautiously in the direction of the wood chopping. Could it be a Bolshevik military section cutting firewood? He felt for the pistol tucked in his coat pocket.

The chopping sound ceased when Joshua calculated they were around a hundred yards away. He wiped the rain from his eyes and peered into the semi-gloom of the forest ahead but could see nothing. When he turned to speak with the major he was startled to see he was lying on the earth, doubled over in agony.

'You go ahead,' the major said through gritted teeth. 'Make a recce of what is up ahead and return with a report.'

Joshua's instinct was to remain with the British officer but he was also a soldier conditioned to obeying orders. For a moment he was tempted to leave his revolver with the stricken officer but realised he was in better condition to use it. He stepped out to investigate the source of the activity ahead but had only gone a dozen yards when he came across a well-worn track.

Careful to stay off the track, Joshua followed it on a parallel course until he came to a cleared area carefully concealed among the tall stands of the taiga. He crouched in a thicket of ferns from where he could observe the log hut. Smoke hovered over the sod roof of the cabin and firewood was piled in great stacks outside. There was clearly much more than required for use by the inhabitants and Joshua guessed that he had stumbled on a woodcutter's hut. Confirming his suspicions, he noticed a broad-shouldered and heavily bearded man dragging a heavy log towards one of the stacks. He was unarmed. Joshua quietly slipped from his place of concealment to make his way back into the forest.

'Looks like a log cutter's cabin ahead,' he said, kneeling down beside Locksley who he had helped prop against the trunk of a tree. Joshua's description appeared to brighten the expression on the officer's face.

'It sounds promising,' Locksley gasped. 'All you need to do now is return and see if you can spot a young woman in the vicinity. If you do, you are to return to me. Hopefully I will be able to get my strength back and join you.'

Joshua accepted the command and made his way back to the hut where he resumed his hiding position. He had a clear view of the front entrance. The rain soon eased, making the task of sitting and watching less miserable, but the biting cold did not go away. Joshua remained in his hide for a good hour, listening to the wind swishing through the wet branches around him. After some time the door opened and a young woman stepped out. Joshua was only twenty yards from the cabin entrance and could clearly see her features. He was struck by her large blue eyes and fine profile. She did not seem to have the slightly Asiatic features that he had noted in many of the Russian women he had seen. She was much more European in appearance and beautiful too. He guessed the girl to be around twenty years of age. She wore a long dress and was bare headed, her long tresses piled into a bun on her head. Her rosy cheeks looked pinched, by either hunger or possibly some inner pain. Was this the girl the major had wanted him to find?

The young woman walked to the wood pile and selected an armful of cut timber. She appeared to carry herself with some grace, and Joshua found himself admiring the young woman. When the girl had returned inside the cabin, he once again left his observation point to return to the major and report.

'She was rather tall, brown hair, blue eyes and not a bad looking sheila,' he said.

Locksley closed his eyes for a moment. 'That sounds like her,' he finally said with a wince, followed by a hacking cough. He muffled a yelp of pain. 'Our mission is almost complete. All we have to do now is get to her.'

'I didn't see anyone other than the woodcutter,' Joshua offered helpfully. 'What is it that is so important about the girl?'

'If she is identified as the person I seek,' Locksley said, 'there is no reason for you to ask, sergeant. All you have to do is obey my commands. Then we can make our way back to Archangel and you will be able to rejoin your regiment and steam home to London.'

Joshua was even more mystified. Why would a senior British officer and two soldiers risk their lives behind enemy lines only to find and identify some Russian girl? None of it made sense and he felt irritated by being kept in the dark.

'What happens if we identify her?' Joshua asked.

'No questions, Sergeant Larkin,' Locksley snapped. 'Just help me to my feet and we will pay a visit to the wood-cutter's cabin. Just have your pistol ready.'

Joshua slipped the revolver from his jacket and placed an arm around the British officer's shoulders to support him. Half walking and half stumbling, Joshua led the major towards the cabin. When he reached the front entrance the major pushed Joshua away and stood unsteadily before the door. Although he knew that the Englishman spoke the language fluently, Joshua was stunned to hear the British major suddenly break into what he felt was Russian as only a native could speak it.

After a pause, a male voice from within the cabin

answered, spurring more Russian words from the major. Gripping the pistol, Joshua stood to one side as the door creaked open slowly to reveal the bearded face of the wood-cutter. A wicked-looking axe dangled at his side. The major said something further and the door fully opened to reveal the pretty young woman Joshua had seen before. She entered the conversation and both the young woman and the woodcutter stepped outside to assist the British officer into the cabin.

'It is all right, Sergeant Larkin,' the major said over his shoulder. 'You can enter.'

Joshua slipped the pistol back into his pocket but retained his grip on the butt in case he needed to use the weapon. Inside the cabin was a strong odour of wood-smoke and smoked meat. The small hut was lit by a single kerosene lantern. Its pallid light cast shadows on a rough wooden table and two rustic chairs. A couple of hams hung from the ceiling and in the corner was a bed covered by thick fur blankets. Quickly Joshua scanned the dark nooks of the room but saw that the woodcutter and the girl he presumed was his daughter were the only occupants.

The girl assisted the major to the bed where she lay him down gently. She turned and said something to Joshua, which he did not understand but guessed meant that the British officer was very sick. She placed her hand over her mouth and pantomimed a cough.

Joshua stared into the girl's beautiful serene eyes. 'Could be he is coming down with pneumonia?' he asked, hoping that his meaning was understood. 'Do you speak English?' he added hopefully, but she shook her head and replied in Russian. Her expression suddenly brightened however and Joshua realised that she was asking if he understood French. His tough face broke into a smile.

146

'*Oui, mademoiselle,*' he said warmly and apologised that his French was not very good. She seemed to relax and with her own wistful smile explained that sadly her French was not much better. But at least they had found common ground. Stumbling over her words Joshua learned that the major had identified himself – and that he was expected. The girl told him too that she had nursing experience and that the major required immediate medical help as he appeared to be on the verge of pneumonia. Hence she had ordered him to the bed to rest.

When Joshua glanced over at the bed where the British officer lay he could see that he was sweating profusely and lapsing into some kind of fever. The woodcutter was already pouring water into a battered mug for the very ill British soldier.

'I am Sergeant Joshua Larkin from Australia,' Joshua said in his fractured French by way of introduction. 'What is your name and is the woodcutter your father?'

'I am Maria,' the girl said. 'And the woodcutter is not my father. He is a brave man who has risked his life providing me with a place to wait for help.'

'Why are you waiting for help?' Joshua asked bluntly.

'I am to be taken to England to my relatives,' Maria answered in a somewhat guarded manner. 'I cannot say anything more. I wish I could so please do not ask any further.'

'You must be a person of great importance,' Joshua commented. 'But I will respect your wishes.'

'*Merci,*' Maria answered.

Locksley had drifted into a fevered sleep. No doubt he had developed something akin to pneumonia as a result of his injuries. Serving in the trenches of the Western Front Joshua had witnessed many cases of soldiers falling to the dreaded disease and knew its symptoms well. There was a good chance that Locksley would not pull through, leaving Joshua as the senior man of the mission to make decisions on what would happen next. The question as to the task they had undertaken seemed to be the location and retrieval of this pretty Russian girl so she could be escorted back to England to be reunited with relatives there. This did not make much sense however; there were thousands of Russian refugees seeking asylum in England. She had to be of some vital importance to British interests. For a moment, Joshua was tempted to rifle through the British officer's coat pocket. But he refrained; as long as the semi-conscious major was still alive he knew he was bound by duty to respect his commanding officer's wishes.

'What are we going to do?' Maria asked at his elbow.

Joshua thought about the situation. As far as he knew his friend, George Littleton was probably dead by now, having given his life to draw off the Bolshevik soldiers hunting them. The mad major was also probably dying.

'We will give Major Locksley forty-eight hours to see if he is well enough to travel,' Joshua replied. 'If not, I will carry on as outlined in papers he has in his possession.'

Maria looked at Joshua with fear in her eyes. 'It is dangerous remaining here,' she protested. 'Every day I am here increases the chances that the kind woodcutter may be found by the Bolsheviks and executed for harbouring me. We would also be killed.'

'I am sorry, but I am a soldier,' Joshua said. 'I must think like a soldier and undertake my responsibilities in that manner. My responsibility is not only to why we are here but also to protecting a comrade.'

Maria sighed and turned away to say something to the woodcutter who cast Joshua a hostile look. It was obvious that he was not all that happy providing a roof over the heads of foreign soldiers deep in Bolshevik territory. Joshua ignored him. The woodcutter at least had provided hot soup made from turnips. Maria fed some of the soup to Locksley, gently spooning it into his mouth while Joshua dried his clothing by the open fire.

When night came, the woodcutter fed them slabs of ham and cheese with a coarse, black bread on wooden plates. He took his meal and sat by the fire while Joshua and Maria used the only two chairs to sit at the rough-hewn table.

'What is Australia like?' Maria asked, chewing on a corner of cheese.

'Not like here,' Joshua answered. 'It's warm and friendly.'

'I have learned of Australia in my geography lessons,' Maria continued. 'But I was not a good student. My sisters said that I was more interested in the young soldiers of the palace.'

'Palace,' Joshua repeated. 'What palace?'

'Oh, I spent some time in a palace,' Maria answered evasively. 'There are many palaces in Russia.'

'Was your family members of a palace staff?' Joshua persisted gently.

'Yes,' Maria replied, staring directly into Joshua's eyes. 'We were members of the Czar's personal staff.'

Maybe this was so, Joshua thought. If so, then she must have some further knowledge of the fate of the Czar and his family. The Bolsheviks were not forthcoming on the Russian royal family's current status although there were rumours that they had murdered the Czar himself. So it would make sense to transport a member of the royal staff to England for intelligence gathering.

'I understand,' Joshua said, a little clearer on why he was in this cabin deep in the taiga.

'Have you been a soldier very long, Sergeant Larkin?' Maria asked, changing the course of the conversation.

'It feels like a lifetime,' Joshua sighed, biting into a slab of smoked ham.

'Do your family miss you?' Maria continued.

'I do not have any family to miss me,' Joshua answered glumly. 'My wife in Australia died from the epidemic not long ago.'

'I am sorry for you,' Maria said sympathetically, at the same time impulsively placing her hand on Joshua's arm. 'I understand your pain.'

'Did you lose a husband or someone else close?' Joshua countered.

Turning away, Maria nodded her head. 'Not a husband, my family,' She wiped away tears with the sleeve of her dress.

Joshua guessed that she had suffered this great loss only recently and was not surprised. The Bolsheviks were slaughtering their own citizens by the thousands. 'I am sorry,' he said gently. 'This war raging in your country should not be happening.'

Maria turned back to Joshua, tears rolling down her cheeks. She was so vulnerable, Joshua thought, realising that his heart was going out to her. In any other circumstances he might have taken his interest further. It had been a long time since he had felt anyone touch his heart. Yet he felt a little guilt for the memory of his dead wife for as much as he tried to remember her face he found that it grew harder with every passing day. It was as if continuing his life as a soldier had helped erase the memories of his past. After all, had he not volunteered with this hope in mind?

'You are a kind and gentle man, Sergeant Larkin,' Maria said. 'You are the first Australian I have ever met.'

'Well,' Joshua smiled weakly. 'You are the first Russian girl I have met who speaks French and has lived in a palace.'

This time, Maria reached for Joshua's arm and her hand remained. 'You have the look of a man who is wise and strong. I feel a little safer for staying. I admire that you would not desert your sick friend, regardless of the fact that you may be risking your life by lingering here.'

'He is my commanding officer – not my friend,' Joshua said, glancing over at the bed where Locksley lay sleeping fitfully. 'But I swore my duty to him when we took this mission to find you. We will get out of here and I will ensure that you are returned to your relatives in England.'

'I pray that you are right, Sergeant Larkin,' Maria said, withdrawing her hand. That night Joshua was given a fur skin blanket to use as a bed by the fire while the woodcutter selected a corner of the cabin to sleep. Maria placed her blanket by the fireplace a short distance from Joshua. He gazed at her face as she slipped into a troubled sleep.

Joshua remained awake for a long time thinking about his decision to wait two days to see if the major's condition improved enough to move him. A wolf howled in the distance and the patter of rain grew louder against the stout walls of the log cabin. Joshua's mind whirled with thoughts for George and then he found himself gazing once more at the flickering shadows dancing on Maria's face. She had a serene beauty unlike that of any other woman he had known. Even though they had really only just met, Joshua already felt that he would give his life willingly to protect her.

At last Joshua fell into a deep sleep. When morning arrived with the bleak sun showing between broken clouds,

Joshua sat up, throwing off the blanket that he had wrapped around himself. Maria was no longer sleeping by the fire and the woodcutter was also absent from the cabin. Locksley still lay in the bed when Joshua went to check on his condition. Although sweat beaded the major's forehead he appeared to be less in the grip of the illness than he had been the previous evening.

Joshua walked towards the closed door of the cabin but froze when he heard the scream from outside. He knew immediately that the sound of terror had come from Maria and the revolver was in his hand. He pushed the wooden door ajar to peer through it.

'Bloody hell!' he swore under his breath.

In the yard only twenty paces away three armed men he presumed were Bolshevik militia were wrestling Maria to the wet earth. Her long dress was being dragged up over her hips, revealing the smooth, pale flesh of her thighs. There was no doubt in Joshua's mind what the three men intended to do as they laughed and jostled with each other. Maria was forced down screaming until one of the men slammed his fist into her face, silencing her cries of distress. Joshua was about to put his life on the line for the young woman yet he did not hesitate.

FIFTEEN

Valley View
Present day

The tents sprouted like mushrooms in the camping ground along the creek of Valley View. Caravans crowded the park by the showground and long beards adorned the faces of floppy-hatted men. The annual folk festival had arrived along with magnificent spring days of wildflower-covered paddocks. Beer-drinkers from the town's hotels spilled onto the pavements and tourists strolled up and down the quaint streets gawking at the reminders of a century when local stone was the building material of choice.

A festival air pervaded among the lovers of folk music and Senior Constable Morgan McLean was relieved that the average age of those who had flocked to the small rural town in the hills was thirty-something plus. He was even enjoying the sight of the colourfully dressed tourists in their casual clothing somewhere between new age and country. He cruised the main street. The crowds of people appeared relaxed and friendly, sharing in the festival's down-to-earth atmosphere.

So far so good, Morgan thought. The extra two police that would be sent to assist him with crowd control that evening would probably not be earning any overtime. If this friendly mood persisted at the dance to open the week of music, folk art sales and old-fashioned barbecue stands, everyone would have a good time.

Monique Dawson and David Greer mingled with the crowd at the folk festival. It was not often that David could take time off from his busy schedule to share some time with his partner. The weather had been so perfect and the gaiety of the event drew them to the many little stalls already displaying T-shirts, leather hats and strings of colourful beads. Laughter and the sound of banjos, fiddles and guitars from the visiting musicians filled the air.

Monique stopped in front of a stall where beads and bangles attracted her eye. David walked a few paces on to gaze at a stand selling leather-crafted hats. The tired expression on the middle-aged seller's face suggested that the festive atmosphere had little to do with the fact that he had to make a living from selling his wares.

Monique was considering a bracelet when someone in the passing parade of pedestrians bumped her. She turned, immediately thinking about the expensive bag slung over her shoulder; along with the honest attendants at the fair there were also those who made a living off pick-pocketing. Glancing into the open bag Monique noticed a letter sticking up from among her personal items. She scanned the people immediately in her vicinity but all she saw were a sea of faces; young people, children, middle-aged couples and a dog or two being led by skinny elderly ladies.

Frowning, Monique pulled the envelope from her bag and slipped out the typed sheet of paper addressed to her. Her frown deepened as she read the letter. David was still examining the hats two stands away. Her first instinct was to call out to him, but she almost immediately changed her mind. What she had just read was an inherent threat. Instead, Monique slipped the letter back into the bag and walked over to where David was now trying on a hat.

'What do you think?' he asked, grinning at his image in a mirror hanging from the tent pole of the stallholder's tent. 'Makes me look like a real cowboy or what?'

'It doesn't suit you,' Monique mumbled, causing David to cast her an inquiring glance.

'Are you all right?' he asked, sensing Monique's sudden change in demeanour. Only moments earlier she had been laughing at a wisecrack David had made about the local fair.

'I have just a bit of a headache coming on,' Monique replied. 'I feel like something to eat. Can we go to the pub?'

'Sure,' David said, passing the hat back. 'We can walk up to the top pub and get a bite.'

Monique nodded and attempted a weak smile of appreciation. She would need time to consider the letter's contents. More importantly, she desperately needed someone who might have the experience to help her decide a course of action. Morgan McLean's name came to mind and she wondered whether she should contact him.

As they made their way back from the paddock covered in tents and stages to the main street and away from the bulk of the tourists and market people Monique saw Morgan standing beside his police truck chatting with a young couple whose haversacks displayed the Canadian flag. Back-packers, Monique thought idly, all the way from Canada. She frowned again. The note was written by someone whose first language was not English, she was sure, and the thought made her uneasy.

As they passed Morgan, Monique noticed him turn in her direction and beam her a friendly smile. She raised her hand and waved to him.

'Our local Mr Plod will have his work cut out for him this week,' David said, noticing her gesture.

'I wouldn't say he was any kind of Mr Plod,' Monique retorted, surprising herself at having defended Morgan's reputation.

'It doesn't take much to be a cop,' David replied. 'All you need is more brawn than brain – everyone knows that – and be able to spell "speeding fine".'

'You forget that I was once a nurse,' Monique said. 'I saw at first hand in the casualty ward what the police had to put up with. Drunks wanting to fight, psycho druggies and people in the most distress that they will ever experience in their lives.'

David was scowling. Her defence of the local police-man was being taken personally by her partner. She slipped her arm into his to reassure him. She did not know why David would need reassurance; he was everything a woman could want: handsome, suave, rich and successful. Why would he want to belittle a simple country cop? She wondered if her contact with Morgan had been behind the tirade against the police. There had never been any-thing untoward in her contact but in a small town people may well have interpreted the most casual of meetings as lustful encounters. Whatever it was, David had no fear of losing her. After all, Morgan McLean was nowhere near

156

as handsome as David, and his police salary would never make him a wealthy man.

Monique and David were not surprised when they reached the pub that they had to wait to order a meal. After their order was finally placed, David took their drinks outside, where they were lucky enough to snatch a small table under the wooden latticework at one end of the beer garden. For an hour Monique attempted to forget the letter in her bag but Morgan's name kept cropping up in her thoughts. She wondered if he would be on duty at the dance in the local hall that evening. If so, it might give her the opportunity to make contact with him and even show him the letter. Surely he would know what to do.

The walls, roof and wooden floor of the local hall vibrated under the pounding of booted feet. Whoops and yells echoed across the nearby paddocks while the squeal of fiddles blended with banjos, drums and the vocals of a folk song harmony. The odours of sweat and beer mixed with wisps of marijuana smoke inside the hall where the dancers were carried away by the music that was at the heart and soul of the Australian psyche. The old 'South Australia Bound' had the audience up on their feet in no time and Morgan watched from the rear of the hall as the crowd enjoyed themselves, spurred on by the professionalism of the popular band from Sydney. It was foot-tapping music he enjoyed and he hoped that the happy atmosphere would continue without fights or injury to those in the hall. He was alone at the dance as the two police sent out from the district station were out patrolling Valley View's streets and camping grounds.

'You ought to get out and dance,' a pretty young girl

shouted to him as she swirled by with her partner in some parody of an old-fashioned Scottish reel. Morgan smiled. Being a small town cop meant missing out on what most people took for granted – the chance to have a few drinks and get just a little drunk; he was always on call in this job.

He slipped from the hall unnoticed, making his way across to his vehicle.

'Could I speak with you, Morgan?' Monique queried.

Morgan stopped and turned to see her following him from the hall.

'Sure,' he replied. 'How can I help you?' He could see that she had dressed up for the dance, wearing a cheesecloth dress that flowed around her calves.

'I would like you to read this letter I received earlier today at the markets.'

Monique produced the sheet of paper, handing it to Morgan who opened the door of his vehicle and flicked on the interior light.

'You should have brought this to my attention as soon as you got it,' Morgan said, looking up at her. 'There is a threat of some kind in the words. Did you see who passed this to you?'

'I felt a bump and by the time I turned around the letter was in my bag. It could have been anyone near me at the time,' Monique answered. 'Do you think it is some kind of bad joke?' she asked, hoping for reassurance that she had nothing to worry about.

Morgan bit his bottom lip, pondering the meaning of the directions and the warning in the typed words. 'It says that your life is in danger,' he said. 'And that you are to produce the diary and all documents pertaining to Joshua Larkin. Whoever wrote this knows a lot more than any practical joker.'

'You know that I only have copies of the diary – as you do,' Monique said. 'I couldn't comply with the demand even if I wanted to.'

'You must not arrange any meetings with whoever wrote this,' Morgan said, folding the paper along its original lines and placing it in the glove box of the police vehicle. 'And you are to keep me informed of anything and everything that you think is suspicious. I will be making extra patrols out your way to keep an eye on your place. Does David know about the letter?'

Monique pulled a face. 'I haven't told him about it,' she replied. 'I don't think that there is any reason to alarm him. I want you to promise me that you will tell no one else about it,' Monique continued. 'If I feel that there is some real threat to my life I will promise you that I will leave Valley View for somewhere safer.'

Morgan took a deep breath before answering. 'I can't promise that I will not reveal the letter to colleagues,' he finally answered. 'But I will keep it to myself until I ask around a bit. I have a feeling that the author is a foreigner – maybe from Eastern Europe, judging by the wording.'

'You are definitely *not* a Mr Plod,' Monique mused, catching Morgan off guard.

'It may be wise to tell David about the letter, so that he can help keep an eye on you,' Morgan said, wondering about what she had just said.

'I feel safe enough knowing that you are handling the matter,' Monique answered with genuine trust in her voice.

'What did you tell him about your visit to the UK?' Morgan asked.

'I told him that I was visiting a sick relative in England,'

159

she replied defiantly, cocking her head to one side. 'He knows that I have family in England. I should get back to David,' she continued. 'Otherwise, the good people of Valley View will say that you and I are having an affair.'

'Yeah, it doesn't take much around here. I have to admit that I sometimes miss the big smoke. You will have to excuse me,' Morgan said when he heard his call sign on the police radio in the car. 'Sounds like I've got a job but I will catch up with you later.'

Monique turned and walked back to the hall that by now was shuddering on its foundations thanks to the rowdy treatment it was receiving from its temporary occupants. Morgan watched her walk away. The thought that he might be having an affair with her was not unappealing, he thought wistfully. But it would never happen, he reminded himself. He had a duty to Monique and it was no different from the one he had to the rest of the Valley View residents. He was here to uphold the law and protect the people. Now he would have to use every skill he had as an investigator to track down the source of the letter and its author. That vague feeling that he had weeks earlier when he had held onto the diary was being solidified. He was already working on his first angle of the investigation. Maybe Cheryl at the service station might be able to help him.

Morgan slid into the driver's side of his vehicle, unaware that he was being watched. Satisfied that the local police officer was driving away from the hall, a dark-clad man disappeared into the shadows of the car park. All going well his mission would be completed that night and Ms Monique Dawson would no longer be considered a threat to British national security.

SIXTEEN

The taiga
South-east of Archangel
August 1919

Maria was attempting to fight off her would-be rapist, but a blow from his fist stunned her, ending any
resistance.

Inside the cabin Joshua gripped the revolver, quickly
assessing the situation with a soldier's eye. He could not see
the woodcutter – only three men, one on his knees between
Maria's bare legs with his pants pulled down and his rifle
lying next to him. The other two were laughing, watching
their comrade take the first turn with the helpless girl. Both
had their rifles slung over their shoulders and Joshua wondered at their carelessness. They had not cleared the area
before engaging in their savage act. Either they were poorly
trained or just downright stupid.

Joshua stepped from the doorway of the cabin with his
pistol raised and pointed at the three scruffy-looking Russians. One saw Joshua emerge, and immediately reached for

his rifle. The act took away precious milliseconds in which time Joshua had fired off two shots at the man kneeling between Maria's legs since he was the only one of the trio who could have snatched up his rifle to threaten Joshua. He grunted his surprise before collapsing on the semi-conscious girl.

Calmly, Joshua continued advancing on the other two, whose fear he could see behind their grimy beards. The first man to unsling his rifle had now brought it level with Joshua who fired two shots into him. The man staggered but remained standing to bring up his rifle again. Instinctively Joshua fired his last two remaining shots into the man, this time seeing him drop to the ground. The third man was the final threat, having unslung his rifle and worked the bolt to chamber a round. The precious loss of time in not having his rifle already loaded was time enough for Joshua to realise that his pistol was empty and that he would not have time to reload himself. As he was now only four paces away, Joshua flung the empty pistol at the Russian's face, causing him to flinch. Joshua was now on him with all the force he could muster. As both men crashed to the ground Joshua could smell the stench of rotten meat in the man's breath on his face.

Joshua found himself straddling his opponent and smashed his fist into the man's face as hard as he could. The blow caught the man in the nose, rupturing it in a spray of blood. Without hesitating, Joshua closed his hands around the struggling Russian's throat. To his horror, a fourth Russian had come into the small clearing and witnessed the attack on his comrades. He halted, unslinging his rifle from his shoulder. Even if Joshua killed the man under him the fourth would surely kill him.

Joshua's surprise translated into loosening his grip on the man's throat. The Russian suddenly raked at Joshua's eyes with his right hand. Joshua ducked his head, avoiding the filthy, long-nailed fingers seeking his eyes and was able to bite down on the outstretched hand, crunching through to the bone. The man screamed in agony and Joshua resumed choking the life out of the Russian, spitting out the severely injured fingers of the Russian's now useless hand. The crack of the bullet beside his face alerted Joshua to the fact that the fourth man had fired at him. His aim was bad but Joshua knew he only had to close the distance of about fifty feet and shoot him at point blank range. At least he would kill the third man before he in turn was killed. His only regret was that Maria would be left to the mercy of men who knew none.

The Russian's struggle grew weaker but Joshua kept his hands around the man's throat to ensure his death. When he looked up he could see that the fourth Russian had advanced to within ten paces, his face a mask of fury. He was screaming curses at him, spittle forming on his thick lips. Joshua felt his heart beat even more heavily. Behind the Russian killer was the woodcutter wielding an axe over his head and running at the armed man. His yells caught the fourth man by surprise and he swung around to face the threat. The bullet meant for Joshua caught the woodcutter in the chest from only two paces away and he crumpled on the spot, the axe falling from his hands. Before the Russian could eject the spent case and chamber a fresh round Joshua had scooped up one of the rifles from the ground. He could not afford to pull the trigger as it may have an empty chamber and in the time it would take to work the bolt he knew the other man would already have a round ready to fire. Instead, Joshua reversed the rifle, swinging it like a club at the Russian. The rifle butt caught the startled fourth man on the side of his head, felling him.

Without hesitation, Joshua stood over the semi-conscious man groaning in pain and brought the rifle butt down between his eyes. His forehead smashed open with a sickening crunch of bone and a sharp hiss escaped the felled man's throat while his eyes closed.

Panting from the adrenalin rush, Joshua stepped back to scan the surrounding forest. The forest appeared silent and serene in the early morning shadows so he recovered his revolver, quickly reloading before going to Maria whose eyes were opening as if from a deep sleep. Shoving the dead Russian aside, he kneeled and cradled her head in his lap. A trickle of blood ran from her lip, split from the punch to her face.

'Are you badly hurt?' Joshua asked gently.

Maria shook her head weakly, sitting up and pushing her dress down over her thighs. Gazing around, she could see the carnage in the small clearing. When her eyes came to rest on the woodcutter she let out a small cry of distress. Joshua helped her to her feet and immediately she went to kneel beside the dead man's body.

'Oh, Ivan,' she said softly, stroking his face tenderly. 'I have cost you your life.'

Joshua stood behind her, still alert to any other threat emerging from the forest. 'I think we will not have time to mourn,' he said, his hand resting on her shoulder. 'I suspect that if we have four of the Bolshies here there must be more not far away.'

Maria stood up stiffly and stared at the bodies sprawled in the mud of the clearing. 'I don't think these men were Bolshevik militia,' she said. 'I think they may have been deserters from either the Bolsheviks or the White Army. I remember when they caught me one of them said something like, this is better than taking orders from the officers.'

Joshua tended to agree with her, given their very slovenly appearance. Deserters flowed across the countryside from either side and when they were in transit they acted as bandits raping, looting and murdering helpless non-combatants. If nothing else, the fact that the dead men may have been deserters gave Joshua a glimmer of hope that he would not immediately be facing more disciplined Bolshevik troops carrying out operations in the area. No matter what he considered, one matter stood out – they could not remain any longer in the district. Despite the gravity of his illness, Major Locksley would have to accompany them – or remain to face his fate in the taiga.

'I am sorry for the death of the woodcutter,' Joshua said sympathetically. 'But he must have thought his sacrifice worthwhile to do what he did.'

'Too many people have died because of my family,' Maria retorted angrily, wiping at the tears streaming down her face. 'I wonder if my life is worth more than theirs.'

'It is to me,' Joshua answered, reaching down for a rifle and stripping a bandolier of ammunition from a dead Russian. 'Do you know how to use one of these?' he asked Maria who also picked up the rifle lying beside her would-be rapist.

'Of course I do,' she said haughtily, quickly recovering from her introspection.

'That's good,' Joshua said with a slight smile as they returned to the cabin to ascertain the British major's state of health and prepare to leave for the trek to Archangel. 'We might pass as Bolsheviks if we have to.'

The horses splashed through the swamp while their riders held on with the expertise of men trained to cavalry.

George Littleton had little difficulty keeping his seat as polo had been a game he had played often before his commissioning into the Australian army. He had in fact left a string of polo horses at one of his father's many properties west of Sydney at Camden. Lieutenant Andrej Novotny spurred his mount forward to join George at the front of the column. 'Corporal, you ride well,' he said. 'You sure you not cavalry?'

George shifted in his saddle to greet the cheery Czech officer. 'I failed enlisting in our Light Horse contingent,' he replied.

George had been finally accepted by the Czechs as being what he purported to be – an Australian NCO serving in the British army. As such he had befriended the young Czech officer who liked using his rather good English to reminisce about his student days in England before the war. He showed an interest in George's life in Australia and they realised that they were gentlemen in the old tradition. A trust grew between the two men of different cultures but similar social worlds.

It had been two days since the attack on them in the forest and George had been given a horse that had belonged to a Czech killed in the short but sharp assault on the flank of the Russians which had succeeded in killing many of the Bolsheviks and routing the rest. The handful of prisoners captured had been executed and George had been made to stand aside as the helpless men were forced to kneel before being shot.

'We cannot take them,' Andrej had explained calmly as he walked away from ensuring all their prisoners were dead. 'We are cut off and must travel light.'

George understood the military rationale; it was no less than what the Bolshevik commanders were doing to their own troops if they did not press and attack with what they considered enough enthusiasm.

'Why were you out here?' Andrej asked.

'I was with a fellow Australian and a British major on a special mission,' George confided, knowing that as he did not know what the mission was for he could not be divulging any military secrets. 'I last saw them when I volunteered to lead off the Bolshies from pursuing us after we did some damage to them at a village some miles from where you found me.'

'What was mission?' the Czech officer asked bluntly.

'I honestly don't know,' George answered, kicking his horse out of the swamp and onto dry ground covered in long grass. 'Just to get to some place. After that – I don't know what we supposed to do.'

'We were supposed to search for someone,' Andrej said, signalling a halt to his column of men who drove their mounts onto the dry ground, dismounted and checked their equipment.

George dismounted too and patted the nose of his horse. She was a tough little mare with a long scar Andrej said had been inflicted by a Russian sabre weeks earlier in a skirmish east of their current position.

'Funny,' George said. 'I always had the feeling that we were on our mission to find someone.'

The Czech officer rolled his head and waved his arms to loosen the muscles which had cramped during the difficult crossing of the swamp. 'We hear story that Russian princess escape from Ekaterinburg when we take the city,' he said. 'I put in charge, tasked to find princess. But no good. Just find many Bolsheviks and kill them.'

George pondered the Czech's explanation of his mission but dismissed his own as not having anything to do with searching for surviving members of the Czar's family. After all, why would the British army only send three men on such an important mission? Like the Czechs they would have assigned at least a battalion to sweep an area if this had indeed been their mission. It had to be a coincidence that the Czechs were in the same area for that purpose, he thought, even if the fate of the Russian royal family was still blurred in mystery. The high command of men such as Lenin and Trotsky had not admitted to killing them all, only the Czar.

After a short break Novotny signalled to his men to mount up and the column moved out. The port of Archangel beckoned and it was the safest way to evacuate from a land quickly being swamped in the red of a socialist revolution. Although George would have liked the Czech officer to assist him in finding his comrades he was powerless to convince him to do so. The Czech's first priority was to his mission and secondly to his men. Searching for a couple of Allied soldiers was not in his orders.

Joshua propped the British major up in the bed and spooned him cold soup left over from the night before. Locksley still had a fever but his eyes burned with resolve.

'You up to making it back to Archangel with us, sir?' he asked.

Locksley sipped the soup and gripped Joshua by the sleeve. 'We leave here together, but there is something you must do before we leave,' he said with fierce determination.

'What is that, sir?' Joshua asked.

'You are to execute the girl,' the major whispered. Joshua thought that he had misheard and leaned forward.

'Sorry, sir, but I thought you said execute Maria.'

Locksley gripped Joshua's sleeve with all his strength. 'That's right, Sergeant Larkin. You are to execute the girl. You are under my orders and my orders come from the highest circles in London. Do you understand?'

Joshua pushed the major's arm from his sleeve and stood up. He glanced around to see if Maria was within earshot but she was outside placing a posy of wildflowers on the body of the dead woodcutter.

'Why in hell would we kill an innocent girl?' Joshua flared, thinking that the British officer might be delirious from his fever. There could be no other explanation as they had risked so much to find her. How could a mere girl be considered of such importance that the British army would assign three valuable men to seek her out just for the single purpose of killing her?

'You have my orders, Sergeant Larkin,' Locksley reiterated. 'It is not your position to question them.'

Joshua shook his head, glaring at the British officer. 'You would have to have a bloody good reason for me to shoot Maria,' he said. 'Your orders alone are not legal – under military law as you well know.'

Locksley fell back on the bed and stared up at the dark ceiling. 'I would have done it myself if I could,' he said. 'You do not realise just how dangerous it would be for British interests if the girl was able to reach England. It is not my decision but sanctioned at levels beyond simple soldiers. Just carry out my orders and we can return to England and report the mission was accomplished. After all, it appears it has already cost Corporal Littleton his life. Don't make your friend's sacrifice be in vain.'

'Sorry, sir,' Joshua said. 'I refuse to obey an order I consider to be unlawful. You have not justified why the girl should be executed.'

169

'If you won't do it, then I order you to hand over your service revolver, Sergeant Larkin. That is a direct command.'

Joshua hesitated. He might be able to disobey the order to kill Maria but he could not refuse to hand over his revolver to a superior officer. Joshua reached in his coat and withdrew the pistol. Locksley stretched out his hand for it and the pistol slipped into the major's grip.

'I am not going to shoot you, Sergeant Larkin,' he said with a sigh. 'But you will have to answer to a court martial for your actions here. I appreciate that you saved my life back in that village but you and I have a duty to the Crown.'

Joshua shook his head in disgust just as Maria entered the cabin unaware of the tense situation between the officer and NCO. Locksley raised the pistol. It all happened in a split second.

SEVENTEEN

Valley View
Present day

Miss Dawson,
Is a warning life in danger. I am friend who will make
contact with you. This is not jest. Remember this when I
contact you. Is about your trip to London.
A friend.

Morgan re-read the note, wondering about its meaning. His experience with the SAS Regiment had put
him into contact with former Warsaw Pact soldiers now
selling their secrets to the wealthier capitalist West. Joshua
Larkin had a good ear for nuances in language and this message too had an Eastern bloc accent to it. From what he had
read of Larkin's diary it was almost as if history was repeating itself. An eerie feeling that ghosts really existed crept
into his mind, causing him to glance around at the shadows
in his office. But he was alone and only the distant sound of

the dance in the local hall pervaded the room. Who wrote the note and why? Morgan's suspicion was that Monique must be a direct descendant of the highly decorated former Australian army captain and his wife Maria who, according to Larkin and the translated papers, was the Princess Maria of the Russian royal family – the only survivor of the slaughter which made Monique a claimant to any estates or the throne. But, as Russia was now a federation and no longer a dynasty, any claim would be moot.

Morgan stood up to stretch his tired body. So how could she be considered a threat to anyone? She was English born and Australian raised and as far as he knew, had no links to Russia. After all, there were plenty of examples of members of former European royal families overthrown after the Great War who now lived as private citizens. But there was something else that did bother Morgan's police instincts. Larkin's journal outlined an incident in a cabin in the Russian taiga when he had been commanded to kill Maria. But he had never explained who was behind the order other than the British major. Had Locksley been operating on his own? He was after all, a Russian by birth and may in reality have been working for the Reds. Over the years, the British intelligence services seemed to have a dubious record of having highly placed traitors in their ranks.

Normally any stranger to town would be noticed by the locals, but the folk festival had changed all that. The town was flooded with tourists, not only from Australia but also from overseas.

Morgan glanced up at the clock on the wall and wondered if Cheryl's service station would still be open. He was in luck. Cheryl was in the process of closing down when

172

Morgan pulled up. One of her assistants was a boy that Morgan had recruited for an Army Reserve unit and he greeted Morgan warmly as he wrestled with a rack of oils he was trying to get inside the shop.

'Young Matt,' Morgan said. 'How is the army going?'

'The unit is going on a two-week exercise to Hawaii in January, Mr McLean,' Matthew answered enthusiastically.

Morgan smiled. The boy had rarely gone any further than the main town down the road from Valley View and now he was about to travel overseas with his unit and see a bit of the world.

'I need a bit of help,' Morgan said conspiratorially, catching the young man's attention. 'I am looking for someone who speaks a bit like this: "Is good, da."'

When Matthew blinked Morgan realised that he must have sounded silly. 'I am looking for a man who speaks with what we call a Russian or Eastern European accent. They sound a bit like that.'

Matthew's face broke into a broad smile. 'I know what you mean,' he said. 'There is this wrestler on cable TV who is the Red Terror and he talks like that.'

Thank God for TV, Morgan sighed to himself. At least it taught Matthew what a Eastern European accent sounded like. 'Have you had anyone in the shop who sounded like that?'

Matthew frowned. 'I have only been on since three this arvo,' he answered. 'But Cheryl has been on all day. She might have.'

'Well, if you do come across anyone with an accent – male or female – give me a call. Better still, if they are driving a car take note of the numberplate. I will have a talk to Cheryl.'

'Will do, Mr McLean,' Matthew said, wiping his hands on his trousers.

Morgan had a similar conversation with Cheryl and knew that the next day he would be repeating it in places all over town. At least he was now creating his own counterintelligence organisation, recruiting members of Valley View's population.

When Morgan returned to his station he met with the two police constables sent out from Hume City to assist with crowd control at the festival. Morgan did not mention his search for the Eastern European speaker as he hoped for Monique's sake to keep the matter at a local level. The last thing she needed was publicity if news got out about the mysterious note.

It was after midnight when Morgan decided that the town was settled enough for him to complete the car log and then head home. He had hardly dragged the blankets over him when the phone rang on the bedside table.

'Senior Constable McLean speaking,'

'Morgan, are you out of bed?'

Morgan recognised the female voice at the other end as that of a radio control operative from Hume City police station. 'Just got in,' he answered. 'What have I got?'

'We have just been notified by the ambulance that you have a fatal about five clicks south of Valley View. A single vehicle accident and one dead occupant. The vehicle is registered to one of your locals – a Miss Monique Dawson.'

Morgan sat up as if he had been shot.

'I am on the way,' he said, dropping the cordless phone back into its cradle.

Monique dead! He gasped, overcome with guilt. Maybe he should have alerted Ken to the note and sought help. In seconds he was dressed and racing to the garage for his vehicle.

★

Petrov Batkin flipped the glowing cigarette butt onto the ground and with the heel of his shoe, ground it out. People were coming and going around him at the entrance of the hall where the dance was grinding down to the last brackets. The air was chilly and the night sky ablaze with the stars of the southern hemisphere. The man that he had been shadowing was still inside as far as he knew and he would wait for him to exit before determining where he was staying.

The email Batkin had received had come with an attachment displaying the man's photo and a resumé. Russian hackers had been able to show the world that no one is safe in cyberspace. Links to Batkin's neo-Nazi group had been able to tap into MI6 for a short time when the firewalls had been compromised by a highly skilled Russian hacker and what they had learned confirmed their suspicions of British intentions in Australia.

Batkin had emailed back in a coded message, seeking permission to terminate the man he was following, but permission had been denied. The mission must be kept as low profile as possible and the death of a British agent on Australian soil would cause too many questions to be raised. Even what appeared to be an accident might open a door to things better concealed almost a century after the events in Russia.

Frustrated by the things going wrong with his mission, Batkin decided it was time to go inside to pick up the trail of the man he was shadowing. As far as he could ascertain, the girl he had recruited to assist him had not yet arrived and that annoyed him. It was almost impossible to complete his mission without Sarah Sakharov and it had been he who was forced to deliver a message that was meant to be Sarah's task. His English was not as good as her grasp of the language. At one stage in the afternoon Batkin thought he had caught a glimpse of her in the milling crowd of festival-goers but when he hurried to catch up with the girl she was gone from sight. He had expected that she would have contacted him immediately upon reaching the town. She had no reason to avoid him.

Batkin entered the hall to see the dance floor strewn with paper streamers, empty plastic cups. Drunken revellers were falling over themselves. He scanned the room and was disturbed to see that the British agent was nowhere to be seen. With a Russian curse for his lack of alertness, he turned and stormed from the hall. Mr Daniel Kildare had slipped by him. Was the British agent aware he was being shadowed or was he better trained than Batkin had estimated?

The Russian stepped into the night and made his way back to the hotel. At least he would meet up with the girl in the morning, he consoled himself. Her email promised that much.

Blue and red flashing lights cast an eerie glow in the distance as Morgan sped to the scene of the reported traffic accident. He slowed on the corners of a treacherous stretch of road winding through a series of hairpin bends in the hills until he came out on the scene by the road where the two officers who had been assisting him with crowd control at the festival held up traffic travelling in both directions. Morgan used his lights and siren to make his way past the stalled traffic to a point near the scene where he brought his vehicle to a halt. He leaped from the police vehicle and was met by a young constable he knew from Hume City.

'We were on our way back when we got the call,' the constable said, waving a long, black metal torch. 'The ambulance got here first. A driver heading to Hume City saw the accident happen. I've got his name and address for a statement.'

Morgan felt empty, staring at the crushed saplings at the side of the road, indicating that the vehicle had gone over the edge into a shallow gully.

'Where is the body now?' he asked.

'Still in the car,' the constable answered. 'The ambos are going to remove it.'

Morgan slipped his torch from his utility belt and clambered down the gully where the white-uniformed ambulance officers and blue-uniformed police officers were working together to prise open the smashed car's door. It appeared that the car had slammed head on into a giant gum tree and from the extent of the damage Morgan guessed it must have been travelling very fast. He came to a stop next to the driver's side and peered inside to see the body slumped forward. The head was smashed open and blood soaked the clothing of the dead person.

'It's not Monique!' Morgan gasped with relief.

He recognised the dead boy as one he had strongly suspected over a couple of stolen vehicles in recent weeks. Glancing at where the ignition key should have been, Morgan noticed it was missing. The car had been hot-wired.

'Know him?' an ambulance officer Morgan knew well asked.

'Yeah,' Morgan replied. 'Guess I will have to go back and tell his mother.'

'Rather you than me,' the ambulance officer grunted as a couple of officers from Highway Patrol helped the ambulance officers to drag the dead boy from the driver's seat. His body flopped onto the ground and Morgan could see from the unnatural angle of his legs that the impact had also smashed his lower torso. Bradley Smithers was his name,

Morgan remembered. Aged seventeen and his mother was a single mum. No doubt the rebellious juvenile had somehow stolen the vehicle although it was not yet reported as missing. As the accident had occurred in his patrol area Morgan knew he would be lumbered with the investigation for the coroner's court. It would be a matter of calling the Accident Investigation Branch to carry out their own investigation as to possible cause of the tragedy. But first he would have to inform the dead boy's mother and arrange for her to make a formal identification of young Bradley's body.

Strange, Morgan thought, that the vehicle would be stolen this night and totalled. Just a coincidence, he attempted to console himself, knowing that only the expertise of the police traffic investigators would be able to answer his questions as to the cause of the collision. After collecting as much information from the young constable as he could, Morgan returned to his car. He was about to undertake the worst job in the police force – telling a mother her son was dead. Better to face an enraged knife-wielding lunatic than have to knock on a door and say those dreaded words.

EIGHTEEN

Northern Russia
August 1919

The bullet slammed into the wooden door frame beside Maria as Joshua chopped down with the edge of his hand, catching Locksley's wrist, forcing him to drop the pistol. 'You mad bastard,' Joshua screamed at the British major, swinging around to ascertain Maria's condition. She was pale and shaking. Joshua scooped up the pistol as Locksley collapsed back on the bed. In a couple of steps he was beside Maria and placed his arm around her shoulders. She had suffered enough this day.

'It was an accident,' he attempted to soothe with a lie. 'The major is still in a fever and did not mean to shoot at you.'

Her mouth agape, Maria stared at the British officer lying on the bed, gazing at the ceiling.

'You must kill her, Sergeant Larkin,' he said in a calm voice. 'That is an order.'

179

'What did he say?' Maria asked, not understanding English.

'Nothing of importance,' Joshua answered, slipping the pistol back into his jacket. 'He is still delirious.'

Maria did not look convinced but allowed Joshua to guide her to the chair to settle from the shock of being so close to death once again that day. She remained sitting while Joshua rifled through the cabin for anything of value to carry on the trek to Archangel. He cut off a sizeable slab of the smoked ham hanging from the ceiling and pocketed a slab of cheese along with a small loaf of hard, black bread. Satisfied that he had retrieved everything of assistance for the trip he told Maria to gather up anything that might be of importance to her. All that Maria collected was a small leather satchel and a bulging linen belt, which she secured under her clothing. Joshua wondered at both items.

'Wait outside,' he said quietly to Maria.

'What about the major?' she asked with fear in her eyes.

'He is too ill to travel with us,' Joshua answered. 'I will speak with him when you are outside.'

Maria understood that whatever transpired between the two men was not meant for her to witness but this did not reduce her fear. She did not want to ask the Australian soldier what he intended to do with the major. She had seen the ferocity of Joshua's handiwork in the front yard.

'You will not kill him,' she blurted. 'He is a very ill man.'

'I promise you that I will not harm him,' Joshua answered.

Maria nodded and left the cabin while Joshua walked over to the British officer.

'I'm sorry, sir,' he said. 'But I think that you are too ill to travel with us and in your present condition I see that you may harm the girl – or even yourself. I am going to leave you with food, water and one of the Russian rifles. It is my intention to get the girl to England to join her relatives there.'

Locksley's soft chuckle turned into laughter. 'When I rejoin the army at Archangel I will have you arrested and charged with disobeying a direct order while on active service, Sergeant Larkin, and you know what that means. You are no longer in the Australian army but under British military law. You can be shot for your disobedience but you still have a chance to kill the girl and redeem yourself.'

'You have not given me any justification for executing an unarmed civilian, sir. Under the King's regulations I am justified in disobeying your unlawful order.'

'If you only knew what you have got yourself into, Sergeant, you would see the justification behind my order,' Locksley said, staring at the ceiling.

'Then, who is the girl?' Joshua demanded, leaning towards the British officer. 'She will not tell me, except to say that she once had contact with the Czar's family.'

For a moment Major Locksley appeared to consider answering the reasonable question truthfully but finally he said, 'You are a soldier in the King's army and have to accept that all orders from senior officers are made without the necessity of conferring with the lower ranks. That is all you have to know.'

'I saw enough of that same bloody mindedness on the Western Front,' Joshua growled. 'I saw good men die on the whims of staff officers who had never set foot in the trenches, so don't give me that rubbish. Goodbye, sir, I hope you make it back to Archangel.'

With his parting words, Joshua turned on his heel, leaving a rifle and spare ammunition beside the bed.

'Oh, I will get back to Archangel,' Locksley shouted after him. 'And when I do, Sergeant Larkin, I will hunt you and the girl down and complete my mission. Be assured of that.'

Joshua heard the words fade as he trudged away from the cabin with Maria. He doubted that the major would live as he was still a long way from recovery and it was very possible that the Bolsheviks would stumble on him even if he survived the fever. The chances of him leaving the taiga were negligible. But at least Joshua knew that Maria had been the reason for their dangerous mission and that the major was indeed mad to want her dead. No, he would get her to Archangel where the higher authorities would arrange for her to be debriefed, and sent to England to join her relatives there. Joshua did not know why she was of interest but suspected she must know something of vital importance.

Maria was strong and easily kept up with Joshua on the march into the depths of the forest. They would need a lot of cunning and luck to avoid the Bolshevik patrols but he felt that the girl beside him was up to the long and arduous journey.

'Thank you,' Maria said as they walked. 'You have saved my life and you have not broken your word to ask no questions of me or my past.'

'That's up to you,' Joshua sniffed angrily as they walked. He could not get out of his head that the girl had a link with the probable death of his friend and the confrontation with the major.

Maria fell silent, sensing his brooding thoughts.

'We have to make another path,' Lieutenant Novotny said, stabbing at the ground with his sabre. 'The enemy are deployed in force to our front.'

George swallowed a mouthful of thick, black bread-crumbs from the ration he had been allocated, followed by a swig of brackish water from a canteen.

'Not a chance that we could wait until night and slip through their ranks?' he asked hopefully. They were within a few days' ride of Archangel but the Bolsheviks were deploying in strength from what they had been able to observe from the cover of the forests.

The Czech officer shook his head. 'I am sorry, my friend, but I will have to double-back through the last two villages we past through. Our path will take us back to a place not far from where we found you. It is what the Bolsheviks will not expect.'

George's training as an officer told him the young officer's planning made sense although it was disappointing to be so close to the safety of the city on the sea. There, he knew, the Allied armies would be in enough force to resist an attack.

Novotny gave the order and his men remounted. They were weary but showed no sign of despair. George had to admire the fighting spirit of these mounted soldiers who he had learned had been fighting in Russia since the fall of the Czar.

George swung himself into the saddle. His soreness was less today and he was even feeling at home astride his horse as the column moved out without the traditional jangle of equipment. Novotny had ensured that all of his men strap down anything that might make the slightest noise as they rode and the column moved silently with the exception of the occasional snorting or heavy breathing of the horses.

On a compass bearing taken by the Czech officer that would lead them back to the vicinity where he had last seen Joshua and the major, George mused that they might bump into the two men again. But he quickly dismissed the thought as ludicrous. Russia was a big place and the forest swallowed all life. What were the odds?

Joshua pulled together fallen timber to make a tiny hide for the night. Maria assisted by fetching the foliage to cover the spaces between the tree limbs. It was placed in a small depression to help conceal their temporary home and when the job was complete, Joshua invited Maria to crawl inside with him. Dark, heavy clouds were forming on the horizon and Joshua prayed that the storm would hold off as the hide would become very wet if it rained. Their concealment made it virtually impossible to see at ground level and he was relying on this to get a good night's sleep as anyone lurking in the area would have to literally walk over them.

'No fire,' Joshua warned when Maria was facing him only inches from his body. 'We eat the ham and cheese and get a full night's sleep.'

Maria accepted the intimate conditions, knowing what Joshua meant. They would not have to take turns staying awake as sentry duty. Her exposure to soldiers had taught her much about military tactics.

Joshua produced the ham and cheese, cutting off slabs with a small sharp knife he had found in the woodcutter's cabin. He passed Maria the food and they ate in silence, listening to the night sounds of the forest. When he pulled his coat over both of them, Joshua could smell Maria's breath on his cheek.

'What did you do before you became a soldier?' she asked, breaking the silence.

'I was a pencil pusher. A clerk in Sydney.'

'You do not act like a clerk,' Maria said. 'You are as brave and good as my father's imperial guards.'

'Your father was an officer?' Joshua asked.

'My father was the Czar of Russia,' Marie replied quietly. 'Your King George and his family are who I am to join in England.'

At first Joshua thought that he was hallucinating. 'Your father was the Czar Nicholas?' he echoed disbelievingly.

'Yes, I am Princess Maria,' she replied simply. 'All my family were murdered at Ekaterinburg by the Bolsheviks – except for me. I was kept alive as a hostage but I was able to escape.' She paused and Joshua sensed that she was remembering something she would rather not be. Maria turned away, tears streaming down her face. Joshua wrapped his arms around the girl and held her to him. Maria sobbed in his arms as he stroked her hair. He was confused and did not know what to think of her story.

'How did you get this far?' he asked gently.

'Just after I fled the city I was found by a hunter. He knew who I was and helped me journey between villages until I was able to reach the woodcutter's cabin. He was able to smuggle a message through the Bolshevik lines to Archangel. When you came for me I thought I was saved but I fear that there must be people in England who want me dead and I do not know why.'

Joshua's mind was still reeling from what Maria had told him about her identity. He was sure that it had been the major's intention to kill her but that still did not make sense. Why would the British want the last surviving member of the Russian royal family dead? The answer was beyond Joshua's comprehension and so he dismissed the idea. The British major had been truly insane, Joshua convinced himself, and now it was up to him to deliver Maria into the hands of the English.

That night as they huddled into each other for warmth

185

Maria whimpered in her sleep and when she did, Joshua would soothe her with soft words. She awoke in the early morning hours to hear his steady breathing. She could not see his face in the dark but every line was burned into her memory. Maria wondered at this man from a place so far from Russia. He had asked nothing of her and had proved his readiness to sacrifice his life to defend her – even when he was not aware of her royal status. He was handsome in a rugged way, she thought. And both gentle and savage. Maria felt a growing attraction towards the Australian, realising that he alone stood between her future and the possibility of a cruel death in Russia. Impulsively Maria reached over to stroke his whiskered chin. Joshua stirred briefly, scratching at his chin but fell back into a rhythmic breathing. She felt such deep affection already for this man whose very existence protected her. She sighed. It was easy to feel safe in the arms of this Australian.

The skirmish with a mounted Bolshevik patrol took the lives of four Czech cavalry men. They had bumped the enemy patrol crossing a clearing and both sides were taken unawares. The disciplined Czechs charged the Bolsheviks who outnumbered them at least two to one, but they were able to smash into the enemy's assembling line before they were fully formed to resist the shock of the Czech attack. In the ensuing hand-to-hand fighting from horseback George had fought with a ferocity that impressed his comrades and the column had succeeded in routing the Bolsheviks. Novotny had roared the order to allow none to escape alive and the Czechs rode down the Bolshevik survivors who threw up their hands in surrender.

Led back, the surviving enemy were ordered to dismount

and Novotny gave the order to shoot the bewildered men who were standing in a close circle. They fell, screaming for mercy. George no longer felt pity for them. The column had just passed through a village that the Bolsheviks had occupied where all the town's male population over ten years of age had been forced into the local Orthodox church and burned alive. It had been a lesson to the surviving women that all Russians who were not actively with them would be considered counter-revolutionaries. The local men had not even been given the choice to join the revolution. This mattered little to the Bolsheviks who stood by, impassively listening to the agonised cries of the men and boys inside. Nothing could be too brutal to further the aims of the revolution.

It was when the Czech column had entered the devastated village that George lost any pity he may have had for enemy prisoners. He only hoped that these men they had executed were part of the Bolshevik party that had carried out the atrocity in the last village.

'They will not tell of our presence,' Novotny said, delivering the coup de grâce to one of the Bolsheviks who had not died in the hail of gunfire from the mounted men. 'But their absence from their unit will be noted,' he said, swinging back onto his horse.

He led them out of the clearing and back into the forest. For a day they rode in a great sweeping arc until near nightfall a rider on the flank rode back to report a cabin in a small clearing ahead. What was notable about the vicinity was the presence of the bodies of enemy dead before the hut. Novotny knew that they would need to bivouac for the night and decided to reconnoitre the area first.

George accompanied the Czech officer with two escorts to observe if any other enemy may be in the vicinity, but doubted it as they would have at the least buried their comrades. In a way it was a good sign that the Bolsheviks were absent from the area.

From the edge of the forest they sat quietly scanning the surrounding trees for any sign of an ambush, but saw none. One of the escorting Czech cavalry men suddenly hissed a warning, drawing their attention to the cabin where they saw a figure emerge unsteadily, a rifle in his hands.

The soldier who had hissed raised his rifle. 'Bloody hell!' George swore and turned in his saddle to warn off the Czech steadying his rifle for a shot. 'Don't shoot!'

Novotny heard the warning and snapped an order to the Czech who lowered his rifle.

George spurred his horse forward shouting over his shoulder, 'It's Major Locksley, my commanding officer.'

He brought his horse to a halt directly in front of the British officer and swung himself down. The major was filthy and unshaven, but he was on his feet, and for a brief moment did not seem to recognise George.

'Sir, it's Corporal Littleton,' George said. 'Thank God we have found you alive.'

Locksley blinked and a smile crossed his face. 'It is you, corporal,' he said. 'I cannot tell you how good it is to see you. Is Sergeant Larkin with you?'

George shook his head. 'Sorry, sir, I thought he was with you. I was fortunate enough to be found by our Czech allies some days ago and have been with them since. This is pure luck finding you.'

Locksley stepped out from the doorway and stared past George to the three cavalrymen emerging from the forest and picking their way past the bloated, decomposing bodies of the men Joshua had killed.

'Lieutenant Novotny, this is Major Locksley of the British

army,' George introduced. The Czech officer snapped a salute which Locksley returned. 'It seems that you have put up a good show here, Major Locksley,' Andrej Novotny said, surveying the front yard.

Locksley followed his line of sight but made no comment. 'Is a Sergeant Larkin and a Russian girl with you?' he asked again, eliciting blank looks from both the Czech and the Australian.

'I presumed that he was with you, sir,' George answered, wondering at the mention of a Russian girl.

'He has a day's march on us,' Locksley said. 'I must call on your services as an ally to assist me in finding them,' he continued, addressing Novotny.

'Is this important?' Novotny asked, displaying some irritation at the request. He had his own orders and they were to fall back to Archangel. Any further mission might disrupt that plan.

'I would not ask it,' Locksley said, 'if it were not important to the outcome of this campaign. I can assure you, Lieutenant Novotny, that my request would be immediately sanctioned by your higher authority if the mission was revealed. It is of vital importance to the war here but I am not at liberty to tell you why I make this request for assistance.'

George was elated to hear that Joshua was still alive, but was decidedly uneasy at the tone of the major's voice. Something had happened and George was certain that it was not in his friend's nature to leave a wounded or ill fellow soldier behind.

'Sir,' he said with a frown, 'is there something we should know about?'

Locksley turned on him. 'Nothing more than that Sergeant Larkin will be caught and arrested for disobeying orders, and deserting a superior officer on the battlefield. That is all you have to know.'

Stunned by the accusation towards his friend, George did not answer but shook his head in disbelief.

'I will comply with your request, Major Locksley,' Novotny said after considering the possibilities. 'Only if the search for Sergeant Larkin and the Russian girl is towards Archangel.'

Locksley smiled grimly. 'I can assure you that will be the situation. If my guess is right, they are fleeing in that direction as we speak.'

Novotny nodded and wheeled his horse away to bring his men into the clearing. George stood staring at the British major, the look that passed between them sparking distrust and suspicion. Whatever had occurred at the cabin days earlier, George had a feeling that Locksley was not about to take his friend alive.

NINETEEN

Valley View
Present day

Senior Constable Morgan McLean found himself buried in paperwork. He had knocked on the dead young man's mother's door at 2 a.m. and gone through the procedure of informing her that her only son was dead. Morgan had prepared for the task by first waking the next door neighbours who he knew were close friends and having them on standby to console the poor woman with soothing words and cups of tea. He had worked through the rest of the night making the telephone calls required to fill in the boxes of the reports.

The sun was rising as he pushed himself away from the computer screen. In the distance he could hear the sweet call of a butcher bird greeting the dawn. Soldiering with the SAS had trained him to snatch sleep in small packets and without bothering to return to his bed he dozed in the office with his head on the desk. He did not know how long

191

he had been asleep when the phone rang as he expected it would before he put his head down. Groping for the phone, Morgan forced himself awake.

'Valley View police,' he answered through a fog of half-reality.

'Morgan, this is Phil from the Accident Investigation Unit. Just thought I should tell you that from our preliminary check of that car brought in last night it looks like the braking system had been sabotaged. No wonder the car was totalled at Spencers Bend.'

Morgan shook off the last of the fog and rubbed his eyes. The seeming accident now took on the nature of a murder inquiry.

'Have you got onto your local D's?' the man from the Traffic Accident Investigation unit asked.

'I'll call Ken Barber straightaway,' Morgan replied. 'Thanks for the news,' he added with a touch of sarcasm in his voice.

'Anytime,' Phil answered, knowing that his news meant a lot more paperwork than just a traffic accident. 'I am not about to give anything out to the press,' he continued. 'You can do that at your discretion.'

'Thanks,' Morgan said, replacing the phone.

He immediately called Hume City police station, leaving a message for Detective Senior Sergeant Barber to contact him as soon as he got into his office, then stood and stretched. It was time for a shave and shower and a change of uniform. He would commence this new investigation by interviewing Monique, as it had been, after all, her vehicle involved in the incident. Whatever had happened the night before involved her, and Morgan was sure that she had been the target of sabotage. The note in his desk drawer had taken on a very sinister significance. He would have to

192

double his efforts and locate that man or woman with an Eastern European accent.

London
Present day

Harry Stanton stared out the pub window at the people on the street scurrying under umbrellas against a sleeting rain. So many foreign faces, he reflected. It was not the London of his youth. The Scotch and soda on the table in front of him was hardly touched but at eleven o'clock in the morning he did not expect to drink it. He was an after five social drinker and he had chosen this out-of-the-way public house to meet with the man from some obscure department in the civil service.

Around Harry, a crowd began to spill into the pub from the surrounding office blocks for lunch and an ale. Young men and smartly dressed women chatted and flirted. Harry checked his watch and when he looked up he saw the man he was to meet. He was grey in every aspect – his hair, suit and skin tone – and he carried a government-issued brief-case. They exchanged looks and the contact from the civil service sat down at Harry's small table by the window.

'We will move to a corner over there,' Harry said, rising with his drink in his hand. 'Just an old habit when I am meeting with someone.'

They moved to a corner of the pub where they secured another small table.

'Are you having a drink?' Harry asked. His contact shook his head. 'Sorry, old chap, a bit early for me.' No names had been exchanged, nor any formal greetings. 'We would like to have a sitrep on events in Australia,' he said without preliminaries.

'Our man on the ground is active,' Harry replied.

The grey man leaned forward. 'You realise that there must be no connection with events there and the government here,' he said quietly, pursing his lips. 'You have to appreciate that the PM has no knowledge of the operation. This is simply a continuation of something that should have been resolved by your department in 1920. The threat to European stability is greater now, than it was then. We already have a suspicion that a Russian nationalist movement knows of her existence.'

'I can confirm that suspicion,' Harry said, eyeing his drink and wondering if it was not too early to have a sip considering the clandestine nature of their business. 'But we are on top of that. We have been for some time now.'

'If those mad Ruskie nationalists are able to prove that a direct descendant of Czar Nicholas is still alive it will prompt many Russians to rally to their cause. If that happens we could very well have a civil war on our hands and that is not good for the stability of world politics – or our own interests in a united Europe. Civil wars have a bad habit of escalating and spilling over into neighbouring countries. It is bad enough that the Russians have to face trouble from their old territories but this would strike at the very heart of the present administration in the Kremlin. It is vital that we remove any reason for the nationalists to raise up the old imperial standard.'

Harry fully understood the implications of the Russian nationalists producing a living heir to the old imperial throne. Since the fall of communism Russia had been left open to all kind of influences. All had not been better under the new, democratic regime as many had lost the modest but secure income promised by a socialist state. Crime had spiralled and the poor saw the rich as examples of the decadence the old Soviet communists had warned them of. At the heart of Russia beat a nostalgia for the even older order of Russian imperialism. Religion was still the blood that oozed in the deeply spiritual culture and that the imperial princess had been since sanctified in the Russian Orthodox church meant a lot to the poor and dispossessed of the sprawling nation at the strategic edge of Europe. It could only take an icon like a surviving descendant of a Russian saint played by the right people to cause another revolution. Harry knew this well, as did many others who had lived in the world of ensuring checks and balances remained in place for the peace and security of Europe. As much as he was suspicious of the so-called democracy emerging in Russia, he realised that he was a player in making certain it had a chance to grow and mature. Russia and Europe did not need the return of the old imperialists' myth of a grand Russian empire.

'You can make your report that we are on top of it,' Harry reassured. 'We have had one little hiccup but the man I have assigned will rectify the situation. All we have to do is get possession of a certain journal and some identity papers to make the situation go away.'

'I hope so,' the grey man said, standing to leave the pub. 'Your next report should be that the situation is fully under control.'

He said no more and made his way out of the crowded hotel to step onto the grey streets of London's busy business heart where he merged with the grey day outside.

Harry remained for a short time brooding on the whole operation. He knew it was messy but so far had confined it in his department to himself and Daniel Kildare. MI6 was still smarting from the ludicrous accusations in a royal commission that they had been instrumental in having Princess Diana assassinated on the command of the English royal family. That was purely James Bond stuff to feed the tabloids hungry for sensationalism guaranteed to drive up sales and hence profits for the media. No, black operations were aimed at far more important things than news for the trashy tabloids. Black ops were aimed at retaining world stability and this situation in far-off Australia was a case in point. Harry realised the magnitude of what he was overseeing and wondered about his predecessors in the old Secret Intelligence Service of the 1920s. Had they felt the same bile-inducing feelings he was now experiencing when they had attempted to hunt down and eliminate the only surviving Russian royal? But their motives had been different then and if the press had been as active pursuing that case then they would have had a royal scandal to boost sales. Now it was simply a case of attempting to covertly assist the Russians in maintaining some stability.

Harry picked up the Scotch and soda and swigged it down in one gulp. The liquor hit his stomach, producing a warm glow. It was time to return to his office and monitor the situation at some Aussie folk festival in a place on the other side of the Indian Ocean. He dutifully filed his report and sent it into a secret place in cyberspace where only he could retrieve it – or so he thought.

Valley View
Present day

Morgan's investigation inevitably led him to the doorway of Monique's house, where he was greeted by David, who ushered him inside.

'I have come about Monique's car,' Morgan said.

'We have already heard it was involved in a terrible

196

accident last night,' David said. 'We did not realise that it was stolen until this morning when I went to pick it up from the hall. Monique left it there last night because she had a few drinks and a friend gave her a lift home.'

Morgan accepted the explanation. The locals were very conscious of obeying the drink-driving laws and aware that the police patrolled the streets at this time of the year well into the early hours. 'I will still need Monique to come down to the station and make a statement,' he said. 'The earlier the better as the matter will be under investigation by the coroner because a death was involved.'

'You don't think Monique had anything to do with it?' David asked indignantly.

Morgan hurried to reassure him. 'Not at all,' he said. 'It's just so we can clear Monique at this early stage of the investigation.'

'She is a sleep but I will tell her as soon as she awakes,' David said.

Morgan nodded and was about to leave when David spoke again.

'You know,' he said hesitantly. 'It's like this place was cursed or something.'

'What do you mean?' Morgan said.

David frowned. 'Ever since those skeletons were dug up in our backyard things seem to be going wrong in our lives.'

'What things?' Morgan asked but he could see from the expression on his face that David had closed down on any further questions.

'Nothing of real importance,' he replied.

As Morgan walked back to his car he wondered about what David had said. Life had been pretty simple in Valley View until the discovery of the two unidentified bodies. It

was as if ghosts had been released from their sleep to res-
urrect an old curse left over from the Great War and its
aftermath in Russia. The world had changed so much yet
human nature remained the same. Whatever had activated
the current events swirling around him had its roots in the
snows of 1919 Russia. That much he did know, and he also
knew that Monique was central to this drama now being
played out. He just wondered how he had been caught up
in it.

When Morgan returned to the station he was met on the
steps by Ken Barber.

'What in bloody hell is going on around here?' the detective senior sergeant barked. 'All I can guess is that it's got
something to do with you and that sheila, Monique Dawson.'

'Want a cuppa, Ken?' Morgan asked politely, brushing
past the burly policeman.

'That would be a good start,' Ken Barber replied more
mildly. 'I would rather have a bloody beer.'

'It's not lunchtime yet,' Morgan retorted.

'See, you would never have made a detective,' Ken
grumbled, following Morgan inside the station. 'It's got to
be lunchtime somewhere in the world. But for now maybe
we can figure a few things out.'

Morgan clicked on his hot water jug. He knew that to a
point he would have to level with his senior officer before
the situation got out of control.

'I have to admit that there are a lot of weird things happening,' Morgan said, pouring hot water into two mugs.
'And I have to admit that there might be some link to the
bodies dug up at the Larkin house.'

Ken Barber accepted the mug offered him. 'Let's see
how it all shapes up,' he said, placing his coffee on the edge
of Morgan's desk to cool down. 'A few weeks back a couple

of skeletons are dug up at what you call the Larkin house. They still remain unidentified although there is Buckley's chance of closing a probable murder case, considering the time that has elapsed. Still, it would be nice to have the bodies identified so that the coroner can make a finding and the paperwork in my pigeonhole will go away. Last night we have a car accident that appears to be the result of brake failure due to sabotage which makes it murder. The car belongs to one Ms Monique Dawson who happens to be the current title holder of the Larkin house. This might not be so suspicious if it weren't for the fact that the media runs with a story some weeks back that some Russian princess might have lived there for a short while.'

'I was able to quash that story,' Morgan said. 'There was nothing in it.'

'Except that a uni department in Sydney has photocopies of documents purporting to prove her existence in Valley View back in the 1920s. Couple that with some leaked photocopied pages from this Captain Larkin's diary, and I start to smell something as fishy as dead carp on the side of the Murray River.'

'You remember that matter some years ago about the so-called Hitler Diaries,' Morgan smoothed. 'I suspect that someone is out to try and make a killing in the collectors' market with the story of the Russian princess surviving the massacre.'

'Okay, produce the journal and documents and we can have our documents department prove – or disprove – their authenticity.'

'Mrs Harrison denies that she has any documents or diary,' Morgan lied. 'It's all a hoax.'

'I bet she is a sweet old lady who makes scones for the church fete,' Ken sneered.

'Yeah, something like that,' Morgan confirmed, taking a sip from his coffee and wondering just how much the senior detective believed of his explanation.

'Mate, if you are lying to me I suspect that you'll have got yourself in a hole you will not be able to crawl out of,' Barber said. 'You just might see the faces of the internal affairs people staring down at you from the top.'

Morgan flushed at the warning, knowing that the detective was correct. He was hiding information but felt he did not have enough in the way of facts to send the matter any higher. At the back of his mind was the need to keep the matter in a low-profile mode to protect Monique from any unwanted attention from the media, especially considering the sabotage of her car.

'Ken,' Morgan said, 'I agree that what happened last night was meant for Monique Dawson. But we don't have enough to confirm our suspicions.'

The detective senior sergeant smiled grimly. 'What else?' he asked in a way that intimidated suspects but not Morgan.

'There could be some truth in the Larkin journals that Princess Maria of the Russian royal family did live here for a short time,' Morgan conceded. 'I also think that she and Joshua Larkin were involved in the disposal of the two bodies on their property which, of course, implicates them in the killings.'

'That doesn't explain much of what is going on as regards the possible attempt on Ms Dawson's life last night,' Barber said.

'Maybe not,' Morgan answered. 'But for some dumb reason I get the feeling history is repeating itself. It's like we disturbed ghosts who are out to settle matters today.'

A broad grin spread across Barber's face. 'Have you been down to those bloody hippie tents and had a touchy-feely session with one of those new age people? Or is it time you applied for a transfer back to Sydney to escape the isolation of Valley View?'

'Yeah, well, laugh if you like,' Morgan growled. 'Not everything in the world can be explained by scientific facts.'

'You really believe in ghosts?' Barber asked with just a touch of wonder in his question.

'Not per se,' Morgan answered. 'But I believe that whatever happened here in Valley View almost a century ago has something to do with what is happening now.'

'Okay,' Ken said, leaning back in the chair, causing it to creak dangerously. 'So, who is lurking out there threatening Ms Dawson?'

'That is what I am trying to ascertain,' Morgan replied. 'And when I do, you will be the first person to know.'

Barber placed his mug on the table. The coffee was as bad as anything he had drunk at Hume City police station. 'Do that,' he said. 'At this stage I will commence an investigation into the sabotage of Ms Dawson's car. I doubt that we will be able to keep it out of the papers.'

'I just hope that we don't get some headline happy journo picking up on the story and speculating a link to the old story of the Russian princess,' Morgan groaned, foreseeing another wave of media people arriving in town and nagging him for a few facts.

'Not if I can help it,' Ken said, standing to leave. 'As far as the media are concerned we will run with the story that it was an accident. By the time the coroner releases the real facts you should have solved the case of who wants to do mischief to Ms Dawson.'

Morgan knew that he was being sarcastic, but appreciated his help in keeping the lid on the investigation.

'By the way,' the detective senior sergeant said with a leer. 'Are you screwing this Dawson sheila?'

'In my dreams, Ken,' Morgan answered. 'In my dreams.'

The departing policeman shrugged and stepped onto the verandah.

Morgan poured the remains of his coffee down the sink and sighed. He was running out of time to find a suspect. The needle in the haystack seemed as elusive as it had always been.

TWENTY

East of the Dvina River
Northern Russia
Late August 1919

Joshua calculated that they were east of the Dvina River
and south-east of Archangel. Much of the taiga had given
way to windswept plains dotted with small farms and villages
that appeared to be caught in the feudal times of Medieval
Europe. Joshua had elected to dispose of the rifles they carried as the number of Bolshevik patrols had increased, and
from his military knowledge he knew they would soon be
coming up against larger concentrations of enemy troops,
attempting to cut Archangel off from supplying the Allied
troops in the field.

Maria had suggested that he pose as mute if they were
accosted by Bolshevik forces. He had falsified papers identifying him as a Russian worker and their chances of breaking
through the enemy lines would be greater if they were not
considered anything more than refugees plodding a course
to Archangel.

For seemingly endless days they trudged poorly marked, rutted roads between villages where Maria obtained food and lodgings for them with a stash of silver coins she produced from the linen belt around her waist. Despite the workers' revolution, both revolutionary and counter-revolutionary still accepted the cash she carried.

Little conversation occurred between them as they journeyed in the direction of the port city but at nights they would huddle together in some lice- and flea-infested room at the back of a villager's home. Occasionally they saw Bolshevik troops in the villages and luck was with them as they were able to steer clear of the enemy. But their luck ran out one morning as they were about to leave a village where they had stayed for the night. They were stopped by a roaming patrol of Bolshevik soldiers searching for potential recruits to be conscripted to their army; Joshua and Maria had no warning until they stepped around a corner and into the path of the advancing patrol. The leader shouted something in Russian to them and Maria hissed from the side of her mouth that they were to halt or be shot.

Standing in the muddy track that was the main street of the unnamed village, Joshua felt the chill of fear even more biting than the cold wind that moaned between the wooden, thatched huts. The villagers had disappeared inside their hovels to peer fearfully at the young man and woman who had spent the night in one of the houses.

'You have papers?' the commander of the patrol of armed men demanded. Joshua did not like his appearance as he was not one of the typically burly Bolshevik soldiers he had encountered before. This man looked more like a school-teacher with his clean-shaven face, bald head and thin-framed spectacles. There was a dangerous fanaticism burning behind the eyes that appraised them and although

Joshua did not understand the conversation between the man and Maria, he had a fair idea that she was pleading with him to accept that they were refugees escaping the former Czar's loyal troops. Joshua prayed that he would not be searched as he still retained his service issue revolver.

'He is my brother's friend,' Maria answered when asked why Joshua did not seem to respond to directions. 'He is a mute from birth and we escaped the White Army to the east.'

The commander of the patrol examined the papers Maria produced and held his hand out to Joshua who understood by the gesture that he wanted his too. Joshua passed him the well-worn documents, which the man examined. It was obvious that he could read.

'These papers do not say that your friend is mute,' the commander said menacingly. 'Nor do I accept that you are simple refugees. You speak like a bourgeoisie and you have the manners of one to match.'

'I am the daughter of a landholder,' Maria replied, desperately seeking a way out. 'My family were sympathetic to the plight of the people and were killed by the Cossacks of the Czar's army.'

The intense demeanour of the commander terrified Maria and she had trouble controlling her trembling. His scrutiny of her was like a searing flame burning the skin. He did not hand back the papers.

'I do not believe you,' he said coldly. 'You and your companion will be held under arrest until you are interrogated more fully. Men, escort these suspects to the house at the end of the street.'

Joshua was suddenly aware that the patrol were pointing their bayonet-tipped rifles at him. He noticed Maria's despairing glance in his direction. She dared not speak to

205

him as that would have confirmed the commander's suspicions. He fell into step and allowed the patrol to prod him in the direction of a hovel at the end of the village. They had come so far to be intercepted in the middle of nowhere, Joshua thought bitterly. And they were outnumbered; their chances of escape almost nil. More importantly, if they found his revolver and the money Maria carried in her linen waist belt they would incur the wrath of the Bolsheviks; simple peasants fleeing the civil war did not carry money and guns.

'Go in,' the commander snarled at them and Maria grabbed Joshua's hand as a bayonet pricked him in the back.

They stumbled into a filthy, dark room that stank of animal waste and sweat. The door closed behind them and Joshua could hear the boots of the enemy marching away in the squelching mud. Through a crack in the door he could see that they had left only one guard and guessed that they had continued their search of the village for any other people suspected of not being committed to the revolutionary cause. When Joshua turned back to Maria he was startled to see that they were not alone. Huddled in a corner he saw an old man and two young boys in their early teens staring at them with frightened eyes.

Maria spoke softly to the three and ascertained that they had been arrested that morning on the riverbank and brought to the village by the patrol currently conducting search operations in the district. They said that they were simply fishermen attempting to carry on their work to feed starving families and were not counter-revolutionaries as they had been accused. The commander was well known to them.

'His name is Grigory Tarasov,' the old man offered. 'He was once a public official in a village not far from our own. He knows that we are not enemies but that does not stop him settling a debt against my family. He once accused me of cheating him in a sale of fish to his family and now plans to kill us as his revenge. I am Lazar Sidorov and these are my sons, Kuzma and Ipati.'

Maria relayed what she had learned of their captor and Joshua nodded in understanding. It figured that there would be men who would use the revolution as an excuse to settle old scores.

'What can we do?' Maria asked, wide-eyed.

'It seems that our captor is either arrogant or careless,' Joshua smiled grimly. 'He has not yet searched us.'

Maria was hardly aware of this small but vital oversight, such had been the almost paralysing fear that she had felt upon interception by the Bolshevik patrol. But Joshua was right and for the first time since being stopped by the patrol she felt a glimmer of hope. She gazed at Joshua's face in the gloom and felt her spirits soar. He was her rock and she knew that while she was in his company she would be safe. She had total trust in his proven courage and resourcefulness.

'What do you know about our three companions?' Joshua whispered, lest he be heard by the guard standing outside the door, only a few feet away.

'They are fishermen who were taken on the river before dawn this morning,' Maria whispered. 'They are innocent people.'

'Ask them if they have a boat,' Joshua said. 'And if so, where is it?'

Maria turned to the three other prisoners and relayed Joshua's questions. The old man rambled off an answer. Maria turned to Joshua.

'They said that they last saw their fishing boat secured to the bank of the river where they were taken,' she said. 'The river is only about a mile away.'

Joshua pondered the answer. 'Would they be able to guide us to their boat in the dark?'

Maria relayed the question and Joshua noticed the senior man look at him and nod.

'What if they search us?' Maria asked fearfully.

'I think that they will inevitably do so,' Joshua replied. 'But so far we are safe and for the moment we can conceal the money belt and gun in the straw here.'

'Should not we attempt to escape?' Maria asked. 'There is only one guard outside the door.'

'That would not be wise in broad daylight,' Joshua answered. 'They would hunt us down easily and kill us. Our only chance is to wait until it is dark and then make our move. God willing, no search will be made of us.'

For a moment Maria bit her bottom lip. She turned her back on the three men in the corner and slipped the linen belt from around her waist, laying it in front of Joshua. 'I think that you should carry this,' she said, flipping over the fabric to reveal rows of multi-coloured gemstones and a few silver and gold coins. Joshua almost gasped at the sight of the small fortune before his eyes; diamonds, sapphires, rubies and emeralds caught the faintest of light filtering into the room and threw off mesmerising fires.

'I have carried this since my imprisonment in the Ipatiev house,' she continued. 'Now it has become our means for survival and I will trust it to you for safekeeping.'

Joshua stared at the sparkling stones. 'Are you sure that you can trust me?' he asked softly, closing the linen flap to hide the stones and coins.

'With all my body and soul,' Maria replied, gazing into his eyes. 'If it had not been for all you have done until now I would have been violated and killed back at the wood-cutter's cabin. And you saved me from your major.'

Maria passed him the small satchel containing her identity papers to hide as well. Joshua reached over to squeeze her hand. 'We will escape from here and you will still have your inheritance.'

Tears flowed down Maria's cheeks, pinched with the rigours of their trek. 'I have not truly thanked you for all that you have done for me,' she said, squeezing his hand. 'I have never met a man as kind and brave as you before. No matter what happens I have prayed to God that you will enter heaven with me.'

Joshua shrugged off the heartfelt gratitude but now completely believed her story of who she was. Who else could be in possession of what appeared to be a royal ransom? 'We aren't about to go to heaven for some time,' he said with a savage grin. 'There is only eight of them and one of me. I see that as about even odds.'

Maria wiped at her tears and tried to smile at Joshua's bravado and she wondered if he was a typical Australian male. If so, they must be a tough and courageous race of people.

'What are we to do?' she asked.

'We will wait until dark and I will kill the guard. Then we will flee with the Sidorov men, but they will have to trust me, as I do not intend to head straight for the river. Anyone pursuing us might guess that is where we would be going.'

Maria listened to the plan which depended on two critical points: one, that they were not searched between now and dark; and secondly, that they were left alone until then. She had little doubt that their three fellow captives would agree knowing full well the alternative was to be executed by the vengeful patrol commander.

The long daylight hours slowly passed and it seemed as

if Joshua's plan might have a chance to work. The guard at the front of the door was relieved by another, but he seemed to pay little interest in their welfare. No food or water had been offered and Joshua guessed that their captives thought it a waste of time to look after the needs of already doomed prisoners.

Throughout the day, Maria chatted with the other prisoners and learned much about their families and their lives. She was pleased to find that the men were all loyal to the Romanov dynasty, and felt that their lives would be worse under the new dictators, despite their promises of a workers' utopia. So far the Bolsheviks had not demonstrated any concern for the individual and they were intelligent enough to see what was ahead in the new order of things.

Eventually, Maria snuggled up to Joshua for comfort and he held her against his broad chest, stroking her hair absentmindedly while his mind raced with the terrible things that could go wrong in the next few hours. His unspoken fears came true when, just on dusk, Grigory Tarasov flung open the door of the hovel.

'You,' he said, pointing at Joshua. 'Come with me.'

Joshua did not understand the command and attempted to look dumb and confused.

'I will come with you,' Maria said, standing unsteadily, leaving Joshua truly confused by what was occurring.

Maria did not look back but was wrenched from the hut by Tarasov. Joshua watched helplessly as she was dragged away, leaving only the single guard at the entrance. Now he was alone with three other men he could not communicate with and the linen belt and leather satchel Maria had left him. Earlier, he had carefully removed his revolver and hidden it under straw near his hand. Joshua reached for it, realising that an attempt to shoot his way out of the village with daylight remaining was suicidal. He felt tears of frustration in the corner of his eyes. Not for his own life – but for what might happen to Maria.

The Bolshevik patrol had elected to use a large storage shed as their temporary headquarters. It was filled with bags of grain and had been the last of the villagers' food supplies. Now the grain was forfeited to the revolutionaries.

Maria stood under the flickering light of a kerosene lantern while Tarasov ordered his men outside to make a last sweep of the village for any who may have been able to conceal themselves during the day, and attempt an escape under cover of the approaching night.

Now he was alone with the girl he had taken prisoner. He had intended to kill her male companion first but when she volunteered to go with him he thought that he had seen the glimmer of co-operation in her gesture. Grigory Tarasov was not a really committed Bolshevik but an opportunist who knew where his future survival lay. He could foresee that the Czar's former soldiers and their foreign allies were on the verge of defeat and that those in Moscow flying the red flag would assume power, and he had immediately displayed his loyalty by announcing a soviet in the village he had once administered on behalf of the former Czarist government. His natural intelligence and ability to take on the demeanour of a zealot had cemented his position with the district soviet. In a short time he had personally overseen the killing of those he nominated as class enemies of the revolution. It had been easy to betray former friends and colleagues when his own life had been in jeopardy because of his former position in the government. In the backwaters of Russia he was not alone in taking advantage of chaos and

211

his position had privileges far beyond his previous life as a clerk. Now he could possess what he wanted in the name of the people's revolution so long as those in Moscow saw a share of his small victories in seizing men and material for the cause. Tarasov knew from dealing with a cross-section of Russian society that the girl standing before him was no *kulak* or peasant.

'What is your name again?' Tarasov asked, barely interested in the answer.

'Maria,' she whispered, her throat dry with fear.

Tarasov walked over to her and reached down to lift the hem of her long dress. Maria flinched away from him but he simply looked up and slapped her face. The crack resounded in the confines of the musty smelling shed. Maria reeled from the blow but remained standing. She knew that her capture had nothing to do with her possible counter-revolutionary ideals. This man was simply a criminal who had the political power to force himself onto her. She tried to remember a prayer to recite but nothing came. Fear swept over her when she felt his hand reach under her dress and up between her thighs. His fingers hurt when they were forced inside her.

'Please, God,' she began to pray aloud.

'Haven't you heard,' Tarasov sneered, standing to breathe into her face. 'We do not believe in God. Comrade Marx has taught us that religion is the opiate of the masses. God will not help you – but I can.'

'What must I do?' Maria pleaded, knowing that the answer would not be pleasant.

'You can pull up your dress and lie on your stomach on that pile of bags there,' he said. 'If you do not, I will have my men go to the hut where your companion is and bring him here to be shot in front of you. Would you like that?'

Maria could feel the heat of his lust on his breath. She

closed her eyes and shook her head. She did not want anything to happen to Joshua considering that he had a chance to flee. But now the situation had turned against them and she prayed silently that she could at least delay the leader long enough for the night to come and Joshua to make his escape.

Her face was swelling from the vicious back-handed blow Tarasov had delivered, but she hardly felt the stinging effects compared to what she knew was inevitable. Maria walked unsteadily to the pile of bags and bent over, pulling her dress up over her bare hips, revealing herself to Tarasov. She lay face down and felt his bodyweight on her back. Maria closed her eyes and tried to take herself to a place she remembered as a girl with her family in the Crimea. There were fields of flowers and the sound of honey bees. The scent of the flowers returned to her until the first agonising thrust. Maria had been a virgin until this moment and now something had been taken from her that could never be returned. She screamed, causing the panting man behind her to thrust harder. Joshua, her guardian angel, could do nothing to help her just now.

TWENTY-ONE

Valley View
Present day

Morgan recognised young Matthew's voice over the telephone. 'I think I got something for you, Mr McLean,' he said. 'I was talking to Mr Barry down at the pub and he told me a Russian kind of guy was booked into one of his rooms. His name is Mr Olev.'

'Thanks, young Matt,' Morgan replied. 'You have done a good job.'

'It was not a problem,' Matthew said. 'Anything I can do to help, you only have to ask, Mr McLean.'

Morgan bid him a good day and placed the phone on the cradle. When he looked up he saw Monique walk through the door.

'David said that you would need a statement from me about my car being stolen,' she said. She appeared pale and shaken.

'Would you like a tea or coffee?' Morgan asked, walking over to the front counter of his office to meet her.

'No, thank you,' she replied. 'I am fine and I am sure that you are a busy man with all that is happening at the moment around Valley View.'

'What is wrong?' Morgan asked, sensing that she was acting in a very distant manner towards him. 'How about you come in and take a seat. I will close the station.'

Monique stepped behind the counter and took the seat he offered. She had been crying.

'I just had a slight upset with David. Nothing much, really.'

'How much does David know about what's going on in your life?' Morgan asked, taking a seat near her chair.

'I have not told him very much,' Monique sniffed. 'I don't want him to worry. I know David and all that is happening would be too much for him.'

'What does he know?' Morgan persisted.

'He just knows that I went to London and that my car was stolen last night. I am having trouble coping with the fact that that poor boy was killed in it.'

'There is not much I can say to console you on that matter,' Morgan said. 'It was not your fault that he should hotwire your car and get himself killed at Spencers Bend.'

'What happened?' Monique asked, staring at Morgan through misty eyes.

Disconcerted, Morgan would have preferred to avoid answering but knew he must use the tragic incident to warn her away from Valley View. 'Is it possible that you might like to visit Sydney and stay with friends or family for a while?' he countered, sucking in words that he did not want to utter.

'Why would you say that?' Monique asked. 'What is happening?'

'The brakes on your car were tampered with,' Morgan exhaled. 'It could be that someone wanted you dead. But it was a clumsy attempt and I doubt that whoever was responsible would hang around Valley View knowing that we would eventually recognise the sabotage.'

'I don't know why, but the moment I heard that my car was involved in a fatal accident, I just knew it was not really an accident,' Monique said. 'It all has to do with that warning I received, and my link to the Larkin name.'

'So you know that he is your great-grandfather?' Morgan asked.

'I suppose I should have trusted you more,' Monique answered, looking past him to the posters on the wall displaying missing persons and wanted people. 'I am about ninety-nine per cent sure that Joshua was my great-grandfather and all I am attempting to confirm now is that my great-grandmother, his wife, Maria was my ancestor. As you know I had a DNA test when I was in London as they have a database for the Russian royal family over there.'

'A positive result might confirm that you are the direct heir to the Russian throne – that you are also a Romanov by blood. Authenticating Captain Larkin's journal would be a moot point. Your blood is all the evidence required to prove that Maria survived the massacre.'

Monique looked up. 'It is something I am having trouble coming to grips with,' she said. 'The DNA test might confirm that she was my great-grandmother and as far as family records show there are none other alive who share her royal blood. But why would that be a reason to want me dead?'

Morgan walked over to the counter, glancing through the window of his office at a car that had pulled into a space in front of the police station. He suspected that he would have to cut short his conversation with Monique.

'I can't answer that question,' he answered bluntly. 'But there are a lot of psychos out there who might think that

216

finishing off the last of the Romanov line will grant them immortality. You need to get out of town for a while until I get the chance to try to track down whoever was responsible for tampering with your car.'

Monique rose. 'I will not be leaving Valley View,' she said, passing Morgan to reach the door. 'Matters are bad enough with David and my leaving won't help our relationship. I can only hope that you find whoever was behind the sabotage.'

Morgan opened the door and Monique stepped past an older man whose florid face displayed his pent-up anger.

'You have to find the little bastard who nicked my wallet,' he yelled at Morgan as if he had been personally responsible for the theft. Morgan sighed and led him inside, taking the details of how the man had been at the row of stalls in the paddock where the folk festival tents were erected. Seeking out Mr Olev would have to wait for the moment.

Sarah Sakharov was not only strikingly beautiful but had an intelligence quotient worthy of a physics professor. Sarah knew that she turned heads when she entered a room and her private school education, followed by Swiss finishing schools gave her that educated accent Aussies referred to as posh. Dressed in a pair of designer jeans and silk blouse, Sarah could have passed as the poster girl for the folk festival.

But Sarah was more than just a beautiful young woman attending the festival. As her name implied, her family roots were in Russia, albeit before the turn of the 20th century. Her fascination with genealogy had inspired Sarah to study the Russian language and in her spare time visit the birthplace of her blood. Now she spoke in fluent Russian to the man who had recruited her to the mission. They sat opposite each other at a wooden bench in the Valley View park by a city of festival tents and sipped coffee from cardboard cups. The muffled sound of singers and banjos drifted to them along with the aroma of sausages sizzling on a barbecue stand.

'There was a car crash involving Miss Dawson's car,' Petrov Batkin, aka Olev said. 'They are trying to dispose of her.'

Sarah sipped her coffee and gazed around at the crowds of people drifting into the tent city, seeking souvenirs, sausages and songs. 'I have read about the accident in the local paper but did not know it was Miss Dawson's vehicle involved.'

'Kildare must have got to her car,' Batkin growled. 'I blame myself for losing him at the dance in the hall. Somehow he was able to identify and sabotage the car.'

'How do you know this?' Sarah asked. 'It did not say in the newspaper report that her car had been sabotaged.'

'I was passed a report from our people in St Petersburg,' Batkin replied. 'They have been able to tap into the local police computer network and read their reports. It has taken a lot of money to buy the right hackers for that job.'

'Then we must assume that the British MI6 is involved in a black op to eliminate any trace of the Romanov blood,' Sarah answered. 'In the meantime we should avoid contact as much as possible.'

Batkin gazed around the pretty town of green, rolling hills and a gentle river running past the edge of the village limits. 'I doubt that we have much to concern us with Australian intelligence monitoring our activities,' he scoffed. 'This place is so far out of the way I doubt they know it exists. As far as my reports go it also appears they are not aware of what the British are doing in their country. No, this is between us and the English.'

'Do you wish me to make contact with Miss Dawson today?' Sarah asked. 'In the light of what has occurred with her car I suspect that she will be open to meeting me. I will arrange for a meeting today. I doubt that she will feel threatened considering who I am.'

Batkin could see that Sarah was exuding confidence. His organisation had scored a coup when she had joined their ranks to train in urban warfare and assassination. He had schooled her in how to become an opportunist killer – she could turn readily available items found in any house into weapons. She was the perfect choice for this mission with her cover of freelance journalist and her ability to blend in with the crowds attending the festival. His recommendation had been enthusiastically accepted by the board of wealthy businessmen in St Petersburg, who Batkin well knew were really Russian mafia. He despised much about this organisation but was realistic enough to recognise that it was they who really controlled Russia, their money being their power. They needed political legitimacy and Batkin's shadowy organisation needed political clout. Strange fellow travellers with a common aim. Had not Hitler been brought to power and supported by the German industrialists before the Great Patriotic War? As an avid student of history, Batkin knew his organisation would accept criminal money but in the end, when they had achieved political legitimacy, they would turn on the hand that fed them just as Hitler had done to his financial supporters who mistakenly believed they could control the man. Monique Dawson would be the core symbol of their struggle to re-establish the Old Order of imperialism that Russia once knew. Batkin understood the power of icons in his country and she would be a living icon – descended from a Russian princess now sanctified by the Orthodox Church. All she needed was to be convinced that they could protect her against the anti-Russian forces out to kill her and they could expose her existence to the world.

Sarah finished her coffee and pushed herself away from the bench. 'It is time to assume my role here,' she said with a faint smile. 'It is one that I will enjoy.'

Batkin watched her walk away. He was feeling sluggish from his stay in the hotel and felt the itch to exercise. For the rest of the day he would take in the events organised for the folk festival and track down the English intelligence agent, Daniel Kildare.

Morgan's shift was coming to an end and he welcomed the two young constables who had been sent out from Hume City to relieve him. After briefing them on the events of the day he left them in the station to return to his accommodation and change into shorts, his old singlet with its faded SAS insignia emblazoned across the front and running shoes. It was time for his hard run out of town and up the road to Connors Hill. The last few days he had slipped in his regime and looked forward to being alone, out of town, running with the sun setting over the tree-covered hills.

Morgan stepped out to a wolf whistle from the female constable behind the counter. She was barely twenty and pretty so Morgan accepted the compliment as good for his ego.

'Not bad for an old guy,' she said with a broad grin.

Morgan waved to her as he set out to follow his usual route north of town past the Larkin residence. He passed crowds of festival-goers, meandering their way back to the caravan park and camping ground, and continued on until he was outside the town's last row of houses. Now he was jogging along the bitumen, past paddocks and the occasional farmhouse set back in a field of flowers. The road wound into the hills north of the town and Morgan knew his challenge lay ahead, steadily climbing the road to the top of the range. It was an extremely tough track but one that he had conquered many times. He passed the Larkin house and noticed a car parked in the driveway. By the look of it, it was a hire car. Monique and David had visitors, he thought idly as he continued to jog, sweat running down his face and body despite the cool nip to the still, spring air.

Past the house Morgan was finally away from civilisation, and felt the road bite with the increase in the incline. He was breathing steadily and knew his pulse was beating at a safe rate, and as he pushed himself for the climb to the top he was surprised to see a distant figure ahead of him, jogging as he was. Never had he seen anyone else take this route for a run since he had been at Valley View. It had to be one of the more physically minded tourists. At least he would have company. He suddenly felt an urge to catch up and pass his sole competitor for the right to reach the top first. With a savage grin, Morgan pushed just a little harder to close the gap between himself and what he could make out was the figure of a man around his own age.

The runner ahead glanced over his shoulder and noticed Morgan fighting his way up the hill, attempting to overtake him. For over a half kilometre both men pushed each other until the unidentified runner finally reached the top and reeled into the lookout that had sweeping views to the valley below. He was bent over and forced himself to stretch, taking in extra air to his lungs.

Morgan was not far behind him and also staggered into

the tourist stop. The sun was three-quarters behind the distant hills, bathing them in an eerie blue haze.

'You ran well, my friend,' Batkin complimented Morgan as he remained bent over, trying to bring his breathing back to a normal pattern. 'You are soldier?' he then queried, noticing the faded SAS emblem on Morgan's old singlet.

'No,' Morgan gasped. 'I am the local copper.'

'But you have army sign, yes?'

Batkin frowned, recognising the emblem of the Special Air Service. It had been, after all, that the Russian military had chosen the British SAS in the early 1970s as a model for their own special forces soldiers, but they had not been granted an emblem in order to disguise the fact that they actually existed.

Morgan glanced at the tough-looking man speaking to him and noticed a faded, tattooed parachute on his right bicep. From the stranger's accent and demeanour Morgan made a calculated guess that his rival for the honour of the hill was a former Eastern bloc soldier who once belonged to Warsaw special forces – possibly even Spetsnaz – as the only symbol they could claim was that they were para trained.

'Not good for man to carry SAS sign,' Batkin said, shaking his head. 'Unless he member of unit.'

'You're right,' Morgan said, standing straight and eyeing the other man. 'I was once a member of the regiment, but that was a long time ago. Were you Russian special forces?'

Batkin grinned at Morgan. In the serenity of the dying day, so far from the rugged mountains and valleys of Afghanistan and his own former Communist forces, it did not seem to matter that he admitted his former service to another who he suspected had also once served his country as a special soldier.

'Afghanistan, when your Yankee brothers from the CIA gave the Taliban the means to eventually cause us to withdraw.'

'The Gulf War, when our Yankee brothers went to war to fight the fundamentalists,' Morgan said, holding out his hand to the stranger. 'The ones you guys failed to kill. Morgan McLean.'

Batkin accepted the extended hand and his grip was strong. 'Petrov Olev,' he said.

Morgan almost recoiled. He had found the man he had intended to search for and question about the message passed to Monique and the sabotage of her car.

'Is long time to meet a man, who know what is like to serve country as we did,' Batkin continued, still gripping Morgan's hand and staring him directly in the eyes. 'We should share drink, yes.'

Morgan retrieved his hand. 'May be a good idea,' he replied. 'Where are you staying?'

'At public house at other end of town,' Batkin replied.

Morgan already knew the answer to the question he had asked. This was not the place or time to question his suspect, however, and Morgan continued to play dumb. 'I will look you up,' he said. 'I reckon you and I could swap a story or two.'

Batkin nodded. 'I must continue run or I will get cramp,' he said, turning to jog down the hill.

Morgan allowed him time to get ahead before setting out to return to the town. As he passed Monique's house he noticed that the unidentified car was still in the driveway. He memorised the registration number. In the back of his mind was the nagging thought that Olev had once been a member of the feared Spetsnaz forces although he did not admit to it directly. But old habits die hard among former

223

special forces soldiers and maintaining a high standard of physical fitness was one of those habits.

Batkin had not considered that the local town policeman could have been a former member of an elite fighting force. This previously unknown fact now nagged him. His intelligence had informed him that the local town police officer was involved in the investigation of the two bodies that had unleashed the ghosts of the past to wreak havoc in the present. Batkin cursed those who had briefed him for the oversight. He would have to do something to change the current situation.

TWENTY-TWO

Northern Russia
Late August 1919

Joshua watched through the cracks in the wall as the armed patrol sauntered past, their rifles slung. It was obvious that they were not well trained soldiers from the way they carried themselves and the Australian soldier suspected that his captors were probably poorly trained militia. Night was falling and it had been about an hour since Maria had been taken from the hut by the Bolshevik commander. Inwardly Joshua raged at the sun for being so slow to set. As each minute dragged by he fretted about Maria's fate at the hands of the militia commander.

Finally, it drew dark enough for Joshua to act. He could no longer see the patrol which had returned from a final sweep of the tiny village and ambled down the street out of sight. He guessed that they were returning to their night quarters. Joshua drew the revolver from beneath the straw and pushed up against the wall. Through a crack in the wooden slab, he could see the back of the guard's head only inches away. Carefully, Joshua pushed the end of the barrel of the pistol through the crack and sighted the guard's head. He knew that he must act fast and already had a plan to help him search for Maria. What he would need after pulling the trigger was a diversion.

When he squeezed the trigger the pistol bucked in his hand and he had the satisfaction of seeing the guard crumple without knowing what had torn through his skull. A fine spray of blood filled the air and the three men with Joshua yelled in their fright. Joshua kicked open the rickety wooden door.

'Get out!' he screamed at his three fellow prisoners who, although not understanding his words, recognised the opportunity for freedom. Scrambling to their feet they pushed past Joshua and fled into the night.

Joshua slipped from the hut and made his way behind it. As expected, he saw the remaining militia men tumble from a building at the other end of the village which Joshua remembered was a storage shed. They had their rifles unslung and immediately rushed to the hut. From his position Joshua watched the men mill about, shouting and arguing. As he had guessed, they immediately set off in the direction of the river, calculating that their prisoners were making a dash back to the boat they had left there.

Joshua waited until the last of the Bolshevik militia were deep into the darkness before emerging from his hiding place. He had been right about their poor training and made his way cautiously down the street where dogs were barking at the uproar. He found the shed and noticed that the lights were still blazing inside. With pistol in hand, Joshua found the door and eased it open. Through the crack he could see two men. One was sitting at a desk made from a slab of timber and supported by barrels writing, while the second man stood behind a pile of grain bags with his rifle slung over his shoulder. Joshua recognised Tarasov sitting at the improvised table. Scanning the inside of the shed he attempted to see if any other threat remained beside the two men he could see. Satisfied that they were alone, Joshua burst into the shed, firing three shots at the man with the rifle. His aim was true and one of his bullets struck the armed man in the throat before he could unsling his rifle to retaliate. Even as the man grabbed at the mortal wound to his throat, Joshua swung his pistol on the seated Bolshevik commander whose face registered his shock and terror. Then Joshua heard a moan from near where he had shot the first man who was now kneeling and making gurgling sounds as the blood ran back down into his lungs. Joshua saw Maria lying on the dirty floor, her dress thrown across her like a blanket. With the pistol still levelled at Tarasov, Joshua walked across to her, kicking the dying Bolshevik in the head as he passed him to reach Maria.

'Have they hurt you?' he asked, still keeping the pistol levelled at Tarasov who had enough sense not to move.

'Oh Joshua,' Maria sobbed. 'I prayed that God would take me. I prayed that you might fly from here and reach a place of safety. Why did you not flee?'

'Have they hurt you?' Joshua asked once more in a cold voice, knowing already from the way she'd been thrown into the corner of the shed with her clothes piled on her, that she had probably been raped by one or more of her captors.

'I want to die,' Maria sobbed. 'Please, leave me and let me die.'

Joshua left Maria to walk over to Tarasov and forced the pistol into his mouth. The terrified Bolshevik commander attempted to mumble a plea for his life but the gun went off and he was thrown back from the shot. Toppling from his chair, the man fell to the earthen floor to twitch away his life in a pool of blood. Joshua kicked him in the face and quickly ejected the empty cases to reload the revolver before returning to Maria who was still huddled in a foetal position under her dress. Joshua squatted down beside her and gently stroked her hair matted from the filth of the shed.

'You will always be safe with me from now on,' he soothed with words. 'You will get dressed and we will leave here and we will reach Archangel. The man responsible for your pain has been sent to hell for his sins.'

Maria stood, pulling the dress up to her bare breasts. Joshua turned aside to allow her to clothe herself in privacy and kept the doorway covered with his pistol. When Maria was dressed, Joshua offered his hand to lead her from the place. She did not resist. God had returned her guardian angel to guide her from this place of torment and into the light.

'We will travel away from the river and north,' Joshua said to Maria. In the distance and coming from the direction of the river, Joshua could hear the faint pop of rifle fire. He shook his head and sighed. It did not seem that his fellow captives had made their escape after all, but he knew that would be the outcome when he had manufactured their freedom. They had been his diversion to allow him to free Maria, who now gripped his arm at the sound of gunfire.

'It is nothing,' he whispered. 'We must go on.'

Maria wondered about the fate of the three men who had been with them in the hut and she prayed that they had made it safely to their boat. But Joshua insisted they could not go in search of them; they must set off immediately in order to make good headway.

They trudged through the short night until Joshua found

a place in the woods where he felt safe enough to snatch some sleep for a few hours. According to his calculations it might be safe enough to attempt to change course and head for the river. There they might be lucky and find someone to take them down to Archangel. Civil war or not, the river still had a life and men must ply their trades. Fish was still in demand and, Joshua guessed, so were the silver coins that he now carried around his waist.

The advance to Archangel through mostly enemy dominated territory had taken its toll on Lieutenant Novotny's column. Skirmishing had gradually whittled his command down to himself, five of his cavalry men, George Littleton and Major Locksley. Of the five men, two had sustained serious, but not fatal wounds. Food was rationed and ammunition all but spent.

For the moment they rested outside a village in a copse of woods. Novotny had wisely decided to hold up until he could conduct a two-man recce of the area ahead of them, leaving the British major and George with the rest of his men.

The pursuit of Joshua and the Russian girl had long been side-tracked in favour of just reaching Archangel alive. Not even the major who was possessed of a burning need to find the renegade Australian sergeant had objected when the Czech officer told him directly that his duty to his men had priority over the major's search. They were now just fighting to survive.

Locksley had not discussed with George his obsession to locate Joshua but George needed to know what drove it. Waiting among the trees, George decided it was time to confront the British officer and ask for an explanation.

Locksley was sitting on the ground with his back against a tree when George approached.

'Sir, if you don't mind, I feel that you might tell me what happened back at the cabin.'

Locksley looked up at the Australian corporal standing over him. 'Sergeant Larkin disobeyed a direct order to carry out the task that I had been given for our mission, corporal,' he said in a tired voice. 'A mission that put your life and mine in grave danger, and after refusing to do as he was commanded he then deserted me and only luck has got me this far. If you survive and I do not, you are to continue with the mission and, despite any personal friendship with Sergeant Larkin, you are to kill him and the Russian girl he may be with. It is imperative to the national interests of the Empire that this be done.'

George almost reeled under the shock of the words so casually uttered. 'Sir, I am a soldier and former commissioned officer sworn to my oath of office, but I must know the justification for such an order,' he said.

Locksley cocked his head, as if digesting the Australian corporal's response. 'I wish I could inform as to the reasons you must endeavour to carry out the order,' he sighed. 'But you were selected for this mission on the understanding that as a former officer you would remain loyal to the King. I can only appeal to your sense of honour to comply with my order and do your best to bring about the authorised outcome of this mission. Believe me, it is not something that I relish.'

George shook his head, realising that he would not receive any explanation. He was torn between his bond of friendship to Joshua and his duty to the King. Had not duty been a word he had grown with? His father had forever used the term to educate him about the meaning of life. But had it not also sent over 60 000 Australians to their deaths as they complied with the need to demonstrate their duty to the ideals of the British Empire? Had not he volunteered for the same reason – duty? Would he adhere to duty and carry out the major's direction if he ever met with Joshua again? The frightening thought echoed that he just might do as the major had commanded if duty meant more than friendship. He walked away to the edge of the trees to scan the marshes and strips of dry land between them. He could see Novotny returning on foot with his escort and his attention was suddenly drawn to the blue sky above. It was small and circling overhead, but George recognised the markings on the wings of the Fokker triplane. It was a Bolshevik fighter and it had spotted Novotny who suddenly heard the distinctive droning sputter of the aircraft engine behind him.

'Enemy fighter!' George screamed and the Czech officer broke into a sprint as the plane swooped down, levelling for a strafing attack on the three tiny figures below.

The patter of the twin machine guns mounted forward of the pilot could be heard over the drone of the aircraft's engine. Dirt flew up dangerously close around the men as they ran for their lives. Suddenly, one of the running men cried out and pitched forward. A bullet had found its mark. Novotny stopped, spun back to bend over his fallen man. George immediately sprinted from the relative safety of the trees to assist Novotny as the enemy aircraft climbed in a circle to make another run on its targets below.

George fell to his knees beside Novotny and the mortally wounded Czech soldier. The bullet had passed through his back and exited his chest. George grabbed the Czech officer by the sleeve. 'We have to leave him before that Bolshie bastard has another run at us,' George pleaded, tugging the reluctant Czech to his feet.

The Fokker was turning to dive again when George spotted something else coming out of the sun. He immediately recognised the shape of a De Haviland DH9A twin-seater biplane and its markings identified it as a British aircraft. Normally the British aircraft would not be a match for the faster Fokker but it had the element of surprise and the sun behind it, as it now swooped on the enemy fighter concentrating its efforts on the targets below.

Fascinated by the sudden turn of events neither Novotny nor George moved. They could hear the machine guns of the British aircraft stuttering away before the Bolshevik fighter could fire its own. The distance between the two aircraft closed to within a hundred yards and George could see the impact of the British bullets striking along the enemy aircraft fuselage. The Bolshevik pilot slumped forward over his control panel and his aircraft rolled over, to spiral into the ground a quarter of a mile from where they crouched. A splintering boom signalled the death of both pilot and plane.

Both men stood and waved frantically to the British plane that swooped so low over them they could see the leather helmets and goggles of the pilot and his observer. George was jumping up and down, hoping that his display of enthusiasm for the British kill would indicate that they were on the side of the British airmen.

The aircraft climbed and waggled its wings. George waved back and the aircraft circled around to feather its engine for a landing on a strip of dry ground. George could not believe their luck. The pilot must be a brave man, George thought. He was taking the chance that those on the ground he had saved were allies and not Bolsheviks.

The plane bumped to a stop and turned around for a quick take-off if necessary. The pilot did not turn off the engine but idled as the observer behind him turned his ring-mounted Lewis gun towards them. Without hesitation, George dropped his rifle on the ground and ran towards the aircraft, his hands above his head. When he reached the aircraft he stopped and roared over the noise of the engine. 'Corporal George Littleton, British army, temporarily attached with Czech army.'

The pilot signalled for George to approach. 'Pilot Officer Randall, RAF,' he yelled. 'Are you chaps lost?'

George broke into his broadest grin. 'You could say that, sir,' he replied. 'We are trying to get back to Archangel.'

'Well, old chap,' Pilot Officer Randall said. 'If you continue on a westerly bearing you will hit the railway line to Archangel in about three miles. From our patrol I can tell you that you have a safe corridor on that route. There is an armoured train due along in about six hours' time and a company of our boys currently doing a clearing patrol along the track. I will leave you and drop a note to our boys to expect you fairly soon. Just give me the details of your current strength et cetera and you should get a good cup of tea when you arrive.'

George reached into his pocket for his notebook and a pencil. He quickly scribbled down a quick outline of their circumstances and handed it to the pilot who passed it back to the observer behind him.

'Well, old chap, good luck,' he said, pulling the throttle back to increase his revs for the take-off. 'Just do me one favour,' he added before departing. 'See if you can retrieve something from the Bolshie plane to identify it. I need some proof that I shot the bugger down. The boys back at the squadron might not believe that we bagged a Fokker.'

George agreed and stepped back, waving as the tiny, fragile aircraft bounced down the strip of level earth to bump into the sky and fly west. He walked back to Novotny who had witnessed the exchange at the aircraft.

'We are almost there,' he said. 'Only three miles to the track to Archangel.'

True to his word, George retrieved the dead Russian's pistol from the body still slumped in the shattered aircraft. He also was able to find some papers identifying the dead man as a pilot of Fokker aircraft. And true to the British pilot's direction they were welcomed by a company of British troops clearing the railway track of enemy interference. George and the major were each handed a mug of hot, steaming tea. It had been something they had not tasted since departing on the mission three weeks earlier.

TWENTY-THREE

Valley View
Present day

Paranoia was not simply the trait of dictators. The two men simultaneously considered their meeting as more than coincidence. In his hotel room, Petrov Batkin brooded about this new factor in the equation. Why would a former special forces soldier be the local policeman? Had the Australian intelligence services known about Monique Dawson's family connection to Czar Nicholas all this time? Even as he questioned himself about Morgan McLean the subject of his interest stood under a shower and considered the man he knew as Petrov Olev. Olev had to be the one who passed the warning note to Monique days earlier and thus some kind of threat. Was he behind the sabotage of Monique's car?

Morgan turned off the shower and stepped from the cubicle to grab a towel. Drying himself, he shook his head. It did not add up – to warn a target, then attempt to kill them. So who was behind the sabotage. Dressing in his uniform, Morgan continued to let the pieces swirl around in his head, as he attempted to make sense of what he already knew.

The telephone extension rang and Morgan picked up the receiver. Ken Barber was at the other end.

'Young Morgan,' he said. 'We have opened a possible murder case on that car accident. I will be out with Davo and Springer tonight to interview any witnesses. Have you talked to the Dawson sheila yet?'

'I have her statement,' Morgan replied. 'She left her car at the hall on the night and the first thing she knew of the car being involved was when she heard it from a friend the next morning. I doubt that she has anything to do with the tampering with the brakes.'

'I doubt it too,' Ken replied dryly. 'But it makes me think she was the target. What do you think of that?'

Morgan knew that the senior sergeant was no fool and agreed. There was only so much he was able to keep to himself without seriously jeopardising himself if he hindered the investigation.

'Well, put on the kettle and we will see you within the hour.'

Morgan replaced the phone and walked to his office. He was met by the young policewoman and her male partner, eating potato chips and fried chicken purchased from the local café. They greeted Morgan by pushing the greasy chips towards him.

'I got a call back from a car rental company,' the policewoman said, wiping her hands on a tissue and handing Morgan the information she had scribbled down. 'It seems that the car you got the rego off is currently hired by a Ms Sarah Sakharov who is a citizen of the UK.'

Sakharov. Morgan frowned. Another Russian name. The numberplate he had recorded from the vehicle parked in Monique's driveway when he went for his run had been put through a computer search of traffic records and come up as a hire car, as he'd suspected. He had called the car hire company immediately with a request for information but the girl on the other end had politely declined unless he could verify that he was actually from the police. He gave her the phone number of the Valley View police so she could confirm it and suggested she could call back. He had waited and then opted to have his shower. The hire car girl had called back in the meantime and the relieving policewoman had taken the call.

'Is there anything we should know about the driver and vehicle?' the policewoman asked.

'No, nothing really,' Morgan replied. 'I thought it might have been stolen,' he continued lamely, hoping that his explanation would quash any further questions. 'I am just going to head out and have a look around town,' he added, pocketing the keys to his police vehicle.

Morgan drove directly to Monique's house, hoping that she might be alone. He had an excuse with the investigation into the accident now it was a murder case. When he pulled into the driveway in front of the house he could see no other vehicle and guessed that David must be away. The lights were on in the house and he booked off the air.

Morgan strode across the driveway to knock on the door. Monique answered.

'Just out to speak with you about your car,' he said, taking off his cap before entering.

Monique held open the door for him to pass inside. 'Have you had anything to eat?' she asked, surprising Morgan with the invitation.

'I, er, am keeping an eye on the calorie intake,' he answered.

'Pity,' Monique said with a grim smile. 'I made David and myself a nice quiche and salad and opened a bottle of good red wine but David seems to have other plans for tonight. It would be a waste otherwise.'

'In that case, I guess it wouldn't break any regulations for me to help you eat the meal. But, alas, the wine will be out for me.'

Monique smiled with more warmth. 'We were just going to eat in the kitchen – if that is okay with you?'

'Anywhere would be fine,' Morgan answered.

Monique was wearing a very sexy almost see-through dress that clung to her body. In the back of his mind Morgan felt that there had been some kind of disagreement between the two as her smile was not all that happy. He sat down at the already prepared place at the table and noted the unlit candle beside a posy of wildflowers.

'I presumed that you had come out here on business,' Monique said, removing a delicious smelling quiche from the old wood combustion stove.

'I went for a run past your place earlier this evening,' Morgan said as Monique sliced the quiche. 'And I noticed a car in your driveway.'

Monique placed a fine china plate in front of Morgan and took a bowl of crisp salad from the refrigerator.

'That was probably Sarah's car,' she said, placing the salad bowl on the table and sitting down. Fresh bread rolls and curls of butter accompanied the quiche and salad. 'She is a journalist working freelance and wanted to do an article on the history of this house. It seems that she picked up the story of Joshua Larkin on the internet and decided that she would combine business with pleasure. She is a folk music devotee. Why? Is something wrong about that?'

Morgan buttered a roll. 'You know,' he said, avoiding the question, 'this would have to be one of the nicest spreads I have seen in a long time. Thank you. David is a lucky bloke.'

Monique made no comment confirming Morgan's suspicion of a rift between them.

'I am a cop and curiosity is a trait they encourage in the job,' he said. 'You know that I am concerned for your welfare and anything unusual has to be investigated considering what has happened lately. What kind of questions did she ask?'

Monique pushed at her quiche with a fork. Her appetite seemed to have diminished. 'Oh, just what did I know about Captain Larkin and his wife. Was there any substance to the rumour that Maria was in fact Princess Maria of Russia. Questions like that.'

'What did you tell her?' Morgan asked, biting into the bread roll and savouring the cold butter on his palate.

'I told her that I knew very little – that her research before interviewing me probably revealed more than I knew.'

Morgan felt his mobile phone vibrate in his pocket. Excusing himself, he flipped open the phone to talk. It was Ken Barber and he was waiting for Morgan. Morgan pulled a face of genuine disappointment. 'I must apologise, Monique, but I have been called back to the station.'

'The second man to reject me and my cooking tonight,' Monique sighed. 'I can take a hint.'

There was just something very vulnerable about her as she stood to escort him to the front door and Morgan felt a desire to hold her to him. 'I doubt that I would be stupid enough to reject either you or your cooking,' he said light-heartedly. For a second he thought he saw a flash in

Monique's eyes that dared him to expose his hidden feelings. 'Well, back to work,' Morgan said, turning to walk away.

Monique followed him to the door and waved to him as he drove away. He felt light-headed and cursed himself for not knowing more about the body language of women. He blamed his many years in the tough world of soldiering and the jobs of labouring he'd taken before joining the police force. How did a man know what was in a woman's mind? He was afraid that if he had acted on his impulse he would have embarrassed – if not frightened – Monique.

He drove back to the station heavy in thought about the freelance journalist who had turned up on Monique's doorstep but dismissed his troubled thoughts. Someone was bound to ask Monique sooner or later about the rumours of royalty, especially considering the information about the discovery of the two bodies that had already been released to the media.

It only took a few minutes to return to the station and Morgan could see the detective's vehicle parked outside. Ken was standing on the verandah smoking a cigarette.

'G'day, Morgan,' he greeted. 'Looks like you have a job. A call just came in that there has been an assault and rob on one of your locals. Your relief crew are in attendance.'

'Have you got a name?' Morgan asked, unlocking the front door to the station.

'Yeah, a Mrs Gladys Harrison. There is an ambulance on the way.'

'The museum?' Morgan asked.

'Seems so,' Ken Barber replied following Morgan into the station, cigarette in hand. 'I have a strong feeling that it has something to do with the journal she was not supposed to have anymore.'

'What else would you suggest?' Batkin shrugged. 'We lost valuable time when you failed to appear in Sydney to meet me.'

'I was delayed,' Sarah countered. 'There was a mix-up with my passport.'

Batkin accepted the young woman's explanation and stubbed out the end of his cigarette. It was time to give some thought to the British agent and the Australian policeman. Both would have to be dealt with if he was to get Monique Dawson out of the country.

Gladys Harrison was in the back of the ambulance when Morgan arrived at the museum. A crowd of curious bystanders had gathered to view the spectacle. The combination of police cars and the ambulance usually meant something serious had occurred.

Morgan could see from the blood-soaked bandage around her grey hair that the gentle woman had sustained a savage blow to the head. He clambered into the back of the ambulance to sit beside Gladys on a stretcher.

'We have to get Mrs Harrison to the base hospital,' the ambulance officer attending to her said, 'But she is going to be all right, aren't you, Mrs Harrison?'

Gladys Harrison provided a weak smile of reassurance and Morgan admired her courage. She reached out to him indicating that she wished to say something in private. The ambulance officer slipped into the front to radio to his base, leaving Morgan alone with her for the moment. Morgan leaned forward, his ear against her mouth.

'Whoever attacked me in the museum demanded that I give them Joshua Larkin's journal,' she whispered. 'But I did not tell them where it was.'

'You should have,' Morgan replied, squeezing her hand. 'It was not worth your life. Gladys, you said they,' he continued, 'was there more than one man involved in the attack on you?'

'No,' Gladys replied. 'It was a man and a woman. I did not see them very clearly in the dark but I remember a woman's voice just before she struck me with something over the head.'

'Got to go,' the ambulance officer said to Morgan. 'Do you want to come into Hume City, in the back with Mrs Harrison?'

'No,' Morgan replied. 'Got to stay around here tonight, Steve. Last night of the festival.'

Morgan climbed out the back of the ambulance and closed the doors. A man and a woman, he thought. Who in hell could the pair be? Whoever they were, the blow that had been inflicted was potentially capable of killing the elderly woman. And somehow they were linked to the ghosts at the Larkin house.

TWENTY-FOUR

Northern Russia
Early September 1919

The vastness of the land could be intimidating. Joshua sat at the edge of the great river flowing north. He had kept watch for over half a day and was yet to see any traffic on its waters. Four days had passed since he and Maria had escaped from captivity in the little village to the east and on their dogged journey Maria had said little of her horrific experience. Joshua guessed that she had been raped but did not mention it. Instead, he would talk optimistically about reaching safety in Archangel and his soothing words seemed to have an effect on her. She would at least register interest and at night still nestled into him for warmth against the bitter chill. The short nights were lengthening as winter threatened in the weeks ahead and Joshua was aware that they would not survive their trip if winter came early.

'You have seen nothing,' Maria said, settling down beside Joshua on the soft, green grass.

'A river this big has to have fishermen and maybe a ferry,' Joshua replied. 'Something will crop up.'

'When we reach Archangel I will ensure that you are richly rewarded,' she said quietly. 'You have been my guardian angel.'

'I don't expect any reward,' Joshua answered. 'It was my duty to find you . . . I don't know why, but it was meant to be. That's all I know.' He turned to look at Maria, whose sobs broke the soft stirring of a wind over the grassy plain behind them. 'What is wrong?' he asked, gently placing his hand on her arm.

'I do not think that we will live to see Archangel, and if we do I know I must seek out those who will help.'

'Well, we will survive and we will reach Archangel. From there the British government will get you safely to England and you will be able to sort yourself out.'

'What will you do, Joshua?' Maria asked.

'First, I will have to convince the British army that I am not a deserter, and then I will have to make a report of all that has occurred since setting out on the mission to find you. I doubt that my friend George or the mad major will be alive to corroborate anything. Then I want to go home to Sydney. I have finished with war. I have heard that my government is giving out parcels of land to returning soldiers to farm. I would like to go back to the country. City life never much appealed to me. I was born on a farm near Goulburn. I only left because my older brother inherited the property when my dad died.'

'You have been many things,' Maria said. 'I think God is looking after you.'

'More like the Devil,' Joshua snorted. 'Considering how I feel about you.'

His statement startled Maria. She knew what he meant and shrank away.

Joshua reached out to her. 'You must know how I truly feel about you,' he said.

Maria rose to her feet, a look of confusion written across her pretty features.

'*Stoy!*'

The dreaded Russian word to *stop* hit Joshua like a lightning bolt. It had come from around a hundred yards away through the tall grasses behind them. 'God, not again,' Joshua moaned, reaching for the pistol in his coat.

He attempted to drag Maria down but she resisted and he could see a strange expression on her face. It was not fear but disbelief.

'They are imperial soldiers,' she uttered. 'They are White Army soldiers.'

Cautiously, Joshua slipped the pistol back into his coat and rose to peer across the plain at the advancing company. He too recognised the uniforms as those of their Russian allies.

Maria reached down to grip Joshua's hand. 'We have been saved,' she said and with her free hand wiped at the tears of joy rolling down her cheeks.

Joshua stood and a middle-aged officer waving a pistol gestured for them to approach. When they were close enough to speak Maria addressed the officer.

'I am the Princess Maria and I am the only survivor of my family,' she said. 'I have proof as to my identity and this man with me is a member of the British army who was sent to find and save me. I would like us to be taken to Archangel.'

Joshua had not been able to follow her speech as she had spoken in Russian but did note that the Russian major burst into laughter. Joshua did not take this as a good sign and felt that he might have been better off fighting a Bolshevik platoon rather than fall into the hands of a White Russian company.

'Girl, you are a lunatic and could also be a Red sympathiser,' the Russian officer said, scanning the identity papers Maria had hastily retrieved from her skirt. 'You will both be escorted to the regiment's HQ for questioning and depending on what you say you will either be released or executed.'

From the shocked expression on Maria's face Joshua guessed that all was not well with their supposed saviours. 'I am a British soldier,' he said loudly. 'Does anyone here speak English?'

The middle-aged Russian major swung on Joshua with his pistol and Maria stepped protectively in front of Joshua, at the same time speaking hurried words. The officer lowered his pistol and turned to call back to the soldiers spread out in a skirmish line behind him. One stepped forward and saluted. He was a young man with a thin face and wispy moustache. Shouldering his rifle he came forward to the major then turned to Joshua.

'I speak English,' he said. 'Who are you?'

'Sergeant Joshua Larkin of the British army. I have identity discs concealed on me to confirm my identity and this young woman is the Princess Maria and should be shown the utmost respect.' His statement caused a look of shock on the face of the young Russian soldier who turned to the major to translate. A frown spread over the major's face and he spoke softly to his translator.

'Our company commander says that you are to go with us to our HQ where you will be handed over to a more . . . how you say . . . senior person for further interrogation and examination of identity papers. Please to come with us.'

'You speak very good English,' Joshua remarked. 'Where did you learn?'

'You would not know the place because it is far from England,' he replied. 'I learn English when I am with Russian diplomatic post in Melbourne, Australia before the war. I was cook.'

When Joshua burst into laughter Maria was startled, but even more so when he slapped the young soldier on the back. 'No kidding,' Joshua said. 'I am from Sydney. I am an Australian.'

The young soldier burst into a beaming smile. 'I think you sound like an Australian but not think so when you say you are British. Do you know who win Aussie Rule grand final last year?'

Joshua shook his head. 'Sorry, old chap, I don't follow Victorian football but it is good to probably meet the only Russian for a thousand miles who knows where Australia is.'

'My name Grigor,' the young soldier said, extending his hand which caused further alarm to the Russian major. 'Good to meet an Aussie again.' He turned and rattled off a long speech to the major whose face finally broke into a smile. The Russian officer stepped forward and slapped Joshua on the back in a fraternal manner.

'My major think you okay. That you are an ally,' Grigor said. 'Is true that the woman is Princess Maria?' he asked in a more awed tone.

'She certainly is – but it is a long story,' Joshua answered. 'We need to get to Archangel.'

'The major says he can do but he is not convinced girl is Princess Maria,' Grigor cautioned. 'He will treat you well but I convince that you are truly British. He not understand that you Australian.'

'Well, that's a start,' Joshua said, noticing that Maria was looking at him with some admiration for the way in which he had turned their situation around so she felt safe once again.

British HQ
Archangel
Early September 1919

Major James Locksley had been seen by an army doctor and cleared for inactive service for the time being as he had not fully recovered from his broken ribs. He had been able to obtain a new uniform and the trappings of his rank. Pale and gaunt, he waited patiently to be debriefed by Colonel Kingston, the liaison officer for the Secret Intelligence Service in northern Russia. Locksley sat outside the colonel's office while smartly dressed staff officers strolled past to the many offices in the marble and gilt building.

'You can go through now, sir,' an NCO acting as an orderly room clerk said.

Locksley stood and marched to the office at the end of the huge, echoing foyer. He entered the colonel's office and saluted smartly.

'Good to see you in the land of the living, old chap,' the colonel said warmly. 'We had almost given up on you but I believe that you had somewhat of a hot time getting back to Archangel before the evacuation of our forces.'

'I had some good fortune in remaining alive,' Locksley replied dismissing the praise for his capacity for survival deep behind enemy lines. 'But I failed to complete my mission.'

Colonel Kingston gestured to an ornate chair. 'Have a seat, old chap,' he said. 'I am still being kept in the dark about the purpose of your mission by those in London but it seems that they want you back as soon as possible – and some Australian chap, Corporal Littleton.'

'Ah, yes, Corporal Littleton,' the British major said. 'I have recommended him for a decoration for his role in the affair. I expect they will give him something like a DCM if he is lucky – an MM at the least. Pity he still did not have his commission. It would have been a DSO or MC if that had been so.'

'From what I have read of your report he will be the lucky one considering what you have written of this Sergeant Larkin chap. He will be fortunate if he doesn't get a firing squad if we ever catch up with him, although naturally a court martial will come first before we shoot the bugger.' The colonel lifted Locksley's report from his desk and waved it in the air. 'But I doubt that he would have been able to survive long with that girl with him. I strongly suspect that the Reds would have killed them a long time ago.'

'I would not presume that, sir,' Locksley said. 'He is a rather resourceful and tough chap for a colonial. It must be that convict blood they all seem to have.'

The colonel burst into laughter at the joke. He had a prejudice against anyone who was not born in Britain of Anglo-Saxon blood. In his opinion, those former Anglo-Saxons who had left England's shores for whatever reason had relinquished their claim to any equality. They had been, after all, the dregs of English society. His grandfather had been a magistrate and had sentenced many of his countrymen to transportation to the penal colony on the other side of the world.

'Well, we shall be on the look out for the blighter if he does turn up in Archangel. He will be immediately arrested if he does.'

'Sir, if he is arrested in Russia I feel that those in London would not want him to be interrogated by anyone here,' Locksley cautioned. 'He is a matter for national security to deal with. I think that you will understand. If he happens to be with a Russian girl at the time we would rather she be discreetly dealt with. She may attempt to claim that she is the Princess Maria but we have proof that she is an impostor. You can imagine that if she is left to run around free she could cause us a lot of embarrassment.'

'You can assure those in London that should either turn up on our doorstep I will ensure that they are dealt with in the appropriate manner,' the colonel said, touching the edge of his nose in a conspiratorial manner. 'Here are your movement orders and those of Corporal Littleton,' he concluded, handing Locksley a bundle of papers. 'Have a good trip home and I will hopefully have the opportunity to invite you to my club when I return very soon.'

'Thank you, sir,' the major said, rising to accept the papers and salute the colonel. 'I would be happy to join you at your club for a drink.'

Locksley left the office and walked out into the foyer. He accepted a salute from the orderly room NCO and stepped out into the chill of the street where George Littleton had been waiting in the cold.

'Well, sir, are we returning to London?' George asked.

'Not only are we returning to London, Corporal Littleton, but I suspect that you will be invited to Buckingham Palace to receive a gong I recommended for your service to our mission,' Locksley said, stunning George. The mad major was a man of many facets, and George felt a surge of gratitude. He would return to his family from his military service a decorated hero.

TWENTY-FIVE

MI6 HQ
London
Present day

'Harry, you are wanted upstairs in the chief's office ASAP,' a fellow department head said, popping his head around the door to Harry's office.

Harry cast his colleague a questioning look but received a shrug in response. He had a bad feeling about the order to see the head of MI6. Dame Susan Perry, DCB – Dame Commander of the Most Honourable Order of the Bath, QC – was a formidable woman. She had once practised constitutional law before entering public service where she distinguished herself on many boards overseeing Britain's foreign policy. She was also known as a staunch supporter of the Labor Party. Having been appointed the head of MI6, for the last year she had settled into intelligence politics as easily as if she had been orating in the Supreme Court. In her late fifties, she dressed conservatively and looked like the modern grandmother that she also was. It was rare for her to summon individual department leaders to her office unless a matter needed clarification. In this case Harry had a horrible premonition his requirement to be in her office immediately had something to do with the operation he was conducting in Australia.

When Harry was ushered into the chief's office he noticed a man he recognised as one of the accountants from the pay office bending over her desk, pointing at a sheaf of papers. When he looked up at Harry he was frowning.

'That will be all, thank you, Mr Cunningham,' the chief said. 'Please, sit down, Mr Stanton,' she added when the bean counter had exited the office. 'Do you know why I have requested your presence here today?'

Harry knew that she was expecting him to reveal something she may not have known. He would not fall for her fishing technique. 'I am afraid that I do not, Ma'am,' he replied, hoping that he had his nerves under control.

'It has been brought to my attention that we are paying Ms Sarah Locksley to have a holiday in Australia with your endorsement,' the chief said ominously. 'I do not remember her trip to Australia being mentioned at our last meeting of department heads.'

Harry was suddenly confused. The last he knew of Sarah Locksley was that she had been working under cover in St Petersburg, infiltrating a radical nationalist movement apparently led by a former Spetsnaz soldier. He had signed her off for the mission under her old family name of Sakharov. He did at least remember that the target of her infiltration was one Petrov Batkin and he was also in Australia – according to Daniel Kildare.

'I was not aware that Ms Locksley was in Australia but I think that she is with a target, a Russian by the name of Petrov Batkin. I assume that she is following her directive to keep as close to him as she can. Other than that I am as much in the dark as you, Ma'am.'

The chief's gaze had the piercing effect of a laser. Harry was aware that his explanation left him open to the accusation that he was not in control of his operations.

'So, it could be said that you do not really know what is going on with your people,' Dame Perry said. 'I only became aware of Ms Locksley being in Australia when our accounts department was being randomly audited by Mr Cunningham who noticed that her travel costs were not being properly signed off.'

Harry frowned and leaned forward. 'I confess that her presence in Australia is a surprise to me but I will immediately make contact and demand an explanation from her,' he said. 'She will be counselled about her reporting procedures as soon as she returns to us.'

'We cannot afford to make mistakes, Mr Stanton,' the chief said. 'Our role forces us to live in a very secretive world but that only extends to public perception – not within our own ranks.'

'Yes, Ma'am,' Harry dutifully responded. 'I will investigate the incident as a priority one matter and inform you immediately the situation is resolved.'

'I expect that you will, Mr Stanton,' the tough but fair head of MI6 responded. 'That is all I have to say about the matter until I hear from you within the next twenty-four hours – and no later.'

Harry stood up and walked stiffly from the office. What in hell was Sarah Locksley doing in Australia? No wonder she had ceased to report back to him from Russia. Locksley! Suddenly the name set off an alarm and he vaguely remembered an old report archived in MI6's deepest basements. It was a name that had slipped from his consciousness until the Larkin file had been activated.

Harry quickened his pace to the lift. He slumped into his chair behind his computer, and after coding in his password, called up the Larkin file. He read through the photocopied pages transcribed to a disk to find the name Locksley. It stood out and Harry Stanton scanned the report referring to the decorated former officer of the King who had been recruited to the Secret Intelligence Service in 1919. It was not a flattering report of a man who had marital problems and who had disappeared while on a trip to Australia. The original conclusion on the former British major was that he had run off with some woman he had met in Australia. It was not a very honourable ending to the career of a man who had distinguished himself in the Great War.

Harry read on and in the notes saw the name Sakharov. It appeared that Locksley was of Russian heritage. Suddenly the MI6 department head was hit with a gripping fear. Sarah had so readily adopted the undercover name for her missions in Russia. She must therefore be a relative of the mysteriously disappeared former British major and intelligence officer. But why would she be interested in the current case – nearly a century old? Or was she simply sticking with the man she had been assigned to get close to? Was the link to her family simply a coincidence? Harry Stanton was not a believer in things just happening and the answer that echoed in reply made him very uneasy. Was she in the private business of settling old scores and completing a family mission almost a hundred years old? If so, she had to be stopped. He knew his next step was to get his hands on her vetting documents for departmental clearance. It would either confirm or deny her links to the disgraced Major Locksley.

★

Valley View
Present day

The telephone call came through on Daniel Kildare's mobile in the early hours of the morning. He was annoyed at having been awoken from a deep sleep and fumbled for the phone next to his bed.

'Hello,' he mumbled, rubbing the sleep from his eyes.

'Kildare, are you alone?'

Daniel Kildare glanced around his spartan but clean hotel room, recognising Harry Stanton's voice. He was free to speak as the mobile phone he carried had a special scrambling device fitted to encode any conversation. 'Yes,' he answered. 'You know what time it is over here?'

'I wouldn't have called if it was not a matter of vital importance,' Harry snapped. 'Have you seen Sarah Locksley?'

Kildare pulled himself into a sitting position. 'Certainly, you assigned her to work with me.'

'Did she say that?' Harry queried.

'Well, yes,' Kildare replied. 'She told me that she is continuing with her work covering Petrov Batkin. Why? What is wrong?'

At the other end of the world Harry thought about his response to the question. 'Maybe nothing is wrong,' he replied. 'She is not answering any calls so when you see her next tell her she is to report to me immediately. I mean immediately.'

'Okay, consider it done.'

'Have you succeeded in retrieving the items?' Harry asked.

'Not as yet,' Kildare replied. 'But I have a fair idea where to look.'

'Well, there is nothing else for the moment,' Harry said, closing off the call.

Kildare snapped closed his mobile phone and glanced down at the woman beside him who had been listening to the conversation. It did not pay to inform one's superior that a trusted operative was sleeping with a colleague. MI6 had rules concerning the behaviour of its agents on foreign assignments.

'It seems that you have caused a bit of a stir with old Harry,' Kildare said. 'Apparently you have been a naughty girl and not kept up your reports to home. He wants you to make contact as soon as possible.'

In the dark, Sarah frowned. She should have known that this moment was bound to come once her silence from Russia had been noted. She would have to hasten her mission.

One very important reason Petrov Batkin was good at staying alive was because he was a non-trusting type of person. Sarah Sakharov had been recruited by him and seemed ideal for the mission to bring Monique Dawson over to their cause. After all, in his opinion it was Monique's duty to support them in their quest to re-establish the imperial order of old Russia since she carried the blood of the Czars.

The fact that Sarah had been late for the assignment caused his first suspicions and now that he had covertly tracked her to her hotel he'd seen her meet with the British MI6 man. It set off alarm bells for Batkin. His thoughts that she may be an agent of the British were strong – but not confirmed. It was no wonder that the British were active on the case, he mused as he sat on the edge of his hotel bed in the dark. The long hours of just sitting around in his hotel room or visiting the folk festival were almost as tortuous to this active man as being shown the interrogation cells of the old KGB. But from his knowledge of his former comrades working in intelligence, this was part and parcel of their world. Only in the English James Bond books were things different. Batkin decided to complete another set of physical exercises before retiring for the night.

The following morning Morgan drove to Hume City to speak with Gladys Harrison at the hospital. He was not interviewing her in an official capacity, as that had already been done by the first police on the scene.

He was directed to her bedside where she lay against the pillows surrounded by vases of colourful flowers and sat down in a chair by her bed. 'How are you feeling, Gladys?' he asked with genuine concern in his voice.

'Oh, I will be all right,' she replied with a smile, although her head was still swathed in a great bandage. 'It is at times such as this that you realise just how many friends you have,' she said, touching a bloom in a vase on the cupboard next to her hospital bed.

'Can you tell me what you remember of the attack on you?' Morgan asked.

'I remember that I had to go to the museum to collect the petty cash tin for our fundraising,' Gladys replied. 'I unlocked the door and it was dark inside. I think I saw the beam of a torch and when I turned on the lights to the office where we keep our cash tin I was shocked to see two figures standing in there. They both wore masks, like you see people wearing who are skiing. Balaclavas – that's it,' she exclaimed, remembering the name. 'I was shocked and they seemed to be surprised by my appearance. The bigger of the two grabbed me and started to shake me. He was asking about Captain Larkin's journal which you know I do not have. I told him so and it was then that I heard the voice of the second person asking if I did not have the journal, where would they find it. I remember it was a woman's voice and that both of them had English accents. I think I said something like you can go to buggery . . . you must remember that I do not swear and will have to go to confession for saying what I did. Then I do not remember anything else after that until that lovely young policewoman came to my assistance and called the ambulance.'

'You are a very brave woman, Gladys,' Morgan said, reaching over to squeeze her hand. 'I feel guilty about putting you in the situation but promise I will find whoever did this to you and arrest them.'

Gladys returned the squeeze. 'Don't feel bad about what happened. It was not your fault and it is a bit exciting to think that we have people desperate to get hold of Captain Larkin's journal. I bet that they are spies.'

Morgan grimaced. The mention of spies was the last thing he wanted to hear but something did ring true in the elderly lady's statement. At least the tourists packing up and leaving town was like draining a waterhole. What strange fish would be left in the empty pond in the next few days? And floundering fish are easy to catch.

'Is there anything that I can do when I get back to Valley View?' Morgan asked, rising from the chair.

'Nothing, dear,' Gladys replied. 'If you could just drop in on my husband and make sure he has taken his medicine, that would be a good help.'

'Promise I will,' Morgan said.

He returned to the police vehicle and dropped off at the busy Hume City station to pick up any departmental mail due to be sent out. It was also a good chance to swap gossip with the shift before setting out to return to Valley

View. If it were true there were spies in town, Morgan mused, they would be Russian and English ones replaying some old Cold War game – but in a very innocuous theatre.

TWENTY-SIX

Archangel
September 1919

Although not totally convinced that Maria was who she said she was the White Russian commander treated both Joshua and Maria with respect. He had a small detachment of soldiers escort them to Archangel for Maria to prove her identity and Grigor was assigned to accompany them.

Joshua could see Maria's spirits soar when she sighted the golden-domed buildings. She took Joshua's hand as they approached the city.

'We will go to Archduke Basilevsky,' Grigor said to Maria when the five soldiers escorting them entered the outskirts of the city.

'Cousin Anton!' Maria exclaimed. 'He is safe.' She turned to Joshua and explained that they were to be taken to a relative who would be able to confirm her identity.

'Then you will be able to travel to England,' Joshua replied.

'We will be apart,' she sighed. 'I do not know what I would have done without you.'

'I am a soldier and was doing my duty,' Joshua shrugged, casually attempting to conceal his pain at losing her. 'Nothing more.'

He slipped the belt containing the fortune in gems from under his coat and passed it to Maria. 'Your dowry,' he said. 'The only reward I need is just enough to spend in the first bar I find in Archangel.'

'When I am in England I will ensure that you are truly rewarded for helping me,' Maria said, retrieving a handful of coins from the belt and passing them to him.

'That's more than enough for me to drink until 1930,' Joshua said, eyeing the pile of gold coins in his hand. From the corner of his eye he could see the awed expression on Grigor's face. 'Make sure that the Princess Maria is kept safe,' he said to Grigor. 'I guess that the future of Russia may lay in her hands.'

Grigor nodded his understanding. Unlike his commander he was sure that the pretty young woman was in fact the Princess Maria and was proud to be of assistance to a member of the royal family.

'Well, I guess we part here,' Joshua said.

'What will you do now?' Maria asked.

'Have a drink then report back to my regiment,' Joshua replied. 'I guess there will be a lot of people who will want to talk to me.'

'I will always remember you in my prayers, Joshua Larkin,' Maria said, trying to force back the tears welling in her eyes. 'I will never forget you.'

Deep inside him, Joshua felt a pain that brought back memories of losing his wife. It was as if he was losing Maria in the same way.

'I would like to have a drink with you, Sergeant Larkin,' Grigor said. 'Where you go?'

'Do you know the bar near the big church?'

'Da, I know,' Grigor answered. 'I see you there when Princess go to the Archduke house.'

'Good luck,' Joshua said in parting and turned to walk away. Maria had tears in her eyes, but he did not look back and continued walking until he was at the end of the street. He turned a corner, passing soldiers wearing the uniforms of many Allied countries. Limbered guns passed him on their way to the shrinking front around the city and columns of troops marched towards the wharves. They hardly paid any attention to the dirty, unshaven civilian they passed. Joshua was acutely aware that he would have to keep an eye out for the red-capped military police who patrolled the streets in search of deserters. But the need to have a drink and wash away the last few weeks from his life over-rode the fear of the provosts.

He found a bar that he and George used to frequent when on leave in the city. It was filled with the uniforms of Canadians, Yanks and Italians. Alcohol flowed and the raucous voices of men celebrating the impending evacuation from Russia filled the smoky room. Joshua pushed his way to the bar and ordered an English beer from a hard-faced Russian whose knowledge of English was limited to demanding payment for the product he sold. Joshua handed over a coin and gulped down the beer. It tasted good and he settled in to drink some more, refusing to allow the thoughts of Maria to haunt him.

Joshua had his head down on a wooden bench in the bar when he felt his shoulder being shaken.

264

'Sergeant Larkin, wake up.'

Joshua lifted his head to focus on Grigor standing over him with an expression of deep concern. 'Was up?' he asked.

'The Princess Maria, I think she in trouble,' Grigor replied.

Joshua attempted to shake off the effect of the three bottles of English beer. He was not drunk but still felt the effects of the alcohol.

'What do you mean?' Joshua asked, rising to his feet.

'We take her to the archduke,' Grigor replied. 'He tell us we must fetch English soldiers. He lock the princess in his house.'

'Has anyone gone for the British?' Joshua asked.

'*Da*, the corporal go for to tell the British. I make excuse and come here to fetch you.'

Joshua wiped his face with his hand, cursing the fact that he had not seen the predicament coming. It was obvious that there were Russians who had a reason to betray Maria. But why this one? After all, the man was her blood relative.

'Come on, Grigor,' Joshua said. 'Take me to the archduke's house.'

The two men left the bar and hurried along the street with Grigor leading, trailing his rifle. Joshua instinctively felt for the revolver in his coat and was reassured by its presence. He had no idea what he would do when he reached the house but knew that he had to have a plan.

'How many people does the archduke have?' Joshua asked Grigor.

'Archduke has personal staff. Servants. I know not how many,' Grigor said.

'Are they armed?' Joshua asked.

265

'I do not know,' Grigor replied. 'But I think he has guns. All nobles have guns.'

When they stood before the magnificent house, Joshua scanned the imposing building. It opened onto the street and the great wood-panelled front door was closed. No doubt locked, he guessed.

'You need to tell the archduke that I am an agent from the British HQ.' Grigor gave him a doubtful look – not surprising, considering the dishevelled appearance of the Australian sergeant.

'I think this not work,' he replied.

'Just give it a go,' Joshua answered, slipping the pistol into his hand and holding it behind his back. They were lucky as the street was deserted and there would be no witnesses.

'Okay,' Grigor shrugged and knocked on the door.

A voice answered from inside and Joshua listened as Grigor exchanged words with whoever was behind the door.

'Servant open door to us,' he whispered from the corner of his mouth.

Joshua nodded, bracing himself as the door creaked open slightly. Joshua threw himself at the door, forcing it wide and crashed past the startled servant, a man in his old age. Grigor followed.

'Ask him where the Princess Maria is?' Joshua said, pointing his revolver at the terrified man's head.

'He say she upstairs with archduke.'

Joshua glanced across the ornate marble-floored room to a magnificent staircase. He was halfway up when he was confronted by a tall man wearing an expensive tailored suit. From his arrogant, aristocratic demeanour Joshua guessed that this must be the archduke. He shouted something in Russian and Joshua noticed Grigor bring up his rifle to cover the man.

'Do you speak English?' Joshua demanded, covering him with his gun.

The man shook his head and Joshua asked the same question in French.

'I speak French,' the man answered coldly. 'I am the Archduke Basilevsky and you have no right to break into my home with weapons. You will pay for your impertinence.'

'Where is the Princess Maria?' Joshua asked. 'And I don't have time to listen to any lies because I think I am getting a hangover, and that makes me dangerous.'

The archduke glared at Joshua contemptuously, turned his back and commenced to walk up the stairs as if dismissing him. Joshua fired once and saw the Russian collapse. The bullet had struck him in the lower leg as Joshua intended.

'The next one will be in your head,' Joshua spat, standing over the Russian noble. 'Your choice.'

The archduke glared up at Joshua with pure hate. 'You will pay dearly for this,' he gasped, the pain biting at his leg from the wound.

'One more time,' Joshua said, placing the tip of the barrel against the man's head. 'Where is the princess?'

For a moment their eyes locked and the Russian noble considered the possibilities of the threat. But what he saw in the Australian soldier's eyes was frightening and he knew he had no choice. 'She is in the bedroom at the top of the stairs.'

'Why were you about to betray her to the English?' Joshua asked.

'Because they will assist me to settle in England if I hand her over,' he said. 'The Bolsheviks will rule this country and anyone such as myself will be executed if I remain.'

An idea crept into Joshua thoughts. 'Where is the treasure that the princess had with her?'

The question startled the archduke. 'It is safe in my keeping,' he replied, knowing that the mad man with the gun at his head was capable of killing him on a whim.

'Grigor,' Joshua said. 'The archduke is going to take you to fetch something. Go with him.'

Turning to the nobleman Joshua explained how the soldier would help him to retrieve the small fortune in gems. Grigor slung his rifle and helped the archduke to his feet. Assisting him up the stairs, Grigor was led to a room at the end of a long hall. Once they were out of sight Joshua knocked on the door where the wounded Russian had said he would find Maria. When the door opened Joshua was stunned to see Maria wearing a lavish dress that gave her the regal appearance she was due.

'Joshua!' she gasped in her surprise, her eyes wide with happiness. 'I thought that I heard a gunshot. The duke has forbidden me to leave his house and has taken all my possessions. I do not understand what is happening.'

Joshua stepped inside the room. 'Your cousin was about to hand you over to the British and steal your family treasure. It appears that Major Locksley was right when he ordered me to kill you. For some reason the British do not want you to live.'

The shock registered on Maria's face. 'But the king of England is a relative,' she said. 'How could he want me dead?'

'And your cousin is the archduke and was about to help the English get rid of you. This place is crawling with dirty deeds. We are going to get you out of Russia somehow and maybe to France. Grigor is at the moment retrieving your jewellery.'

Without questioning Joshua, Maria followed him from the room. They were met by Grigor holding up the linen belt in one hand and the Russian noble in the other.

'I have the thing you wanted,' Grigor said triumphantly.

'Good,' Joshua answered, taking the belt from him. 'Now, all we have to do is get out of here before the British arrive.'

'You will not get far,' the archduke snarled. 'The city is crawling with patrols.'

'Maybe,' Joshua shrugged. 'But so was the countryside and we survived that.'

'You cannot go with this man,' Basilevsky said to Maria. 'He is a commoner who wants to steal your inheritance.'

'No, cousin,' Maria answered sadly. 'It is you who I cannot trust. You would betray me – your own flesh and blood.'

The Russian nobleman fell silent.

'What do we do with him?' Grigor asked, with some apprehension.

'Well, he isn't going to run after us,' Joshua said. 'We will let him live. It's time to get out of here.'

'Where can we go?' Maria asked. 'It is not safe any-where in the city.'

'First, all we have to do is get out of this house and find a place to hole up. I suggest that you change back into your travelling garb. You are going to have to look like a peasant girl again.'

Maria nodded and ducked back into the room while Joshua and Grigor waited anxiously; any time now they could be disturbed by the arrival of a British patrol assigned to detain Maria. But she was quick and appeared at the top of the stairs in her old peasant dress.

The three made their way to the street, leaving the wounded Russian nobleman at the top of the stairs. When they were in front of the house, Grigor spoke. 'I think I know where we can go and be safe for now. I spend my early years growing up here. I have friend who has book-shop not far from here. He can help.'

Joshua slapped Grigor on the shoulder gratefully. 'Thanks, old cobber.'

Grigor beamed. 'I no hear that since Australia,' he said. 'You my cobber.'

They hurried down the street until they reached a thoroughfare bustling with crowds of troops and Russian civilians streaming into the city as refugees from the advancing Red Army. There, they were able to lose themselves in the parade of people. Joshua did not have a plan beyond following Grigor to the safe house. All he knew was that he was with Maria again and that he loved her more than even his own life.

TWENTY-SEVEN

Valley View
Present day

'The car was parked over here,' Detective Senior Sergeant Ken Barber said, standing at the edge of a paddock beside the community hall. 'No lighting and easy for someone to slip under and do some mischief without being noticed. But no tyre tracks or shoe prints that we can see.'

Morgan stood beside him taking in the sweep of flattened grass, a legacy of many feet and car tyres crushing the open area during the folk festival.

'I asked around among the locals but they didn't see anything on the night.'

'Bloody investigation going nowhere,' Barber growled, shaking his head. 'What about any potential witnesses to the bash and rob at the museum. Do you have anyone among your locals good for the job?'

'Not really,' Morgan answered.

'What do you know?' Barber asked, turning to Morgan.

'That I was born and will pay taxes until I die,' Morgan answered. 'Other than that all I know is that we have a GBH and the probable murder of a car thief.'

'Well, I will leave it with you,' Ken Barber said, turning to walk back to his car. 'Probably the most exciting things to happen in this town, since that apparent double murder in 1920, if you ask me.'

Morgan watched the big detective stride away, pondering the detective's parting words. He had an eerie feeling that the discovery of the skeletons had indeed unleashed weird events in the present time. He was sure that there was a link between what had happened so long ago and the events of now, although he would be at a loss to explain why. But when he put little bits together he had an unconfirmed, direct descendant of Princess Maria living in the same house as her great-grandmother had. He had also seen the journal with damning statements about the role of the British authorities in a conspiracy to kill the sole survivor of the Russian royal family, and documents that could possibly prove the authenticity of what the late Captain Joshua Larkin wrote in his journal. Morgan well knew that courts of law required the primary source and not photocopies as evidence. So as long as the journal and documents remained out of legal hands nothing could be proved. But if the documents did become public property they could seriously rewrite history in a way not very flattering to the British government of the time.

Coupled with this was the presence of a former Russian special forces soldier attending an Aussie folk festival. Olev was a fish out of water and good cops were able to pick up what didn't fit in the picture. It was time to talk to Petrov Olev again.

★

On his way to the hotel where the Russian was staying Morgan spotted the man walking along the footpath in the direction of the town's one and only general store. He parked the police vehicle and alighted in front of the Russian.

'Mr Olev,' Morgan said. 'Do you have a moment to spare?'

Batkin eyed the policeman suspiciously. 'Ah, my friend,' he said. 'It is a beautiful day and I have time to talk with you. Are you still going for your run up the hill out of town?'

'Not lately,' Morgan replied. 'But things are settling down and I hope to hit the hill again soon.'

'Good, we can run together,' Olev answered with a disarming smile.

'What business brings you to Valley View, Mr Olev?' Morgan asked. 'It does not seem the type of place that would hold any interest to a Russian citizen.'

'I have always wanted see Australia,' Batkin replied calmly. 'I hear of Aussie folk festival when in Sydney and, how you say, get feel for Aussie culture by coming.'

'But you are still here and the festival is over,' Morgan countered.

'I like town,' Batkin said, spreading his arms to encompass the surroundings. 'Is good. I might buy property here one day and retire.'

Morgan shook his head. 'I'm not a fool, Mr Olev,' he said. 'We both know that you have little interest in retiring here so just give me something I can believe.'

Batkin's smile disappeared. He sensed that the man standing before him was no fool and could be dangerous.

'I think in your country I no have to answer questions,' he said calmly. 'You must arrest me first.'

'Just a friendly conversation, Mr Olev,' Morgan said with a faint smile. 'You are free to walk away at any time.'

'I think I do so,' Batkin said and brushed past Morgan to continue his short journey to the store.

As Morgan watched him walk away he wistfully thought about how good it would have been to be a member of the old KGB. Now, there was an organisation that didn't have to worry about the rule of law. But Morgan had what he had come for. He was now convinced that the Russian was a fish out of water and that put him at the top of his list of suspects in the attempted murder of Monique. All he had to do was get proof.

What worried Morgan was the statement given by Gladys Harrison concerning her assault at the museum. She had been adamant that she had been attacked by a man and a woman with distinctive English accents. He knew from speaking with her that the break-in had been to find the journal of Joshua Larkin. Was it possible that the British government or one of its agencies was involved? The thought did not sit easily when he remembered how the French many years earlier had used agents to sabotage the *Rainbow Warrior* Greenpeace ship in a New Zealand harbour. That had caused the downfall of the French government of the time. Surely the Poms weren't that stupid.

London
Present day

In the true tradition of all good intelligence agency practices, the next contact Harry Stanton had with the government grey man was in a small Asian food mart in a London suburb. The two men walked slowly along the cramped aisle,

274

sometimes side by side, occasionally stopping to seemingly examine the produce.

'You called this meeting, Mr Stanton,' the grey man said.

'We have . . . what I can see . . . shaping up to be a situation,' Harry said, picking up a jar of Chinese pickled vegetables. 'Something unforseen has cropped up in Australia.'

The grey man did not look at Harry when he spoke but pretended to be interested in the tins of Chinese mixed vegetables too. 'Is it a situation that might cause embarrassment to the PM?' he asked.

Harry took in a deep breath. 'It might if what I suspect is about to happen goes forward.'

This time the grey man looked at Harry. 'I think that you should elaborate.'

'I am not saying it is inevitable that anything will ever be traced back to us,' Harry replied, placing the jar back on the shelf. 'I have mechanisms in place to prevent any threat to our security in the matter. But I am reluctant to initiate a counter-strike unless absolutely necessary. And even if our blocks failed we still have the fact that the Aussie authorities may not put two and two together. After all, Australia is a long way from here.'

'Not in this age of global communications,' the grey man replied. 'You should be very aware of that. After all, was it not the internet that opened this matter after such a long time dormant?'

Harry nodded. A call across the Indian Ocean was all that was needed to activate Daniel Kildare to carry out a mission on behalf of MI6 – except that it would not really be MI6 that authorised any killing of a British subject in a foreign land. He could not authorise murder – only conspire to abet such an act.

'It could be that you are right,' Harry said quietly. 'We cannot take the chance. I will initiate an action to cut off any potential threat to the government. Leave it with me.'

'I feel that it has gone somewhat pear-shaped,' the grey man said. 'Just remember that all this can only be traced to you if the PM's department is pushed into a corner. If that event occurs I doubt that you will be on the list of next year's honours for a gong.'

Receiving a decoration from the Queen was the last thing on Harry's mind, although he currently held an MBE and was hoping for a higher honour in the announcements on the New Year list. There were rumours that such a decoration was in the wind for his services to MI6.

The grey man departed with his little shopping bag under his arm, leaving Harry to think on the call that he would make to Daniel Kildare's mobile phone. He felt sick and trapped but he had no choice now.

Valley View
Present day

Daniel Kildare stared through the window of the bar onto a view of the main street. Very few vehicles passed by, a contrast to the week just gone when the main street was packed end to end with cars and pedestrians. He had failed to locate the journal and knew that his presence in the town would not go unnoticed by the locals. He was a stranger and any questions regarding the possible whereabouts of the journal would raise suspicion among the normally taciturn drinkers propping up the bar. He would have to use every skill he had ever learned with MI6 to find a way into their trust as he was certain that someone in town knew where the book might be.

276

But the major matter occupying his thoughts at the moment was the call from Harry Stanton. What he had been ordered to do was causing him grief. More grief than Harry would have comprehended. Kildare had not let on that he was currently having a passionate affair with Sarah. Such a relationship would not be viewed with favour by his department.

He continued gazing out the window, the glass of beer in front of him on the bench under the window hardly touched. It was, after all, just on midday and Kildare had a long day to go.

Then he saw her crossing the street towards the pub. She was wearing jeans and a tight-fitting blouse. Kildare was aware that the other drinkers in the bar had turned to watch her as she walked in and sat down on a stool beside Daniel. They looked more like father and daughter than lovers.

'Did you miss me this morning?' Sarah beamed, disarmingly.

'I was rather too busy to notice,' Kildare replied, feebly attempting to appear aloof to her charms.

Their affair had commenced in Sydney when she unexpectedly arrived at his hotel room to announce that she had been assigned to shadow Petrov Batkin and assist Kildare with his case involving the same subject. A shared dinner under subdued lighting in the four-star hotel restaurant, a couple of bottles of good Aussie wine and it had happened. Kildare had not been able to believe his good fortune. She could have stepped off any catwalk in Milan into his bed. The lovemaking had been ferocious. Sarah had a liking for inflicting pain and when Kildare had eventually staggered out of their shared bed the next morning he had both a hangover and a trail of bite marks all over his body. He gave a short prayer of thanks that he was single and would not have to attempt to conceal the marks to a wife when he returned to England.

But he would have to conceal the affair from his departmental supervisor, Harry Stanton if he were to keep his posting, and killing Sarah was something he was not sure he could do – despite Stanton's direction. Sarah now sat beside him, chatting cheerily about how wonderful the spring weather was in Valley View and how quaint the town was.

Kildare brooded. 'Sarah, did you get a clearance for this assignment?' he asked, cutting across her chatter.

Her expression registered a look of surprise. 'I was directed to get close to Petrov Batkin, and when he chose me to accompany him to Australia, I had no other choice but to follow him,' she replied. 'I am still working to my original assignment. That it has brought me here is purely coincidental. Why do you ask?'

'I had a call from Harry,' Kildare answered. 'He is a bit annoyed that you did not report your sudden move over here to him.'

'I may be guilty of not following procedures to the letter,' Sarah said. 'I wanted something substantial to report before I made contact with the department.'

Her excuse sounded too hollow to be true, Kildare knew, and he wondered why. What was she really up to? This question nagged him because of what Harry had told him over the encrypted phone call. 'Are you related to a Major James Locksley, formerly of the Secret Intelligence Service?' he asked bluntly.

Sarah's calm composure shifted slightly. 'He was my great-grandfather,' she answered. 'Why should that be of any interest in the present day?'

'Well, we know the reason we are in Australia because he failed to carry out his assignment over here in 1920. In fact,

I suspect that one of the bodies the Aussie coppers found in Valley View is probably his. Tell me that you didn't know that?'

Sarah gazed through the window at the fluffy white clouds boiling up in the sky. They threatened a late afternoon thunderstorm, as the morning had been so sultry.

'I didn't know anything about the case until I was told by Batkin when I reached Valley View. All I was told in St Petersburg was that my skills were needed for an unspecified mission in Australia. I was in the dark until I got here. The rest is pure coincidence although I will admit what I have learned since has held some fascination. Are we going to order a counter lunch or do I go down to that terrible little café at the end of the street and eat alone?'

Kildare thought over what Sarah had said. Harry must have it all wrong. Sarah's explanation made a lot of sense and her motives appeared innocent. After all, she had worked closely with him to search for the journal. Even risking capture by the local police over the break-in at the museum and the bashing of the woman who had walked in on them. He would need to contact Harry and explain what he had learned from Sarah. Hopefully he had found a way out of the most disturbing order Harry had left him with. Kildare had no desire to dispose of the girl who was seen as a threat to Britain's security service; that would be cold-blooded murder. Despite the beautiful young woman's role in MI6 she exuded an innocence that he was in love with, and he hoped that she could see that.

Petrov Batkin was bored. There was only so much one could do in a tiny rural village so far from any real civilisation. As a good former Spetsnaz soldier he had already walked every street and lane in town, noting the buildings, high ground and escape avenues into the hills should the need arise. Sarah Sakharov had disappointed him. Monique Dawson had made no move to contact his organisation and Sarah, the English girl of Russian imperial sympathies, was sleeping with an English MI6 agent. When he had confronted her with his knowledge of the affair she had owned up, saying that it was part of her cover. He should be pleased that she was able to seduce the English agent and be in a position to learn what he knew over the pillow talk. Under other circumstances the honey-trap technique employed by the old KGB in the Cold War might have been considered a good move, but what worried Batkin most was how she knew Daniel Kildare was an MI6 agent, when he had not passed on that information to anyone.

Sarah had, however, told him that Kildare had admitted to attempting to kill Monique Dawson by tampering with the brakes of her car the night Batkin had been shadowing him at the hall. That was an important bit of information, confirming Batkin's theory that the English would attempt to eliminate the last in the line of the Romanov dynasty. It only spurred him on to wrap up his mission before the English were successful in silencing the woman. Time was running out, however, and Petrov Batkin was now questioning Sarah Sakharov's role in his mission. Maybe he had been a bit smitten by her looks and charm. He was, after all, still a man and the young woman had the kind of allure that could seduce St Basil himself.

And there was that local cop, Senior Constable Morgan McLean. Who was he really? Paranoia had indeed kept Petrov Batkin alive through many dangerous situations. It was again time to submit as much as he could to the organisation in Russia and let them dig up as much as they could on Morgan. Batkin began to undress and slip into his jogging gear. It was time to explore the countryside as any good former special forces soldier would. A place was needed to discreetly dispose of a body. He suspected Sarah Sakharov of double dealing. It would take a lot for her to prove her loyalty to her Russian heritage.

TWENTY-EIGHT

Archangel
September 1919

Grigor located his friend's bookshop and they were fortunate that the man was still operating in a city increasingly seen as doomed by those who knew that the Red Army was gaining strength in northern Russia.

The bookseller Grigor introduced as Lev Fedorov was a little man, bald, and wearing glasses and a threadbare jacket. Joshua guessed the man to be in his fifties – if not older. He did not smile when he saw the three standing on his doorstep but Grigor spoke rapidly, gesturing down the street that they had just walked up.

At length Federov turned to Joshua and said in English, 'My old friend tells me that you need help, also some preposterous story that the young lady with you is the Princess Maria.'

Joshua was surprised at how fluent he spoke English and as if to answer Joshua's unasked question, Federov continued,

'I have lived many years in England,' he said. 'I made the mistake of thinking that I should return to Archangel to sell English published books here. Grigor was a loyal customer – if you can call a young man who sits in your shop all day reading your books without paying such a person.'

Joshua looked at Grigor who ducked his head. 'I help Mr Federov around the shop to pay,' he said sheepishly.

'No matter,' Federov said and ushered the three into his shop, closing the door behind him and placing a closed sign in the window.

Joshua could see that the bookseller was either unpacking or packing books given the wooden crates that took up most of the space on the floor. He guessed it would be the latter considering what he had just said.

'Grigor has told me that you need temporary refuge before leaving Archangel,' Federov said, leading them through the crates to a tiny back room that served as bedsitter and kitchen. He placed a large well-used pot on the tiny stove and Joshua could smell tea brewing. 'You must realise that I have very little room here and do not intend to remain in Russia so I can give only a little help.'

'Any help is appreciated, Mr Federov,' Joshua said. 'We do not intend to stay long. We need a way out of Russia ourselves, and in saying that I think I can include Grigor. I suspect that he is now a persona non grata as I am probably too by now.'

'On that matter I may be of help,' Federov said, pouring tea into tiny cups. 'I am afraid I cannot offer you cream or milk. Not even lemon for your tea,' he apologised.

Joshua did not mind. It was hot and strong. He noticed that Federov was eyeing Maria with great interest.

'If you will excuse me for the moment,' Federov said, placing his cup on the tiny sideboard cluttered with newspapers. He disappeared back into his store and a few moments later reappeared with a large, flat book in his hand. It contained many photographs and Joshua recognised them as being of the Russian royal family. When Maria realised what was in the book Joshua noted the change in her expression. It was a mixture of shock and sorrow. Federov flipped the pages and glanced up at her.

'You look very much like the Princess Maria in these pictures of her,' he said in French. 'And if you are she then you will also have a rudimentary grasp of the language I am speaking.'

'*Oui, monsieur*,' Maria replied. 'I was tutored in French by my mother.'

Federov slowly placed the book on an upturned crate by the door. 'I am sorry that I still have doubts about you,' he said, switching back to Russian. 'The Princess Maria was not tutored in French by her mother – a fact you seem to have overlooked.'

Joshua could not follow the conversation but saw the tears well in Maria's eyes. Whatever was being said had caused her normally pale cheeks to redden.

'I will give you all the assistance you need,' Federov said in English, addressing Joshua. 'Maria has told me that you are responsible for saving her life on more than one occasion, Sergeant Larkin. From what she has told me about her family she has suffered so much already that she deserves to escape this sad land.'

Joshua shrugged off the man's words. 'You are also a part of helping the princess stay alive,' he replied. 'As you are planning to get out of this godforsaken part of the world yourself, no doubt you have contacts.'

'I do,' Federov said, taking off his spectacles and cleaning them with a handkerchief. 'But you will not escape from here by sea or land. By land you will have too far to journey through dangerous territory and by sea the shipping is all too well guarded by the Allied naval forces. The only way out for you is by air.' Joshua blinked at the little bookseller's statement. 'Ah, I should explain,' Federov continued, seeing Joshua's confusion. 'There is a man who has an aeroplane. He is a Polish aviator who will fly well-connected people over the Bolshevik lines and anywhere into Europe they choose. But he does not come cheaply. Maria has explained to me that she is able to pay any price required to escape Russia. If so, the Pole is your best way to escape. He has an aeroplane big enough to fly all three of you out.'

'If he is able to deliver what he promises I am sure that we will be able to come to some arrangement,' Joshua said, considering the option. They would be out and away before the British could find them and safe in France if the Pole was able to do so. A flight would reduce the time they would be in Russian territory and exposed to capture or death from either side. 'How do we contact him?'

'You are in luck,' Federov replied in English, replacing his spectacles at the end of his nose. 'He is coming to Archangel tonight to pick up an important parcel for me. He also speaks French which I believe you also speak with some fluency, according to Maria.'

Joshua relayed the plan to Maria in French and Grigor in English, and she responded by saying that she would trust Joshua to negotiate while she would act as their banker.

That evening they left the bookshop in a horse-drawn wagon. The air was bitterly cold but luckily Federov had found extra clothing for them. For Maria, he had obtained an expensive fur coat and for the men a couple of well-fitting leather coats with fur lining.

From his past experiences dealing with the Polish pilot Federov knew what was ahead. Joshua had agreed to pay him for the expenses.

Federov lugged a rectangular, paper-wrapped parcel under his arm. 'The aristocrats are selling cheap,' he said when Joshua stared at it. 'This small collection of art icons is worth a lot of money in Paris and London. My Polish partner knows how to trade.'

Joshua did not reply as the wagon creaked its way along the streets, arousing little curiosity in the refugees now filling the city. They passed White Russian and Allied patrols but they also showed little interest in the people huddled in the back. The wagon driver knew the roads and used the rutted tracks to the tree-lined fields beyond. After a time he indicated that they were at their destination and took the money Federov paid him.

Joshua scanned the countryside and noticed the field was lengthy and flat, an ideal landing area for an aircraft. They did not have to wait long before Joshua heard the hum of aircraft engines. For a moment he felt a terrible fear, recognising the sound of the dreaded 'Gotha hum' so familiar to him from his days on the Western Front when the giant German bombers rained death down on the trenches, slaughtering many Aussie diggers as they cowered helpless. Joshua realised that his hands were trembling and his instinct was to flee for the concealment of the trees.

The German canvas-covered biplane appeared against the horizon, flying low and slow.

'It is the Pole,' Lev Federov said, stepping forward to wave.

The big bomber glided down at the end of the field and

286

bumped along the slightly uneven surface to roar to a stop just a few yards from where the four stood. The engines sputtered to a stop and only the crack of them cooling in the cold air broke the silence across the field. Joshua noted that the aircraft had no national roundels but was painted in camouflage colours to blend with the earth below and the sky above.

From the open cockpit behind a rounded nose area allocated to a front end gunner, a huge man wearing leather jacket, helmet and oil spattered goggles leaped to the turf with the ease of a gymnast. He strode towards the waiting party, slipping great fur-lined gloves from his hands as he did.

Federov stepped forward and spoke with him. Joshua could see that the Polish pilot stood well over six foot and was broad in the shoulders. He was an impressive man. Federov then turned to lead him to his three potential passengers.

'This is Captain Jan Novak,' he said. 'He said he will help you for a price.'

Joshua stepped forward and extended his hand. 'Sergeant Joshua Larkin, sir,' he said. The Pole accepted his handshake. 'You call me Jan,' he said warmly. 'I no longer in army. I now capitalist flyer.'

Joshua guessed that the big Pole was flying for the strong post-war blackmarket, a kind of aeronautical mercenary. 'The deal is that we want a flight to Paris,' Joshua said. 'Can you do it? Money is not a problem.'

'Lev tell me you can pay,' Jan said, surveying Maria and Grigor. 'He Russian?' Jan asked, nodding at Grigor. 'We Poles at war with Russians.'

'The girl is also Russian,' Joshua said quietly. 'She is paying.'

'She is pretty, so she welcome,' Jan said, smiling at Maria.

'She is paying to have all three of us flown out of Archangel,' Joshua continued, ignoring the leer on the Polish pilot's face. 'Do you have room for three of us and can you make it to Paris?'

Jan turned his attention back to Joshua and scratched his head. 'I fly you to Hamburg,' he said. 'First, we go by Riga where I refuel. It will cost a lot.'

'Why not Paris?' Joshua asked.

'Too far and French no like me,' Jan answered. 'I have spare fuel under wings,' he said, pointing to drums slung where bombs were normally loaded. 'Is good to get us to Riga and Hamburg where I have friends who help me. But no friends in Paris. I fly you to Hamburg. I have friends who can get you ship to London.'

Joshua thought about the Polish flyer's idea. The most pressing thing was to get out of Russia and to be able to pick up a ship was a long step away from the dangers around them.

'Okay,' Joshua said, extending his hand again. 'You have a deal. The three of us to fly to Hamburg via Riga.'

Jan eyed Joshua for a moment and accepted the deal with a handshake. 'Good,' he said. 'Now you help me fuel aeroplane for flight to Riga. It a long way and we fly by night. Less chance either Red airforce or your own shoot me down.'

Joshua explained to Maria that a deal had been struck and that they would fly out as soon as the German bomber was refuelled. Grigor accepted the invitation to be one of the passengers with less enthusiasm. He had never flown in an aeroplane before but was convinced to do so when Joshua explained that he had never flown either. Maria surveyed the plane with great interest.

When the refuelling was complete, Jan explained the layout of the aircraft. 'The Russian will man the rear gun,' he said, pointing to an open space behind the pilot's position. 'The girl will sit next to me on the floor. She can hang on. You will man the forward gun,' he said to Joshua. 'You know how operate German 7.92 parabellum LMG 14 machine gun?' he asked.

'I have a pretty good idea,' Joshua answered. 'I saw something similar to the ones you have aboard a couple of years ago in Belgium.'

'Good,' the Pole grunted. 'What about the Russian?'

'Ask him,' Joshua said. 'He speaks English as good as you. I thought Poles spoke Russian anyway.'

'Poles no speak Russian. But we understand it,' Jan replied, indignant. His country had faced centuries of being squeezed between German and Russian invasions but now the Versailles Treaty had granted them recognition as a separate nation. They were fighting for survival against the Bolshevik forces which were attempting to seize their lands as a bridge into Europe so they could spread their socialist creed in the east and engage in skirmishes with the German army in the west over disputed border zones. The Poles were formidable fighters and both the German and Red Army suffered many defeats against them.

'I know how to operate the German gun,' Grigor said. 'Better than any Pole.'

The two glared at each other and Joshua stepped in. 'What range has this got?' he asked. He knew that the Gotha bombers had rained terror on London during the latter part of the Great War and suspected that the range was impressive.

'We fly five hundred mile easy. Then I land and we put more fuel in and get to Riga,' Jan answered. 'I have landing field before Riga.'

Lev Federov stood back and watched as the three were helped aboard. Once in the plane, Joshua could see that the pilot had a position to the left of the fuselage while an open space ran from the front nose area for the gunner to the rear gunner's position. It was possible to walk from the front to the back although it was a very narrow space.

Jan stashed the package Federov had given him under his seat and settled Maria down beside him where her head would be below the rim of the cockpit and out of the wind.

The Polish pilot stared at the sky for a moment, noting the direction of the slight but chilly breeze. Settling back behind his cockpit controls he opened up the two engines and the aeroplane came to life. When he was satisfied that he had the revs he swung the plane around and began his taxi to take-off. The three passengers waved to the little man standing alone at the edge of the airstrip and he returned their parting gesture.

Joshua watched fascinated as the dark field beneath the wheels rushed past under him when he gawked over the front of the plane's nose. By the time they had reached the end of the field the plane had bumped off the ground and was airborne. The earth rushed away and the wind howled past his head, threatening to freeze his nose and ears off. Joshua pulled down the fur hat he had been given with his leather jacket and slipped on the goggles Jan had passed him before they had taken off. Both helped ward off the cold as the plane continued to climb into the darkening night sky. When Joshua glanced back at Maria he could see that she was wrapped in the jacket and only her frightened eyes showed. Joshua flashed her a smile of reassurance and he saw the change. She was smiling back at him.

Below them Russia stretched out east and west. They were flying west and away from the war between the Red and White armies but still across territory where the Red Army was fighting the German one which had been tasked by the victorious Allies at the Versailles Conference to stem the Red tide and prevent it from invading war-weary Western Europe. What lay ahead was hopefully safety for the Princess Maria. Joshua no longer considered his own life. All he knew was that he had not been with his beloved wife when she died. At least he might be able to console himself by keeping this young woman alive. She was the woman he had fallen in love with even if he had little chance of spending the rest of his life with her, since being of royal blood she must marry one of her own kind.

Sergeant Joshua Larkin also did not have to be told that he was now a deserter in time of war and under British regulations could be executed by a firing squad. That he was an Australian would not save him because he had volunteered to abide by the British army rules and regulations when he enlisted in that army.

Now Joshua slumped down, sitting with his back against the inner surface of the gunner's cockpit. He was out of the biting wind and facing Maria. The night was falling and her face was disappearing from view. Soon, he was left in a world of darkness that throbbed with the power of the two pusher engines nearby.

No one could hear Joshua scream when he finally fell asleep, huddled in his world of sub-freezing cold and darkness. Locked in sleep, Joshua was reliving the hell of being pinned down in a trench while Gotha bombers poured bombs down on him and his men. Bloody bits of body splattered about him as soldiers were blasted apart. He wanted death to take him cleanly and not let him live like the man crawling along the trench with his stomach hanging out and his face a bloody pulp.

He felt someone shaking him and saw Maria staring wide-eyed at him. He was vaguely aware that the night was disappearing and that he had slept. But the look on Maria's face was one of terror. Suddenly Joshua understood why when the thud-thud of bullets striking the canvas brought him fully awake. They were under aerial attack.

TWENTY-NINE

Valley View
Present day

Petrov Batkin selected the town's café to meet Sarah and they sat in a corner away from curious eavesdroppers. Batkin spoke in Russian knowing the chance of anyone in the town understanding the language was extremely slim. Sarah ordered a salad sandwich and Batkin a plate of French fries.

'Kildare is still planning to kill Monique Dawson,' Sarah said quietly.

Batkin lifted a potato chip to his mouth. 'How do you know?'

'Because he has asked me to help him,' Sarah replied.

Batkin did not answer immediately but stared out the large glass window to the quiet street. 'I do not know what to believe,' he said, munching into the crisp potato. 'It is almost impossible to hide such a crime in a place as small as this.'

Sarah leaned back from the table as if exasperated by his response. 'I am telling you that the British plan is to eliminate any chance of her working with us.'

'If that is so then we have to protect Miss Dawson,' Batkin shrugged. 'It will not be easy. I would need assistance from our people in Australia to carry out the task.'

'Do you have contacts over here?' Sarah asked.

'Maybe,' Batkin shrugged, knowing that he had been given names before leaving Russia should he need some muscle. Russian organised crime had its tentacles in every Western country and was proving to law enforcement a deadly and intelligent problem to deal with. Its ranks included highly educated former State employees, ranging from scientists to former KGB operatives now seeking the dark fruits of rampant capitalism in their country. But he did not completely trust the woman he had recruited for this mission and was not about to reveal any further contacts that he had. She was, after all, sleeping with the enemy, albeit to learn what the British intelligence was up to. Either, she was better at her job than Batkin gave her credit – or she was a traitor.

'If you give me a gun,' Sarah said. 'I can prove that I am loyal to our cause. I will get rid of Kildare.'

Batkin picked up another chip and stared at Sarah. 'If you kill the Englishman,' he said, knowing that at this stage he had to hedge his bets on her loyalty. 'that will reassure me that you are committed to our mission. I will give you a gun but do not think I will not kill you if anything goes wrong.' Sarah smiled. She did not doubt the former Spetsnaz soldier's threat to kill her but she was used to living on the edge. This mission was little different from the risks she had endured infiltrating his organisation for MI6. She had a game plan and Batkin had played the right card to her. How stupid men were, she gloated. Not only would she remove Kildare but also Batkin. That would then leave her with an open field to play out the rest of her personal mission.

The hard run helped clear Morgan's head and ease the stress of sitting before his computer filling in the many forms required by the coroner. With the folk festival over for another year he was left with the paperwork for the lost and found property hanging over him. He was also due for a station inspection in a week from the commander of the Hume patrol.

He had reached the top of the hill in good time and scanned the horizon beyond the lookout over the valleys of tall gum trees below the steep cliff. A car passed and when it was gone the peace of the fading day returned. A magpie warbled for the last time in the daylight. The thick clouds billowing overhead threatened a late afternoon thunderstorm and Morgan was not keen to be caught in the open. He turned and began jogging down the hill onto the flat that ran alongside the old Larkin house. The large drops spattered around him, hitting the hot bitumen which threw up its distinctive pungent scent. He knew that he would be too late to avoid the storm and when he glanced over at Monique's house he saw her waving to him to come inside.

Gratefully, Morgan pulled off the road and pounded his way to her front door.

'You look as if you could do with shelter and a towel,' Monique said with a cheery smile as Morgan bent at the waist to catch his breath and bring his pulse down to a steady beat.

'Thanks,' he gasped. 'It's not the rain but the lightning I like to avoid.'

'I have a towel for you in the bathroom,' Monique offered. 'Follow me.'

Morgan wiped his jogging shoes on the door mat, following her inside.

'Where is David?' he asked.

'David has left,' Monique answered.

'You mean he has gone to Sydney or something?'

'No, I mean he has left me,' Monique replied, turning to Morgan.

'I'm sorry,' Morgan lied. He had never liked the pompous bastard who he sensed looked down on him. 'I hope it is only a temporary thing.'

Monique shrugged and passed Morgan a towel. 'That is up to David,' she said as Morgan rubbed himself down.

'Would you like a cup of coffee until the storm passes?' Monique suggested. Morgan accepted. He took the mug of steaming coffee she offered into the living room cluttered with paintings and brass objects representing strange animal shapes. Monique seemed distant and he wondered if she was taking the break with her partner well.

'Anything I can do?' he asked.

'I don't know if I will be staying,' she said. 'I feel that something terrible is going to happen and I'm scared.'

'Does it have anything to do with the bodies?' he asked.

'I truly believe that we have released the spirits of whoever was buried out there,' she replied. 'I feel as if destiny is drawing me towards some dark abyss. I know I sound like some crackpot but I believe there are forces around us that are not all good,' she said fixing him with her eyes. 'Morgan, can you truly protect me?'

296

Morgan was startled by her question but could see that it came from the heart.

'I suspect that there is a threat to your life but have to confess that I do not know where it will come from. Leaving town for a while might be a good idea until I get a handle on what is going on. Believe me, I will, this is a very small town and not much happens without someone noticing.'

'It was the interview I did with that journalist, Sarah Sakharov that made me think of my place in this world,' Monique said. 'If I am the direct descendant of the Princess Maria what is my relevance to the world of the 21st century other than as a five-minute item on a television current affairs program? What other relevance do I have to anyone?'

Morgan thought about what she'd said. Who would want to harm her, and why? He sensed that the answer might solve the mystery. It was time to widen his search to net anyone who was not a citizen of the town, let alone Australia. He already had Olev in his sights but were there others? After all, the couple that had attempted to steal the Larkin journal had English accents. There had been many tourists in town during the festival and it could have been someone now long gone from the district although Olev still remained in town.

The telephone rang and Monique answered it. A girl-friend calling, Morgan guessed from the way Monique spoke. He could see that she was caught up in the call and he rose from the couch. With a wave to Monique he let himself out. The storm had been short and sharp and passed on to drench dry paddocks elsewhere. Morgan continued his run back to the police station, Monique's statements echoing in his mind.

A day would pass before Morgan would get an answer. When he did all hell broke out in the sleepy little village.

MI6 HQ
London
Present day

Harry Stanton knew that a request for the background checks on Sarah Locksley aka Sakharov would raise a red flag. So he called in a favour from the records section to lift her file. It lay open on his desk and what Stanton read in her psych evaluation alarmed him. He was not a psychologist but he had an understanding of the term 'borderline sociopath'. Such an evaluation should have excluded her from recruitment but somehow with her skills and charm she had been considered too valuable to let go. She had been attached to Harry's section without his knowledge of her psych evaluation, which by strict privacy laws was classified information, even in the intelligence service. In her capacity of infiltrating an ultra-right Russian nationalist movement she had proved extremely effective and so all else about her background seemed irrelevant for the intelligence she was able to provide to MI6 – until now.

So Harry had a sociopath loose in Australia – and tangled in a very delicate mission. His instincts told him that it was no coincidence that she was in some Aussie village called Valley View. She was a loose cannon, capable of bringing the British government into the international spotlight in a way that was extremely damaging.

And there was another worry. Daniel Kildare had not reported in to him at the prescribed time. A day had passed and when Harry opted to call his agent in Australia the mobile phone simply rang out. Needless to say, Sarah Locksley's mobile phone recorded a disconnected number. In an act of desperation Harry pulled the file on what they knew about the demographics and topography of the little Australian town. There was a police station and a telephone number. Harry glanced up at the clock on his wall. He calculated that it would be night in the eastern states of Australia but knew police were on call 24/7. Harry commenced pushing the buttons on his phone.

THIRTY

West of Riga, Latvia
September 1919

The bullets punched holes in the canvas fuselage above Joshua's head. He screamed over the roar of engines and howling wind for Maria to remain on her stomach on the floor of the cockpit, although he knew that would do little good once he was able to raise his head to peer over the rim from his position at the nose of the aircraft. In the grey sky he could see two fighter aircraft circling for an angle to attack the lumbering former bomber and knew that their machine guns could reach into every part of the canvas and wood giant. Joshua recognised the stubby yet streamlined biplanes as Albatross fighters. He had seen the German aircraft over the frontlines in France and Belgium and had heard from flyers in the fledgling Australian air force that the fighter aircraft were very good. When one of the aircraft turned he could see the black crosses marking them as belonging to the German air force. He was not aware that international politics deemed that the Germans fight on the side of the Latvians to resist the onslaught of the Bolsheviks in their country.

Joshua could see that Jan was forcing his ungainly former bomber into a climb. The twin Mercedes engines roared and one of the attacking aircraft peeled off to slide down below them, while the second made a great sweep to position itself on their tail. Joshua crouched and grasped the pistol grip on his machine gun. Cocking the weapon, he tucked the butt into his shoulder and tried to recall all that he had been taught about defending against aerial attack. He was to aim in front of the aircraft, he remembered, so that the enemy would fly into a spray of machine gun bullets. But he also realised that the aircraft he lined up was well out of range and sliding behind the climbing bomber. Then he heard Grigor open up behind the pilot, firing down a tunnel that ran from the top of the fuselage to underneath. German designers had long realised the Gotha's weakness to attack from below in the hole for the rear gunner to fire through.

Captain Jan Novak knew the only hope he had of avoiding being shot down by the well-armed German fighters was to use the only advantage he had over the smaller fighter aircraft. His bomber could fly higher and he attempted to reach the maximum ceiling of 21 000 feet compared to that of 17 000 feet of the pursuing aircraft.

But the fighter plane attacking from below continued its own climb, firing the twin machine guns mounted on the nose in front of the enemy pilot. Joshua watched helplessly as the second enemy plane pulled into a position on the bomber's tail and the twinkle of fire coming from the twin machine guns became apparent. Both enemy had synchronised their attack to concentrate their firepower on the rear of the vulnerable bomber.

Behind his controls, the Polish flyer simultaneously

cursed and prayed for height as the machine gun bullets raked his plane from stem to stern. From his position in the nose there was nothing Joshua could do but watch helplessly as canvas ripped and plywood splintered under the impact of the bullets hosing their aircraft. All depended on a Polish pilot and a Russian soldier to keep them alive.

Maria, ashen with terror, reached out to hold Joshua's hand. Then suddenly, the ripping, tearing around them stopped and when Joshua glanced over the rim of his cockpit he could see the two enemy aircraft peel away to fall earthwards before rolling over to resume their flight. Jan had succeeded in reaching an altitude beyond that of the lighter enemy aircraft. Levelling off, he piloted his plane towards a cloud bank. It was then that Joshua noticed Grigor slumped on the deck of his firing position. Scrambling over Maria, Joshua crawled rearward to where Grigor lay in a rapidly spreading pool of blood. He was still alive – but barely. Joshua attempted to speak to him but over the noise of the wind and engines around them he had to shout. Grigor simply returned a weak smile and nodded. Joshua could not see where the Russian had been wounded and tore open his leather jacket. He saw the widening splotches of blood on Grigor's heavy woollen jumper. There was more than one wound and Joshua guessed that Grigor had taken at least two bullets in the chest. Even as he examined the dying soldier Grigor's eyes closed and with a rattling sound in his throat he spewed up a fountain of blood. Grigor's head fell to one side and Joshua knew that he was dead. He let go of the body and crawled back to his position at the nose of the aircraft. Marie saw the blood covering his leather jacket and hands. Her eyes widened in fear but Joshua simply shook his head to reassure her.

The flight droned on as Jan navigated towards his first

landing point west of Riga. After about an hour, the Polish pilot began his descent until they were skimming the tops of trees and open fields. The weather was overcast and a fine drizzle stung the occupants of the exposed cockpits. Eventually, Jan spotted his landmarks and followed a winding dirt road until he came to a wide, cleared field which adjoined an ancient farm house.

Expertly throttling back, Jan brought the big aircraft down to bounce along the paddock. As he taxied towards the farm house Joshua could see a man and woman standing by a great wagon drawn by two draught horses. In the wagon, were drums, of what he presumed was aviation fuel.

The aircraft came to a halt and when the twin engines sputtered to a stop the ensuring silence was eerie. Only the sound of farm animals settling down after being disturbed drifted across the field.

'We leave our Russian friend here to bury,' Jan said, removing his goggles and heavy fur-lined gloves. 'He died like a brave Pole would.'

Joshua could forgive the Polish aviator's apparent callous attitude. What else could one do when death had been a constant companion for so many years to them both?

The farmer and his wife urged the big horses forward, bringing up the drums of badly needed fuel. Jan greeted them and spoke in a language Joshua had not heard before. He helped Maria down from the aircraft while Jan strode around his aircraft, examining it for damage.

'Grigor is dead,' Maria said.

Joshua nodded. 'We will leave him with the people here to bury. I doubt that we will have time to hang around. The air around here is lousy with Hun aircraft.'

Maria understood but shed tears when Joshua and Jan

303

removed the stiffening body from the aircraft with the farmer's help and lowered it to the ground. They carefully carried his body to a part of the field well away from the aircraft.

Once Jan was satisfied that the German machine guns had not damaged anything vital to the flying of his aircraft the refuelling went ahead without incident. They were invited inside the farm house to partake of a hot soup of minced beetroot and sour cream, spiced with herbs. The soup was accompanied with hot, crusty bread rolls spread with rich butter. Joshua could not remember the last time that he had eaten such good food and thanked the middle-aged farmer and his much younger wife. Jan had explained that the farmer was a Latvian who also worked for Lev Federov and himself.

When the meal was finished, Jan led them back to his aircraft. They boarded, leaving the burial of Grigor's body to the farmer. Jan fired up the engines and the big aircraft lumbered down the field until he was able to swing it into the gentle breeze. With a roar, the Gotha picked up speed until it floated off the field and into the air. Jan swung the nose around and put his aeroplane on a heading west. He had calculated that they would arrive in Riga within a few hours, just before nightfall.

As the aircraft climbed Joshua settled at his post manning the forward machine gun. After speaking with the farmer, Jan said that they did not expect to see any more German aircraft before Riga. It seemed that the Germans assisting the Latvians retain their newfound national status had pulled back to the city before the advancing Red Army. The latest news from the Latvian Russian front was that the Bolsheviks were being defeated by the combined German Latvian ground forces. Riga could be considered safe for Jan although his own country was at war with the Germans over disputed territory. He had explained that he was in contact with a high-ranking German officer of the Freikorps who had become a kind of partner to the Polish adventurer.

'What is the Freikorps?' Joshua had asked over the meal.

'They are German volunteers, mostly former combat soldiers, who have raised their own unit to fight the Bolsheviks anywhere they find them,' Jan had answered, dipping his bread roll in his soup. 'Tough bunch – best to steer clear of them when we are in Riga. Don't hesitate to kill anyone they suspect of being a Bolshie back in Germany. No trial – just a bullet in the head.'

On the flight west they hit some turbulence and Joshua held Maria's hand to reassure her. She had settled herself in the open nose of the aircraft and sat close to him to keep warm in the biting cold. Both dozed despite the turbulence and when they came out of their sleep they realised that they were descending.

Joshua peered over the aircraft's nose to see another green field by a rutted dirt road. This time there was a truck parked at the end of the field Jan was lining up to land on. Joshua and Maria braced for the impact with the earth but the Pole was a superb pilot and feathered the German bomber onto the field, bouncing a couple of times before roaring back on the power and settling down to a gentle taxi towards the truck. The engines coughed into silence and Joshua could hear the crack of hot metal contracting in the cold air as the engines cooled.

'We will get lift to Riga,' Jan said, leaping from the wing of the aeroplane and helping Maria down. 'I have business there and can give you place to stay for night. Then we go to Hamburg.'

Joshua could not help but like the Polish giant. He was obviously a renegade mercenary who intended to make money out of the turmoil of 1919 Europe. Joshua wondered how Jan had acquired a former German bomber but felt that if he asked he would not get a straight answer.

They walked side by side across the field towards the truck where a thin, slight man stood cradling a rifle Joshua recognised as a German Mauser.

'One day, big plane like mine fly all over the world taking passengers and mail from city to city. Country to country,' Jan said unexpectedly. 'I make money and buy many passenger aeroplane.'

Joshua was impressed by the man's vision and wondered if the passenger planes would need to be armed, considering what they had gone through.

Jan stopped and spoke in German with the man waiting for them. Then he turned to Joshua. 'You get in back of truck,' he said. 'We go Riga. Eat, drink.'

Joshua and Maria clambered onto the open tray of the truck and it set out along the road to the city which they could see in the distance. At least they were now out of Russia if not out of danger, Joshua thought, holding Maria to him. Just on dark they entered the outer suburbs of the beautiful old city built in Medieval times. To Joshua it was like so many of the cities of Europe he had seen since becoming a soldier. The streets were cobblestoned and wide. Monuments sat on pedestals all around the city centre, and Maria nudged him to point out a statue as if they were simply a couple of tourists rather than refugees on the run from just about everyone. Joshua missed the name but could see how being in Riga had sparked Maria's spirit.

'This was once part of the Czar's realm,' she said and then fell into silence.

Joshua could not get used to the fact that her father had once been one of the most powerful men on earth and that the young woman in his arms was a true princess with a lineage dating back centuries.

They drove through Riga passing detachments of heavily armed military men manning barricades, reminding Joshua that Europe was still at war despite the Armistice signed in France. Their driver had no problems passing through the roadblocks, waving some papers at the soldiers and receiving clear passage. Joshua guessed that the Pole had every angle worked out from his operations of smuggling blackmarket goods. Joshua also noticed tough-looking soldiers wearing German uniforms and the sight brought back bitter memories. Freikorps, Jan had said through the opening to the truck's tray. The confident-looking Germans did not have the look of defeated men on their faces, Joshua thought.

Eventually they turned off into a narrower, cobbled street bordered by elegant old three-storeyed houses of ornately carved stone. Stopping in front of one Jan indicated that they should dismount, and led them into a house.

'My place here,' he said, leading them down a corridor. Joshua was impressed by the house's elegance. Paintings adorned the walls and many rooms led off either side of the wide hallway.

'You have rooms upstairs,' Jan said, waving to a broad staircase of finely carved timber. 'Even have hot water for bath. All house is your house. I go see German officer my man in Riga. You can eat at café around corner but be careful. Many patrols and you not have papers. Now I go.'

Joshua accepted the Pole's invitation to explore the house

307

and found two well set out bedrooms. He offered Maria first choice and then went in search of the bathroom. He found a small room with a cast-iron tub. Next to it was a wood burner with a large enamel basin on it. Joshua lit the fire to warm the water and found a straight-edge razor to shave away many days of grime. When the water was hot enough he stripped, and lowered himself into the water and washed away the remaining traces of Grigor's blood and accumulated dirt from his body. Lying back in the tub Joshua luxuriated in the feeling of cleanliness. A knock at the door disturbed his moment of peace.

'You have found the bath, Joshua?' he heard Maria ask from the other side of the door. 'I would like to have a bath also.'

'One moment,' Joshua said, climbing out of the tub to dry himself with a clean towel he found. 'I will change the water and pour you a bath.'

He dressed back into his dirty clothes, gave his newly acquired leather jacket a wipe and was fully dressed when he allowed Maria to enter the room.

'You smell better,' she said with a mischievous smile, brushing past him with a set of clean clothes over her arm. 'Now I will feel better.'

Joshua closed the door behind him and made his way downstairs. When Maria appeared at the top of the staircase some time later she was wearing a colourful peasant dress and blouse.

Joshua immediately complimented her on her new appearance, which brought a girlish blush to her pretty face.

'Now we can go to dinner,' she said, impulsively taking Joshua's arm in her own.

They found the restaurant around the corner of the street

just as Jan had said they would. Joshua was impressed by its elegance in a city beset by war. He felt almost under-dressed when he saw the smartly dressed patrons inside but Maria tugged him through the door where they were met by a young man whose clothes had been patched many times. Beneath the elegant exterior there was poverty, as Joshua could see.

The smiling waiter understood Russian and led them to a table lit by large candles. Cigar and pipe smoke choked the room and when Joshua glanced around he could see many of the patrons were uniformed officers of the German and Latvian army. They paid him little attention although Maria's entrance did turn a few male heads.

Maria examined the menu and placed an order with the waiter. When he left for the kitchen, Maria's face seemed to light up with a serenity Joshua had not seen before and she reached out for his hands across the table.

'Do you know, Joshua,' she said. 'Tonight I truly feel that I am safe. That we will live and be free for the first time in as long as I can remember.'

'We have a long way to go before we get out of danger,' Joshua cautioned.

'Sergeant Larkin, you are such a pessimist,' Maria scoffed gently, withdrawing her hands. 'I am always safe when I am with you.'

Joshua felt humbled by her faith in him and poured them a glass of wine from the bottle brought to the table by the waiter. It was a rich, red wine with no label but Joshua did not care. He had learned to drink 'plonk' in France and acquired a taste for the Froggy drop.

He raised his glass towards Maria. 'Here is to the most beautiful woman in Europe,' he toasted.

Maria looked away uncertainly. She'd piled her hair on

309

top of her head and when she turned away Joshua could see the smooth curve of her neck.

'I do not know what is my destiny,' she said, turning back and taking a sip of the wine. 'Tonight, I am but a woman like any other. Oh, Joshua, I wish I could see into the future and know if it is my fate to return to my beloved Russia when the Bolsheviks are defeated.'

Her words tapered away as she remembered how horrified and helpless she had felt watching her family being executed before her eyes.

Joshua reached over to take her hands in his. 'We have a more important role to play right now – just staying alive and getting out of here,' he said. 'Worry about your destiny when we are finally safe. I will not feel that way until I can once again smell the gum trees and see the heads of Sydney Harbour from the bow of some ship.'

Maria did not attempt to retract her hands from his and he could see that she was struggling with thoughts that wanted to be words.

'Joshua, I cannot go on without confessing . . .'

Joshua pulled away just as the waiter placed two large plates of a finely cooked stew in front of them, interrupting that delicate moment when words might have been uttered that could not be taken back.

They ate in relative silence except to exchange little jokes about their time together. Maria laughed often and it seemed so natural for her to do so. Joshua was pleased that he could make her smile and for the moment feel they could have been anywhere safe in the world.

When the meal was finished they drank the bottle dry and ordered another one. When they'd downed the last drop, Maria paid for the meal and they stepped out onto the bitterly cold street. Together, they hurried back to the

310

house, leaning on each other for support. Bursting through the door, Maria flung herself into Joshua's arms and kissed him on the lips, taking him by surprise.

'Thank you, Joshua,' she said. 'I cannot remember such a wonderful night as we have had tonight. But now we must sleep,' she continued. 'The Pole will expect us to be ready at dawn.'

'I suppose so,' Joshua answered, regretting that Maria had broken the embrace to head for the stairs.

'Goodnight, Joshua,' she said and disappeared into her room.

It dawned on Joshua that this was the first time since he had met her that Maria had not slept in his arms for protection against the cold and the enemies that pursued them.

Reluctantly, he went to his room and lay down on the bed fully clothed to stare at the ceiling. He could not sleep despite the wine and found himself reflecting on his life. Only five years earlier he had been a simple clerk, married and living in Sydney. Five years later he had become a ruthless killer of men; a soldier who other men had followed into hell – and died for their faith in him. He was no longer the Joshua Larkin of five years earlier. War had changed him and he could never go back to his country as the same man he had once known.

He felt the guilt of the survivor but worse, he felt the guilt of treason. He had whored with his men behind the frontlines. The need to smell, touch and taste the purity of a woman's flesh had been his way of reminding himself he was still alive. When the news arrived that his wife had died of the terrible flu pandemic Joshua had been racked with guilt for his betrayal of the woman he loved. He felt the anguish of helplessness at not being by her side and soon after had volunteered for the Russian campaign hoping that death would find him and wash away his guilt. Instead, he had found Maria and a reason to stay alive – despite how impossible his love for her was. If nothing else he would keep her alive until her destiny was fulfilled.

Joshua hardly noticed that sleep was washing over him until he suddenly snapped from his dozy state, sensing that he was not alone in the dark. Someone else was in the room and Joshua edged his hand towards the pistol under his pillow.

'I could not sleep alone,' Maria's voice came to him from a few feet away.

Joshua let the pistol go and turned to see her outline against the flickering candle on the bed stand. But he was truly snapped from the last remnants of sleep when he saw that she was completely naked and shivering in the cold air. He immediately reached up to draw her down to the bed and hold her to him.

THIRTY-ONE

Valley View
Present day

Morgan grappled for the phone beside his bed and hauled himself into a sitting position before answering. From the corner of his eye he could see his digital clock register 2.13 am.

'Valley View police, Senior Constable McLean speaking,' he mumbled, still shaking the sleep from his fogged mind.

'Constable,' the voice at the other end said, 'I realise that it is very late where you are as I am calling from the UK but I am very concerned about a relative of mine, a Mr Daniel Kildare, who I believe is visiting your town to attend a folk festival. My concern is that I have not heard from him for the last couple of days and that is not like him. I am hoping that you could make some inquires as to his whereabouts as I am worried for his welfare.'

'Maybe he is no longer here,' Morgan replied, rubbing his

eyes. 'The festival has been over for the last week but since you have called from the UK I will make some inquires in the morning. What is your name and the number I can call you on?'

'My name is Paul Smithers and you can contact me on my mobile phone.'

Harry provided his telephone number and a description of Daniel Kildare, which Morgan scribbled down on a pad he kept by the bed for messages. Conversation over, Morgan replaced the phone, rolled over and went back to sleep.

In his office on the other side of the world, Harry Stanton leaned back in his chair and noted the name of the police officer he had spoken to, along with the time and duration of the call. He had not given his real name – nor could the mobile phone number ever be traced to him. It was all a habit from his intelligence experience to habitually do such things. Except that he had not recorded the contact for official MI6 records. Harry stared at the wall opposite his desk and the portrait of a young Queen Elizabeth II. He had not updated the portrait, as he liked the look of the Queen when she was a younger woman in her reign over the British Commonwealth. He thought it ironic that she was also the monarch of the Commonwealth of Australia. Some links with England died hard.

But Harry's mind was distracted by the silence from Australia. It was like losing a crew in a capsule in outer space, he thought. The sudden loss of contact and the darkness beyond where those at ground control could do nothing. He rubbed his forehead; he would dearly love a shot of Scotch to ease his troubled mind. Whatever was happening on the other side of the world was now out of his control unless

314

he established communications with Daniel Kildare. Otherwise, something very bad was about to happen. Harry knew it in his bones as sure as the cold, grey clouds covered London in the winter.

Morning came to Valley View and a cloudless, humid spring day once again promised an afternoon thunderstorm. Morgan showered, shaved and dressed in his uniform. A quick breakfast of orange juice, a mug of tea and a piece of toast was all that he needed to start his day. Then he remembered the missing person call he had received during the early hours of the morning and retrieved the scrap of paper from beside his unmade bed.

Daniel Kildare, a Pom. Gladys Harrison was sure that her assailants had British accents. Morgan closed the police station door and made his way to the top hotel. It had not yet opened and he found the publican, Clare Neill in the backyard supervising the unloading of beer kegs from a truck.

'G'day, Morgan,' she greeted him.

Clare was in her fifties but had the figure of a woman in her twenties. She had a face that had seen too much sun in her youth and the years of working behind a bar had hardened the expression in her eyes. As the local cop Morgan had proved himself firm, fair and friendly and she respected him.

'Morning, Clare,' Morgan answered. 'Looks like a good day for business.'

Clare glanced at the sky, before going back to assisting the delivery driver in getting the kegs to the back of the hotel. 'Yeah, could be a hot one.'

'I was just wondering,' Morgan said. 'Do you have a

patron staying by the name of Daniel Kildare – a Pom, I believe.'

Clare ceased rolling a keg and stood up to wipe the sweat from her brow with the back of her hand. 'I did,' she replied. 'But he seems to have done a runner on me. Hasn't been in his room for the last couple of days and owes for a week's accommodation. I was hoping that you might be able to find him for me.'

'Has anyone occupied the room since he left?' Morgan asked.

'Not so far,' Clare answered. 'You want to have a look around?'

'If you don't mind,' Morgan said. He followed Clare into the back of the hotel to walk up the worn carpeted stairs to the second level. She opened a door off the corridor and Morgan followed her in. The bed had been made up and the room cleaned. The room opened out onto the wide verandah overlooking the main street.

'I'll leave you to it,' Clare said. 'Just close the door when you have finished.'

She was about to leave when something came to mind. She stopped mid-way through the door. 'You might talk to the English lass a couple of rooms up,' Clare added. 'I suspect she spent more time in his room than her own. Her name is Sarah Sakharov and her room is Number 3. I am sure she will still be in.'

Morgan thanked her and began his search. He opened an old-style wooden tall boy where clothes were hanging on coathangers. Morgan rifled through the pockets of a pair of trousers but found nothing but a handkerchief.

He tried the drawers of a bedside low boy of similar vintage. The usual Gideons Bible for travellers and a dog-eared, glossy brochure extolling the trout fishing of the local streams in the mountains around Valley View, as well as fliers from various businesses for their products and services. It was evident that if the English tourist had chosen to leave without the intention of paying he would at least have taken his clothes with him. But Morgan saw no other sign of foul play in the room. He had been provided with the missing persons' particulars as to physical description, date of birth and so on by the caller from hours before. Now he would write up a missing persons' report to satisfy the rules and regulations of his job. In the meantime, he would question this Sarah Sakharov whose name he already knew from Monique's mention of her as the freelance reporter who had interviewed her a week earlier.

Morgan closed the door and walked a short distance down the passageway. He knocked on the door. A muffled female voice answered and Morgan declared his occupation and waited. After a short time the door opened to reveal a very attractive young woman whose ruffled hair and pale face indicated that she had been asleep when he knocked. Morgan introduced himself. Sarah held the door ajar but did not invite him inside. 'Yes, how can I help you, Senior Constable McLean?' she asked.

'Are you Sarah Sakharov?' Morgan asked.

'I am,' she replied with a frown of irritation. 'May I ask why you want to know?'

'Nothing to be concerned about,' Morgan reassured her. 'I am just asking some routine questions about a gentleman I have been informed you may know – a Mr Daniel Kildare – and if you have some ID like a driver's licence it would help greatly.'

'Daniel, yes I know Daniel,' Sarah responded. 'But I haven't seen him for the last couple of days. I was actually considering a visit to the police station to see if you could help me locate him.' The door had opened wider and the girl's initial annoyance had seemed to dissipate a little.

'You interviewed Monique Dawson recently,' Morgan said unexpectedly and thought he saw a fleeting look of concern on Sarah's face. 'Is that correct?'

'Yes, I did,' Sarah answered. 'I am a freelance journalist and was attracted to your town by the rumours that the Princess Maria of Russia might have escaped the slaughter in 1918 and eventually settled in your little village. I felt that the story was worth travelling from the UK to research and Ms Dawson's name was prominent in my investigation. It would have been super to actually prove that she was a direct descendant of Princess Maria. It would have been wonderful for my career.'

Morgan was closely appraising her response to his question but could not read deceit in either her voice or body language. Either she was innocent of any misdeeds or she was a very practised liar, he concluded. After all, what were the chances of two British citizens – a man and a woman – being involved in the assault on Gladys Harrison. Here he had both and from what Clare had told him they knew each other. Sarah retrieved an international driver's licence with her particulars, which Morgan quickly scribbled in his notebook before handing the licence back to her.

'If it is convenient,' Morgan said politely and with a broad smile, 'I would like you to drop into the police station to assist us with our search for your fellow countryman, Ms Sakharov. Say, around ten o'clock this morning. I promise that I will provide a good cup of tea when you arrive. You can call me Morgan, if you like.'

Sarah found herself thrown off guard by the Aussie policeman's charm. He was not bad looking for an older

318

man, she thought. Monique had mentioned his name more than once in the interview and she could see why.

Morgan turned to walk away. What had an old sergeant once told him when he had first commenced working the streets — when it came to getting answers from suspects *an ounce of honey is worth a ton of salt.* Morgan had never forgotten the advice.

He was no longer smiling when he made his way down the narrow wooden stairs. His gut feeling was that he had identified who had broken into the museum and viciously assaulted Gladys. The only trouble was that one of his suspects had suddenly disappeared and he still required legal proof before he could act on his instinct. So who was this person who had called him from the UK?

'Gonna be a hot one today,' the barman said to Morgan as he made his way to the front door.

'Looks like it, Marty,' Morgan answered. 'A real stinker.'

As soon as he arrived back at the police station he picked up the phone and dialled a number.

'Ken,' he said. 'I think we might have a couple to put in the frame for the break-in and assault out here. I need to run a couple of names through the UK system. Can you do that?'

When the answer was in the affirmative Morgan supplied the names of Sarah Sakharov and Daniel Kildare along with Kildare's date of birth, explaining that he would have more on the woman after he interviewed her at the station.

Morgan closed the conversation and put the phone down. He wondered if he had any Earl Grey tea bags.

Petrov Batkin took the call on his mobile phone. It was short and to the point. After meetings in St Petersburg the organisation had decided that Monique Dawson must be taken against her will if necessary. It was in her best interests as it was obvious that British intelligence wanted her dead. Batkin would be assisted by a couple of local Russians working for organised crime and based in Sydney. They would arrive that night and Batkin was to brief them on the abduction. Under no circumstances was she to be harmed. A cargo ship steaming off the coast of New South Wales would be available for them to smuggle her aboard before it headed to Singapore.

Everything was in place and all Batkin had to do now was wait for the meeting with the two men arriving from Sydney. He expected them within hours of his call.

Sarah arrived at the police station on time. 'I was hoping that you may have some information on the whereabouts of Daniel,' she said. 'It seems so unlike him to simply leave without telling me.'

'I gather that you two had a more than friendly relationship,' Morgan said.

'That is really none of your business,' Sarah responded coldly. 'Now, if that is all, I will go. I have matters to complete before I leave your town.'

Morgan knew that he could not stop her leaving but needed to learn as much about her as he could without appearing to be conducting an interrogation.

'I'm sorry if I sounded a bit personal,' he apologised. 'It's just that I have been a copper too long to change my manners.' His apology appeared to work and Sarah settled back into the chair.

'When was the last time you saw Mr Kildare?' Morgan asked.

'I think it was a couple of mornings ago,' Sarah said. 'He was in his room and said something about spending the day sightseeing on the northern side of your town. Daniel was a fly fisherman and was interested in checking out your waterways.'

'You used the past tense to refer to Mr Kildare's interest in fly fishing,' Morgan said. 'Do you feel that something may have happened to him?'

'I meant, *is*,' Sarah quickly countered.

'For a journalist you should be more aware of such a slip,' Morgan said, knowing he had caught her off guard. 'Not that I am implying you have had anything to do with his disappearance.'

'Constable, if that is all I think I shall leave,' Sarah said, this time rising fully from her chair. 'You know where to find me if there is anything of any consequence to talk about.'

Morgan watched as she walked out of the station and down the stairs to the street below. He picked up the phone and called the detectives' office in Hume City.

'Got back some info on that Kildare bloke,' Ken Barber said over the phone. 'He came into Australia about three weeks ago on a flight from London via Singapore. Our liaison officer with the Pom police tells us that Kildare is employed as a sales rep for a toy company in the UK based out of London. He has nothing in the way of a criminal record and zero else on him to report. So write him up as a missing person for now.'

'Just got a bad feeling about this one, Ken,' Morgan said. 'I don't think he did a runner on our pub. It's like he has truly disappeared into thin air.'

'Not much else you can do until something turns up,' Ken replied. 'But I do think that your info on the two Poms

321

might have something in it unless you can find two other Poms to fit in the frame.'

Morgan frowned. He had his suspects and no one else in the tiny town fitted the picture so well.

'I will give you a call when we get something back on this Sarah Sakharov sheila,' Ken said in closing. 'In the meantime, just keep an eye on her.'

Not hard to do, Morgan thought. No doubt all the red-blooded males in Valley View were doing that every time she stepped out of her hotel room. He replaced the telephone and found that he was thinking about Monique Dawson. She had told him that she was preparing to leave town for a stay in Sydney. He was wondering if she was still in town when the telephone on his desk rang.

'Valley . . .'

'Morgan, it's me,' the voice cut across.

Morgan immediately recognised Ken Barber's voice and the urgency in his tone.

'Get yourself down to the creek at Paddy's Crossing. A local of yours has just found a body and put it through triple-0. It sounds like your missing Pom. Just contain the scene until we get out to join you.'

THIRTY-TWO

Riga
September 1919

Joshua felt Maria trembling and in the flickering shadows of the candle by his bed, when he looked down at her face he could see fear. Gently, he stroked her hair and kissed her on the forehead. Time in the trenches under fire had taught him that the mind was something very vulnerable. Despite his desire for her, Joshua knew her gesture was not what it seemed. He spoke softly to her with soothing words until her trembling turned into racking sobs, for Joshua had seen in her eyes the horror she had experienced in the village when the Bolshevik militia soldiers had forced themselves on her. It was not that different from the looks in soldiers' eyes when they had just survived an artillery bombardment.

Maria sobbed until there were no more tears and Joshua held her to him. At length she fell into a deep but troubled sleep; she twitched and muttered words in Russian he did not understand. Joshua laid her down carefully, pulled a thick blanket over her and then slid under to hold her until sleep eventually overtook him.

Before dawn his internal clock woke him and he shook Maria awake. She sat up, pulling up the blankets to cover her breasts. Joshua left her to make her way back to her room to dress and they were both ready to leave when the Polish pilot arrived shortly after.

No words about the previous evening passed between them and it was only when they were following Jan from the house that Maria whispered in Joshua's ear the words, 'Thank you.' That was enough for Joshua to know that he had done the right thing.

The day broke with a stiffening wind over the grassy field where the great bomber sat waiting as if it was eager to climb into the sky. Joshua watched as Jan carried out his ritual of preliminary checks on the aircraft.

'We reach Hamburg today,' he said, rubbing his hands together against the cold. 'Not good like Riga. Much trouble with Bolsheviks and Freikorps fighting in streets. You be careful.'

Joshua helped Maria to climb into the cockpit and followed. He positioned himself in the nose but was aware that he might also have to man the rear machine gun if the situation arose that they had to fight off attacking aircraft.

The Gotha bounced down the field with its nose into the stiff breeze and rose like a kite. Joshua thought that the aircraft seemed to struggle a little getting into the air as if carrying extra weight, but the earth fell away to a patchwork of green fields, dirt roads and in the distance the outline of the city on the mighty river snaking its way to the sea. Joshua could also see columns of troops below on the roads and the horse-drawn artillery of an army at war. He did not know whose forces he was viewing from the sky – Russian, German or Latvian – but so long as they were flying away from the troops below it did not matter.

After a couple of hours Jan passed out paper-wrapped bundles of bread, ham and cheese along with a bottle of good, red wine. The skies had cleared and the view was magnificent despite the bitter cold and rushing wind around them.

The flight went well and late in the afternoon Jan signalled that he was going in for a landing. Joshua peered at the horizon and could see glimpses of the sea as well as a sprawling city he guessed was Hamburg. It felt eerie to be flying into the city of a country he had once been at war with.

As before, Jan had a field picked out that Joshua guessed was his depot in Germany. He could see a huge hangar and some small buildings that suggested the place was a former military airfield. This time they would be landing on a cleared strip. As they drew closer, Joshua could see that there were other aircraft adjoining the airstrip, former fighter aeroplanes of the German air force. He noted the tiny figures of people moving about on the ground.

Jan circled his Gotha and waggled its wings. Joshua saw a flare fired from near a tall building with people standing on a platform. The red flare fizzled out as it fell back to the earth and the big Gotha made its approach. With the ease of his expertise behind the controls, Jan drifted into line with the hardened earth and roared to a stop adjacent to the cluster of wooden buildings. A beautiful, golden-haired young woman broke away from a small gathering of men in overalls to rush towards the aircraft. Her long hair flowed in the breeze. When the engines powered down Joshua heard her call Jan's name. Jan leaped from the cockpit to the wing and then to the ground to embrace the woman, lifting her from the earth. She squealed with delight and kissed him all over his oil-spattered face.

Joshua and Maria climbed down and joined them.

'This is Helga,' Jan said, introducing the young woman who thrust out her hand to Joshua. 'She is my wife.'

Jan said something in German and Helga shook Maria's hand also.

'She not speak good English like me,' Jan said, holding Helga around the waist.

The four men standing aside moved forward on a command from Jan and Joshua was surprised to see them pull aside a panel in the fuselage to reveal legs of ham stacked inside. As well as recovering the pile of hams from inside the fuselage they also removed the drums from under the former bomber's wings and opened them to reveal even more legs of ham.

'The Allies continue to blockade Germany,' Jan explained, seeing the question on Joshua's face. 'Many hundreds of thousands German, man, woman, child starve to death. Food more valuable than gold. I get lots of gold for food. But come, you are guests who pay well and Helga good cook. We go my house in Hamburg and eat.'

With little other option, Joshua and Maria accepted the kind invitation and Jan led them behind the sheds to a car.

'Is Ford 1915 Model T touring car,' Jan said proudly as Joshua gazed at the shiny black vehicle with its gold-coloured framed radiator. 'Has electric starter. No more crank car to go. You get in and I drive.'

Joshua and Maria slid into the comfortable leather seat in the back while Helga and Jan took their places in the front. Jan kicked over the engine and was pleased to hear it sputter into life. With a shift of gears the car jumped forward and the Polish pilot flew the Ford towards an open gate out onto a rutted dirt road. Both Maria and Joshua hugged each other as the Polish captain hurtled recklessly along. Joshua guessed that Jan was a better pilot than he was a driver. But Helga screamed in her delight while the rear passengers gritted their teeth against the jolts.

'Is good,' Jan yelled back over his shoulder. 'I get from Yankee ship to port. Make me pay much.'

When they arrived in the outer suburbs of Hamburg Joshua could see what the Pole had meant by starvation. Every face he saw on the sidewalks was pinched and pale. Old people and children held out their hands begging and Joshua could not feel any animosity towards his former enemy when he took in their desperate situation. Anger flared in him when he considered that the Allies had continued their blockade of Germany as further punishment. In Joshua's world, it was putting the boot into a man when he was down. How could the bony, wide-eyed child they just passed sitting in the street be an enemy?

Jan slowed down in the cobble-paved streets and drove cautiously to avoid the pedestrians that ambled across his path with little regard for their welfare. By now Helga's happy mood had turned sombre. Joshua somehow doubted that the food Jan had flown in from Latvia would grace the tables of the people he saw starving in the cold, windswept streets. It was more likely destined for the larders of those who still had old money to spend.

Eventually they reached a modest villa in a leafy suburb and Jan pulled into a lane beside the house. Alighting from the car Joshua and Maria followed Helga and Jan into the house which was far less pretentious than the one Jan owned in Riga, small but comfortable. Joshua felt the warmth of a fire burning in a wood combustion stove. It was strange, he reflected, that they were in Germany and he was relatively safe with Maria.

After a very pleasant evening with Jan and Helga, Maria and Joshua retired to separate rooms, where the clean sheets and thick eiderdown blankets on their beds promised a good night's sleep.

Joshua stripped down to his long johns and pulled the blanket up to his chin. In a short time he fell into a deep sleep but thankfully the nightmares of being back in the trenches did not come to him. In the early hours of the morning however he was torn from his sleep by the sound of crashing boots and shouted words. Joshua reached for the revolver under his pillow and leaped from his bed, standing in the centre of the darkened room attempting to clear the cobwebs of sleep from his mind.

Two thoughts swirled in his head: he must see if Maria was safe and that her linen belt containing the fortune in precious stones and gold coins was hidden. The latter occupied him first as it was at hand. Groping for the belt, Joshua found it and hurriedly searched for a place to secure the fortune. Joshua picked up a small fireplace shovel from nearby a smouldering fire in the hearth and lifted the burning log. He slipped the linen cloth containing the gems into the fire. The cloth burst into flames and petered out but the gemstones and coins were concealed under the hot coals at the back.

He was just about to go to Maria's room when he heard heavy footsteps outside his door. Joshua immediately brought up his pistol to cover the door, which burst open to reveal a uniformed soldier pointing his rifle directly at him. Behind him were two other uniformed soldiers. He was cornered with little chance of fighting his way out.

Realising that he was outnumbered and wouldn't be able to shoot all three men before one of them was able to kill him, he deftly slid his revolver under the bed and the three men fell on him with their rifle butts pounding Joshua into the floor.

Joshua covered his head until the rain of rifle butts ceased when a fourth man entered the room, barking a command in German. Joshua was pulled roughly to his feet. The fourth man was obviously a high-ranking German officer Joshua ascertained from the insignia on his smart uniform. He shouted something in German while the other soldiers made a messy search of the room in the semi-dark, upturning the bed and pulling out drawers spilling the contents on the floor.

Joshua stood still, nursing his jaw where a rifle butt had clipped. His revolver had not been discovered and none of the searchers took any notice of the glow from the fireplace.

'I don't speak German,' he said, rubbing his jaw.

The officer frowned. 'I speak English,' he said. 'Who the devil are you?'

Joshua sized up the square-faced officer standing before him. He was about Joshua's age and seemed to be an intelligent man.

'I am Sergeant Joshua Larkin, formerly of the British army fighting in Russia,' Joshua replied, deciding that telling the truth was the best option, considering the overwhelming edge the Germans had. 'I am attempting to make my way back to England. I missed the boat at Archangel.'

The German officer's expression softened slightly. 'You do not have an English accent,' he said.

'I am an Australian by birth,' Joshua replied. 'I volunteered to fight the Bolshies with the British army and prior to that I was an Australian officer – a captain – in the Western Front campaign.'

'I am Major von Fettermann, at your service,' the German officer said, bringing his heels together. 'I do not know why you would be in Hamburg, Sergeant Larkin.'

'I and the Russian lady travelling with me availed ourselves of the services of Jan Novak to fly us out of Russia. If you want to know I am probably thought of as a deserter by the English. A bit of a mix-up where I was cut off from my regiment near Archangel.'

'You will come with us, Sergeant Larkin, until I sort out your story. I warn you – do not attempt to lie to me.'

Joshua allowed himself to be escorted to another room where Maria and Helga huddled together in their night-dresses under armed guard. Jan appeared to have suffered badly from a beating and was being stood over by more German troops. In the light of the living room Joshua could see that the soldiers wore the armband of the Freikorps.

Maria stared fearfully at Joshua who attempted a crooked smile to reassure her. As he was marched past he whispered one word in French, 'Fireplace.' He hoped that she would understand its significance.

Jan was forced to his feet and prodded with rifles to accompany Joshua out of the villa to a flat-bed truck waiting outside. They clambered onto the tray on the command of their captors and sat down with their backs against the cabin. The captors quickly scrambled aboard and the officer climbed into the cabin. Within minutes the truck had puttered away from the house and Joshua could feel the beating he had taken almost overwhelm him.

'What the hell is going on?' he whispered from the side of his mouth.

'I have trouble with Freikorps tax,' Jan groaned quietly. 'Major von Fettermann my contact.'

Joshua shook his head. If this is how Jan's contact treated them what would a complete stranger do?

Very soon they arrived at a cobblestoned square adjoining a large three-storeyed building. Lights shone on all floors and Joshua had a very bad feeling in the pit of his stomach. A miracle would be required for him to emerge into the square alive once they were taken through the doors.

The truck came to a stop and orders were shouted in German for them to dismount. Jan and Joshua climbed down from the tray and were escorted into the building under guard. Neither man spoke. The German's mood was not worth the trouble of a beating to test.

The interior of the building confirmed Joshua's apprehension. It was manned by uniformed men wearing Freikorps armbands. They sat behind desks shuffling papers or stood around maps. The place had the feeling of a military headquarters and both prisoners were ushered through to rooms at the end of a long corridor that smelled of wax.

Joshua was separated from Jan and pushed into an office. Still in his long underwear Joshua was feeling the cold and shivered when he took a chair in the sparsely furnished room. He had not been alone for long when the door opened and the officer who had identified himself as Major von Fettermann entered and sat behind the desk.

'Can I get you anything, Sergeant Larkin?' von Fettermann asked politely, setting Joshua slightly more at ease.

'I wouldn't mind a smoke right now,' Joshua replied.

The Freikorps officer pushed a packet of English cigarettes across the desk to him. Joshua took one and von Fettermann lit it for him. 'And something to keep me warm.'

'I can arrange a blanket for you,' the officer said, lighting

331

a cigarette himself and blowing smoke into the cold air. 'Strangely, the Pole has corroborated your story about who you are and why you are in his company. If you are a deserter from the British army it is no concern to us but I will still verify who you are before I can release you. You may be a Bolshevik agitator returning to England from Russia and if so I am sure that our English colleagues would like to know about your presence in Hamburg. Now that the war is over we are friends once again.'

Joshua detected a note of sarcasm in the last few words. He had seen the starving children in the streets and doubted that there was any love for the British in this part of Europe.

'If I may ask,' Joshua said. 'Why have you brought us here?'

'Your Polish friend owes what you might call a lot of back taxes for us providing him bed and board in our country,' von Fettermann answered. 'He was supposed to report to me as soon as he returned from Russia but I did not know he was back until a friendly little bird I have planted at the airfield informed me. So, I thought it wise to visit Herr Novak and ask him in person why he was so reticent to see me.'

'So, it's all about money,' Joshua said, breathing a slight sigh of relief.

'Not for you if the English inform me that you are a Bolshevik agitator,' von Fettermann responded mildly. 'You will be executed if that is so.'

In the brighter light of the office Joshua noticed that the German officer was missing two fingers on his left hand. 'Where did that happen?' he asked.

Von Fettermann looked down at his hand. 'A place called Mont St Quentin,' he said.

'I commanded a company at Mont St Quentin,' Joshua

replied, surprised at finding himself in the company of a man from the other side in that terrible battle for the heights. 'It was a bad time for us both. I copped shrapnel in the guts on the hill.'

Von Fettermann suddenly displayed an expression of interest in his prisoner and Joshua realised that two former enemies had found common ground in a way only those who had spent time in hell could understand.

'Ah, my friend,' the German said. 'I hope for both our sakes that you are not a Bolshevik agitator. I would regret executing a man who has known the nearness of death on that cursed piece of ground.'

Joshua noticed that the attitude towards him seemed to have changed after the major left the room and returned with a guard to escort him to a dank cell in the basement. He was still a prisoner but was not being mistreated. He was ushered into a cell with Jan who clearly was not so well respected given the additional bruises and cuts he had sustained since arriving at the Freikorps HQ.

Joshua sat down next to Jan, whose eyes were almost closed from the swelling to his face. Under the current circumstances there was little he could do for either of them but Joshua quietly prayed that Maria might find a way. Now their roles had been reversed, and she would have to be the protector.

THIRTY-THREE

Valley View
Present day

The body lay face down, the legs still in the creek. Morgan was no longer alone protecting the scene as Ken Barber and a dozen police from Hume City had joined him where the water ran over the smooth river stones that served as a base for the dirt road leading into a paddock. Already the crime scene specialists were going about their work, preserving any possible evidence and documenting the immediate area around the water-logged corpse.

Ken Barber stood back from the scene with Morgan. He lit a cigarette and exhaled grey smoke into the sultry late morning air.

'What's the bet this is our missing Pom,' he said. 'The wallet he had on him seems to confirm that he is one Daniel Kildare.'

Morgan gazed up the swiftly running creek to the heavily timbered hills beyond.

'He could have been killed further upstream,' he suggested. 'The creek is pretty deep and wide up to the crossing.'

'Looks like a gunshot entry to the back of the head,' a police officer bending over the body called to Ken, who acknowledged the information with a wave of his hand.

'What calibre?' Ken called back.

The crime scene examiner stared at the wound he had found when he spread the hair. 'Maybe a .22 or .32. It looks like the slug will still be in his head. We should be able to recover it at the autopsy,' he replied with the knowledge of a man who knew his firearms.

'Well, a shot to the back of the head appears to rule out suicide or even an accident to me,' Ken said. 'You got anyone in mind for this?'

Morgan bit his bottom lip, contemplating the little pieces he was putting together.

'He was in the frame for the museum break-in and I have since learned that he was in a relationship with a woman I interviewed a short while ago. The one whose name I gave you, Sarah Sakharov. She is still back in town staying at the Top End pub. She would have to be a good place to start asking questions.'

'We will do that,' Barber nodded. 'See what she has to say about her former boyfriend. I have to say that all this seems to be pointing to a link with your Ms Dawson.'

'Why do you say that?' Morgan asked.

'Nothing I can put a finger on right now,' Barber said. 'Just an old copper's gut feeling about all the strange things happening around your beat since we uncovered those two bodies in her backyard.'

Although Morgan agreed with his superior officer he did not comment on his observation. It was infuriating that the fragments floated around in his head without any glue to tie them together: Monique's sabotaged car, the museum break-in, Russian and English suspects – at least in his opinion, and now a murdered man floating in the creek a mere five kilometres from Valley View.

The gathering clouds drifting in from the west promised a violent storm later in the afternoon. Sweat dripped from Morgan's brow and he thought about a cold drink. He also thought about calling the number in the UK to inform the man who had identified himself as Smithers that Kildare was most probably the dead man they had found but chose not to until the dead man's identity was properly established.

'If you don't need me here anymore I will head back to town,' Morgan said. 'Maybe see you later.'

Ken nodded and Morgan walked back to his vehicle. As far as he knew, this was Monique's last day in Valley View before taking time off to go to Sydney and he had a desire to see her before she left. At least he could disguise his visit as a professional one to ensure that she was okay, he thought.

Morgan drove to the old Larkin house and found Monique at home. But she was not alone. Parked in the driveway was the hire car Morgan recognised as that of Sarah Sakharov. He reached the front door very quickly. The sudden appearance of the beautiful English woman's car at Monique's house alarmed him. Sarah was, after all, a person of interest in the investigation of Kildare's death and it was police procedure to look first at those closest to the deceased; the majority of homicides were committed by someone who knew their victim. Random killings were rare.

Morgan rapped on the door and when Monique opened it Sarah was standing beside her.

'Hello, Morgan,' Monique greeted. 'Would you like to join us for a coffee?'

'Er, that would be nice,' Morgan answered, stepping through the door.

'Well, I should be going,' Sarah said to Monique, sounding annoyed. 'We will catch up later.'

Before Morgan could react Sarah brushed past him and walked out the door.

'Miss Sakharov,' Morgan called after her. 'Where are you off to?'

Sarah stopped with the keys of her car in hand. 'Why?' she asked.

'It's just that a matter has come up we need to speak to you about.'

'You know where I am staying,' Sarah replied, turning to continue towards her car. 'You can find me there.'

'What is going on?' Monique asked.

Morgan turned to her. 'Nothing much,' he lied. 'We just want to ask Ms Sakharov about a missing person. Why was she here?'

'Do you want a coffee or would you rather interrogate me?' Monique asked, a slight smile on her face. 'If you like you can tie me up.'

Morgan burst into a smile at the mischievous expression on her face. 'Sorry,' he apologised. 'I kind of worry about you.'

'In your duties as a police officer?' Monique asked.

'Yeah,' Morgan replied. 'There seem to be things happening around town that don't add up but also appear to have a link to the bodies we uncovered in your backyard. I know you may think that I am crazy but why was Sarah here?'

'If you must know,' Monique said, turning to walk

to the kitchen, 'Sarah was just clarifying a few facts for her story about my possible descendancy from Princess Maria.'

'What did you tell her?'

'I gave her a copy of my family tree back to 1920 which shows that my great-grandfather and grandmother were Charles and Mary Dawson from the UK – not Joshua and Maria Larkin,' Monique answered.

'So how is it that this place could be in your family name back then if it belonged to Joshua Larkin?' Morgan asked.

Monique took a breath. Either she had an answer or was confused. 'When I travelled to the UK I went in search of the records for my great-grandparents,' she said. 'From what I had been told by my parents they came from London – except I did not find anything in the archives about them. I was told that any records concerning them may have been destroyed during World War Two when London was bombed in the blitz.'

Morgan sat down at the table, accepting a mug of coffee. 'I can't see how this place could be legally in your family unless your grandparents and parents could prove title back to Joshua Larkin.'

'Maybe he sold the title to my great-grandparents when they came to Australia,' Monique offered, sitting down in the opposite chair.

Morgan sipped his coffee. 'You know, the DNA test you had could prove if there is a link or not between you and Princess Maria. I read somewhere that the Russians who found the burial pit of the Czar and his family used DNA from Prince Philip – the Queen's husband – to establish that the bodies were those of the Russian royal family. Maybe the same DNA profile might help you.'

'I am still waiting for the results,' Monique said.

'When do you get them?' Morgan asked.

'Anytime now,' she answered. 'I don't know how, but Sarah knew about my DNA test. I guess as a journalist she has access to such things.'

Morgan did not comment. He somehow doubted that this would be the case but the possibility worried him.

'When do you leave for Sydney?' Morgan asked, changing the subject.

'Tomorrow morning,' Monique replied. 'I am just packing a few items as I intend to return when I feel that enough time has elapsed. I still have this eerie feeling that there are ghosts haunting this place. That incident with my car has me a bit spooked too. We both know that someone is trying to kill me.'

Morgan agreed but he did not want to frighten her further. Her leaving was a good idea although he would miss her. He dared not fully admit to himself that he was very attracted to her, the most beautiful woman that he had ever met. After all, he was sure she could do better than a country cop who still suffered nightmares from his time on active service with the SAS.

'Well, I had better get back to the station. We have had a bit of an incident just the other side of town,' Morgan said, placing his half-finished mug of coffee on the low magazine-covered table between them. 'A body was found in the creek at Paddy's Crossing.'

'That's terrible! Is it anyone that I might know?' Monique asked with a worried expression etching her face.

'Doubt it,' Morgan answered. 'Probably just some tourist who fell in the river and drowned,' Morgan lied to avoid alarming her on her last night in town; he could see that she was on edge already. Maybe the media would not have all the details by nightfall and Monique would be far away in Sydney before the full story of a murder was revealed. He hoped so.

Driving away Morgan was still puzzled by the missing link in Monique's family tree. Was it possible that Charles and Mary Dawson were in fact Joshua and Maria Larkin? They had good reason to adopt another identity given what he had read in the Larkin journal.

'Bastard!' Morgan swore, pounding the dashboard of the police vehicle. None of the sinister events happening in Valley View would have occurred had David Greer not dug up the first body weeks earlier. He felt that he was no closer to solving any of the crimes although two names kept cropping up in his mind – both Russian.

When Morgan reached Valley View a few minutes later he saw Ken Barber and an offsider, a young, plain-clothes policeman by the name of Mark Branson, standing by their vehicle in front of his station. Even at a distance he could see the irritated expression on Barber's face.

'Where have you been?' he asked as Morgan stepped out of his vehicle. 'I was calling you on your radio and mobile – you didn't answer.'

Morgan grabbed his phone and realised that he had forgotten to charge it. The reading indicated no power and he had also failed to go off the air at Monique's place. Seeing Sarah Sakharov had distracted him.

'Sorry, Ken,' he apologised. 'I stuffed up – the mobile's flat.'

'No bloody worries,' Ken growled. 'We have been up to the top pub and the publican there tells us that Sakharov checked out this morning. No forwarding address.'

'I saw her only about half an hour ago,' Morgan responded with a frown. 'She was out at the Larkin house.'

'Well, she doesn't appear to be anywhere in town right now,' Ken said. 'And she was our best bet. Any ideas?'

Morgan took a deep breath. 'I have the particulars of her hire car,' he said. 'Maybe we could broadcast a call to the Highway Patrol to pick her up.'

'You know there are four directions she can go from here in the half hour since you saw her,' the detective cautioned. 'Besides, we don't have anything on her other than a suspicion, certainly no evidence to back us up. I have a feeling that Miss Sakharov will be out of the country before we get the body to the morgue – if she has had anything to do with the murder.'

Morgan knew that Ken was right. She was a person of interest – nothing more.

'There is this Russian,' Morgan offered, hoping to placate the angry detective. 'A bloke by the name of Olev. He might be worth talking to.'

'A bloody Russian!' Ken snorted. 'What is this, the Cold War all over again just because a Pom has been murdered. Jesus, McLean, you need to get out of this town, it's making you paranoid.'

'At least it's something for the running sheet,' Morgan said. 'I can't see any of my locals shooting Kildare. Maybe the Russian didn't like the soccer team that Kildare supported. You know how passionate the Poms and Europeans are about their football.'

'I know you are trying to be funny,' Ken chuckled, despite himself. 'We will give this Russian a go and see what shakes out. At least we can justify some overtime to catch up on a cold beer and counter meal while we are out here.'

Satisfied that he had something to start on, Ken Barber

341

turned to the plain-clothes officer with him and threw him the car keys.

'You drive, Mark,' he said.

Morgan watched them drive away and looked up at the sky. The tall, billowing thunderheads rolling in from the west were an impressive sight. They were definitely due for a fierce storm before the day was through. At least the rain would cool the air.

Petrov Batkin was angry. Sarah was not answering her mobile phone and had not returned the .32 semiautomatic pistol he had loaned her. Not that the loss of the gun was of great consequence as he knew the two men due to meet him that evening would be armed. The weapons were not to be used to harm Monique Dawson however but simply were a means to deter anyone who might get in the way. His small hotel room was humid even with the clattering, overhead fan blowing air over him as he thought about Morgan. He realised that if for some reason McLean might happen to be around at the time they abducted the girl they would need some firepower to stop him. The local policeman was no ordinary country cop.

Where was Sarah, he asked himself again just as he heard the knock at his door.

'Who is it?' he asked, rising from the bed where he lay under the cooling breeze of the overhead fan.

'Police,' the deep voice answered. 'We would like to have a talk with you, Mr Olev.'

Petrov Batkin felt a chill and not from the cooling breeze of the fan.

'I will open door,' he replied. 'Please to wait.'

He had given himself a few precious seconds to consider

342

his options. Why had the police suddenly appeared at his room? He knew that the voice was not that of the local policeman. The hotel verandah was on the other side of his window and an escape route. Unarmed, he would be forced to kill with his hands, which he knew he could do very efficiently. But he did not know how many police were on the other side of the door and what he was up against. He opened the door to stare into the faces of Ken Barber and Mark Branson.

'What do you want?' he asked in a surly tone.

'We would just like to ask you some questions about Daniel Kildare,' Ken said, shoving his big foot inside the door so that it could not be closed against him.

'Never heard of man,' Batkin answered, attempting to close the door. 'You go away.'

Ken forced the door back and pushed himself into the room. His action and appearance reminded Petrov Batkin of an old-time KGB man.

'Mr Olev,' Ken said mildly, scanning the small room. 'I would almost think that you have something to hide considering your less than cooperative manner towards New South Wales finest. I only want to clear up a few matters and then we will leave you alone.'

'I am Russian citizen who come on visa to your country,' Batkin retorted. 'I make complaint to Russian embassy about you.'

Ken sat on the bed.

'Now, once again, do you know of a Mr Daniel Kildare?'

'I tell you, Mr policeman, I not know this man. Who is he?' Batkin said, standing and walking to the open window to the verandah.

'Do you have some form of identification?' Ken asked.

Batkin was not sure of the laws of Australia and felt that they had a right to demand identification as occurred in his own country. He knew that he did not have to cooperate but felt that he should produce his passport at the least. He walked over to a small vinyl suit bag and pulled it out. It was so well forged that he doubted the police officer would know that it was a false passport.

Ken took the passport and examined the photo against Batkin – they matched. He scribbled down any particulars that he could recognise from the Cyrillic writing before handing it back. 'Well, thank you for your assistance, Mr Olev. I apologise for the inconvenience that we may have caused you and hope that you have a pleasant stay in Valley View.'

With his parting words, Ken nodded to the young plain-clothes officer. They closed the door behind them as they left and headed for the stairs.

'We can write him off,' Branson said. 'He's not going to talk about anything and I can't see how he would know the dead Pom.'

'On the contrary,' Ken said. 'That Ruskie bastard knows something. Young Morgan was right.'

'How do you come to that conclusion?' the young trainee detective asked, glancing at Ken.

'Because while I was talking to him he was eyeing off a way out of the room,' Ken Barber replied. 'Olev is as guilty as sin about something and was planning on doing a runner if I came on too heavy with the questions. It's time to do a quick check on our Mr Olev with the customs people. I have a gut feeling he's Russian mafia, and if so, what's he doing in sleepy little Valley View?'

Mark Branson did not doubt the older man. Ken Barber was a legend among his peers and idolised by those who had the opportunity to work with him. The trainee detective was learning something about professional observation from an experienced investigator. Gut feeling was something he would have to develop himself.

THIRTY-FOUR

Hamburg, Germany
October 1919

A week had passed for Joshua and Jan in their cell. They had not been mistreated and even allowed visits from Helga and Maria who was able to bring Joshua a set of clothing on the first day. Both men were released from their cell to meet with the women in the spacious foyer of the Freikorps HQ. They were seated at a table, free of restraints, but also realised that any attempt to escape would not get them very far.

On the first visit Maria leaned forward and whispered to Joshua in French that she had found the gems and coins. She also told him that Helga had been of great assistance in putting her in contact with an American businessman visiting Hamburg who had paid her fairly for some of the gems in English sterling.

In the evenings Joshua was fetched to Major von Fettermann's office to dine with him. The Freikorps officer would discuss with Joshua their respective war experiences and a bond formed between the two former enemies despite their present relationship of gaoler and prisoner.

'I hope that I will be able to release you soon,' von Fettermann said over a game of chess one evening. 'You are an honourable soldier – even if the British might consider you a deserter. The British did not treat their colonial allies very well in the Great War.'

Joshua had to agree. 'What are you going to do with Jan Novak?' he asked casually, pushing his knight into a position to counter his opponent's bishop.

'The Pole will be released as soon as his woman raises the money that he owes us,' von Fettermann replied, pondering Joshua's move. 'I suspect that she will have it all within the next few days. The Pole and his aeroplane are too valuable for us to waste. He is what you would call a pirate; he knows no real loyalty to anything other than making his fortune in these times of misery. But to that end he is a very enterprising man and provides us with a good income to further our aims.'

'What are your aims?' Joshua asked, knowing that their friendship had progressed enough for him to be so bold.

'We wait for a leader who will throw off the outrageous shackles the Versailles Treaty has imposed on us. Our people starve to death and we are held responsible for the disaster of the past war. We had no choice when the weak Austrians went to war with Serbia. It is the decadent French who wish to crush us. They know that we are a morally stronger people and with the right leader one day we will crush them.'

Joshua felt a chill at the German major's pronouncement. It was as if he was planning for another war already. But how could anyone want another war when the last one had proved so destructive?

347

When the game was over and von Fettermann had won he poured two tumblers of fiery schnapps and raised his glass. 'A toast that we never face each other on the battle-field again,' he said.

Joshua returned the salute and soon afterwards was escorted back to the cell where Jan sat in a corner on his thin palliasse of straw.

'You have good time with Karl?' Jan asked sarcastically.

'I found out that he is going to let you go free as soon as Helga raises the money to pay him,' Joshua answered, ignoring the Pole's bitterness. 'You have more chance of walking out the front door than I do.'

'What you mean?' Jan asked.

'The major is waiting on an answer from the English government as to whether I am a Bolshie agitator before they free me.'

'You not Bolshevik?' Jan asked suspiciously.

'I would have more chance of getting out of here alive if I were,' Joshua replied. 'I have a feeling that my name is going to crop up in the wrong places.' He did not elaborate but prayed silently that it was not even now being bandied about among intelligence circles of London. He reassured himself that it was highly unlikely that Major Locksley had survived when he left him in the cabin, and at worst he would be listed as a possible deserter.

Major Karl von Fettermann stared at the report on his desk. It bore the letterhead of the British government and was a reply to his own report mailed a week earlier. Von Fetter-mann stood and strode to the single window of his office which had a view of an alley behind the HQ. The expression on his face reflected his concern. The former Australian army officer – and now a British army deserter – was recorded as a dangerous Bolshevik agitator travelling in the company of a Russian woman known also to be a highly placed Bolshevik spy. The Polish aviator's woman had promised to pay the owed funds that day and he would be free to leave, but this letter from London was as good as a death warrant for Joshua Larkin and the pretty Russian girl who visited him each day. Despite any personal feelings von Fettermann was an officer in the German Weimar Republic and therefore must obey orders. He walked to the door of his office and called down the corridor, 'Corporal Heinz, bring the prisoner Larkin to me.'

The German corporal hurried away to fetch Joshua.

Joshua was not offered a chair when he was brought to von Fettermann's office and felt some apprehension at this change in his captor's mood.

'Leave us, corporal,' von Fettermann said to the guard.

Joshua remained standing as the corporal departed.

'Sergeant Larkin,' von Fettermann snapped. 'You lied to me.'

'Lied?' Joshua queried, confused by the question but also wary of any forthcoming answer.

'You informed me that you were not a Bolshevik agitator and yet the letter I have before me says that you are – and that the Russian girl with you is a spy for the Bolsheviks.'

'That's not true!' Joshua exclaimed. 'I am not a bloody Bolshie. The British are lying and I think I know why.'

'It will not matter,' von Fettermann sighed. 'The British are sending an officer, a Major Locksley to handle the matter for them. They have requested that we immediately arrest the Russian girl who visits you.'

'Locksley!' Joshua gasped. 'I know him.'

'How is this?' von Fettermann asked.

Joshua badly wanted to sit down and gather his thoughts. He knew what he said in the next few minutes would either sentence him to death or be a possible way out. It all depended on the German officer's loyalties.

'Major Locksley was my commanding officer on a mission I was assigned by the British,' Joshua said in a tired voice. 'Our mission was to find a person.'

'You should take a seat, Sergeant Larkin,' von Fettermann said sympathetically, sensing that the Australian was speaking the truth.

Joshua accepted gratefully and continued. 'There were three of us but by the time Major Locksley and I found the person he sought we had lost one member of the team to the Bolsheviks. The person we sought is the Russian woman who accompanies me now. But when we found her Locksley had orders to kill her.'

'Because she is a highly placed Bolshevik operative,' von Fettermann interjected.

'No, because she is the Princess Maria of the Romanov family,' Joshua said. 'The last survivor of the Russian throne.'

The expression on the Freikorps officer's face spoke of his shock and disbelief.

'For reasons beyond my comprehension,' Joshua continued, 'it seems that there are some in the British government who would like to see the princess dead rather than reach English shores. But we both know how important it is that she lives to reclaim the throne of Russia. Alive, she is a symbol of resistance to the Bolshies' ambitions to seize Russia and eventually the rest of the world. Your own organisation is devoted to crushing the Bolshies in Germany. Major Locksley is the enemy here, not Maria and I.'

'If you could prove what you say is true then I would not

350

hesitate in protecting the princess,' von Fettermann said. 'But the British major will be here within a few hours and I have had the Russian girl arrested already. I am sorry, my friend. It is out of my hands now. Corporal Heinz, take the prisoner back to his cell.'

'She has identity papers to prove who she is,' Joshua said.

The German officer shook his head. 'I am sorry, my friend,' von Fettermann replied sadly. 'Forged identity papers are easily obtained on the blackmarket. You would need more.'

Joshua rose from his chair and waited for the German NCO to enter the room and escort him back to the cell. His mind was in turmoil as he thought about Maria being arrested. They had been so close to freedom and he had let her down. He did not care about his own life but he did care about Maria.

When the guard opened the door to the cell that had been his home for over a week Joshua noticed that Jan was no longer present. The money had been raised and he was free to continue his activities leaving Joshua alone.

In the late afternoon Corporal Heinz came for him again. This time Joshua's hands were shackled in front of him and he was led once more to von Fettermann's office. When the door was opened Joshua was shocked to see James Locksley standing with von Fettermann by the window. He was wearing civilian clothing and had not changed much from when Joshua had last seen him in the cabin in Russia.

'Sir,' Joshua said, acknowledging Locksley's position. 'I see that you were able to get out of Russia.'

'I was in France when I received news from London that you were being held in Germany, Sergeant Larkin,' Locksley said in a cold tone. 'It appears that you have taken up

subversive activities dangerous to His Majesty's government. I believe the girl is still with you and that Major von
Fettermann is now holding her. I am sure that the British
government is beholden to the Freikorps for the fine job they
have done in apprehending you and the Russian bitch.'

'At least grant her the honour that she warrants, sir,'
Joshua snarled. 'At least refer to her as the Princess Maria.'

Locksley turned away from Joshua, ignoring his retort,
to address the German major. 'I am grateful for you and
your men delivering Sergeant Larkin and the Russian girl
into my custody, Major von Fettermann,' he said. 'I am sure
that my report will sit well in London with my superiors.'

'Will your superiors in London recommend that the
Allies lift their murderous blockade against us?' von Fettermann asked.

'This matter has nothing to do with the deal your government has with mine,' Locksley answered. 'Please arrange
for your men to escort Sergeant Larkin and the Russian girl
to a ship we have commandeered for their transport back to
England.'

'I don't think so,' von Fettermann replied. 'Sergeant Larkin is under German jurisdiction, Major Locksley, and will
remain so. There is little else you or your government can
do about that.'

Joshua was stunned at the audacity of the Freikorps
officer. The tension between him and Locksley had been
rising but now he was defying outright the might of the
conquering allies.

'I will be protesting to our prime minister,' Locksley
spluttered, red-faced and angry, realising how helpless he
was under the current circumstances. He knew that he
would have to retreat and gather diplomatic forces to grind
the German into the ground.

'If there is nothing else, Major Locksley,' von Fetter-mann said. 'I would bid you a good day.'

Locksley glared at Joshua and the German officer before turning on his heel and marching out of the office. Joshua stood silently and after a few moments Karl von Fettermann spoke.

'I fear that you will not have heard the last from your major,' he said.

'I do not know how to thank you,' Joshua said as von Fettermann released the shackles from his wrists.

'Do not thank me,' von Fettermann replied. 'You can thank the combined efforts of the Pole and his woman. They raised a little extra to pay for what we might call your bed and board while a guest of the Freikorps.'

Although the German officer had offered this as the reason for his unexpected release, Joshua sensed that the bond that had formed between the two former enemies had also played its part in his freedom.

'The girl is waiting for you outside,' von Fettermann said, extending his hand. 'So is the Pole. I would suggest that you both make yourselves scarce in Germany. The British occupy us and will have the means to hunt you down. On a second attempt you may not be so lucky.'

Joshua accepted the hand. 'Thank you, Major von Fetter-mann. You have done for the cause of fighting Bolshevism more than you can appreciate right now.'

'What will you do now?' von Fettermann asked.

'Like you suggested, get out of Germany,' Joshua answered.

'It would be dangerous attempting to escape by a ship,' the Freikorps officer said. 'Maybe better to travel overland as our occupiers have the ports blocked.'

Or fly, Joshua thought, wondering how much Maria had been able to make on the sale of the gems.

Minutes later Joshua stepped out onto the street to be greeted by Maria, Jan and Helga. Joshua hugged Maria to him and whispered his gratitude for her efforts to free him.

'Having you around causes me much grief,' Jan said, slapping Joshua on the back as they walked away from the Freikorps HQ. 'Yet I think that I risk all again – for a little more money. But we will discuss that later. You and Maria have a flight to catch. The Gotha awaits us. She is eager to soar in the skies.'

Von Fettermann stood in the foyer of the HQ with his hands clasped behind his back gazing at the group on the street. It had not only been a matter of a well-placed bribe that had convinced him to free Joshua and Maria but also his hatred for the English. Thousands of his fellow Germans had starved to death and now the British had the arrogance to demand that he dance to their tune. Resisting British intelligence in their efforts to take custody of the Australian soldier and the Russian girl was just one small victory against the occupiers of his country. He was not convinced that the Russian girl was the Princess Maria but that did not matter. What mattered was the look of frustration and rage on the British major's face when he was denied his prisoners. It was worth the rift his organisation might have with the British fighting the spread of Bolshevism. Smirking, von Fettermann turned on his heel and returned to his office.

Locksley stood by the door of the British army staff car that had conveyed him to the Freikorps HQ.

'Sir, is that the two we came for?' A smartly dressed

young British lieutenant asked from inside the vehicle, observing the happy reunion on the street.

'Yes,' Locksley snapped, still upset about his humiliating ousting by the German officer.

'Do we proceed and arrest them now, sir?' the lieutenant asked eagerly.

The British major scanned the street where armed Freikorps soldiers were watching him intently in the event of any attempt to intervene in the safe passage of the released prisoners. Locksley sighed, opened the car door and slumped inside next to his fellow officer. 'I am afraid that we will have to allow the guilty to elude us for the moment,' he said. 'I doubt that our PM will want to give the Hun the excuse to start a second Great War. Drive on.'

But as far as Locksley was concerned the matter was far from finished. He was determined to settle it once and for all with the elimination of the Australian sergeant and the Russian princess regardless of what it would take.

THIRTY-FIVE

Valley View
Present day

Petrov Batkin was both angry and confused. Why had the police visited him to ask about the British agent, and why had not Sarah answered his calls on her mobile phone? He sensed something was wrong and was vastly relieved that the police had not searched his room and luggage or they might have found the .32 pistol in his possession. How it had been returned was a mystery to him. Somehow Sarah must have entered his room when he was out and concealed the pistol in his luggage. This made him very nervous as the police had been asking him questions about Kildare and Sarah had requested his gun to execute him. He well knew that if they had found the pistol they might have linked him to Kildare's death. He had also gathered from the police visit that Sarah must have taken care of Kildare before returning the pistol. Why else would the police be questioning strangers in town?

Batkin was feeling more than the humid heat of the day in his hotel room but could not put his finger on the cause of his anxiety. He was counting the hours until his two contacts arrived from Sydney to execute their plan to abduct Monique Dawson and smuggle her out of the country. Convincing her of declaring her heritage would come later once she had the opportunity to consider her importance to the cause of Russia resuming its rightful place as the premier nation among the world's superpowers.

Outside the hotel the gathering clouds rose as columns, drifting from the west across the green fields and low hills of Valley View as Batkin finalised his packing to leave the town forever.

Sarah Locksley sat in her hire car surveying the isolated farm house north of Valley View. It was like so many others with old farm machinery rusting in the yards around the house and the wooden walls badly in need of a coat of paint. She had spent her time making trips around the district to locate a base for her ultimate mission. She knew from a visit a week earlier posing as a lost tourist that this house was occupied by a man in his eighties. He was a recluse who had little contact with those in town or his neighbours on the other side of the rolling hills surrounding his farm. One of the best features of the site was the dirt track that led out of the farm onto roads connecting with the highway that would eventually lead her north to the state of Queensland. She knew avoiding the obvious highways would be important when her mission was completed. From the little contact she'd had with the local police officer she sensed him to be a very intelligent man. Damn him to hell, she fumed. Had he not arrived at Monique's house when he did the descendant of Princess Maria would have been dead by now.

Monique had spoken in glowing terms of Morgan McLean and Sarah suspected that she was possibly attracted to him. She hoped that she would not have to fall back on her contingency plan but Kildare's body had been discovered twenty-four hours too soon and the local cop had forced her to act earlier than she had originally planned.

Sarah stepped from the car and walked towards the battered screen door which opened to reveal the farmer. He stepped onto the small verandah and peered at his visitor.

'It's you, miss,' he said, recognising Sarah. 'Are you lost again?'

'Sort of,' Sarah beamed. 'I was wondering if I could ask a huge favour. I need to call my hotel to tell them that I will be late for dinner.'

The old man was still chewing the remnants of a sandwich and it was obvious from the expression on his face that he was not immune to the beauty of the young English woman walking towards him.

'You can call the pub,' he said, holding the door open for Sarah to pass. 'Phone's in the hallway.'

Sarah stepped up onto the verandah and entered the house. The man was very neat for one living alone; the simple house was clean and orderly. A magazine lay open on the Formica table and a few dishes were stacked in the kitchen sink. Half a sandwich lay on a plate beside a mug of tea on the table top.

The farmer followed her inside, gesturing to the telephone on a small table in a hallway leading from the kitchen. Old-style photos of a young woman and more modern framed photos of a young man wearing a slouch hat hung on the walls.

'Is that you?' Sarah asked, pointing to one.

'My son,' the old man said sadly. 'He was killed in Vietnam a long time ago. His mother never got over the loss and died a year later. I did my service with the army in the Middle East and New Guinea during the last big one.'

Sarah felt no empathy for the man's pain, knowing that she had to remain aloof in order to carry out her mission. 'I am sorry for your loss,' she lied, glancing around the house to ensure that they were alone. 'I will make the call and get out of your way.'

'No problem, miss,' he said. 'I will leave you to your privacy.' He shuffled from the hallway to return to the kitchen and his half-eaten sandwich.

Sarah picked up the phone and listened to the dial tone. She began to speak as if having a conversation, leaning around the corner to see that the farmer had sat down at the table. His back was to her and he was sipping his tea. With a yank of the telephone cord, she cautiously crept up behind him. Twisting the tough cord around his neck she used all her strength to draw it tight.

The farmer instinctively reached up to loosen the cord that was throttling him. He kicked away from the table, causing Sarah to fall to the floor with him. But she did not let her grip falter as the dying man thrashed about on the kitchen floor, attempting to free himself. Sarah rolled him onto his stomach and dropped her knee into his back, using her weight to pull harder on the cord. She held the grip as the old man's struggle grew weaker and finally his throes ceased. Sarah felt the carotid artery to check for a pulse but did not find one.

She rose stiffly. There would be no witnesses to her temporary hide-out and all that she needed to do now was drive the car into the big machinery shed she had observed near the house. It would not be seen from the air should the police mount an aerial search of the district. Not that they should, she mused, dragging the body of the dead farmer into his bedroom and laying him on his bed as if he had been sleeping. She realised that the cord had left a considerable bruise around the man's neck but at first sight it would appear that he had possibly died of a heart attack while resting. The bruises would no doubt lead to an investigation but by the time all that happened she would long gone and on her way back to the UK. From what she had gathered on her first visit, the old farmer he did not receive many visitors and it would take some time for him to be missed.

Killing was easy, Sarah thought. It had been so simple to lure the besotted Kildare out into the hills with a promise of a romantic picnic to watch the sun set. The man deserved to die, she rationalised. A good agent would never have allowed himself to be seduced in the first place. He would be no loss to MI6 and all going well the murder weapon would be found in Batkin's possession after an anonymous tip-off to the police.

Sarah parked her car in the shed. She removed the slim laptop computer from the back seat and took it inside the house, plugging it into the phone socket. At the right moment she would log on and send an email. Then it was a matter of waiting for the email from Sam Briars. By now he should have been able to hack into the DNA laboratory records and find the DNA results for Monique Dawson. In the meantime she would make a cup of tea and after that clean any surfaces of her fingerprints. A quick vacuum of the house was also on the agenda to remove any trace of her ever being there. The contents of the vacuumbag would be disposed of elsewhere. Sarah Locksley was very thorough. Batkin and MI6 had trained her well in the murky world of subversive activities.

When she clicked into her mail box sometime later it was still empty. Briars had not responded to her request for the DNA result on Monique Dawson, but she would go ahead with her deadly plan anyway.

It had not taken long for the local TV station to hear about the body at Paddy's Crossing and Morgan was not surprised to discover that they even had a brief background on the dead man. Their access to information was formidable.

'Does it appear, Senior Constable Morgan,' a pretty young local television interviewer asked, thrusting a microphone in his face on the steps of the police station, 'that Mr Kildare met with foul play?'

'I am sorry,' Morgan answered in police mode. 'I cannot make any comment on the matter until the coroner has cleared us to do so.'

'So it appears that the British tourist has been murdered,' the girl replied smugly.

'I did not say that and suggest that you get in contact with our public relations department,' Morgan replied with a frown. He looked over the shoulder of the young man holding the camera to see Ken Barber and Mark Branson drive up. 'If you don't mind, I have work to do,' Morgan said briskly, thereby concluding the uninvited interview.

'It appears that Valley View has had a spate of deaths in the last few weeks,' the interviewer said to Morgan as he brushed past her. 'Isn't that a bit unusual?'

Morgan stopped and turned to her, knowing that she was attempting to sensationalise her story. 'A traffic accident and a tourist's body do not constitute anything unusual,' he said. 'Even little towns have their days.'

'My sources inform me that the vehicle involved in the

accident had been sabotaged,' she countered. 'That constitutes murder.'

'As I said,' Morgan replied. 'talk to our PR people.' He continued walking towards Ken Barber, who stood next to his vehicle eyeing the TV crew and smoking a cigarette.

'Nice looking sheila,' he said when Morgan approached. 'Hope you didn't tell her anything.'

'Just the usual, talk to our PR people,' Morgan said. 'Somehow she knew about the sabotage of Monique Dawson's car.'

'It happens,' Ken growled. 'Some bloody member of the job leaks it to the media for a quid.'

'How did you go with Olev?' Morgan asked.

'He's got something to hide,' Ken replied. 'Might be Russian mafia and if so, what the hell is he doing in Dullsville? I'm just waiting for a check to come back on him. I've put the inquiry in the fast lane with our people in Sydney to chase up as much as they have on Comrade Olev.'

'Ken,' Mark said from inside the car. 'Just got a call that you should contact this number in Sydney on a landline.'

Ken Barber took the slip of paper from the trainee detective and glanced at the phone number. 'I'll use the phone in the station,' he said.

Ken sat down at Morgan's desk and dialled the number. His conversation seemed to be a series of grunts and monosyllabic replies as he scribbled down the information he received. He put the phone down and looked at Morgan.

'That was our Interpol liaison lady,' he said. 'Their checks with the Russian cops have nothing on Petrov Olev because Petrov Olev has been dead for a couple of years now. So whoever Mark and I spoke to at the pub is someone else. I think it is time that Comrade Olev – or whoever he is – comes clean on who he really is.'

362

Morgan experienced a sudden surge of concern. 'I think that we should find the Russian as soon as possible,' Morgan said.

'We spoke to him in his room,' Ken said. 'Let's hope he is still there.'

When they stepped out onto the verandah, Morgan glanced at his watch. It was almost 3.30 in the afternoon and the sky was now black with clouds. A gentle breeze played with the air, evaporating the sweat on Morgan's brow. Lightning flashed in the west and the green tinge to the clouds warned of hailstones. The rumble of thunder rolling around the hills reminded Morgan of his nights in the Iraqi desert with his section of SAS soldiers. For Ken, it was a reminder of the B52 strikes on distant Vietcong targets.

Morgan followed the detective's vehicle in his own and they were almost at the hotel when Branson thrust his arm out of the driver's side car window and waved him to a stop. Morgan leaped from his vehicle. Ken was holding his mobile phone to his ear. He leaned out the car window to speak. 'We just got a call from the radio room,' he said. 'They received an email from an anonymous sender to say that Olev aka Petrov Batkin is planning to kill Monique Dawson tonight, and that he is responsible for the killing of the Pom. It says that when we find this Batkin we will also find a .32 pistol in his possession that can be matched to the bullet in Kildare. It looks like our hunch was right.'

'We will need backup. This character is most probably a former Russian special forces soldier,' Morgan suggested.

Ken Barber shook his head.

'Olev, Batkin or whoever he is does not suspect that we know about his involvement in the killing of Kildare,' he said. 'I will just approach him in a manner that suggests I am on a routine inquiry. Between the three of us we should be able to handle him. Besides, it will take time to organise backup from Hume City and he might do a runner in the meantime. I'd hate to lose our one and only suspect.'

Morgan understood the rationale but also remembered that the man they were about to approach was potentially very dangerous. But the need to take him out before he could execute any plan to kill Monique over-rode Morgan's caution.

'Okay, we do it,' Morgan replied. 'But I think that we should have a contingency plan.'

Ken Barber smiled. As a former soldier he understood what Morgan was saying.

'How about we do it this way,' he said and laid out a plan to arrest their prime suspect.

The three agreed on the suggested course of action and Morgan returned to his vehicle. But as he did he felt a nagging uncertainty about the anonymous emailer. Who was that person and what reason did they have to inform on the Russian? Something did not feel right, he thought as he slid behind the wheel of his vehicle to follow the detectives to the hotel where Batkin was residing.

THIRTY-SIX

Paris, France
October 1919

The vibrancy was almost tangible even though for Joshua Paris was not an alien city. He had spent leave here after being wounded on the Western Front. Then it had been a place of morbid memories despite the gaiety it had attempted to present to the world. Now, it was truly a place where life oozed from every shop, café and broad avenue. Gone from the boulevards were the endless streams of uniformed soldiers with haunted eyes and the bloody bandages of men returning from the front. Instead, the city continued to rejoice in its rescue from German invasion with the appearance of foreigners flooding the streets in search of a good time.

At great risk, Jan Novak had flown Joshua and Maria into a former military airstrip in Belgium where he was paid off for his duties. But he was generous and used some of the money he had made from them to celebrate in a café in a little village outside Brussels. He had explained that he could not fly them any further south as the French military were still somewhat nervous about seeing a Gotha bomber in their air space.

With back-slapping and a bear-like hug he bid them goodbye when they stepped aboard a train travelling south to France. It was with some sadness that they parted as the bond of facing common dangers had become strong between Joshua and the former Polish officer.

When they had reached Paris Joshua explained to Maria that he had once known a French woman by the name of Francine Dubois in the city during the war. She had billeted him when he was recovering from his wounds. When she saw the French woman Maria realised that she need not have felt any jealousy towards her as she was old enough to be Joshua's grandmother and was very maternal towards him when they met again.

Her modest terraced house was located on the Left Bank and when she took in Joshua and Maria she had one other boarder. He was a slim young man from French Indo China who had sometimes worked as a waiter in Parisian restaurants before the Great War, but was now tied up in politics, she explained, waving her hand as if to dismiss the idea. She said that their fellow boarder was known as Nguyen Ai Quoc – Nguyen the patriot, he called himself. Leading them to their room she further explained that the young man had even attempted to present the American president, Woodrow Wilson with a document seeking freedom for the Indo Chinese people who had been under the thumb of French colonialism at the Versailles conference. 'A stupid idea,' Madame Dubois said. 'Foreigners are incapable of governing themselves. I have even told him so.'

When she opened the door to their room they could see

366

that it was clean and neat with an attic view over the city which sprawled to the river. Joshua paid Madame Dubois a month's rent in advance in English currency. She stared at the notes in her hand with some displeasure but accepted them knowing that she could get a good return on their conversion to French currency.

'We are truly free,' Maria said, gazing out the window over the roof tops of the houses on the other side of the street.

'Not in Europe,' Joshua cautioned. 'The British are not going to take rejection from the Germans very well and I have no doubt that Major Locksley is not about to give up on searching for us. I have seen what he can be like and know that he will continue his mission until he is satisfied.'

Maria turned to Joshua with a worried look and he regretted that he had alarmed her. He walked over to the window and took her in his arms. 'Maria, I love you more than any woman I have ever known before,' he said. 'So long as I am alive, I will fight to keep you safe.'

'I have known a life I could not even explain to you,' Maria said. 'For the first seventeen years of my life I could never have imagined that it would end, but from the time I was a prisoner of the Bolsheviks, I was forced to realise that it was gone forever. Then you came into my life – a man from a different world. I know that I would not be alive today if you had not appeared in that cabin in Russia. Since then we have shared so much pain and suffering together. You held me that night when I was hurting and yet knew that it was the comfort of your arms that I needed most. You did not attempt to exploit my vulnerability on that night. Joshua, I love you also with all my heart and soul and I have carried a terrible secret I must share with you now. When I tell you I doubt that you will wish to be with me anymore but my love for you compels me to share my secret.'

Joshua could hardly believe what he was hearing. Tears welled in his eyes and he held Maria against his chest so that she could not see his feelings erupt in the unmanly act of crying. No more words were needed for the moment. That he could hold her and know that she loved him as he did her was enough. Nothing that she confessed to him mattered as much as the woman in his arms.

London
October 1919

Sitting at his desk in the Secret Intelligence Service office, Mansfield Cumming pored over the reports in front of him. Hundreds of thousands of men were returning to the workforce after their service in the Great War – tough, battle-hardened veterans whose expectations of a better world and meaningful employment were not being met. Instead, unemployment, lack of social services and a government that appeared hardly grateful for their years of service in the defence of democracy comprised the reality they were faced with instead. Disgruntled, the former soldiers and their families listened to the socialist agitators, springing from the despair like mushrooms on the factory floors, in the mines and market places all over the British Isles and the threat of a revolution not unlike that which had recently occurred in Russia hung in the British air.

The British royal family's existence was increasingly under threat from the growing social discontent. How would it appear to the working classes if the King was seen to be supporting the daughter of the late Russian Czar in her claim to the throne, when Lenin and Trotsky were garnering sympathy from the disfranchised of the British Isles? The chief of the Secret Intelligence Service could not take that chance and the silencing of Princess Maria had become of vital national security.

'Major Locksley is here, sir,' the chief's secretary announced after knocking.

'Send him in,' Cumming directed.

Major Locksley stepped inside the office. He was wearing a long coat over civilian clothing and carrying a leather satchel case. Cumming gestured for him to take a seat.

'She slipped through your fingers,' Cumming said.

'The bloody Huns blatantly defied us,' Locksley growled. 'That colonial Larkin is in cahoots with her. In my opinion, sir, we should take action against the Freikorps as a lesson to them.'

'That would not be wise, considering the circumstances in Europe at the moment,' Cumming replied. 'They are a bastion against the Bolsheviks taking over Germany and we cannot allow a Germany under a Bolshevik government. Good God, France would be next and then we would be facing an aggressive system bent on tearing down everything that we hold sacred in England. No, we will maintain our covert links with the Freikorps and for now ignore this sleight against us.'

Locksley was frustrated by the chief's support of the Freikorps. He saw problems into the future with such an organisation gaining political power and toppling the struggling Weimar government. A starving, humiliated country was open to the voice of any man promising jobs and pride. Such a man could emerge from the Freikorps movement to impose a dictatorship as evil as that the Bolsheviks were attempting to put in place in Russia. But no one was really interested in the future of Europe, Locksley reflected. All people wanted in 1919 was a better life free of war and its bitter memories.

'What do we do about Princess Maria then?' Locksley asked.

'Now more than ever we need to find the Princess and silence her,' Cumming answered. 'You still have that mission, Major Locksley. Do you have any ideas?'

Locksley had spent many sleepless nights pondering the whereabouts of Larkin and Princess Maria. What would he do if he were the Australian soldier? Where would he go?

The answer was simple: he would get Maria as far from Europe as possible so as to protect her. Maybe travel to Canada, South America or the United States of America. But it was just as possible Larkin would return to Australia with her. The country was a vast land, easy to disappear into. But it had one weakness: a very small population despite its geographic size. Maybe Larkin had not thought of that, Locksley considered. He leaned forward in his chair.

'I think that a trip to Australia might pay dividends,' he said. 'I doubt that I could find Larkin and the girl in Europe, but the hunted eventually return to known territory. My suggestion is that I steam for Australia and ambush the prey in his lair.'

'If you think that your plan will work I will authorise the documents for the mission,' Cumming replied. 'But you must understand, your trip to the colonies will be seen as a private venture with no association with this office. If anything should happen to you we will disown any relationship we have with you. Do you understand and accept the consequences of what I have told you?'

Locksley took in what the intelligence chief was telling

370

him. He was completely on his own and could not even tell his wife and children of his mission. He would simply disappear from their lives until he returned when no doubt he would be secretly rewarded by a grateful British government. It was worth the risk.

'I understand,' Locksley answered. 'I have been a loyal soldier to the King and I consider this mission as no less important than the orders I obeyed during the war.'

'Good, chap,' Cumming said, rising to his feet and extending his hand. 'I will draft the appropriate papers for your travel to Australia and see to it that your family continues to receive your pay. You will operate on a fund we will set up for you to draw on.'

Major James Locksley left the SIS HQ with a new lease on life. The arrogance of the Germans and their treatment of him in Hamburg still smarted. To be virtually marched out of Germany under arms as if he had lost the war had been too much for the proud British officer. And it had been that colonial upstart who had caused his shame. Locksley had Russian blood and to him dishonour was worse than death. Both Larkin and the Princess Maria would pay with their lives for his ongoing failure to serve his country.

Paris
October 1919

Joshua and Maria were married by a refugee Russian Orthodox priest in a private ceremony in Paris. It had been Maria who had sought out help from the small order of monks at their priory in the Rue d'Allery and arranged the marriage. Although Joshua was a Methodist by birth he did not object being converted to the Russian Orthodox faith if it meant so much to Maria. Like many Australians, he did not put much stock in a man's religious convictions.

Madame Dubois had been invited as their only guest and had fussed over making Maria a wedding dress. Joshua used some of the money from the Romanov fortune to purchase a suitable suit. The priest was a young man with a heavy beard and had been on the Bolshevik death list in his village. He spoke no French but that did not matter. At the end of the ceremony, Joshua realised that the woman at his elbow was now Mrs Maria Larkin.

They celebrated the wedding with a quiet meal in a good French restaurant where other couples congratulated them with a toast of wine. It was a happy day neither would forget and Joshua had even booked them into a good hotel for the honeymoon, albeit only of one night.

As the sun set Madame Dubois said goodbye to the couple with hugs and teary kisses. Wiping at her eyes with a dainty handkerchief she pressed a simple gold ring into Maria's hand. 'This belonged to my son,' she said. 'He was killed in 1915 and it was meant for his fiancée. But she married another and now I would like you to have it for good luck in your life. Maybe it can be passed to your first born son for his fiancée.'

Both were touched by her kind gesture and Joshua hugged the grandmotherly lady in appreciation.

They took a taxi to the hotel and registered for the night as Mr and Mrs Joshua Larkin. Joshua knew that this was dangerous as it meant they could be traced but as he had no intentions of remaining long in France he took the chance to display their names proudly as man and wife. He had yet to tell Maria of his plans. It could wait.

That evening Maria lay asleep in Joshua's arms with an

expression of peace and contentment on her face. Their lovemaking had been gentle rather than passionate and it seemed to Joshua that time and his patience had cured the wounds of the past inflicted on Maria's body and soul. The next morning, as they partook of breakfast in the hotel dining room, Maria's beautiful face beamed with happiness.

'Do you think that we could remain in Paris forever, my old bear?' she asked, breaking open a warm croissant and spooning in rich strawberry jam.

'Old bear!' Joshua snorted, but pleased at the compliment. 'I am only twelve years older than you.'

'You are not really old in my eyes,' Maria said, chewing delicately on her croissant. 'What do you think about my idea to live in Paris? We both speak French and there are many of my countrymen fleeing here.'

'That's the problem,' Joshua replied, sipping his coffee. 'You might be recognised by one of your countrymen and no matter how well meaning they might be about who you really are, the British are bound to find out. I doubt that you would be safe. No, we have to move on.'

The expression of disappointment on Maria's face hurt Joshua but he realised that he could not give in to her whims. His role was to protect and provide for her.

'There is one place as far from Europe you can get,' Joshua said, taking Maria's free hand in his. 'My home, Australia.'

Maria's eyes widened in shock. 'That is at the other end of the world!' she exclaimed. 'I have heard that it is hot and dry.'

'I know a place where it snows in winter,' Joshua said, hoping that his compromise might mollify her fears of an alien landscape. 'With the money we have we could buy a small property and I could become a farmer like my father.

We would be out of reach of the English as my country's government is not always compliant with British interests. We refused to allow the English to shoot our men for desertion during the war as they did their own. There was a lot of pressure from the British for us to fall into line but my government resisted. I doubt that now the war is over the British could get their hands on me for a charge of desertion.'

'There will be snow in winter?' Maria asked.

'There is snow and a wonderful little village in the hills west of Sydney,' he said. 'There we would be safe and happy. A great place to raise children.'

'What is the name of this place?' Maria asked.

'Valley View,' Joshua replied. 'A place of safety.'

THIRTY-SEVEN

Valley View
Present day

Petrov Batkin sensed the danger: a creak on the wooden planks of the floor outside his room late in the afternoon. He slipped the .32 pistol from his luggage at the end of the bed and held it behind his back.

'Police! Open the door!'

Under the considerable bulk of Ken Barber, the door flew open and Batkin brought up the pistol to fire. Barber had hardly burst into the hotel room when it was filled with a small explosion and the acrid smell of cordite. Ken knew the smell well; it had been part of his life as a young soldier serving with an infantry battalion in Vietnam. What he had not experienced before was a bullet smacking into the upper part of his chest just below the collarbone. Behind him, young Mark Branson brought up his pistol to level on Batkin, but the Russian's special forces skills gave the young trainee detective no time to fire. The second

375

bullet from Batkin's pistol took Branson in the lower jaw, causing him to spin around and drop his gun.

So fixed had Batkin been on the two targets bursting through the door, he did not see Morgan smashing through the flimsy screen on the window that opened onto the verandah. He slammed into the Russian from behind, the momentum taking Batkin completely off guard. Before he could recover, Morgan had wrenched the man's arm holding the pistol into an angle, forcing him to drop his weapon. Morgan's other arm was around the Russian's neck and he applied a savage sleeper hold. Batkin attempted to shake the policeman off but to no avail. His struggles decreased as the oxygen was starved to his brain. He went down and with one knee in his back, Morgan yanked the semi-conscious man's wrists into a set of handcuffs.

'You shoulda killed the bastard,' Ken snarled, clutching the wound oozing blood from his shoulder.

The gunshots had drawn attention and voices outside the room called if anything was wrong.

'Everything is under control,' Morgan shouted back, realising that they needed time to review the situation that had gone bad on them. They would need a story for the police integrity investigators because a shooting had occurred, albeit of two police officers by the bad guy. Morgan used his mobile phone to dial triple-0 for an ambulance, explaining in clinical terms the nature of the gunshot wounds then reassured his colleagues despite the blood they were losing they did not have life-threatening wounds and help was on its way.

'You were lucky it was not an AK-47 round,' he said to young Branson, padding his face with a clean towel from the room. 'Otherwise it would have taken your face away. As it is you have something that rates just above a shaving

376

nick.' This was not true but Morgan knew how vain the young officer was about his looks. He fancied himself as a lady's man so Morgan added that the subsequent scar would impress the ladies even more. So convincing was he that the young man attempted a smile, only to grimace in his pain.

As the oxygen once again circulated in his brain Batkin was regaining his wits. Morgan took Branson's handcuffs and secured the prisoner to the end of the iron bed.

'A bloody stuff-up,' Ken said quietly. 'You were right. I should have got backup.'

'Not your fault,' Morgan reassured. 'Just one of those things that goes wrong from time to time.'

'I could have got you all killed,' Ken apologised. 'The bastard was waiting for us when we came through the door.'

'He's a former Russian special forces soldier,' Morgan said. 'It had to be expected.'

'Bloody hell! What has happened here?' a male voice said from the doorway.

Morgan glanced up to see the publican, Paul Barry standing with his hands over his mouth.

'Could do with a hand,' Morgan said. 'Just keep an eye on Mark until the ambulance arrives.'

The publican moved forward to kneel by the wounded police officer and hold the towel to his jaw. He was not a stranger to blood after many years of witnessing bar room brawls. Morgan moved back to examine Ken's wound but he waved him off. 'It's nothing much,' he said in his usual nonchalant way.

Morgan did not like the ashen appearance of the detective's face. Ken might be tough but even a small calibre round could do a lot of damage in the right place.

He turned to Batkin who was now fully conscious and

staring bleakly at the two men he had wounded. Morgan had a desire to smash the Russian in the face with his boot but resisted the rising anger.

'You are in a lot of trouble,' he said to Batkin. 'If you want to help yourself you had better start talking. We need to know about the murder of Daniel Kildare and what harm you had planned for Monique Dawson.'

Batkin stared at Morgan but there was no hate in the Russian's eyes – only a look of confusion and respect. 'You beat me, my friend,' he said. 'We were told that Aussie special forces man was good. You beat me.'

Morgan shook his head. It was not the response he expected. Olev – or whoever he was – considered being overpowered by him as more important than the situation he was in facing having just attempted to murder two police officers.

'What about Kildare?' Morgan persisted, ignoring the rules of interrogation. The detectives would carry out a formal interview at the police station later.

Morgan's mobile phone rang and he found himself speaking with the district police superintendent. Morgan gave a brief explanation as to what had happened, leaving out as much as he could until he had a chance to tidy up loose ends with Ken Barber. He was informed that a team was on its way from Hume City, as well as more senior officers from Sydney who would take charge of the situation. Morgan was to make himself available to them as well as securing the prisoner. When the conversation had finished Morgan turned his attention to Ken. 'That was the district super. Said he tried to ring you but your phone was off.'

'Had it off until we finished picking up the Russian,' Ken said. 'Didn't want it going off when we sneaked up on him.'

378

Morgan returned his attention to Batkin. 'What were you going to do to Monique Dawson?' he asked quietly.

'Nothing,' Batkin lied. 'I did not kill the English agent. You talk to Sarah Sakharov.'

'Agent?' Morgan queried. 'What do you mean by agent?'

Batkin realised that he had let the dead man's identity slip. 'Is nothing,' he replied dismissively.

But Morgan's interest was piqued.

'Are you Russian intelligence?' he asked, only to receive a look of derision.

'Russian intelligence like kill me,' Batkin replied. 'I think Sakharov double-cross me. I think you should find her. She know about Kildare.'

Morgan noticed that the Russian kept coming back to the English journalist who was now well and truly on his radar as a person of interest.

'What if ballistics matches up your gun to the Kildare killing?' Morgan asked, noticing that his question had registered concern on Batkin's face.

'Maybe same gun,' Batkin answered. 'But Sakharov have gun. Not me. She plant gun on me. Look bad.'

'Why did you want to kill Monique Dawson?' Morgan asked.

'Not kill Miss Dawson,' Batkin answered. 'Take Miss Dawson away. Save her from English MI6. They want her dead. We want her alive.'

Morgan was confused by what the Russian's was saying. Not all had been clarified in the hotel room.

'Before the detectives get here I need to know some things,' he said quietly to the Russian. 'This has nothing to do with what has happened in this room.'

Batkin looked at Morgan. 'I shoot policeman but think

379

they harm me,' he said. 'I know I do that but good lawyer help me in your country. I read criminal in your country never get punished. Maybe do a few years in your prison. Better than living in our house estates anyway. I talk to you as soldier to soldier. I did not kill Kildare who was MI6 man. I think Sakharov did that. She take my gun and say she will fix English agent. I think she work for me but I think she, what you say, double agent. I think she work for herself. Not us or MI6. I think you should look to see if Miss Dawson safe.'

As Morgan listened to the Russian's words he felt that he was hearing the truth. But why would the English freelance journalist want to harm Monique? It made no sense.

'I find yesterday from St Petersburg Sakharov not real name of woman I know as Sarah,' Batkin continued. 'Her English name Locksley – not Sakharov.'

Locksley! Morgan stiffened as if he had been electrocuted. The name flashed in his mind. Locksley was the name of the British officer who Larkin had mentioned in his journal as the man he most feared. Locksley had the mission of finding and disposing of the last of the Russian royal family. Ghosts! Monique had been so adamant about ghosts being resurrected. Now it seemed that she was right except this ghost was flesh and blood and somehow related to Major James Locksley. Maybe even a direct descendant, Morgan thought. But what could drive a person to murder over an issue almost a century old? Why put your life on the line to satisfy a mission already long dead? Or did such missions not have a statute of limitations?

Morgan reached for his mobile phone and quickly dialled Monique's home number. All he heard was a dial tone that rang out.

'Ken, you and Mark going to be all right?' Morgan

asked and was relieved to hear an ambulance scream to a halt in front of the pub, followed by a couple of police cars with lights and sirens blazing a passage through the late afternoon.

'Why? Where you going?' Ken asked, holding his shoulder.

'Got an urgent job on,' Morgan replied, returning the mobile to his pocket. 'Haven't got time to explain right now.'

Morgan slipped past the ambulance paramedics as they thumped up the stairs with their bags of emergency equipment. In seconds he was flinging open the door to his vehicle and turning over the engine.

Locksley! The threatening name from the past was now a danger in the present. He had to get to Monique. He had sworn to her that he would protect her – just as a long-dead Australian soldier had promised a Russian princess all those years earlier.

THIRTY-EIGHT

Valley View
November 1920

A year had passed since Joshua and Maria's marriage in
Paris. Maria's small fortune had been able to buy them
papers out of Europe and onto a ship travelling to Australia.
They journeyed via the Suez Canal, Bombay and down the
west coast of Australia before steaming up to Sydney, where
the newly married couple disembarked in March 1920.

Joshua had travelled on a false passport and Maria was
listed as a French national as marriages between returning
Australian soldiers and French girls were not uncommon.
Upon reaching the shores of his home country, Joshua
reverted to his real name as he had faith in the protection
his government would provide against any British attempt
to bring him to their military justice. There had been prec-
edents from the Boer War when the British had failed in
their attempts to extradite alleged traitors to the Empire's
cause of subduing the Dutch farmers of South Africa. Despite

Australian loyalty to the ideals of the British Empire, the Australian people would not abide British interference in their own proclaimed laws.

In Sydney Joshua looked up the former members of his battalion who were very pleased to see their old colleague return safe and sound from the Russian Front. He avoided questions about his service in Russia and even if friends he had soldiered with were curious about the gaps in his experiences they did not ask questions. After all, the popular officer had saved many lives with his leadership. They raised beer glasses to toast his return and his marriage to the very pretty French girl.

Joshua spent some money to purchase a new car and he and his bride set out across the Great Dividing Range, travelling along the rough, hard-packed earthen roads to reach their promised land. They arrived in Valley View, a bustling little village well away from the major centres of Australian civilisation but with every service one would want. The town boasted a butcher's shop, bakery, barber, resident doctor, four hotels, two boarding houses and a regular visit of the travelling movie picture show man who screened the latest silent films in the town hall to an appreciative audience. Wool was the mainstay of the prosperous district so when Joshua made a bid for the large sandstone house outside town with its thousand acres of fertile land used for running sheep it cost them a substantial bite out of Maria's fortune. However, they still had money over to purchase breeding stock and enough in the bank to live comfortably.

Maria had begun learning English and was relatively fluent after a year living with Joshua, enabling her to converse with the curious women of the town's small social elite. At first it had been hard for the former Russian princess but she soon took delight in working alongside Joshua and her love for him grew with each day they were together, as did his for her. The fear of being hunted by the British quickly evaporated under the hot sun of 1920.

Maria had accepted that she would never return to Russia as pessimistic news from the front there only reinforced that the Bolsheviks were winning the civil war. But there were times at night when Joshua would find her weeping by the stove in the kitchen when something had reminded her of her life with her family. He would hold her until the melancholy passed and knew that he would die rather than ever see her hurt again.

In the town Joshua met up with one of his former soldiers from when he had commanded a company in his old battalion. Bill Crawford had returned to Australia in 1919 and made his way home to Valley View where his wife and children lived. He had been a blacksmith before enlisting in 1915 but the new-fangled development of the automobile was threatening his past occupation. Over a few beers in the bottom hotel, Joshua had suggested that he open a garage to service the cars and trucks now churning up the dust of the main street. Bill Crawford accepted the offer and Joshua became a silent partner in his newly opened garage, supplying fuel and servicing the vehicles in the town. Bill had been at the point of despair until Joshua stepped in to assist as he had a growing family to feed and clothe. But Joshua's advice and money had put him back on his feet and he prospered in the new business.

Bill Crawford had strong memories of how Captain Larkin's courage had kept most of his men alive on the battlefield. His decisions had been wise and he had the ability to stand up to some less than impressive senior officers. It was known to all from the company cook to the company sergeant major that Captain Larkin would have lain down his life for any one of them and Bill was quick to tell anyone of influence in the town of the decorated soldier's impressive record.

In the short time they had been in Valley View Joshua and Maria were made feel that they had been living among the townspeople forever.

Life in the isolated village proved to be secure and comfortable for Captain Larkin – as the local people liked to call their resident war hero – and his wife. That was until the first week in November. Joshua was having a drink with Bill Crawford in one of the town's hotels on a Friday afternoon when the barmaid casually mentioned to Joshua that a gentleman with a posh voice had been asking around about him. Joshua took his glass of beer from the barmaid and glanced around the crowded bar filled with farm workers – fresh out of the paddocks – seemingly intent on spending a part or all of their wages for the week.

'Is he still here?' he asked.

'No,' the barmaid replied, already moving on to pour more beers from the tap for the thirsty clientele. 'The bugger is staying at the boarding house owned by Mrs Leonard. A real toff, if you ask me.'

'Did he leave a name?'

'Come to think of it,' the girl frowned, 'he didn't. You owe him some money or something, Captain Larkin?' she asked tactlessly.

Joshua shook his head with a weak smile. 'No, nothing like that,' he said, feeling a chill through his body not caused by the cold beer he swigged.

Beside him, Bill Crawford hardly noticed the change in Joshua's mood.

'Here's cheers,' Bill said, raising his glass. 'To our mates in the battalion – and to those who can't be with us now to have a cold one.'

Joshua raised his glass but his mind was racing. Could it be possible that Locksley had tracked him to Valley View? He hardly tasted the beer he was drinking. It did not seem possible considering the vast distance between Britain and Australia.

There was only one way to deal with the situation: Joshua knew that he would have to pre-empt any move by the British officer – if he was in town. Excusing himself from the shout, Joshua left the hotel and made his way to the boarding house. He had hardly reached the place when the dread of anticipation turned to outright shock. Frozen by the sight of the man opening the iron gate to the board-ing house, Joshua could only stand in the street staring. The man closed the gate behind him and when he turned in Joshua's direction his also was a look of shock.

'George!' Joshua finally gasped and walked towards his old friend. But as he approached he could not see the expression of happiness he expected at the reunion. Joshua grasped George's shoulders but George did not react. The stony expression remained.

'Cobber, I thought you were dead,' Joshua said. 'It is so good to see you again.'

George removed Joshua's hands from his shoulders and stood back. 'I heard from some of your old mates in the bat-talion that you had returned to Australia,' George replied icily. 'I didn't hear any questions as to my welfare.'

'I'm sorry if you think that I forgot you but the last I saw of you over there was when you went off with half the Bolshie militia in pursuit. I didn't think you would have made it but was forever grateful for what I considered your courageous sacrifice on behalf of the mission.'

'You left the major for dead and failed to carry out the mission we were tasked to do,' George said bitterly. 'My sacrifice might have been for nothing because you got caught up with a bit of Russian fluff – thanks for nothing, cobber.'

At his former friend's slur against Maria, Joshua felt a seething rush of anger begin to overtake him and had to force himself not to strike the man standing before him. 'How is it that you got to see the mad major?' Joshua asked coldly.

'I was with a Czech cavalry recon unit that saved me,' George said. 'We came upon the cabin and found Major Locksley barely alive. He told me how you just left him to die and escaped with a Russian Bolshevik agent. The rest is history.'

'You believed him?' Joshua asked.

'Have you got a better explanation?' George countered.

'I have, but am loath to tell you when you seem to have accepted his story without considering who and what I am,' Joshua said. 'You took the word of an English officer over that of a fellow digger. I doubt that we have anything else to say to each other so I will return to the pub and finish a round of beers with a friend.'

Joshua turned on his heel and walked away, leaving his former friend standing alone in the street staring at his back. As Joshua strode towards the hotel he barely took notice of the ominous clouds rolling in from the west.

George Littleton returned to his room and slumped down on the single bed that occupied most of the space in the tiny area. His mind was in turmoil. He had come to ascertain if the same Captain Joshua Larkin he had overheard the former men of his battalion speak of in a Sydney hotel bar was one and the same as the Sergeant Joshua Larkin he soldiered with in the coldest regions of northern Russia. But seeing his old friend once again had shaken him. George had been able to maintain his rage against a man who had callously deserted a fellow soldier to his fate for the sake of a pretty Russian girl.

At first, he had trouble accepting the British major's explanation but the major had shown George nothing but generosity of spirit in recommending him for his Distinguished Conduct Medal. George had returned from the Russian campaign a decorated hero – thanks to Major Locksley – and had stepped back into his privileged life with something to show for his military service. His father had already suggested that his son run for politics. The title, the Honourable George Littleton, DCM had a noble ring to it. George had considered his father's suggestion but one day Major Locksley unexpectedly turned up on his doorstep in Sydney and when George informed him that Joshua was alive and possibly living in a small Australian town west of the Great Dividing Range reminded his former corporal that they still had a mission to complete.

The knock at his door cut across George's reflections.

'Are you there, George?' the male voice asked.

'Come in, major,' George replied.

Major Locksley entered the room carrying a small overnight suitcase. George rose from the edge of the bed and Locksley extended his hand in greeting.

'Good to see you again, Mr Littleton,' he said, using the term reserved for lieutenants by superior officers in the armies of the British Empire. 'I saw Larkin on the street speaking to you but I don't think he saw me. We now have a positive identification of our target. Have you been able to determine where he lives and if the Russian girl is with him still?'

'Both,' George replied in a flat voice. 'He is within an easy march of here.'

'Good,' Locksley answered, glancing around the room. 'As soon as the mission is completed we will leave for Hume City in your automobile and from there I will take the train to Sydney. I appreciate that the task has a lot of risk involved for you but I can assure you that its necessity overrides any personal feelings you may still harbour for Joshua Larkin.'

'We are speaking of murder, major,' George cautioned. 'If my involvement in the killings of Captain Larkin and his Russian bride is revealed I could be hanged.'

'You will only be required to drive to where the man lives and remain outside while I take care of the two of them,' Locksley answered. 'You will not be a witness to anything that happens and so not be culpable. All you have to do is carry out your part of the plan and when it is done your assistance will be very favourably recorded by His Majesty's government in England. It is now more than ever that we must eliminate the Russian girl for the dangerous Bolshevik agent that she is. You know it is not within my powers to explain everything about her.'

George nodded. He was as loyal a member of the British Empire as the next man and reasoned that the risks involved were outweighed by the needs of the Empire's security. 'What time do we cross the start line?' George asked.

'Nineteen hundred hours,' Locksley replied, glancing at his watch. 'I will meet you on the northern edge of town so that we are not be seen together. There is a large tree growing next to a stable, I will be there.'

Their simple plan had been formulated and now all that was required was the execution of the mission. The former British major had left George alone to resume struggling with his confused feelings. Although he would not be

389

directly involved in the killing of Joshua and his Russian wife he would be just as guilty anyway. He may as well be the one to fire the fatal shots.

Maria stood in the doorway of the kitchen staring up at the great flashes of lightning tearing the sky apart. The massive rolls of thunder reminded her of the artillery gun barrages she had heard in Russia during the civil war. She flinched and continued to gaze into the premature darkness. Joshua had not yet arrived home from his Friday meeting with his close friend, Bill Crawford.

She heard the puttering sound of their automobile on the gravel driveway at the front of the house and hurried to greet him at the main entrance. Joshua alighted from the car just as the first downpour roared across the hills and drenched the dry earth beneath.

'I was worried,' Maria said, clasping Joshua to her in a welcoming embrace. 'The storm is so terrible.'

Joshua smiled at his wife's concern and hugged her to him. 'A bit of water was not going to cause me any harm,' he said.

When she broke from the embrace to gaze into his face, Joshua frowned. There was something in her features he had never seen before; a strange, enigmatic expression. 'Are you all right?' he asked, reaching out for her hands.

'We are going to have a baby!' Maria exclaimed, and now Joshua knew why he had never seen that expression before. After all, it was the first time for his wife. For a moment he stood stunned.

'That's wonderful,' he said, grabbing Maria and swinging her off her feet in his joy. 'When is this going to happen?'

'It has happened,' Maria replied, puzzled at the question.

'I am with child, the doctor came today and said this was true.'

'I mean, when is the baby due?' Joshua clarified.

'I think June next year,' Maria answered. 'Our baby will be born an Australian.'

'You should not be on your feet,' Joshua fussed, leading Maria to a couch in the living room. 'I will hire a girl to help you around the house with the chores.'

'That is not necessary,' Maria sighed. 'I am a Russian woman and Russian women have worked in the fields for centuries beside their men when they were carrying a child. I am no different from my peasant sisters.'

As Maria rested her head on Joshua's shoulder, she felt at peace knowing that her child would be born in this new country, far from the horrors of Europe and the past.

Standing under the great gum tree at the edge of town did not prevent James Locksley from getting drenched to the skin. It was a nuisance but little different from past experiences in the snows of Russia or on the Western Front; the former British army officer was used to being wet and cold. He saw the headlights in the pouring rain and sighted the car when lightning flashed on the horizon. When it slowed Locksley edged towards the narrow road to pull himself into the passenger side.

'Go,' he said.

They drove for a short time north until the lights of the house they sought marked their destination. George parked on the gravel driveway behind Joshua's car. Without a word, Locksley alighted and walked stealthily towards the front door. He drew a pistol from the pocket of his coat. Testing the door knob he was satisfied to see that it was not locked. He twisted the knob and pushed the door open to step cautiously inside the house. He could smell bread baking. Moving along the hallway he entered the living room. Joshua was sitting on a sofa reading a newspaper and when he looked up was shocked at the sight of a pistol levelled at him.

'Don't get up,' Locksley commanded. 'Where is your wife?'

Joshua lowered the paper, glaring at the last face on earth he ever wished to see. 'You think I would tell you,' Joshua replied loudly, praying that Maria might overhear his conversation. He knew that she was in the kitchen and also knew why Locksley had invaded his house. Maria would have little chance to survive and Joshua had only this one forlorn opportunity to warn her of the threat in their house. He coiled himself and sprang from the couch at Locksley, knowing at least when he shot him, Maria might hear and wisely flee the house. With any luck she might be able to run to a neighbour for help.

The bullet ripped into Joshua's arm between his elbow and wrist. He spun halfway around towards the British man and instinctively gripped the wound.

'That was meant to kill you,' Locksley snarled. 'It appears that I am out of practice at this sort of thing. Call your wife.'

Joshua was surprised that he was still alive but still hoped the shot might have alerted Maria to the danger. He prayed that she would not enter the room to ascertain what had happened.

'Run, Maria!' he screamed aloud in French and Locksley fired again. This time the bullet grazed Joshua's cheek, clipping the lower tip of his earlobe. He fell back over the couch out of sight of Locksley.

'We can't do this,' a second voice said.

Joshua recognised it as George Littleton's. Raising his

head above the couch, he saw him standing unarmed behind the British intelligence man.

Locksley swung around. 'I told you to stay out of this,' he snapped. 'Now you are a witness.'

Joshua staggered to his feet, clutching his arm. Blood streamed down the side of his face and he could see the look of concern briefly crease George's face.

'So you are going to help the English murder an innocent woman,' Joshua asked.

'What's Joshua talking about?' George asked Locksley.

'Our mission was to kill the Princess, Maria Romanov, for whatever obscure political reason the English wanted her dead,' Joshua said, gritting his teeth against the throbbing pain in his arm. 'I refused to do so and your Major Locksley has obviously recruited you to his cause. I can't stop you killing me but at least you may as well know why you are helping him.'

Joshua felt sure that by now Maria would have either come into the room or fled from the house. He hoped she had taken the latter option. Under the circumstances it would be useless to reason with the former British major and try to explain that she wasn't a threat. Locksley's face bore the look of a man possessed by his mission.

'It matters little why I have orders to kill the woman,' Locksley said, raising the pistol, his arm outstretched, and pointing it at Joshua's head a mere couple of yards away. 'I am executing you for your treachery in aiding an enemy of the King.'

Sighting along the barrel of the pistol, Locksley began applying pressure to the trigger. On its current trajectory, the bullet would impact directly between the eyes.

THIRTY-NINE

Valley View
Present day

Morgan's worst fear was realised when he reached Monique's house. There, in the driveway, was the hire car he recognised as being driven by Sarah Sakharov aka Locksley. He leaped from the police vehicle, unholstering his service pistol as he did so. He reached the front door and without knocking, eased it open. He could hear voices from the living room and gave a short prayer of thanks that one of them was Monique's. He also recognised Sarah's voice. Morgan walked cautiously along the hallway to emerge in the living room, his pistol down by his side.

The women were sitting opposite each other with coffee mugs between them on the small table. They looked up with expressions of surprise, although Morgan thought he saw a flash of anger in Sarah's face. Morgan discreetly returned the pistol to its holster.

'Morgan!' Monique exclaimed. 'What are you doing here?'

Morgan felt just a little foolish and wondered what he would say. 'I tried to call you but your phone rang out,' he replied. 'I was just seeing if you were all right.'

'Why wouldn't I be all right?' Monique frowned. 'Sarah just dropped by to say goodbye before leaving town to return home and I must have been outside when you rang.'

Morgan noticed the overnight bag by Sarah's feet and stepped forward to open it.

Sarah rose to her feet. 'What are you doing?' she protested. 'How dare you. That is my private property.'

Morgan ignored her and rifled through the bag. A change of clothing, a set of surgical gloves, a wig and a pair of sunglasses. There was nothing that could be considered incriminating, certainly no weapons, although the thin, latex gloves and wig bothered him.

'What were you looking for?' Sarah asked coldly. 'Drugs?'

'Nothing like that,' Morgan answered. 'Just checking to see if you were carrying any prohibited weapons.'

'Have you gone crazy?' Monique asked. Then she noticed the blood spots on his uniform and hands. Her anger quickly faded. 'Have you been hurt?' she asked, moving towards him.

'I'm not hurt,' Morgan said as Monique took his hands in her own to examine for wounds, her nursing experience apparent in the professionalism of her approach. 'We had an incident in town. A couple of colleagues were wounded. It is their blood – not mine.'

'What sort of incident?' Monique asked.

'There was a shooting at the bottom pub when we went

395

to arrest a man,' Morgan answered, staring at Sarah. 'A Russian. I believe that you knew the man, Ms Sakharov – or is it Locksley?'

Sarah paled a little but did not lose her composure. This simple country copper was smarter than he looked. She had lured her unsuspecting target and given a few more minutes would have selected the knife from the rack in Monique's kitchen. It was uncanny how the policeman turned up each time to intervene in her murderous plan. If she had been superstitious she might have thought that he was some kind of guardian angel to her intended victim.

'I briefly met the man,' Sarah acknowledged. 'But that is the extent of my contact with Petrov Batkin.'

'That's strange,' Morgan said. 'I was referring to Petrov Olev. He's never revealed his identity as Batkin to anyone that I know.'

Cornered, Sarah remained calm. She had been well trained and silently cursed her critical slip. 'I have Russian ancestry, constable,' Sarah offered, 'Batkin confided to me who he really was and as a journalist I am expected to keep such matters confidential.'

'So, who is Petrov Batkin?' Morgan continued, sensing that he had broken through her well-rehearsed story. 'And who is Sarah Locksley? Not a descendant of Major James Locksley by any chance?'

Sarah's face reddened despite her experience in intelligence work. She was digging a hole for herself and realised that the man questioning her was well versed in interrogation methods. He had once been a member of the Australian Special Air Service, as she knew, and this alone should have been enough warning to avoid him. 'If there is no other matter to discuss I think that I shall bid you both a good day,' Sarah countered. 'Unless you intend to arrest me for being in possession of an overnight bag containing a spare set of clothes.'

Morgan fumed at the English woman's sudden break with his line of questioning. She had been well trained in resisting interrogation methods and besides he had no evidence to hold her on any charge. It was not a crime to be unavailable for a police interview. However, Morgan was suspicious of the items in the overnight bag. And he could see that she was eager to leave the house. She could simply depart from the country and disappear anywhere in the world.

Monique was perplexed by the exchange between Sarah and Morgan. It was like a coded conversation until she remembered something Morgan had said.

'Major Locksley!' she gasped and looked sharply at Sarah. 'Are you related to him in some way?'

'I don't know who this Major Locksley is,' Sarah replied calmly. 'I travel under the name of Sakharov for reasons I am unable to reveal, and I strongly suggest that you do not attempt to prevent me leaving right now as I feel you will suffer severe repercussions from your own government if you do so.'

'So you are British intelligence,' Morgan offered, countering her effort to intimidate him. 'Or else you would not be so confident of protection. I just wonder if our intelligence services know that you are operating here. All I need to do is make a phone call and we can clear up any misunderstandings.'

'Do that,' Sarah bluffed. 'I doubt that you are stupid enough to try to arrest me for no rational reason.'

Sarah picked up her overnight bag and brushed past Morgan to walk out the front door to her car. He followed her, sensing that had he not arrived when he did he would have found Monique dead. He felt the rage of frustration at having to watch her walk away. Sarah was visibly angry as she struggled with the keys of the car to unlock the driver's side door. Morgan's eyes scanned her hire car and settled on the numberplates covered in dead insects.

'Before you leave, Miss Locksley,' Morgan said, striding towards her. 'There is just a little traffic matter to settle.'

Sarah glanced up at him. 'I have a valid driver's licence for your country,' she flared. 'You have seen it.'

'It's not that,' Morgan said mildly. 'It's just the matter of the car you are driving.'

'If you check the records you will see that I have signed a contract to hire the vehicle,' she replied.

'I would ask you to just stand away from the vehicle while I carry out a routine inspection,' Morgan cautioned. 'It won't take a moment, and then you can be on your way.'

Sarah took a step back from the car, her hands on her hips and a scowl on her face, while Morgan reached for the handpiece of his radio through the window of his vehicle. He contacted the operations room in Hume City, requesting a registration check on the car's numberplates. Within seconds he received an answer. He turned to Sarah. 'I am afraid there is a bit of a problem,' he said smugly. 'Although the number-plates on your car are not reported stolen, it appears that they are not registered to this vehicle, but to a local farmer's car. You will have to come back to the station until we contact the registered owner to clarify what is going on.'

Trapped, Sarah swore savagely at her mistake. She had been so careful, changing the plates from the dead farmer's car to confuse anyone who might note the number when she fled the Larkin house. With a sigh, Sarah held her hands forward to be cuffed.

'You have been watching too many Yank cop shows.

We don't do that for traffic offences,' Morgan said. 'And I suspect that you have a lot of questions to answer about how you got hold of the plates on your car. You will need to come with me to the station.'

Sarah complied, her mind racing to think of how she could extract herself from the situation. No doubt the police would find the farmer dead on his bed and also notice the marks on his neck. This did not prove that she had killed him – as she had been careful to clean up before leaving – but the damned registration plates incriminated her. A matter so simple had brought her down. She would need a good lawyer and a lot of luck to get off a murder charge.

Morgan escorted her to his police vehicle and drove back into town which by now was swarming with police cars and the local television crew. Police shootings always became the lead story for any TV newscast. As Morgan drove down the main street to his station through the crowd of locals now milling around the armada of emergency and media vehicles, hardly anyone gave him a second look. Their attention was fixed on the hotel where all the action had happened. Then the storm clouds rumbling around the valleys and hills broke, scattering the curious crowd of onlookers to the protection of the shop overhangs.

London
Present day
Early morning

It only took a few hours before the arrest of Sarah Locksley hit the desk of Harry Stanton. It was the first item left on his desk by the previous shift. According to the report lifted from the Australian media on the internet, it seemed that she had been picked up on a minor traffic matter which led to her arrest for the murder of a farmer at his isolated house north of Valley View. The report went on to say that she was also linked to the murder of a British citizen, Daniel Kildare, whose body was found on a riverbank near the town.

Harry let his coffee go cold. The bile in his stomach was playing hell with his hiatus hernia and he reached for the anti-acid pills in his top drawer. So Sarah had finally turned up and if she talked he knew that MI6 was threatened with exposure of their covert operation to the world. It had all gone so wrong. Her private mission threatened relations between Canberra and London. It was time for damage control and some discreet approaches to the Aussie government to explain how she was a rogue agent acting on her own. But no matter what they attempted to do to calm the situation it would leave a sour taste between the two governments.

How had she stayed one step ahead of him? Harry bit down on the sweet tasting pill. It was as if she was keeping in contact with MI6 for her information. He stood and walked to the window with a view of the Thames below. He knew that he would not be remembered as one of the great British spymasters after this debacle but he would find whoever was responsible for keeping Sarah Locksley updated on their moves.

'The chief wants you upstairs, Mr Stanton,' his personal assistant said, after knocking and popping her head around the corner of his door. He nodded, groaning inwardly at what the summons meant to his career. No doubt the chief had been briefed on the fiasco in Australia and he would be on the carpet answering some very tricky questions.

Sam Briars!

The name hit him like a sledge hammer. It had to be Briars who had been feeding her the information to keep her one step ahead of his efforts to sabotage her attempts to kill Monique Dawson. Harry remembered how the young computer man had been seen drinking with her in a wine bar in London's inner city. The information had been a line in a routine security check on the movements of staff and it had been his duty to review the report in the spirit of maintaining security.

Harry returned to his desk and sat in front of his computer. Coding in his security clearance, he pulled down the file on his screen and read the report. Not only had Briars been observed socialising with Locksley but the observer had noted he also appeared to be besotted by the beautiful young woman. Some damned computer geek had screwed him and Harry was not a forgiving person. Gathering his thoughts, Harry Stanton left his office for the meeting with the chief. Briars had been judged and found guilty in the span of minutes by the experienced MI6 man. It was up to him to address the issue of the young man's treachery.

FORTY

Valley View
November 1920

It all happened in the beat of a heart. Joshua was staring at certain death and steeled himself to die. But he did so knowing that Maria must have fled the house, as she had not appeared at his side after the shots had been fired. His oath to always protect her had been satisfied.

Locksley had no expression on his face as he pointed the pistol directly at Joshua's head.

'This is not right,' George said. 'It's bloody murder. There are questions to be answered. I am not going to let you gun Joshua down like some mongrel dog.'

He advanced on the major and only a pace separated them when Locksley realised the danger he was in. He swung around and finished squeezing the trigger. The bullet slammed into George's forehead and he crumpled with a look of surprise on his face. Immediately Locksley swung back to fire at Joshua, who had little chance given the severity of his wounds to overpower his would-be executioner.

'Joshua!'

Joshua half-turned his head to see Maria step into the room, his old service revolver in her hand and raised in the same manner as that of Locksley, whose expression of shock was now clearly written in his features. The shot that reverberated in the room dropped the British agent. Maria's aim was true and the bullet smashed into Locksley's brain, killing him instantly.

Joshua could feel his heart pounding in his chest as if he was back on the battlefields of Europe. Maria stood with the service revolver still outstretched, her face ashen as Joshua slowly made his way towards her and took the pistol from her hand. She was shaking and he held her to him, whispering soothing words. Joshua knew that their haven of peace and security was no longer. If Locksley had found them, who was to tell if others would not follow to complete the unfinished mission.

'We have work to do,' he said to Maria. 'Pack all that we will need for a long journey.'

Joshua kneeled hopefully by George's body but quickly saw that he was dead. While Maria put together the essentials for what she knew was ahead of them, Joshua dragged the two bodies out of the house. The rain had eased to a drizzle and he took a shovel to dig two graves. He toiled in pain until he was satisfied that the graves were deep enough to conceal the bodies for all time. He rolled Locksley's body into the first hole and unceremoniously shovelled soil onto his corpse.

He gently lowered George's body into the earth and crossed his hands on his chest as a gesture of respect for an old friend who had sacrificed his life to save them. Joshua stood back and tried to think of what he should do next. He remembered his military identity discs in his pocket. Joshua had long considered them as his good luck talisman.

'Thanks, cobber,' he said, quietly placing the discs on George's chest. 'You were a great soldier and a true mate. Take these with you to heaven and I will get them back when we next meet.' It was all he could think of to say.

When the task of concealing the bodies was complete, Joshua turned his thoughts to disposing of the automobile parked in his driveway. Although the killing of Locksley was done in self-defence Joshua had no intention of reporting the matter to the local constabulary. His priority was to leave Valley View for Maria's sake; any police investigation would only expose their existence to the British intelligence community. Too many questions would be raised and that would put Maria in dire jeopardy.

Joshua went inside where Maria was packing suitcases. 'I will go to see Bill Crawford,' he said. 'I will not be away for long.'

Joshua drove George's car to Bill's garage in town and knocked on his door. It was late but Bill had been working on a tractor repair job.

'Bloody hell!' he said when he saw Joshua's hands. He held the door open. 'What happened to you?'

Joshua slumped into a rickety chair by a work bench covered in greasy car engine parts. 'You got a beer to spare?' he asked.

Bill hurried away to fetch two bottles. They were not very cold but the bite of the beer in his throat made Joshua feel better. In the space it took to consume the brew Joshua told the story of how George and Locksley had been killed. He also explained why.

Bill's eyes grew wide. 'Jeez, it's all so hard to believe,' he finally commented. 'But if you tell me it's true then I have no reason to disbelieve you, skipper. How can I help?'

'I need to dispose of the car,' Joshua said. 'And I need someone to manage the house and estate for me. Maria and I will be away for a long time. I will post documents back to you to authorise your position as manager. Maybe rent out the house and sell the stock. Can you do that?'

'Given all that you have done for me from the trenches to home you know that is a stupid question,' Bill replied, finishing the last of his beer.

'You also know that you can never speak of what has happened tonight,' Joshua cautioned. 'Our lives would be in dire peril if you did so.'

'Skipper, if you had not been our boss back in France then I would not be here today – need I say anymore.'

Joshua rose from his chair and extended his good arm to his friend and business partner. 'Bill, you don't know how much your friendship means to me,' he said, gripping Bill's hand firmly. 'It was an honour to lead you and the rest of the mob during the war.'

Bill Crawford looked at his friend, tears welling in his eyes. 'We are going to miss you, skipper,' Bill said. 'You need to see a doctor about your arm.'

'It's no big deal,' Joshua shrugged. 'You and I saw worse on the front and know that the army sent men back into action with less than this. Maria is capable of cleaning up the wound and stitching it.'

Bill accepted Joshua's explanation and went outside to look at the vehicle. 'I need a few spare parts,' he said. 'In a couple of days the automobile will not exist.'

Bill drove Joshua home and when the sun rose the next day he came back to the house to find that it was deserted. Bill found a bucket, mop and scrubbing brush to clean up the blood in the living room and in his search for the cleaning items came across a battered journal. He slipped it into his pocket. By the time that he had finished in the house he knew it would be ready for renting; he had removed every trace of the bloody events of the night before.

Closing the door behind him, Bill stopped to peer across the Valley cloaked in a sheen of green shoots. The storm the night before had brought life to the town and promised prosperity to all. Bill might never see his friend return in his lifetime but he would be faithful to his memory. It was the least a former soldier could do for the man who had been closer than a brother in a time when they had shared a place in hell.

EPILOGUE

Valley View
Present day

A month had passed since the biggest day Valley View would probably experience for another hundred years. Morgan, Ken and Mark had been thoroughly Q & A'd. The internal inquiries department of the police force had plenty of questions about the shooting. But the three had walked away with a clean record for the arrest. Even though Petrov Batkin was able to provide an alibi for the murder of Daniel Kildare, he faced charges of attempted murder, malicious wounding and being in possession of a prohibited firearm. His case was still before the courts.

Sarah Locksley faced a murder charge over the death of the farmer but it was tough providing forensic evidence; she had made few mistakes other than the switching of the registration plates. Despite their suspicions and circumstantial evidence concerning her role in the death of Daniel Kildare the police had trouble finding any substantial evidence to link her to the crime. It was not the clean result of a conviction that the police would have liked to have but at least they had the consolation that they had done their job.

A leading Queens Counsel was put on Sarah's case. Who was paying his substantial retainer was not known, but Morgan suspected the woman was a British intelligence agent, and the money was coming from the coffers of the British government. If nothing else, they would want to get her out of Australia and deal with her on their own grounds. Morgan was certain the beautiful young woman would charm the jury and she would walk free.

Monique appreciated how close she had come to being killed. If Morgan had not arrived when he did she felt that she would have lost her life at the hands of the great-granddaughter of Major James Locksley over nothing more than a matter of family honour. Monique had been able to put all the pieces together and see that the ghosts of who-ever had been unearthed in her backyard had reignited an old mission. But Monique had also discovered something magical – thanks to the efforts of Gladys Harrison and her little group of amateur historians who had continued to dig into the history of Valley View.

'So, where are you taking me?' Morgan asked as Monique drove her car west of the township.

She had arrived after his routine jog and asked him to get dressed and go with her on a short journey although she would not tell him where or why.

'We will be there soon,' she replied. 'Just be patient and don't ask any more questions.'

Morgan rolled his eyes and gazed out at the paddocks now baking under the hot sun of an early summer. He knew the road that petered out into a dirt track of loose gravel but he also knew there was little along the road other than the occasional lonely farm house well set off the road.

'Did you get the results back of the DNA test?' he asked, despite her request to desist from his questioning.

'I did,' Monique answered, staring ahead to avoid the potholes in the road, and not elaborating any further, much to Morgan's irritation. 'We are there,' she added.

Morgan peered through the dust-covered windscreen as she turned off the road.

'It's the old Valley View cemetery,' he said in a puzzled voice. 'What the hell is out here to get you so worked up about?'

Monique stopped the car and turned off the engine. The only sounds they could hear in the lonely place were those of the wind in the grass and the distant warble of a magpie.

They stepped out of the car and Monique took Morgan's hand. He was surprised at her gesture; nothing so intimate had passed between them before. She led him beyond a few tumbled-down grave markers until they came to a corner of the little cemetery.

'There,' she said, pointing to a tombstone wide enough for two names and covered in dry lichen. Morgan stooped to read the weathered inscription.

Captain Joshua Larkin MC, DCM, MM 1889–1931
Maria Larkin 1901–1952

'I'll be damned!' Morgan said quietly, touching the stone as if expecting to feel the flesh of those buried in the ground at his feet. 'How in hell did they end up here? From what I read I thought that Larkin and his princess would have remained overseas, rather than risk returning.'

'It seems that my great-grandfather asked to have his body returned – and his son obliged,' Monique said. 'I expect that Joshua thought the last place the British would look for him was here. From what I have read of his story I suspect that he was a daring man. He changed his name in England but kept in touch by mail with his old friend, Bill Crawford. They still have his letters but the family have always honoured Bill's oath to keep them secret. Our family was well off and when my great-grandmother was dying, she requested to be buried beside her husband. Bill Crawford made the arrangements at this end. He was a loyal friend to my great-grandfather to the end. You asked me if I got the DNA results back,' Monique continued, holding out a sheet of paper. 'It's copy of a letter translated from French into English and was written by my great-grandmother just before she died. I found it last week when I went through a pile of family papers that have been stored away in an old shoe box.'

'What does it say?' Morgan asked.

'In the letter, Maria admitted that she was never a royal princess but an impostor.' Monique explained. 'That Yakov killed her family, sparing her, because she looked almost identical to the real Princess Maria. According to her she was to be passed off by Yakov as the princess if the Czechs captured his family. But she also realised that she would be disposed of after Yakov evaded the invading Czechs, and when she escaped she was able to take a substantial amount of the Romanov family fortune Yakov was holding, supposedly to support her royal story. She believed, albeit falsely, that the English would pull out all stops to save her and she could live the life of a real royal princess. In Paris, before they were married, she confessed to Joshua Larkin who she really was – Maria Smirnoff, a girl from a wealthy family distantly related to the Czar. So the Brits were always chasing a ghost. But in his journal Joshua always referred to her as his princess.'

'I guess she was his princess,' Morgan smiled. 'I'll be damned.'

Monique nodded and tears welled in her eyes. 'At least we know that my great-grandfather was not one of those bodies buried in my backyard, but I guess we will never know who they were, just as we will never know their full story.' She stepped forward and kissed Morgan on the lips and he responded.

'You were like the spirit of my great-grandfather when he swore to keep my great-grandmother safe from harm,' she said, leaning on his shoulder.

'What about David?' Morgan asked clumsily, feeling foolish for bringing up his name.

'It is well and truly over between us,' Monique replied. 'I think you were in my mind from the moment I first set eyes on you that day at the police station when you changed over my driver's licence. It was as if destiny meant us to be together – just as it had for my great-grandparents. You see, ghosts are real. I think that you have the spirit of Captain Joshua Larkin and I that of my great-grandmother, Maria. It is as if we were destined to play out their story.'

The sun was setting in a cloudless sky and the horizon took on a soft, orange hue. Morgan embraced Monique, his arms around her. 'I think your great-grandparents are watching us now,' he said with a broad grin. 'I think that we should find somewhere private away from their prying eyes.'

Hand in hand they walked towards the car. For a moment Morgan thought he heard a soft voice on the late afternoon breeze, rustling the dry grasses of the old cemetery. But graveyards could have that effect on even the most rational of men.

London
Present day

Sam Briars knew that he had drunk too much. The crowds around him in the hotel bar were mostly young executives, celebrating the end of the working week. He pushed his shot glass of vodka away, glaring with rheumy eyes at the attractive young woman. If only she knew what he had done for his country she would be impressed, he thought. But he knew that his past employment by MI6 meant a lifetime of grey silence.

'Unfair,' he muttered, slurring his words, and the pretty young woman wearing the set smile and expensive clothes moved to increase the space between them. Unfair that Harry Stanton had hauled him into his office and accused him of breaching every protocol of the organisation. That he had been dismissed for leaking harmless information to Sarah Locksley was an insult. How could what he had done been construed as a serious breach of security? She was, after all, one of them. But he had had the last word when he stormed from his supervisor's office. Oh, yes, he would show them all how pompous and ridiculously arrogant they were for picking unfairly on him. His story of MI6 incompetence would be leaked to the media. The world would know of a modern-day attempt to kill the last Romanov. He was smarter than those lesser humans whose knowledge of computer technology only extended to knowing how to click onto the porno websites. Everything was trafficked through cyberspace nowadays and he had enough to sell his story.

Sam felt ill.

'You have had enough, mate,' the barman said. 'You ought to go home while you can.'

Sam focused on the barman, a tough-looking type straight out of a gangster movie.

'Go'in now,' Sam slurred, shifting away from the bar and reeling through the packed, happy crowd, into the biting cold of a London night at the onset of winter.

He was vaguely aware that he was on the narrow sidewalk merging with the Friday night revellers seeking taxis, or walking arm in arm singing football songs and kicking at imaginary footballs. Despite his drunken haze Sam realised that the group approaching him were spread across the footpath, blocking his way. He wisely chose to step onto the roadway to avoid a possible shove from one of the football followers.

But he was not aware that he had strayed into the centre of the road until he saw the blinding headlights of a car travelling at high speed towards him. The impact hurled Sam into the air and back onto the footpath.

A girl in the crowd screamed. The drunken football fans suddenly felt a false sense of sobriety. Already blood was spreading from the smashed head of the young man at their feet.

Later witnesses were unable to recall much about the vehicle that hit the young man and continued without attempting to stop. The incident became just another fatal traffic accident on a busy Friday night. Samuel Briars would never get to tell the story of how a secret unit within MI6 bungled an operation in a friendly nation to kill the last Romanov descendant who was the descendant of an impostor anyway. It was much ado about nothing.

AUTHOR'S NOTES

Most Australians pause on the eleventh hour of the eleventh month of each year to reflect on the sacrifices made by our servicemen and women in what was known as the Great War. If they happen to be near one of the many war memorials erected following the global conflict they would most likely see inscribed: *The Great War 1914–1918*. But not all our war memorials are inscribed with these dates. There are many, such as in my former home town of Finch Hatton in Queensland's beautiful Pioneer Valley, that have etched into the stone the dates of the Great War as *1914–1919*. Very few query the discrepancy.

The inclusion of 1919 on some memorials is to recognise the many hundreds of forgotten Aussie soldiers who fought in the Russian campaign, in support of the Russian White Army – those loyal to a non-socialist government overthrown by Lenin and Trotsky's Bolsheviks. The Aussie soldiers were recruited into the British army to campaign in northern Russia as part of a multi-national expedition-ary force composed of many Western nations and Japanese troops from the east. The British commanders allowed the Aussie soldiers to wear their distinctive uniform, even though they were actually under British army orders. When withdrawn by October 1919 the soldiers returned to Aus-tralia and their courageous service was hardly recognised in a nation that wanted to put the war behind them. Two Aus-sie soldiers earned the award of the Victoria Cross for their bravery in the Russian campaign while serving with British army units: Corporal Arthur Sullivan and Sergeant Samuel Pearse (posthumously).

The story of the execution of the Russian royal family would be well known to many of my readers and some may remember the Anastasia affair that generated many novels and even Hollywood films of a young woman who feigned to be the Princess Anastasia having survived the massacre of her family. She had even been able to fool many of those related to the Russian royal family but DNA tests later proved her to be an impostor. However, for many years after the exhumation of the pit containing the remains of the Czar and his family the DNA could not be identified for his young son and daughter Maria. It has only been since 2008 that the heir to the throne and his sister Maria's DNA has been finally identified, putting to bed any rumours of their survival. That mystery inspired this novel.

Although the guns fell silent on the Western Front on 11 November 1918 they did not in the rest of Europe. Many small but vicious wars continued with Poles fighting Germans, Russians fighting German-supported Latvians, and Russians engaged in a bloody and ruthless civil war while also fighting invading Western Forces are just a few examples of the conflicts that were off-shoots of emerging nationalism in Europe. The echoes still reverberate today.

It is beyond the scope of these brief notes to explain the politics and personalities behind the intrusion into Russia by the Allied Forces, but for those interested in the subject I can recommend Robert Jackson's *At War with the Bolsheviks: The Allied Intervention into Russia 1917–1920* (Tandem, London, 1972). My novel depicts only a fraction of a campaign that saw so much happen in those turbulent years of our Aussie link to the modern-day nation of the Russian Federation.

ACKNOWLEDGMENTS

My heartfelt thanks go to my publisher, Cate Paterson, my editor, Catherine Day, and publicist, Jane Novak. Special thanks also to Jan Hutchinson and Deborah Parry for their work in the production of this book. And I would like to wish Paul Kenny all the best in his new job and thank Jeannine Fowler and James Fraser for their years of support.

As always, my thanks to my agent, Geoffrey Radford, for his tireless work on my behalf – here and overseas. I would also like to send out thanks to a special team of people: Irvin Rockman CBE, Rod Hardy and Brett Hardy, who are working to bring my stories to a wider audience.

A special thank you to Glen Jones, former homicide detective with the NSW Police, for his advice to a pre-DNA police investigator. Mate, I will take the flak for any errors in the homicide investigation procedures in this book.

I would like to single out Fran McGuire and Wendy Rose at the Maclean Library for their very generous assistance in providing the material for research. Thank you, ladies.

I would also like to thank the following from Maclean who have been of great support throughout the year: Graham Mackie, Mick and Andrea Prowse, Kevin and Maureen Jones, John and Isabel Millington, and Tyrone and Kerry McKee. And to all at Corowa and Finch Hatton – you are not forgotten.

Since the release of my previous novel I have lost two wonderful people from my life: my mother, Elinor Watt, who passed away in January 2008, and a good mate, Mel Lowth from Finch Hatton, who passed away in July 2008. Both will be missed.

A special recognition goes to my brother, Tom Watt, his wife, Colleen, and my nieces Shannon, Jessica, Sophie and Charlotte from Hazelbrook. An overdue mention is now rectified.

Not forgetting a friend, colleague and favourite author alongside Bev Harper – Tony Park, whose latest novel, *The Silent Predator*, is well and truly in the Wilbur Smith tradition.

Finally, my sincere thanks to all the readers who have contacted me over the years to express their kind thoughts on the books to date. You keep me writing.

Peter Watt
Cry of the Curlew

I will tell you a story about two whitefella families who believed in the ancestor spirits. One family was called Macintosh and the other family was called Duffy . . .

Squatter Donald Macintosh little realises what chain of events he is setting in motion when he orders the violent dispersal of the Nerambura tribe on his property, Glen View. Unwitting witnesses to the barbaric exercise are bullock teamsters Patrick Duffy and his son Tom.

Meanwhile, in thriving Sydney Town, Michael Duffy and Fiona Macintosh are completely unaware of the cataclysmic events overtaking their fathers in the colony of Queensland. They have caught each other's eye during an outing to Manly Village. A storm during the ferry trip home is but a small portent of what is to follow . . . From this day forward, the Duffys and the Macintoshes are inextricably linked. Their paths cross in love, death and revenge as both families fight to tame the wild frontier of Australia's north country.

Spanning the middle years of the nineteenth century, *Cry of the Curlew* is a groundbreaking novel of Australian history. Confronting, erotic, graphic but above all a compelling adventure, Peter Watt is an exceptional talent.

Peter Watt
The Silent Frontier

Lachlan, John and Phoebe MacDonald, three young children
tragically separated after the massacre at the Ballarat goldfields, try
to make their way in a world filled with poverty and war.

John is determined to find his lost siblings and works hard to make a
name for himself. A business partnership leads to riches and rewards
that he never dreamed of.

Lachlan has always known what it is to struggle for survival. But even
a life of bare-knuckle fighting and destitution cannot prepare him for
the war he finds himself in against the Maori of New Zealand, nor the
feelings he has for his commanding officer's sister.

The Silent Frontier is a tale of courage, hope and forbidden love
set against the backdrop of the New Zealand Maori wars and an
emerging Australian nation.

Peter Watt
The Stone Dragon

It is the turn of the twentieth century – an era of tumultuous change.
What is it that draws Tung Chi, a former Shaolin priest in the service
of the Chinese emperor, to the Australian colony of Queensland?

This mystery ensnares local businessman John Wong, who fears
for his daughter, living across the world in Pekin at a time when a
revolutionary force known as the Boxers is on the rise. Together
Tung and John, with his son, Andrew, embark on a dangerous
journey that will lead them into a conflict in which everything is at
stake, but allegiances uncertain. The sleeping dragon of China is
awakening . . .

From the tropics of Queensland to the heart of the Chinese empire,
The Stone Dragon is a gripping tale of rebellion, survival and the
powerful influence of loyalty and love.

PHOTO: DEAN MARTIN